Stealing Angel

by

Terry Wolverton

Spinsters Ink Books

2011

Spinsters Ink
P.O. Box 242
Midway, Florida 32343

Printed in the United States of America on acid-free paper
First Edition

Editor: Katherine V. Forrest
Cover designer: Judy Fellows
Cover photo: track5/istockphoto.com

ISBN: 13 978-1-935226-45-1

To TLC, who showed me the Baja

Chapter 1

Perhaps the stupidest part of all the stupid things I am doing this afternoon is taking Angel to Mexico. Crossing international borders automatically adds years to one's sentence, doesn't it?

Spirit, show me the right thing to do. Show me the path you intend and give me the courage to walk it.

I could still turn back. What I've done is problematic and might get me into trouble, but it's not irredeemable yet. I could make some excuse, talk my way out of it. There's still time.

I'm sweating as my silver Accord idles in a long line of cars waiting to cross the border. The late April afternoon sun is warm but not enough to create the sheets of perspiration sliding down my rib cage, pooling under my too-big boobs, soaking the cropped hair at the nape of my neck.

In my wilder youth, I crossed this border half a dozen times with a lid of pot rolled in paper towel stuffed into my underwear like a menstrual pad and never worried about getting stopped. But it was the seventies then, and we didn't expect to find terrorists around every corner. Since 9/11, the border is tougher. And of course, my contraband today is much more precious.

"Why are we stopped?" Angel complains from the passenger seat beside me. It's an almost-eight-year-old's impatience, restless with the confinement of the car, the long (to her) drive from L.A. to San Ysidro, the stasis of waiting. It's not that she's anxious to arrive; she has no idea of our destination and the truth is, I scarcely do myself. Or rather, I do know where we're headed, in some blind, instinctive way, but I haven't yet allowed myself to formulate a vision of it, a concrete plan. Nor have I worked out what we'll do once we've arrived. Yoli always hated my impulsiveness, my tendency to leap before I looked. This would certainly qualify as one of those times.

"Sometimes the police need to look inside a car," I tell her, "just to make sure everybody is safe." I try to locate a reassuring register for my voice. I don't tell her how fervently I hope that our car will not be one of the ones pulled over to be checked. *Spirit, if I'm meant to do this, please just let us get a green light.*

I try to imagine the perspective of the border guard: My ten-year-old but still well kept Accord will project an image of middle-class respectability. He'll peruse me, a too-large woman in T-shirt and jeans with short-cropped graying blond hair and Ray-Bans covering my eyes. Due to my age—forty-five this year—it's just possible he'll see "soccer mom" and not "dyke." As if to underscore this impression, I pull my lip balm from my jeans pocket and swipe it across my lips, bringing the slight sting of menthol to the tip of my tongue.

But then that border guard will look at Angel—Angela Davis Washington, according to her birth certificate—her caramel skin, her kinky, slightly reddish curls, and what will he see? Will his vision allow him to see her as mine?

The name in the blank after "Mother" on Angel's birth certificate will not match the one on my passport. *I'm taking her to her mother, down in Los Cabos,* I could tell him. It would be the first time Angel has ever seen me lie. *Only the truth can create right reality*, Guru Tam says. And would the guard believe my fabrication? Will he even speak English? And if he notices the bruises on her, what will he see then? Will he make a phone call and find out Angel's missing and pull a gun on me?

No, it's too soon, isn't it? Only a couple of hours since someone would have come for her at school. Even if somebody called an Amber Alert, the cops don't work that fast, do they?

I wonder if Yoli will call the cops on me. There was a time when I wouldn't have worried about this. However much she might have disagreed with me about my life choices, she knew I was on her side. She knew I was on Angel's side—our daughter. It was a bond we continued to hold in common, even after Yoli decided that being a lesbian was no longer her "scene."

"I'm sorry, baby, we've had some good times." This was how Yoli referred to the seven years we'd spent together, three prior to Angel's birth and four subsequently. "But this alternative lifestyle thing just isn't my scene. You always knew that, Maggie."

I knew it and I didn't. I knew Yolanda Marion Washington wanted to be a singer more than she wanted anything else in the world. I knew when I showed up at her club dates, she always introduced me as her "friend Maggie," and never brought me with her to industry parties; she feared being labeled a lesbian would ruin her chances for stardom. I knew that Yoli got pregnant by a concert promoter during our third year together.

It isn't every lesbian who would be so understanding if her girlfriend came home with the news she was pregnant. Not by a turkey baster, not by *in vitro* fertilization, but by a man in snakeskin boots and a gold belt buckle the size of my hand.

I can still remember that afternoon, eight years ago, Yoli coming home too early. I was working on a client, an actress whose name you would know; her idea of a beauty regimen was to rely on daily saunas and a weekly lymphatic drainage massage to undo the ravages of her coke habit. She always chattered all the way through the massage, too, and I used to wonder whether she got any benefit from it at all. But every time she'd roll up from the table with a wide-eyed, "That was *fantastic!*" (Perhaps the very same line she'd give the ever-changing sex partners that were always rumored in the pages of the *People* magazines Yoli kept in the bathroom and read religiously.)

After the actress had dressed and let herself out the patio door, I was changing the sheets on the massage table when Yoli waved at me from the garden. I let her in to the converted garage that housed my massage business.

Yoli was temping in offices in those days, to keep her schedule open for auditions and the session work that came her way sporadically. But on this afternoon she wasn't dressed for work; she wore loose Capri-length red cotton pants and a gold T-shirt that burnished her cocoa skin. Her straightened hair was unstyled, the ends hanging stiff as if carved. As many times as I'd asked her not to, she plopped herself onto my massage table.

"I just changed those sheets," I complained mildly.

She ignored this, gazing at me intently, her eyes both fearful and resolute. "Maggie, I got some news, and I don't know how else to tell you 'cept straight out."

One of the things I liked about Yoli was her blunt style. She never made you guess about what was going on with her. "Okay," I said.

"I went to the doctor today, and," she paused to draw in her breath, "I'm pregnant." Her eyes narrowed. "I ain't havin' no abortion, so don't go there."

As if I would; she must be confusing me with someone else. But I was a few steps behind her. "Pregnant? How?"

"The *usual* way." She looked at me like I was a bigger fool than she'd even imagined.

I was already practicing with the Light Beings in those days, so rather than react to the avalanche taking place inside my chest, I closed my eyes and took a deep breath. *Spirit, give me the strength to handle this. Give me the courage to respond to this with love.* "I guess I mean, with whom?" I worked to keep my voice neutral.

She'd gotten together with this concert promoter, a white dude, a coupla' months ago, it was a one-time thing, it was a mistake, she was sorry, but she'd understand if I wanted to throw her out. No, she didn't want to tell him, was I crazy? And she was definitely keeping the baby.

Of course I wouldn't throw her out. When I look back on it now it seems our relationship was all about my promising Yoli unconditional love and Yoli's continually testing that promise. *Will you still love me now? How about now?* I knew she'd occasionally slept with men during the time we'd been together, but mostly she'd made at least minimal effort not to throw it in my face. This was different. There was no denying where this baby had come from.

I was stunned and hurt, but I kept praying and meditating, and I told myself that what she'd done had nothing to do with us. After all, I loved her.

So, yes, I knew my girlfriend was still attracted to men; I knew she believed too that they could further her musical ambitions. But I also knew the way she opened herself to me at night with the full moon spilling onto our mattress. I knew the sound of her singing in the shower, not the pumped up stage voice with the phenomenal range everyone got so excited about, but sweet and sleepy and slightly off-key. I knew the street she grew up on in Detroit, and the name of her best friend in the third grade, and that she would run away and hide behind the library when her mom invited strange men over to the house. I knew that potato chips are her favorite food in the whole world. I was sure none of the men she was with were familiar with her in these ways.

So I'd realized it was a tenuous balance, but I hadn't known just which way the scales would tilt for her, until I was left weightless.

By that time, though, I had Angel. I was there in the delivery room when our daughter was born. Through a friend of mine in the massage community, we found a doctor who would deliver our baby in water, a lukewarm tub calming to both mother and child, under low lights instead of hospital-bright fluorescents. Meditation music played on the boom box we'd been allowed to bring in, and for once, Yoli didn't complain about the sound of "New Age crap." Angel's first utterance was not a scream of terror, but a warm gurgle of contentment. I was the first one to hold her.

She already had some reddish fuzz on top her head, and

as I held her against my heart, a recognition shot through me like the proverbial bolt from the heavens. Guru Tam talks about those moments when the universe speaks directly to you, gives you the blessing of knowing your true purpose. As I held this newborn in my arms, I felt surrounded by a warm kind of golden light. I understood then that she was the reason I'd been put on earth, to shepherd and guard and nurture this being. My difficult relationship with Yoli, even the hurt of this and all her other betrayals, had yielded this remarkable gift—what I had been born to do—and I was grateful.

From that time on she was mine. Not that Yoli didn't love her daughter; she did. But she was never the one to get up in the middle of the night for a bad dream, or spend the time to cut the crusts off grilled cheese sandwiches, Angel's favorite. She couldn't miss a concert just because Angel had a fever. Yoli's tie is biological, and I never question that, but Yoli has another mission, another destiny to fulfill, her music. I have only Angel.

So even when, four years later, Yoli went off with Tyrone, her manager, having decided that being my lover was no longer "her scene," she didn't try to disrupt my bond with Angel. She knew it was to her advantage to share custody; auditions, club dates and recording sessions are hard things to pull off with a child in tow. Men tend to not want to watch you change diapers, especially the kind of men who might be in a position to offer one a record deal.

My friend Charlie warned me at the time. "Get it on paper, girlfriend. You need to adopt that child, make it legal." He's been a gay rights activist since he came out at the age of twelve, right after the Stonewall Riots in New York City. And I knew I should listen to him. But I hate paperwork, and the legal system, and its assumption that everyone is a potential adversary. I want to live in a world where people trust one another, and keep their word.

I say that, but look at what I'm doing. Breaking my word, breaking the law. Committing what some might see as a heinous crime. I think about the Buddhist concept of Right Action. Can what I am doing in any way be seen as right action?

Behind me, a horn bleats. I nudge the Accord forward another two inches.

And how can one maintain that principle when the actions of others are so wrong? I would never have imagined the day a few weeks ago when Yoli came to retrieve Angel from my house. I always picked up Angel after school; there was a note in her file that they could release her to Yoli or me. Her teachers were always introduced to both of us, and either of our signatures might go on report cards, permission forms, or excuses for absence. Yoli left it to me to explain that we were former partners who, though separated, were still co-parenting. Luckily, Angel's school had a lot of parents in the arts, the entertainment industry. They were accustomed to all manner of blended families, gay and straight, even one father who'd become a woman.

Half the time Yoli came to get her from me before Angel's bedtime, and half the time Angel spent the night; that was our arrangement. The particulars of this schedule varied depending on Yoli's gigs. I was willing to be flexible. I don't have another girlfriend, I can schedule my massage clients at my convenience, and I was always more than happy to keep Angel whenever possible.

But on that afternoon three weeks ago, Yoli didn't hug me at the door like she usually does. In fact, she wouldn't look me in the eye as she sat down stiffly in one of the rattan chairs in my living room.

"Where's Angel?" she wanted to know.

"She's over next door with Khandi and the new puppies." Since that litter was born it was all I could do to get Angel home for dinner in the evenings.

"We have to talk," she announced, her acrylic nails lightly fiddling with one long beaded earring.

I noticed she looked tired; there was the slightly ashy cast to her complexion that she gets when she's been partying too much. She'd bleached blond highlights into her dark hair, which today was swept up into a French twist that was starting to come undone. Her eye shadow was sea green, a beautiful contrast to her brown skin, but smudging into the lid's crease. Her copper lipstick needed freshening.

"Listen, I got into the touring company for *Aida*. I'm understudy to the lead." She should have been on the ceiling with glee; I couldn't understand the wariness in her voice.

"Yoli, that's incredible!" I jumped up to hug her, but she waved me back.

"Chicago," she added. "The contract is for four months, but maybe they'll extend it."

"Don't worry," I reassured her. "Angel can stay with me until school's out, and then maybe we can fly up to visit you if you've got a day off."

She shot me a harsh look. "Look, Maggie, usually, I would ask you to do that, and you've been really great about helping me out with her…"

I interrupted. "It's not helping out, I mean, she's my girl, too…"

"No," she stopped me. "She's not. She's *my* girl, and I need to be making the decisions about how she's raised…"

"Meaning what?" My fingers had gone stone cold, and I was surprised at the knife in my voice.

"Meaning, Daman thinks…" Perhaps she saw my grimace at the mention of her new boyfriend, perhaps not. At any rate, she stopped to correct herself.

"Daman and *I* think, now that we're together, we need to build Angela's sense of family around this relationship. You and I have been over for a long time, yet Angela still asks me when you and I are going to live together again. It's too confusing for her."

Family. The implications of her words eddied around me, threatened to suck me under. I tried to stay focused on the immediate issue. "So what are you proposing to do while you're in Chicago?"

"Daman's sister has offered to keep her. Lurlene lives in Tujunga, and she's got three other kids, one just about Angela's age; it'll be good for her to be around other kids. She's too spoiled as an only child."

"That's crazy! What about her school?" *Breathe*, I told myself, *stay calm and find your compassion.*

Yoli sighed, smoothing back the stray strands of her hairdo. "We'll keep her in her school till the end of the semester. It's just another six weeks or so. Lurlene has agreed to drive down every day to take her."

She was speaking as if this were just a matter of logistics to be solved. She was talking about taking away my right to be with my little girl, yet she acted as if this was something that could be reasoned.

"What about her sense of stability? You're going to go away and leave her with *strangers* just because your boyfriend is threatened by me?"

Yoli wouldn't dignify this last remark. "Kids are resilient. She'll adjust."

Here then was the difference in our parenting styles. I tried to create a climate in which our daughter could grow and thrive; Yoli felt Angel should adjust to whatever new turn her mother's life was taking.

I tried another tack. "I know Daman put you up to this. What, does he think Angel shouldn't be raised by *a lesbian?*"

At least she had the grace to blush. Still, she remained unmoved. "It's all arranged," she insisted.

But beyond appealing to her sense of fairness, which had apparently deserted her, what recourse did I have? My friend Charlie had been right; I had no legal entitlement to my own daughter. Some part of me tried hard to cling to calm beneath my growing panic; I knew I needed to not antagonize Yoli.

Spirit, help me, I implored. I closed my eyes, concentrating at the third eye point. I felt a tingling there, as I forced my breath to deepen. I could hear the words of my teacher, Guru Tam: *It is in situations of extreme conflict or stress that we need most to call on the Divine for guidance. Unfortunately, these are also the times when we are most likely to forget that we are not alone, that we are always guided by Spirit. When we forget, we are spun into chaos.*

For Angel's sake, I chose to surrender. No sense dragging a child through a battle, pulling and tugging at her loyalties. It was going to be hard enough for her to adjust to this change. And given Yoli's track record with men—Daman was her sixth boyfriend since she'd ended our relationship, and the white producer for some rap labels—I was pretty sure that it wouldn't be long before Angel was back with me.

"Make sure," I told her, and my voice sounded like all the breath had been squeezed out of me. "Make sure those people are going to treat her well. I'm going to hold you personally responsible."

"What, you think I don't look out for my own daughter?" Yoli was belligerent.

I could have summoned a dozen examples of occasions where Angel didn't get picked up from her play date because the session ran long, or Angel didn't get dinner because Yoli was stuck in rehearsal. But once I started down that road, I wasn't sure I could stop. Instead, I called Angel from next door and after she'd hugged Yoli hello, I told her, "Be sure to take DogBear with you tonight when you go." This stuffed toy of indeterminate species was the one she could not sleep without.

"That's right, sweetheart." Yoli knelt beside her. She put on the fake voice she uses with Angel when she's trying to get her to do something she doesn't want to do. Yoli doesn't even know that Angel is already wise to this tactic. "Bring alotta your stuff. You're gonna go stay with Lurlene and her kids for a little while, won't that be nice?"

"I don't want to," Angel said immediately.

"Of course you do, honey. You'll have Kimmerlee and Justin and Baby T to play with."

"I don't want to! I want to come back tomorrow and see the puppies!" Her voice escalated a register. Kids have a sixth sense for when their worlds are about to change. Tears were starting to well up in her eyes.

Yoli glared at me as if this were somehow my fault.

I knelt down beside my girl, kissed the tears from each of her cheeks. "Listen," I murmured, wrapping my arms around her. "Sometimes we have to do things we don't want to do, and sometimes they turn out better than we thought." I have always been scrupulous about not lying to Angel, and I weighed each word carefully before letting it slip from my lips. "Just go and visit Lurlene and the kids. You might like it."

Her small arms enfolded me and she sobbed into my shirt. "I wanna stay with you!"

Yoli tried to pull her away, but that only made Angel scream and cling to me harder. Yoli hates it when Angel has a fit. She retreated to the other side of the foyer, sulking. "This is exactly what I'm talking about, Maggie." She glanced at the watch on her slender arm.

I held onto Angel as she cried out all her feelings. I wanted to join her in one long howl that would drive Yoli out of the house, off to wherever it was she had to be next, but I continued to let each breath fill me with the light of the Infinite, visualized it entering the crown of my head, spilling down my arms, into my heart, soothing myself, willing that energy to surround my girl and soothe her too.

When Angel was at last more composed, I took her gently by the shoulders and faced her. Looking deep into her hazel eyes, I said, "Mrs. Havisham?" It was my pet name for her and even now it made her giggle.

"Mrs. Havisham, I love you more than ice cream. I love you more than sunny days…"

This was one of our routines, and Angel broke in, "I love you more than macaroni and cheese!"

"So whether we are together or not, there is always that love between us, like an invisible thread that binds us, right?"

She nodded.

"Just look at any flower, and I'll be there. Okay?"

She nodded again. I picked her up and handed her to Yoli. "And here's someone else who loves you more than she loves the stars in the sky! Mrs. Havisham, I hope to see you soon."

To Yoli I asked, "Do you need me to pick her up from school?"

As if each word were a sliver of glass against her tongue, she said, "It's probably better if you don't for a while." She wouldn't look at me anymore.

And then she left, her high heels tapping down the walk, my girl in her arms.

It took every ounce of my discipline, every fiber of neutral mind I could muster to let them go. After that I pictured myself as an empty vessel for breath, flowing in and flowing out. If I could just keep breathing, I would not implode. Breath now became my purpose, minute by minute, as the days passed.

I kept appointments with my clients, pressed my hands into their muscles and sinew as if I might find answers there. It became part of my daily practice to keep from driving by Angel's school, to keep from calling or driving by Lurlene's house. Of course I had made the calls to find out where she lived—Lurlene Fraiser, Silverton Avenue, Tujunga—but I kept myself from physically going there.

I meditated until my third eye swirled in my forehead like a pinwheel. *Spirit, what is the meaning of this test you have given me? What am I supposed to learn? How am I to endure it? Spirit, please keep her safe.* The chants of the Light Beings were the only sounds that could drown out the mantra of curses against Yoli and Daman that were a steady stream in my thoughts.

I found myself sleeping with Mickey, the stuffed Disney mouse Angel had loved until she was five and a half, until one day she abruptly and completely lost interest. In my dreams, she was lost in the supermarket, on a busy street corner; I called for her in ragged screams and woke, sweating with fever. In nearly eight years I had never been separated from Angel for more than a couple of nights.

Then this morning, I got a call from Sumiko, Angel's second-grade teacher. This was the kind of school where kids called teachers by their first names. "Maggie," I heard Sumiko's voice, breathless, "I wonder if you would be free to come in and talk to me today, perhaps on my lunch break?"

I was there at 11:30, pacing the corridor, sneaking little glimpses through the door of the classroom, looking for Angel. When the bell rang and the kids poured out of the room, I hid in the stairwell, so she would not see me. Only when the halls had cleared again did I enter Room 114.

Sumiko was a young teacher, just a few years out of school, with a bright open smile. Slender and delicate. I was always aware of my own ungainly height and girth around her. Today she wore her sleek black hair in two red barrettes, but her expression was somber, nervous.

"Sit down," she said, and gestured toward one of the children's desks. I did my best to fold my long limbs into its small contours. "I don't know if I should have called you or not. I understand Yoli is on tour." She paused as though waiting for me to make a comment, but I had nothing to say yet. She continued, "I didn't know what to do. Angela says the bruises are from falling down..."

"Bruises?" I was on my feet.

"Yes, they are on the backs of her thighs, her buttocks. I saw them when she changed her clothes for gym class. I don't think she could get them from falling down. They seem...very bad."

I felt myself spiraling, but I drew in my breath until the world uprighted itself.

Sumiko looked concerned. "I hope it isn't bad for me to call you. I didn't know what else to do. I didn't want to call Mrs. Fraiser. Maybe that's wrong.

"We're supposed to report these things," she continued, "but then Children's Services gets involved and..." She looked down at her desk, apologetically, "I wouldn't like to see Angel get caught up in that system."

My heart was nearly cracking open with gratitude for this young teacher who was putting her career on the line for my girl. I knew she might lose her job.

She said again, "I hope it wasn't bad for me to call..."

"No, it's not bad. It was the right thing. But you might still get in trouble for it, Sumiko." I smiled ruefully. I wished I could reassure her further.

"I'm not worried about my trouble. Only that of my students."

Bless her, Spirit.

"Sumiko," I asked, "am I still on record for being able to sign permission slips for Angel?"

"Yes. To my knowledge, nothing has been changed in the records. Except that Mrs. Fraiser can pick her up from school." She was clearly embarrassed to talk about these delicate issues.

"I need to take Angel to the doctor, to make sure she's okay. Is it possible for her to be excused about a half hour before school gets out? About two thirty?" I wanted to get there before Lurlene arrived to pick her up.

"I just need a note from you."

I borrowed a sheet of notebook paper, lines widely spaced to accommodate a child's printing, and in my own awkward scrawl wrote the excuse. I didn't yet know what I was going to do, or perhaps I would not have left such an obvious paper trail. On the other hand, I'm not a criminal. It's not as if I would try to deny what I was doing.

"I'll be back for her in a couple of hours," I promised.

Walking the hall to the exit, I retrieved the gold pocket watch from my jeans. Its case elaborately carved, it belonged to my great-grandfather. I've promised it to Angel when she turns thirteen, which was enough to motivate her to learn to tell time. Its fragile hands told me I had little more than two hours. With no plan formulated in my conscious mind, I began to enact steps as if I had drilled them my entire life, the way we used to practice for fire when I was a kid, or the way Angel and I have trained ourselves in what to do in an earthquake. Perhaps I had been rehearsing these steps in my unconscious ever since the night Yoli carried Angel from my living room.

While driving to the bank I used my cell phone to call my clients and cancel their sessions for the rest of the week. In many cases it was their personal assistants I was calling. When I became a bodyworker I never imagined I'd end up with a Hollywood clientele. It's something I've been complaining about lately, but today I'm grateful because I had no qualms whatsoever about canceling. In a stroke of luck, I reached answering machines for all of them, so I didn't even have to come up with an excuse for not rescheduling.

At the bank I withdrew the money from my savings; bodywork is a cash business, by and large, so I didn't have that much in my checking account. I had more at home, stuffed into a sock in my sock drawer, and as I drove away from the bank, I was trying to calculate in my head just how much that sock might hold.

I stopped home next, phoning my neighbor Khandi to tell her I'd been called away unexpectedly, would she keep an eye on the house? I knew she would; we did this kind of thing for each other. Although I suppose it won't be anytime at all before the house is crawling with police trying to find some evidence of what I've done and where I've gone. They won't find much. I've never been one for paperwork, and I keep most phone numbers and addresses in my head.

Then it was time to pack. Angel didn't have many clothes at my house now; Yoli had come to pack them up before she left town. I brought only a few things of my own, too. I didn't want to have much more than Angel did; I wanted to be able to travel light. Then I made sure to find my copy of Angel's birth certificate and my own passport. I hoped a birth certificate would be enough to get her across the border.

I knew right away that we would head for Mexico. Baja California Sur. I spent a lot of time there in my twenties; my girlfriend at the time was a surfer. There were little towns all up and down the peninsula with enough gringos where Angel and I wouldn't be too conspicuous. It would be harder to find us, maybe harder to bring us back. And almost all the gringos there have left something behind; there wouldn't be a lot of questions.

But was I crazy to think my daughter and I could simply plunge ourselves into a fugitive life? Especially in a foreign country, and without friends there. It was then I remembered that Guru Tam now lives in the southern Baja; a whole community of Light Beings established themselves there about five years ago. I would go there, I decided, and ask for an audience with the Teacher. Guru Tam would be able to tell me how best to deal with this set of circumstances.

Los Angeles is a city with no shortage of opportunities to explore one's spiritual life, some more credible than others. I'd been introduced to the Light Beings by a client, a producer who swore their practice of meditation had cured his alcoholism; he'd practically dragged me to one of their Sunday night gatherings, now almost ten years ago. Up until that point, I hadn't had much of what you would call a spiritual bent, but I found myself calmer after participating in their sessions, and I liked how it gave me a different perspective on things, less bitter, more kind. Over time, I found myself growing more intuitive in my work with clients. But I've never been a joiner or a devotee, so this quest to see the Guru came somewhat out of the blue.

My daughter was happy to see me when I returned to her

school. This time I walked into Room 114 while class was still in session, and Angel's downcast mouth stretched into a big grin. She was wearing her favorite red shirt, and a pair of corduroy pants, too warm for the season, but long enough that no one could see the backs of her thighs. I could imagine Lurlene getting her dressed this morning, insisting that she wear long pants. She was thinner, and no one had bothered to comb her hair today. It stuck out from her head in random patches. Sumiko called her up to the front and in a quiet voice told her to pack her books; she was getting out early today. Angel eagerly turned to go back to her desk to gather her things.

Help me, Spirit, help me to be calm. Don't let me scare her, or make this any worse than it is.

I walked Angel to the car. Usually she was full of chatter about her day, what new thing she had learned, what she did at recess. Sometimes she asked me to tell her stories about the actresses I'd worked on that day. Today she was silent, gripping my hand as tight as she could.

Once we got in the car, she looked at me accusingly. "Where have you been? Why did you leave me?" Even this, though, was spoken in a tone of plaintive defeat, not the fiery confrontation of which my girl is capable.

"I'm sorry, honey. I couldn't help it." I wondered to myself if that was true. Should I have fought Yoli's decision harder? Had I given in too easily? "I'm here now, baby, I promise."

Angel lapsed once more into silence as I drove away from the school. She didn't ask where we were going or why she was leaving school before the rest of her class. She didn't twist in her seat to look out the window as the school receded from view.

While it seemed important to get on the road as quickly as we could, I knew I needed to talk to her first. I couldn't just change her life utterly without giving her the chance to object. From the cooler in the back, I pulled a Rice Dream bar that I'd stopped at the health food store to get; it was just beginning to melt.

Biting into the chocolate coating to the cold sweetness inside, Angel said, "Mmmm," with just a speck of enthusiasm as I navigated into Griffith Park. I drove up past the merry-go-round and found a place to park under a tree. She rolled down the windows, settling into the relative peace of the place, though the white noise of the freeway was ever-present.

"Honey," I began, "I need to ask you something."

She looked afraid. "Am I in trouble?" she wanted to know.

"You are absolutely not in trouble, Mrs. Havisham. But I need to know, how did you get the bruises on your legs? Sumiko told me about them."

The crease of fear returned to her forehead. I have always taught her not to lie, assured her that she could always tell me the truth about anything at all. She hesitated, trying to figure out a way to respond.

"Miz Fraiser told me to say I got hurt when I fell playing," she ventured, barely loud enough to hear. It was a truthful enough statement.

"Is that what really happened?"

There was another long pause, as Angel studied the carpet under her feet. The rice milk dripped down the popsicle stick onto her fingers, then onto the car seat.

At last she raised a pair of agonized eyes to meet mine. "Miz Fraiser said I'd get in really bad trouble if I told. She said Mommy would get in really bad trouble too." The fingers holding the popsicle stick had started to tremble; she was terrified.

If it had been Yoli sitting there instead of me, she would have barked, "Angela Davis Washington, you tell me right now what happened!" And maybe Angel would have. But I don't believe in making a child do something she doesn't want to do, a quality that has often infuriated Yoli.

I reached both my arms around my daughter. There was a slightly acrid scent on her skin, fear mixed with perspiration. "Okay, sweetheart, I don't want to get you or Mommy in trouble. But let me ask you this: do you want me to take you home to Mrs. Fraiser's house now?"

In a voice tiny as an angel's whisper, my daughter said, "Please, no." She looked as if she expected to be struck for even revealing this much.

That was all I needed for now. I inhaled a deep breath and leaned back to look at her.

"Okay, baby," I told her. "But here's the thing. If I don't take you back there, I'm going to be breaking the rules. We're not going to lie to anybody about it, but we're going to do something we're not supposed to do. And your mommy might be mad. What do you think about that?"

"Will we get punished?" A hunk of her ice cream bar was barely holding its grip on the stick; just in time she caught it in her mouth.

Again, I had to be careful not to mislead her. "*I* might get punished, honey, but I will do everything in my power to make sure you're not. I'm the adult, so I'm responsible."

"I don't want you to get in trouble!" She was alarmed. This level of fear was a new thing, as was the preoccupation with punishment; it wasn't the way I'd raised her.

"Well, I might not. But even if I did, it's worth it to me to have you feeling safe and happy."

She was quiet a minute, taking this in. Then she said, "I love you more than Khandi's puppies."

"And I love you more than fresh-picked cherries." I leaned over to kiss her cheek. Beyond the windshield, an older man in a yellow sweatshirt was walking an Irish Setter. I imagined that later he would tell police, "Yes, I saw a silver Honda in the park, but I didn't pay any attention to it."

"Do your legs hurt?" I asked Angel.

She nodded, her expression gone sad again.

From my bag on the front seat, I pulled a tube of Trau-Med cream. "I use this on my clients when someone is sore or has gotten hurt. It'll help the bruises heal quicker, and take pain away," I offered.

I unleashed her seat belt. She slowly squirmed around in her seat, burying her head in my lap while her legs stretched toward the passenger door. As I rolled down the waistband of her pants, I bit the inside of my cheek to keep from crying out. There were thick diagonal striations across the back of her thighs, extending up to her buttocks; she had been hit with an object, a cane or a stick. The skin was purple and hot to the touch.

Maybe I should have taken her to a doctor, I thought, but I knew a doctor would have to report this, and the Department of Social Services would have taken her into custody.

She whimpered a little when I started to rub the cream onto her thighs, but she's always been stalwart about pain. "This must have hurt you really badly," I crooned, "my brave girl." Then, without compromising her code of silence, "Nobody is ever going to do this to you again."

I offered a silent prayer of thanks to Sumiko. And hurled a torrent of unspoken curses at Yoli and Daman and Lurlene. Forgiveness was a concept of Guru Tam's teachings against which I still struggled.

In my head I heard my friend Charlie's voice. "You should take pictures of this. You'll need proof later on," but, of course, I hadn't remembered to bring a camera.

Before I'd left my house this afternoon I sent two e-mails: one to my friend Charlie, telling him a little about what had happened, and what it seemed like I might be about to do. It's probably not good to involve him this way, but he's a fighter from way back. He cut his teeth on AIDS activism and hasn't stopped fighting the system since. I longed to talk to him now, but I didn't want to risk it. It was only after I'd already hit "send" that I realized the police would search my computer and easily retrieve this message. So I unplugged the computer and threw it in my trunk.

The second message I sent to Yoli. "Yoli, it appears that Angel has gotten hurt at Daman's sister's house, and if it's what I think it is, I can't let her go back there. I want you to be assured that Angel is safe with me. I'm not trying to hurt you, Yoli, and I want to be able to work this whole thing out. I need you to remember who I am, to you and to our daughter, and know that I would never take this step if it weren't absolutely necessary. I will contact you again when I can." I refrained from typing *you fucking pathetic fame-starved bitch.*

Maybe it was stupid to tip her off, but no matter how mad I am at her, I can't bear for Yoli to just think her girl has disappeared and not have any idea why.

"All right, Mrs. Havisham, do you want to go on an

adventure with me?" I screwed the cap back on the tube of Trau-Med cream.

Angel nodded, turning her body around to look up at me, her head still in my lap.

"We might be gone a while. You'll miss school—is that okay with you?"

A small cloud passed over her face. "We're s'posed to have puppets tomorrow. Will I be back for that?"

"No, Mrs. Havisham. If we go, I'm afraid you'll miss the puppets."

She sat up to think this through, needing a more neutral space than my lap to consider this possibility.

"Are there any puppets where we're going?" she wanted to know.

"There might be. I don't know for sure. We could look for some."

"Okay," she told me, and a small brightness began to return to her eyes. "Let's go."

"There's one more thing..." I cautioned.

Yoli has always thought I was crazy, the way I try to give Angel the option of "informed consent." I think kids should have a say in their own destiny; she thinks I put too much burden on Angel to decide things that a child can't understand. I tend to think children understand everything.

Angel looked at me, impatient now to be on our way. "What?"

"I don't know when we'll see DogBear again." I hoped to avert a crisis at bedtime.

Her face broke into a smile. "He's coming too!" she crowed, and pulled him from her backpack.

I was glad to see him—his worn brown fur, his oft chewed-upon ears, his red vest. "DogBear is going to school these days?" I asked.

Her smile evaporated. "I didn't want to leave him at Miz Fraiser's when I was gone," she said in the quietest little voice.

It hurt my heart. I ran my hand over her cheek. "Good thinking," I told her, "plus DogBear really needs to work on his spelling."

From the backseat I retrieved a pillow for Angel to sit on,

which she agreed was "much cushier" than the "scratchy" upholstery of the car seat. I wiped the remainder of Rice Dream from her mouth, pulled the car away from the curb and, moments later, entered the stream of afternoon traffic on the Golden State Freeway. I thought about driving down the hill to the Albertson's market to buy a disposable camera, but it would take too long—the parking, the standing in line, the exchange of money. And people would see us. I suddenly felt an urgency to get on the road, to get away from this city as fast as we could.

Considering the time of day, the beginning of Southern California's six-hour span of evening rush hour, we made good time to the border. Angel was uncharacteristically quiet most of the way; I could scarcely draw her out with my questions about school or my update on Khandi's puppies. Around Anaheim, she fell into a fitful sleep, head slumped against the passenger window, and every once in a while she would emit a pitiful little moan, as if her dreams were troubling her. This worried me, but I was relieved to have her with me.

Even with all that I've done, I could still turn the car around. I could get out of this traffic jam; I could get back on the 5 and head back to L.A. Maybe we'd even get there before dark.

I could go back and confront Lurlene, or get Yoli on the phone and tell her to get her career-driven ass on a plane tonight. I could take Angel to a police station and explain the situation. I could give up this whole crazy idea, blame my hormones; everyone knows women in their late forties are nuts. I'd probably get a suspended sentence, a few hundred hours of community service.

But I think again about the bruises on the back of her thighs, and how she said, "Miz Fraiser said I'd get in really bad trouble if I told," and my stomach turns over. I'm not the one who's crazy here.

Lurlene would just deny everything; who knows anymore what Yoli might do? And the police would take Angel into "protective custody," which means a foster home. Any other step I could take would only ensure that I would never again have Angel in my care.

Spirit, guide me in my quest to keep my daughter safe. Show me what you want me to do and give me the courage to do it.

Suddenly the line in front of me is moving. "Sit up, baby," I tell Angel, and she does. Then I am slowing down for the border agent, sitting in his cramped booth. I search for his eyes behind mirrored, wire-rim sunglasses. But it's not his choice; it's random. He motions me to press the button that will signal a stop or clear passage. I extend my arm from the driver window, holding my breath. The light is green. The guard barely glances into the car, registers the two of us, and with crisp dip of his wrist, welcomes my daughter and me to Mexico.

"Green light!" Angel chirps and high-fives me. She must have learned that at Lurlene's.

Though I celebrate this victory with her, I know too this is just the first hurdle. As far south as we're going, we need to stop and get tourist cards. My memory of the last time I did this—at least fifteen years ago—is that it was routine; you show your passport, pay some money, and go. But I search in vain for a sign that indicates *Immigración*. The stretch of road just beyond the border is a tangle of cars and tiny stores selling auto insurance and who knows what else.

I creep along, straining to see where I need to go. The SUV behind me honks, impatient. It's hard to park. Have I gone too far? It's impossible to turn around; the road is divided by a tall fence; on the other side, several lanes of cars are lined up to leave Mexico. Vendors are selling blankets, baskets and sombreros from car to car, last chance for a souvenir.

Finally, I just pull over; I'll need to ask someone. I hate to leave the car here with everything in it, but I can't see what else to do.

"Come on, Mrs. Havisham," I tell my girl.

"What are we doing?" Angel whines. The traffic noise, the unfamiliar landscape, and my own confusion have her cringing. She's already had way too much adventure for one day.

"We need to find the office of immigration, so we can get our papers." I'm looking around for someone to ask.

"Why do we need papers?" she complains.

"It's another country, baby girl. We're in Mexico."

Ordinarily this would launch a barrage of questions from my inquisitive daughter. It is an indication of her degree of distress that she accepts this statement without curiosity. She merely sighs.

"Take my hand, please." I reach for her. In the midst of the noise and traffic, the confusion of smells and unfamiliar sights, she does.

A man in an undershirt and work pants approaches.

Digging for my high school Spanish, I ask, "*¿Donde esta la oficina de la Immigración?*"

It's only after I pose this question that I realize he's completely drunk. His eyes don't quite focus and his stance is unsteady. I draw my daughter a little closer.

"Tha' way," he points back toward the border in heavily accented and heavily slurred English. I guess it makes sense that this close to the border most people would speak English.

"Wan' I watch your car? Fifty pesos!" He grins at me. The grin suggests that if I don't pay him to watch it, he may do a whole lot worse to it.

"If you're still here, I'll pay you when I come back," I tell him, not wanting to appear intimidated. I'm starting to remember something about how to be on this side of the border.

Gripping Angel's hand firmly, we begin to walk back toward the border, past storefronts offering tourist information and insurance. I'd already decided not to purchase the Mexican auto insurance; I don't want to leave any more of a record of my presence here than I have to.

It's a long walk before we reach the block that contains a bank and the immigration office. As we step inside, we are the only ones in the dusty office with mismatched furniture and a small desk in the corner, save for a tired looking man with a gray mustache, smoking a cigarette with at least an inch of ash. My nose prickles from the acrid odor; when you live in California, it's easy to forget that most places in the world, people still smoke in public buildings. Angel sneezes.

"*¡Salud!*" I tell her, and to the clerk I say, "We need to purchase tourist cards, *por favor.*"

Unimpressed with my efforts at Spanish, he reaches a laconic hand toward me, indicating a request to see our documents. I hand him my passport, Angel's birth certificate.

"She needs a passport," he says flatly.

"Her birth certificate isn't enough?" *Spirit, help me!*

"Every child over age two need passport." He takes a drag on his cigarette. The ash trembles but does not dislodge. "And she needs a letter, *del notario publico*, with her father's permission for her to travel."

Her father! If he only knew. I suppose this policy is designed to thwart cases in which one immigrant spouse snatches a child and hightails it back across the border, leaving the other parent little recourse to regain custody. It's a policy designed to thwart exactly the thing I am in the midst of doing.

My heart beats faster; for a second I imagine he can see it thumping under my T-shirt. I take a deep breath. "She doesn't have a passport, and I don't have a letter," I tell him quietly. *Please let us in, please let us in,* I pray inside my head as I maintain eye contact with him, keeping my expression calm.

He shrugs. "Those are the rules, *señora.*"

Except in Mexico, rules are broken all the time, I want to shout at him, but I know I won't get anywhere acting like just another asshole from the States. I wonder if giving him money will help or hurt my cause, and I wonder how much to offer.

Perhaps sensing underhandedness afoot, Angel has strayed from my side to look at some faded posters on one cinderblock wall of the tiny room. The text is in Spanish; still, she studies it intently. I wonder if she wants to distance herself from what she sees me doing.

Should I tell him a story, and let Angel hear me lie?

Should I slip him a hundred dollar bill? I haven't changed dollars for pesos yet. Or will this insult him, or worse, make him think that something is more amiss than faulty documents?

Should I ask Angel to show him the bruises?

Spirit, if this is what you mean me to do, help me to find the way around this obstacle. Give me a sign. Show me what I am to do.

Just then the ash falls. Nearly two inches long, it lands on the desk with a barely perceptible sound, but I jump as if it had been a steel girder dropped from a great height. He regards it with curiosity, as if it were an omen of something.

"*Niña*," he addresses my daughter across the small room.

She turns to regard him.

"Is this woman, Maggie Seaver, your *mama?*" He studies the obvious physical differences between us, the discrepancies in the names on the documents.

My daughter answers, "She's one of them. I have two mamas—Maggiemama and Mommy."

He ponders this, drawing in the last of his cigarette. I haven't a clue what he makes of this, whether such a situation is as common in Baja these days as it is in the rest of California. "*Y tu papa?*" he wants to know.

"I never met him." Angel shrugs.

"And your 'other' mother—" He scans her birth certificate, "Yolanda Marion Washington. Where is she?" His tone remains gentle with her, for which I am grateful.

"*No se*," my daughter says. She must have picked up a little Spanish from one of the kids at school.

The man breaks into a broad grin underneath his fringe of mustache. "*¡Que bueno!*" he exclaims.

"*Gracias*," my daughter responds.

Without another word, he pushes two forms across the desk at me. I can scarcely believe it. "Fill these out, go next door to the bank and pay the fee, then bring them back." He at last relinquishes the butt of the cigarette, jabbing it into a small ashtray at his elbow.

Spirit, thank you for this blessing! Please guide this journey; please keep us safe.

Outside, I tell her, "You are a most excellent speaker of Spanish!" and she giggles with pleasure.

When we return to the car, our "guardian" is nowhere to be found, and the Accord is seemingly undisturbed. I thank Spirit for this as well. I take the opportunity to apply another coat of lip balm to my already-peeling lips.

Once inside, seat belts buckled, tourist cards safely tucked in my knapsack, I ask Angel, "Why did you say you didn't know where Mommy is? You know she's in Chicago singing in a play."

My girl's eyes grow sad again as I pull the Accord back into traffic. "At school I looked on the map," she says, "I looked for Chicago, but it was so far away. It's just the same as not knowing where she is at all."

Her desolation of her voice robs me of my momentary relief, reminds me that our problems are so much more complex than crossing a border. Yes, we've cleared one hurdle, but this is just the beginning, and we have so many more to go.

Chapter 2

Even when my only goal is to reach the highway that heads south along the Baja, I almost always get lost in Tijuana. The density of this border city has a stupefying effect on me, as does the squalor, which remains shocking to my United States-ian sensibilities no matter how many times I've driven through. I always seem to miss that entrance to the traffic circle that leads from the border to the highway, and too often have ended up navigating the narrow alleyways of crumbling hilltop tenements.

Today, though, I am guided to make the correct turns, to follow the signage to the right road, to ease the Accord through the urban sprawl, to shield Angel from the sight of the worst of it. Still her hands have gripped the dashboard over which her widened eyes peer. "Where *are* we?" she wants to know.

The two-lane highway seems to skirt an industrial part of the city, giving us an unrelieved view of garbage-strewn lots and graffiti-strafed corrugated metal fences. To our right is some huge complex, an oil refinery maybe, or some kind of processing plant. It's an unwelcoming vista.

"Tijuana, honey. We're in Mexico." I pronounce it the way my friend Adelita taught me—"*Tee-whana*, not *tee-a-wa-na*," she used to chide me, "You don't want to sound like some dumb gringo. *Meh-hee-co*." Adelita and I used to trade bodywork when we were both in school learning our trade.

Angel looks at me, momentarily impressed. Just like that, we're in another country. But her curiosity can't fully offset her dismay. "Mommy would hate this, wouldn't she?"

"Yes, my petunia, I'm sure she would." I keep my tone light.

"Does Mommy know we're here?" she wonders.

"No, sweetheart. She doesn't. She knows you're with me," I assure her, "but she doesn't know exactly where we are." I decide to level with her, as I always do. "Truth is, Mrs. Havisham, I don't want her to find us until I can talk to her and make her understand why you can't go back to Mrs. Fraiser's."

With this my daughter is struck silent, whether by the prospect of hiding from Yoli or that of returning to Lurlene's I can't say. She reaches for DogBear and clutches him across her chest. She says nothing for a few minutes.

"Why is it so ugly!" is her next comment. I wonder if she is really talking about what she can see outside her windshield, or about the situation in which we find ourselves, but I answer as if it were the former.

"People are poor here, sweetheart. They can't afford to have everything nice. Besides, it's not all ugly." I slow down to point out a stucco building, new-ish looking, painted turquoise; a bough of purple bougainvillea snakes up the wall toward a red tile roof. "You just have to look a little bit to find the beautiful parts."

"But how come they don't pick up the trash? Don't they know they're s'posed to recycle?" She beams at me, superior in what she knows. They talk a lot about recycling at Angel's school. She drives Yoli nuts sometimes, following her around, pulling bottles and tinfoil and wads of Kleenex out of the trash, trumpeting, "Mommy, you forgot to recycle!"

"Maybe they don't know," I offer lamely. I am praying that we don't find ourselves driving past one of the dump sites, mountains of trash where some people earn their livelihood by scavenging, where others live in makeshift huts.

I am relieved to find the entrance to the toll road, which carries us away from the squalor of Tijuana. It's always been a conflict for me. Like any parent, I want my daughter to have the best we can provide for her, but I don't ever want her to take it for granted, or assume that her way of life is the norm. Yoli says, "Show her people who are better off than her and encourage her to aspire to that," but I contend, "Show her those who are worse off, much worse off, and teach her to be grateful, teach her to help."

Yoli and I had fierce arguments when it was time for Angel to enter kindergarten. I wanted her to go to public school.

"Are you crazy?" Yoli had whirled around, one hand on her hip. "I do not want my daughter going to school with a bunch of hoodlums."

"Yoli, they're five-year-olds. I doubt any of them have boosted their first car yet."

"Those little five-year-olds will have babies of their own before they learn to read," she'd insisted. "No way is Angela going to public school."

So Angel goes to private school, and although an effort is made to achieve a mix of income levels and cultural diversity among the students, I can't help but notice how sheltered these students are, how unthinkingly accustomed they are to things being "nice."

I wonder now who will be paying for that tuition next year, now that Yoli has decided to remove Angel from my care. Daman? That's rich! Of course I would go on paying it, if Yoli asked me. But maybe he'll decide the Tujunga public schools are good enough. As if that upper-middle-class suburban wasteland was a place for a half-Black child to grow up. Or any child for that matter.

And is Mexico any better, my inner voice mocks. I can feel myself lapsing into bitterness and negativity. I need to stop that. It's probably the thing I struggle with most in terms of my spiritual practice, especially since Yoli left me.

Spirit, lift the darkness from my heart. Help me to embrace all things as part of your creation.

The new toll road makes the drive to Ensenada much easier; it's wide and multi-laned like a freeway in the United States, a vast improvement over the old two-lane road, and was built, no doubt, to lure the gringos down to Baja. Ensenada is where I plan to stop for the night. The sun has set, but the sky still carries a bit of light as the road cuts over to the ocean—I want Angel to find some beauty in this country to which I've brought her.

"Maggiemama, what's for dinner?" Angel implores.

"You have a choice, Mrs. Havisham. In the cooler I have a peanut butter sandwich…"

"With bananas?" she interrupts.

"Of course with bananas," I assure her. "What do you think I'd use—jelly?"

"Miz Fraiser puts grape jelly on everything," she informs me, disgust nearly dripping from her mouth.

I really don't know what to say about Lurlene Fraiser at this moment, so I continue, "And I have an apple. You can have those right now. Or, behind door number two…" I pause for dramatic effect, "if you can wait about a half hour, we can stop in Rosarito and get a quesadilla."

"Why can't we stop now?" There's a petulance in her voice that lets me know she's getting tired. I'm running on adrenaline, but she's just been dragged out of hell into the unknown.

Without waiting for my response, she adds, "I hafta go."

"Peeing or pooping?" I silently curse myself for not anticipating this while we were still in Tijuana. The last time I'd pulled over had been at a Starbucks near Irvine, now almost two hours ago.

"Peeing," she tells me.

That's the good news. The bad news is that there aren't many opportunities to exit the toll road, which, like most expressways in the United States, has very limited shoulder access.

"Hang on," I tell her, "We just need to find a place to pull off."

"Maggie, I can't wait!" I know she's annoyed with me when she calls me Maggie instead of "Maggiemama" or just "Mama." My own mother used to resort to "Margaret" to signal to me that I'd incurred her displeasure.

"Let's think about something else," I try cajoling her. "Tell me what you learned in Sumiko's class today."

"That's not working!" My daughter's face is screwed up in misery, and her voice contains rage and tears. I can see she's heading for a meltdown.

Luckily, a sign signals an exit not far up ahead.

"Just another minute now," I promise her as I take the ramp that leads down to the Libre, or free road. From here I can pull off the highway and she can go by the side of the road. If she will, that is.

I remember the one time I tried to take Yoli camping. This was early in our relationship, a few years before Angel. When my girlfriend learned there was no toilet facility at our campsite, she made me take down the tent and drive thirty miles in the dark to spend the night in a motel. "I ain' no bear," she'd declared emphatically, "I ain' gon' squat on no ground." Yoli could speak with perfect Anglo diction when it suited her, but when she got into a mood she almost always drew upon street English.

When at last I stop the car on the shoulder of the old road, Angel looks around. "Where's the bathroom?"

"Wait one second," I tell her. I exit the car and come around to the passenger door. I retrieve a roll of toilet paper from the back. "Now watch," I instruct. Letting the Honda shield me from the view of passing cars, I pull down my jeans and panties, squat with my back against the quarter panel. A stream of pee releases between my legs, hissing into the dust beneath.

Angel is torn between shock and fascination. "Maggie!" she squeals a combination of protest and delight. Her giggle has a fair share of nervousness to it. Peeing outside is nothing anyone has ever told her she could do.

I wipe myself dry and fold up the wad of toilet paper, not

wanting to leave it in the landscape. Others who've been here before me have not been so considerate.

"Just like Sadie," I tell her. Sadie is the mother of the neighbor's puppies, a black Lab. "Okay, your turn." Angel looks skeptical.

I continue, matter-of-factly. "So, the key is not to pee on your clothes or on your feet, so you want to keep your butt way back, okay? That's a girl—take your pants down; it's okay, there's no one around to see you." I'm grateful that it's twilight now, and that there are no other cars on the old road at the moment. "Now lean way back, sweetheart, get your feet nice and wide, that's right. Okay, let 'er go!"

Up to this point, Angel has done everything I've asked. But now she balks. "I can't!" she wails.

"Sure you can. I'm going to be right here, but I'll turn around so I can't see, okay?" I do this. "Now I want you to think of everything wet. Like last week, when it rained, remember. The rain fell out of the sky, and it streamed down the windows and it puddled on the ground. The rain came down and down and down, and it fell into the river, and that river ran all the way to the ocean..."

I hear the stream of urine as it pours onto the dirt. She pees for several seconds; poor baby, she held it a long time. When it stops, I hand her a wad of tissue and say, "Wipe, please." When she hands it back to me it is neatly folded as mine had been.

"Good job! Doesn't that feel better?"

She nods, awed and a little scared by her accomplishment. I deposit the used paper into a plastic bag designated for trash, and return the roll of toilet paper to its box in the backseat. I pull out a couple of Wet Wipes, and we both clean our hands. Then I retrieve her sandwich and apple from the cooler, along with a little box of soymilk.

"How come everybody doesn't just pee outside?" she wants to know.

Oh boy. Yoli's going to want to kill me for putting this idea into Angel's mind. "Well, it's more the kind of thing you do when you're alone and out of the country. In the city you'd have to do it on the sidewalk, and nobody would like that."

Angel laughs so hard she spits up a mouthful of her soymilk.

I haven't eaten since breakfast, I realize, and what was that—a protein shake? Food is the last thing I want, but it won't do for my energy to crash before I get to Ensenada. Navigating in the dark will be more of a challenge as it is. I take another box of soymilk for myself, stick the plastic straw in the top; at least I'll get some protein.

Once Angel is settled in, I retrace our steps and steer the car back onto the toll road. Every once in a while I take sidelong glances at her chewing, the look of concentration on her face. I am once more riddled with doubt. How can I possibly care for the needs of my child on the run in a foreign country? What about her school? What if she gets sick? What am I going to do when the police come after us?

Spirit, this one is in your hands. I am trying to take the steps I'm guided to take, and I just pray they don't lead to any harm to this little girl.

The next time I look over, Angel has fallen asleep, her head resting against the passenger window, box of soymilk still in her hand. I gently take it from her, drink the remainder of it, and put the empty container in the trash bag in the backseat. I rummage behind me with one hand until I retrieve a blanket to drape over her. The moon glimmers above the Pacific, but my daughter will not witness it this evening.

It's past nine thirty when I reach Ensenada. I wonder if it's too late to show up at the address I scrawled on a scrap of paper earlier today, the Light Beings' ashram in Ensenada. The Internet lists centers all over the world—Japan and Canada, Italy and Spain, others in Mexico. But I can't be sure it's still a good address; the Internet can't be counted on for up-to-date information. And how will I be able to find my way there in the dark?

Ensenada is a resort town on the Pacific; if you've only got the weekend, it's the farthest south most gringos venture into Baja. Aside from fishing, tourism is its major industry;

as a result, hotels line the beachfront, and the town is full of restaurants and shops, most of which appear to be still open as I steer through the crowded streets. It's bigger and more upscale than when I used to come down in the 1980s, but as I drive down one main thoroughfare, I recognize a restaurant I used to go to, the El Sol. I remember my first visit. I was in my twenties, and everything seemed foreign and dangerous to me, including Dagmar, my surfer girlfriend. I remember I was so relieved to find that the El Sol served *manzanilla*, or chamomile tea.

If I'd had more time to plan this I would have gone to the Auto Club for a map before I left L.A. Exactly how did I suppose I would find my way to the address tucked in my pocket? I drive down a few more streets, making random turns, hoping I guess to stumble upon the street, or receive a sign from Spirit. But the street signs are small and hard to see in the dark. And it certainly can't be one of these small residential houses, can it?

Finally I decide to stop at a hotel to ask directions, a desk clerk being my best chance of finding someone who speaks English. My Spanish is minimal. At home, the gardener tolerates my efforts to speak his native language with more amusement than comprehension. That might have been something to think about before deciding on Baja as my destination.

I'm grateful Angel isn't awake to observe my uncertainty, as I navigate my way back to Boulevard Costero, and pull into the parking lot of Hotel Misión Santa Isabel, one of the large hotels that caters to tourists from the States. Angel is sound asleep, clutching the red plaid blanket around her. I can't bear to wake her, but there is no way I am going to leave her alone in the car. Even though Baja is much less crime-ridden than the U.S. (despite popular belief to the contrary), tonight I am hyperaware of every possible threat to this child. Instead, I pull up to the valet in the front.

A young man in a red jacket approaches my door, *"Buenos noches, señora."*

"¿Habla Inglés?" I ask, hopefully. Of course, I am the stereotype of every stupid gringo who hasn't taken the time to learn the language of the people next door.

"A little," he replies.

In relief, I begin, "I'm not checking in, and I just want to know if you have directions to this address..."

His blank look tells me I have already taxed his comprehension level, and perhaps his patience. The driveway is busy; hotel guests are departing for late evening plans, deeply tanned women in tight white dresses, men in dress shorts and open collared shirts carrying open bottles of beer.

I try again, unfolding the scrap of paper from my jeans pocket. *"¿A donde?"* I push the paper toward him.

He studies it for a moment, nods, then begins an enthusiastic torrent of Spanish in response to my request. I hold up one palm, *"No comprendo."*

He shrugs, then has another idea. From his breast pocket he takes a pencil, and on the back of my paper he begins to draw lines and arrows, a map from where I am now to where I want to go. In a surprisingly neat hand he pencils street names, then attempts to talk me through it.

I understand perhaps half of what he's said to me, but he's given me something to work with, and I reach into my back pocket for a five-dollar bill with which to tip him. This far north, U.S. currency is accepted routinely, but it occurs to me I'm going to need to change some money soon. I add it to my mental list of things to do in the morning.

Then, too, I wonder if I'm crazy to be carrying so much cash on me. I've got a few thousand dollars rolled in paper towel pinned inside my underwear—a trick Dagmar taught me for smuggling pot over the border twenty-odd years ago—and several more in an envelope taped under the dash of the car—about fifteen thousand in all. It's a huge risk, but credit cards are traceable, ATM transactions too. I know about this from watching cop shows on TV. I don't want to leave an electronic trail.

The valet is happy with the bill I've placed in his hand. *"Gracias, señora,"* he says before he dashes off to greet a BMW convertible that's just pulled in behind me. He calls me *señora* because of my age, because of the sleeping child, despite the fact that my ring fingers are conspicuously bare.

In the bright light of the driveway I study the hand-drawn map, trying to memorize it before I embark. His directions guide me out of the downtown area and into a residential neighborhood of small houses, and finally to what appears to be the outskirts of town, east and into the hills, where the lots are bigger and the houses set farther apart. There are no other cars on this road. If this address turns out not to be what I think, how will I ever find my way out of here?

At last I pull up outside a white wooden fence that is draped in night-blooming jasmine. Its scent enfolds me as I stop the car. In the dark, I can't tell much about the house behind it, but lights burning inside indicate that some of its occupants may still be awake. I open Angel's door and slowly scoop her into my arms.

"Huh?" she asks sleepily.

"We're here," I tell her. "Don't wake up."

She obliges, nuzzling her head into my neck, arms draped heavily on my shoulders, legs wrapped around my waist. I make my way through the gate and up a few steps to the front door. I knock.

Immediately I feel relieved at the sight of the woman who answers. She wears a simple floor-length shift in pale blue. Her head is covered with a drape of the same shade. Around her neck she wears a simple silver heart that matches the one I wear. She wears no makeup, yet her face glows with a serene beauty. Her hazel eyes take in the stranger, the child, with no hint of alarm.

Thank you, Spirit, for the blessing of your guidance.

"Peace begets peace," I greet her in the customary way.

"Peace returns peace," she replies with a slight bow of her head. She opens the door to let me in. Before she has to tell me, I remember to kick off my sandals in the entryway.

Inside there is the scent of Indian spices, perhaps from a meal recently cooked. In the large living room there is a fountain at one end, its water flow creating a soothing sound. A large rug covers most of the tile floor, and thick pillows are set before a long low table. There are a couple of ornately carved cabinets, and several paintings of Hindu gods adorn the walls.

I lower Angel to the floor, atop a heap of pillows, and she curls into a ball on her left side.

"I wonder if you might know of someplace we could stay tonight? Just tonight, I think."

"You can stay here," the woman responds. "My name is Amara."

"Maggie," I say. I've never taken a spiritual name.

Amara leads me down a darkened hallway, pointing out a door on the way and saying, "That's the bathroom." A candle flickers from within. "Remember," she cautions, "no paper in the toilet. You've been to Baja before, yes?" I have, but I had forgotten this feature, how the plumbing in Baja is not equipped to digest even toilet tissue. Instead, every bathroom has a closed receptacle where one discards used tissue. I need to remember to tell Angel.

Amara next guides me to a room near the end of the hall, with a double bed covered in a pleasant comforter, also in pale blue. There is a chest of drawers, and a low table on which rests a short stack of Guru Tam's books and a clear glass pitcher of water and two glasses. At first I wonder with a start if they might somehow have anticipated our arrival, but then I realize that they keep this room at the ready for their visitors.

"There are towels in the bottom drawer," Amara offers. "Do you or your daughter need anything to eat?"

"No, thank you. I'll just go out and bring our stuff in from the car."

"You can come and go through this door," she tells me, pointing to a door at the very end of the hall. She's about to take her leave of me, when she turns to say, "Morning prayers are at three thirty, in the front room."

When I first began practicing with the Light Beings, I went a couple of times to morning prayers. I'd get up in the dark, surprisingly alert, and drive myself to the ashram. The lights would be on low, and those who lived on-site took turns leading the warm-up stretches followed by two hours of chanting. After, I would re-enter a dawning world, light tinting the sky pink, feeling virtuous and serene. Then, around ten a.m. I would start to feel psychotic from lack of sleep and it was all I could do to function for the rest of the day. No matter how elaborate the promises about the benefits of observing this ritual, I've never been able to make it a regular part of my practice.

Still, I watch Amara's retreating back with a heart full of gratitude. Guru Tam has always said, "No one in need is a stranger," but it is immensely comforting to have that confirmed in this moment.

A series of low chimes awakens me, and for a few moments, blinking in the dark, I don't know where I am. Angel's back is pressed against me, her body curled into a ball. She barely stirs as I slip from between the covers. The room is chilly; February can often be warmer than April along the Pacific coast. I rummage for a sweater to add to my sweatpants and T-shirt, and aim a swipe of lip balm at my lips.

I worry about leaving Angel; what if she wakes and is scared because I'm not there? But I remember this is a safe place, and I quietly step from the room. I step lightly back along the hallway, moving toward the front room into which we entered last night, lit now by the glow of a few dozen candles.

I join a loose, wide circle of eight others. One couple looks Mexican, and one woman appears Asian, maybe Japanese. The others look like Anglos. The Asian woman swaddles an infant; a toddler dozes beside one of the men. Most everyone at this hour is either in sweats or modest pajamas; but all wear their headgear, a long draped cloth like a wimple for the women, a turban for the men. Although we're told to keep the crown chakra covered, I've never worn the headgear. I wouldn't be caught dead wearing the women's, and I never had the nerve to ask to wear the men's.

Amara smiles to see me join them, and walks over to me with a simple white bandana, which I obediently tie over my cropped hair. Evidently they must keep these on hand for errant guests.

A moment later, three more people enter, kicking off their shoes at the threshold, a woman and two men, but they are completely dressed in their pale blue gowns. The men wear theirs shorter and belted at the waist over white pants that cling to the legs. One of the men sits on a low platform I hadn't noticed last night; the others join the circle.

We join hands then and close our eyes, beginning a deep, cleansing breath. I am curious to see how similar this will be to what I've experienced at the ashram in L.A., and what aspects might be different. After five minutes or so, the man on the platform leads us through a short series of callisthenic stretches and yoga postures. It feels good to stretch and move after the tension and confinement of the car yesterday. I have another long drive ahead of me today, so I'm happy for the chance to unwind the knots in my muscles and get the blood moving. Stretched backward into camel pose—one of the more challenging poses for me—belly and heart and throat arching to the sky, I pause to give thanks to Spirit for providing this practice that keeps me limber and healthy.

One of the tenets the Light Beings offer is the notion of being grateful for everything in one's life, not just the good things that come our way, but the hard stuff: the challenges, the obstacles, the defeats. "Be grateful," Guru Tam instructs, "for these are your teachers."

I am trying to find gratitude for the situation in which I now find myself: a fugitive, kidnapper of my own child. *I'm grateful that she's safe. I'm grateful that she's with me. I'm grateful that I have the means to do this. I'm grateful to have been taken in at this ashram last night.* I wonder what Guru Tam will have to say about the lesson these events hold for me.

After the physical practice, we sit once more to begin the lengthy sequence of chants that constitutes the morning prayers. There are specially designated chants for this time of the day, different from those given in yoga classes or other meditation sessions. Because I've only been a few times to these morning services, I don't know all the words to these chants, which are in Sanskrit. I let the sounds wash over me, picking up small strings of syllables and mumbling those as I can, almost falling asleep in my sitting position.

I'm always amazed at people who can sit like this for hours.

My hips are too stiff to get into lotus position, and even cross-legged, my legs keep falling asleep after about fifteen minutes or so and I have to stretch them out straight in front of me for relief. I feel self-conscious; no one else is wriggling the way I am, but the others seem so deep in prayer they don't notice. One of the things I've always loved about the Light Beings is their lack of judgment or reproach.

Each of the eight morning chants lasts for about fifteen minutes, and they move from one to the next with only one deep bow, forehead to floor and back up, in between. We are partly through what I think is the seventh—I have dozed off a couple of times—when Angel pads into the room. I hear her immediately, and open my eyes to watch her as she takes in the scene. Her eyes scan the room, looking for me, frightened for an instant that I might have left her here, as Yoli left her with Lurlene. Wanting not to be distracting to the others, I make a little wave at her, and put my index finger to my lips, to indicate quiet.

She tiptoes over with exaggerated carefulness, and plops onto my lap. I fold myself around her, whispering to the back of her ear, "This is a prayer. You can chant it, too." Then I attempt to form the syllables as I hear them.

She picks it up faster than I do, and I hear again in her clear little voice how she's inherited Yoli's musical talent. *I hope she hasn't inherited her selfishness to go along with that.* Then I chastise myself. *Spirit, help me to cleanse the negativity and resentment from my heart.* "When we judge others," Guru Tam has said, "it is because we fail to love ourselves."

Angel gets bored with it after a while, though, and once she starts to fidget, I stand with her and usher her back to the bedroom. "What are they doin', Maggiemama?" she wants to know.

"They're chanting the sun back into the day, Mrs. Havisham."

"Really?" Her eyes get big. "If they don't do it, is that why we have cloudy days sometimes?"

"No," I tell her. "Even when there are clouds, the sun is still there. It's just hiding. Did you get enough sleep?"

"Nooooo," she prolongs it to register that it should be obvious. "It's really early," she complains.

"Well, go back to sleep."

"I hafta pee."

I nod. "Do you remember where we went last night to brush our teeth?"

She shakes her head emphatically.

"Come on, then, let's find the landmarks." I take her hand.

Finding the landmarks is something we've been doing since she was three. I wanted her to feel like she could get around in the world, like she wasn't just being dragged from place to place, but knew where she was. At the door to the hall, I ask her, "Okay, now, do we go left or right?"

She looks both ways. To the left is the door that leads outside; to the right, the hall leads back to the front room, where the chanting still continues. Angel pulls me toward the right.

"Okay, now count the doors—one door, two doors, three doors. Here's the bathroom!"

"One door, two doors, three doors!" she repeats, delighted with this information. I put my index finger to my lips to signal her to whisper.

"Can you get back to our bedroom, or do you want me to wait?" I ask her.

"I can do it!" she replies impatiently, and louder than I'd wish.

"Remember," I whisper, "don't flush the toilet paper. Put it in the little blue trash can."

She makes the same face she made last night.

Morning prayers have ended, and Amara comes down the hall as I am entering the bedroom.

"Peace begets peace," I greet her.

"Peace returns peace. Do you need anything this morning?" she offers, "Aside from breakfast, that is."

"You're very kind," I murmur. "I'm afraid there is." I find out from her the nearest place to change money, where to buy a prepaid cell phone, the best store to purchase a few items of clothing and some sandals for Angel. "Also, might it be possible to use your telephone? I need to call the U.S., but of course I'll pay you for the call."

It is then that Angel returns to the room, wearing only her shirt and underpants. In the waxing light, the bruises on her legs are clearly visible.

Amara's eyes take them in.

"We had to get away," I say, without further explanation.

She nods in agreement and, without asking any questions, leads me through another door off the hallway, behind which is a room set up as an office. Flicking on a lamp next to a tidy wooden desk, she points toward the phone.

"Do I have to dial anything special besides the country code?"

She shakes her head, and leaves me alone. The office is very neat, with a computer on the desk and a shelf of books on one wall. In one corner of the room, a large brass gong stands mounted on a frame. I want to call my answering machine, but I can't risk it. The police might have already put a tracer on it.

There is some small chance they haven't gotten to Charlie yet, though, and I decide to go for it. It's way too early to call him; he's a night owl who stays up until three or four a.m. But he'll understand, I tell myself, as I dial his number with trembling fingers.

The phone rings only once when he answers, "Maggie?"

"How did you know it was me?" Maybe the FBI is sitting in his living room, waiting for me to call.

"Who else but a fugitive would call me at this ungodly hour of the morning?" I have never yet seen Charlie in a situation in which he couldn't muster at least a shred of humor. "I'm just sitting here watching you on TV."

"What do you mean?" Anxiety bolts through me like electrical current, and I drop into Amara's desk chair. Reflexively, I reach for my lip balm and apply it.

"Kidnappings are big news, honey. You're the 'estranged former lesbian partner' who snatched the innocent child. The evil sister, from whose loving care you snatched Angel, has been on, all self-righteous, talking about how she drove all the way from Tujunga to pick up the girl at school, only to find she wasn't there! The school principal has your note asking for early release because of a doctor's appointment. They're still looking for the doctor..."

"Didn't they say anything about her bruises?"

"There's nobody here to plead your case, sugarplum." Does that mean he thinks I shouldn't have taken her away?

"Charlie, I couldn't go to the cops..." I begin.

"Sweet cakes, I am the one person to whom you *don't* have to justify yourself about that. A crazed and vengeful lesbian ex-lover makes wild allegations about a perfectly respectable heterosexual mother of three—gee, I wonder whose side the cops are going to be on?"

"Family values, ya gotta love 'em." My voice drips venom. "I knew I should have taken photos."

"Photos of what?" Charlie wants to know.

"Of Angel's legs, Charlie. The bruises...anyone could see they're not accidental. I thought about doing it, but I didn't have a camera and I didn't want to take the time to get one."

"Well, it's not too late. Those bruises didn't just heal up overnight. Buy one of those throwaway cameras and shoot the film and send it to me. I'll give you a post office box number."

Maybe Amara will do me one last favor and mail it for me. It's a risk, though, because the postmark will show where I am. Or, at least, where I was. But Charlie will be smart enough to throw away the envelope. I turn to my next worry.

"What about Yoli?" I ask.

"'Efforts to notify the girl's mother have not yet been successful,' is what the broadcaster keeps saying."

"Isn't that typical!" I snort. Still, I wonder where Yoli could be.

"It's the lead story!" Charlie actually sounds impressed.

"That's not good news," I warn him.

"Of course it is! A big story will give you a big platform to make your case about the rights of lesbian co-parents!" He's already turning this into a cause. He's probably been on the phone to some gay rights organization about my legal defense.

"Did this break last night or this morning?" I need to know how close they are behind me.

"Not on the six o'clock, but on the eleven o'clock news. Listen, honey, find a way to dump your car; they're broadcasting a description and license number about every minute and a half."

"Shit," I say, "I'm in…"

"Don't tell me. I can't help you at all if I know any more than I do. And listen, from now on don't call me on this number. It's only a matter of time before they start talking to everyone you've ever known. Here's a number you can use…" He gives it to me as I scramble for pencil and paper in Amara's desk.

"You're not using your cell, are you?" he wants to know, "Because they can trace you that way."

"Hey, I watch cop shows too." I don't explain that my cell won't work outside the U.S. anyway.

"Okay, dumpling, you can call me on this number anytime. There's no voice mail on it, so unless I'm at the police station or having sex, I'll pick up. And you should get a prepaid cell phone and give me the number."

"I'm getting a phone this morning, but are you sure you want the number?" If I give him that, he'll definitely know what country I'm in. It's one thing to put myself at risk, but I don't want to ruin my friends' lives.

"Maggie, you can't do this on your own. You're going to need someone here who can monitor what's going on here and keep you apprised. Especially if and when you decide to come back. And since it's me you're calling in the middle of the night, I figure I'm the one."

"Oh, Charlie…" *Thank you, Spirit, for this friend.*

"Listen," he adds, "it's probably not good for Angel to see all this on the TV. Can you keep her away from it till the story dies down a little?"

He thinks I'm holed up in a motel somewhere in another state. "Not a problem, Charlie," I say without further explanation.

"Okay, I'm going to try to get a little beauty sleep now, lovebug. Call the cell and let me know your number when you have one. And don't worry!" he admonishes.

"Don't worry?" Can he possibly be serious?

"Yeah, just do your meditating hoodoo or whatever it is you do, and leave the justice part of it to me."

"Peace begets peace, Charlie."

"Yeah, yeah, whatever." He signs off and, in the blankness that follows on the other end of the line, I already miss him.

My hands are sweating as I leave the office, and find Amara in a large open kitchen, where three blue-clad women work to serve a breakfast of granola and sliced fruit and yogurt and toast. The granola looks homemade, as does the bread. It wouldn't surprise me if the yogurt is too. The men are nowhere in sight; no doubt they'll reappear when it's time to eat.

"I spent several minutes on that call," I say apologetically to Amara. "I haven't changed money yet. Do you have any use for dollars?" I hold out a twenty.

"You keep that," she says simply. She smiles, and I notice a dimple in her left cheek.

"I'm afraid I need to ask you for a couple of other things. Do you think you could mail something to the United States for me?"

She assures me this will be no problem. "Though it might take a week to get there. Mail service from Baja isn't what you're used to."

"That's okay. The other thing is I need to sell my car and get a new one, not a new new one, just another one. But..." I hesitate, not sure how much I should implicate myself, "it would be best if the transfer didn't involve any paperwork."

She's quiet for a moment, taking this in. I hold my breath. If she protests now that I've gone too far, taking advantage of her trust and hospitality, putting the Light Beings at risk, I won't blame her.

"I don't know much about any of that," she answers, and I marvel at the way she seems to meet every event with this kind of equanimity. "I think you could ask one of our neighbors, though. There's a man and his brother who live about a half-mile away, and their yard is always full of cars and trucks. I'm pretty sure Shanti bought a truck from them and felt like he got a good deal. He can take you over there after breakfast. Now, are you and your little girl hungry?"

Amazingly, I am. The granola has bits of toasted almond and coconut, and I can't wait to crunch my teeth against it. As I go back down the hall to fetch Angel, I feel lifted up with gratitude for the way Spirit is guiding me every step of the way. For the moment, this lightness overwhelms the heavy pounding of my heart.

It is just after seven thirty, and I am following Shanti's white Ford truck down a rutted road. A tall, skinny man, bearded as are all the male Light Beings, Shanti is not happy about starting his morning with this errand. I overheard his protests from the pantry, followed by Amara's quiet insistence. Whether it is the illegal nature of my errand, or merely the interruption of his own agenda that he objects to, I don't know, but I hate to feel like I'm imposing.

Amara, on the other hand, was insistent that I leave Angel with her while I take care of this business. I don't know if she felt like she needed to shield my daughter from the negative karma I'm accumulating in this transaction, or whether she just wanted to free me up to get through my list of tasks more quickly. Although Angel at first objected to being left behind, she was easily swayed by the prospect of helping to milk the goats.

The Ford is better suited than my Accord to weather the bumps, and Shanti is making no effort to go slowly, but still I manage to follow him to a small cinderblock house painted a faded turquoise with no panes in the windows. The house is set on a large lot littered with cars and car parts, surrounded by a barbed wire fence.

The white Ford slows, and a pale blue clad arm emerges from the window of the cab, signaling me that this is the place. I suddenly realize that Shanti intends to drive off. I turn off the ignition and dash out of my car.

"Shanti!" I wonder if there is something less familiar I should be calling him? I race to the driver's side door. His eyebrows are pushed together in a scowl.

"Shanti, I hate to ask you this, but could you please stay? My

Spanish is very bad and I need to make sure they understand what I am asking for." His gray eyes darken like a sky beset by storm clouds.

"I could pay you for your time," I offer, "or make a donation to the ashram." It has never been easy for me to ask for help from anyone, another thing Yoli used to hate. Now here I am begging the assistance of a total stranger.

I watch him press his eyes shut, and I know he is praying to keep his temper. When he opens them again, he turns off the ignition and swings open his door, without ever answering my request.

My desperation allows me to feel grateful for his help instead of outraged by his sour manners. I walk behind him through the opening in the gate and into the dusty yard.

A small man in a tight green T-shirt walks toward us, wiping his hands on a greasy rag. *"Buenos días,"* he greets Shanti, and nods politely in my direction. The two men exchange a few words, and then the man in green comes over to me. His head barely reaches the level of my shoulder, and I feel awkward, a giant.

"Señora—*ita,*" he amends after a quick glance at my hands. "José Ordoña," he introduces himself with a courtly little bow. "You need a car?"

At first I don't realize he's speaking English, but then it takes me a few seconds to understand his words through his accent. I hope he doesn't think I'm stupid, or worse, rude.

Speaking with exaggerated slowness and care, I explain that I need a car. "I want to trade in my Accord," I point to the silver car parked outside his fence. Is "trade-in" a concept people use here? Am I ridiculous to think he even wants my car?

I explain further that I want something with Mexican license plates, but that I don't have time to register it. I keep my expression blank so as not to indicate that I'm aware that I'm asking him to break the law.

José is unfazed. "I got a good car for you!" He smiles. "But you don' want Mexican plates *porque* some cop's gonna stop you, say why is this *gringa* driving a car with Mexican plates? Cost you a big fine, plus mix you up with the law."

"But—" My voice cracks. I can tell how tired I am by the fact I nearly burst into tears with this new obstacle. I breathe and regain my steadiness. "I don't want to keep the plates that are on my car now."

"Not a problem!" He beams. "What you want—California, Arizona, Texas?" I wonder for a moment if I'm getting myself in even worse trouble; the car I'm about to buy is probably stolen, maybe the license plate comes from a stolen car too. Is that how I want to get busted?

But I remind myself that I'm in Mexico, where it's unlikely that cops spend their time tracking down cars stolen in *Los Estados Unidos.*

Shanti looks at me like *Now can I leave?* and I nod and mouth "Thank you." He bids goodbye to José, climbs into his truck. "Peace begets peace," I call to his disappearing taillights. Now I'm on my own.

"Felipe!" José calls toward the house. A much taller man emerges. He wears a dusty pair of black cowboy boots. "My brother, Felipe," José confides to me. The family resemblance escapes me, but I can't imagine why he would lie to me about this.

"She wants to buy the Chevy Caprice," José informs the tall man. "Give her California plates."

I want to stop him. How does he know that's the car I want to buy—we haven't talked about it at all. We haven't talked about options, or price, or the trade-in value of the Accord. Then I catch myself and laugh—as if I have bargaining power here. Without knowing one thing about me, José Ordoña has sized up my situation.

Buying a car is always a perilous activity, especially a used car, especially for a woman. I always feel like the salesmen are gathered in the back room, plotting about all the ways they can screw me. It makes me furious to feel helpless to stop my being taken advantage of. But auto mechanics is a skill I never acquired, and for that choice, I pay the consequence. *Every choice has consequences,* Guru Tam always says.

Felipe rounds the corner, piloting a Chevrolet that's seen better days, but not recently. Its paint job, perhaps originally red, has faded to a dull brown with no finish left.

"Nineteen eighty-eight!" José announces. "Classic!"

I've known women who could look at the front bumper or the shape of the taillights and know whether or not this was the vehicle's true vintage, but I am not one of those women. Perhaps Yoli would have liked me better if I had been more butch in certain respects. So I have to take José's word for it; after all, if he were going to lie to me, would he tell me the car was sixteen years old?

"Caprice," I think with dispirited irony, as if the word could somehow make this vehicle seem less like the junker it is. I walk around it, as if I'm supposed to know what I'm looking for. The tires seem decent, not new but not bald either. Should I make a display of opening the hood and poking around at the engine, or should I not even attempt the charade?

"Felipe rebuilt the engine himself!" José boasts.

And who am I to say he didn't?

"May I drive it?" then wish I didn't sound so tentative. Of course, I need to drive it before I commit myself to this transaction.

"Of course," José says, but his face bears a trace of regret, as if I have wounded him with my lack of blind trust.

Felipe opens the driver side door, and unfolds his long limbs from behind the steering wheel. The vinyl seats are cracked; there's a gaping hole in the dash where once a radio might have rested. Am I really going to exchange my beautifully maintained Accord for this? The acrid smell of oil pervades the interior, perhaps the residue of where the car has spent its retirement, or perhaps signaling an oil leak. This makes me nervous.

Leaning out the window, I tell José, "I'm driving all the way to Cabo. Are you sure this will get me there?"

He waves away my concerns with a flap of his rag. "You could drive this car all the way to Tierra del Fuego," he assures me, but somehow I am not comforted.

I turn the key and the engine starts up with a roar, as if the car is a wild animal ready to devour the road. It's been years since I drove a car with eight cylinders. Felipe's legs are even longer than mine; I have to strain to reach the pedals. It's impossible to adjust the seat without a passenger on the other side.

I move the gearshift, and awkwardly navigate my way out of the yard. I have no idea where I'm going, and it occurs to me that whatever I might discover on these rutted roads will in no way prepare me for the highway. Still, I check for what I can: The brakes are tight, at least at low speeds. The muffler is noisy in a worrisome way. The odometer and speedometer appear to work. The suspension is no worse on this road than it was in my Accord. I'm certain the gas mileage will kill me.

Although I'll need to adjust them, all the mirrors are intact. Wipers—check. Lights—check, but not the map light inside. The kind of things women check for—cup holders and vanity mirrors. It makes me furious.

I drive about a half mile up the road, turn around, drive back. I don't know what else to do to protect myself. Maybe it does come down to trusting the Ordoña brothers, or at least, trusting Spirit.

Show me a sign, I beseech. *Let me know if this is what I am supposed to do.*

But the sky is cloudless; no bird or insect crosses my field of vision. No animal cries. My own instincts are too fraught with nerves—the pressure to dump the Accord, the need to move south, the urgency to reach Guru Tam—to provide a reliable indicator. I'm going to have to just decide and hope I've done the right thing.

A few minutes later, I return to the litter-strewn yard of the Ordoña brothers, and, with a knot in my stomach, agree to purchase the car. They should pay me, is what I'm thinking as I unpack my possessions from the backseat, the trunk, and, of course, the envelope taped under the dash. The Silver Cloud, Angel always called my car. It breaks my heart to let it go, but I remind myself that attachments are the primary cause of human suffering. I agree to pay them $1,000 cash, $10,000 *pesos*, plus the Accord, in exchange for this decrepit Caprice.

A car is such a repository of memory—places I've driven, people who've ridden by my side, a container of my identity these past nine years. The Accord was the first car I bought new, an indication that I'd achieved adulthood, some measure of stability. For all of Angel's life, this has been the car I've driven. In an hour it will be sporting Baja plates and by tomorrow it will be painted green.

As I watch Felipe drive it onto the lot, this feels more irretrievable than anything I've done so far. No matter what ends up happening with Angel, even if Yoli forgives me and I return to my life in Los Angeles, I will never again be that person, the one who drove the Silver Cloud.

The Ordoña brothers are kind enough to provide me directions to get downtown, arguing vigorously between themselves about which route is easiest. I end up relying mostly on my instincts—"Let's see, the ocean is *that* way"—to make my way to Avenida Juarez, where I set about my errands. The most challenging turns out to be buying clothes for Angel; it will be far too hot where we're going to keep her in long pants, yet I don't want her bruises to be visible and raise suspicion. All the girl's shorts on sale seem to be scandalously short, presumably tourists from the States want their prepubescent daughters decked out in hot pants. I end up buying her a couple of pairs of brightly colored boy's nylon trunks, cut to fall to the knee. She'll have a fit if she finds out I bought her boy's clothes—one way she takes after Yoli and not after me. I buy her some girl's T-shirts and a pair of bright pink flip-flops to make up for it. At the last minute I splurge on a beautiful embroidered cotton blouse that I think she'll love.

By ten thirty in the morning, my wallet is stuffed with nearly ten thousand pesos—the exchange rate is approximately ten to the dollar—minus what I've spent on sundry purchases. The rest of my dollars are repacked in my underwear; Amara reminded me about the army checkpoints that dot the highway all the way down the Baja. Although the bored young soldiers don't always search your vehicle, they can, and there would be nothing I could do to stop them from pocketing whatever they found in the search.

I have shot a roll of film documenting Angel's bruises; I

cajoled her with the prospect of having her picture taken with the goats on the community's land. This film is packaged up and addressed to Charlie, ready for Amara to post.

And I have a prepaid cell phone, with one thousand pesos worth of time. That won't go far; calls to the U.S. run about a dollar a minute. I wish I could check my e-mail, to see if Yoli made any kind of response, but the longer it takes the authorities to figure out I'm in Mexico, the better the chance I have to disappear. Or am I kidding myself? I've never been the kind of woman who drew a lot of attention for my looks, and somewhere early on in life I think I decided I was invisible. That idea used to crack Yoli up. "You're six feet tall, girlfriend. You're an Amazon. You think people don't notice that?" Perhaps at the first checkpoint, the soldiers will have been alerted to watch for someone who looks like me.

Now I know I'm in fantasyland. Nothing is that well organized in Mexico.

I check one more time to make sure I have the map of Baja that Amara has been kind enough to mark: towns that are worth a visit, likely places for checkpoints, a good place to stay tonight.

"You should be able to make Santa Rosalia before dark," she advises, "if you don't make too many stops along the way. If not, Guerrero Negro is okay too."

I cannot begin to express my gratitude to this woman, who has welcomed us into her home and her community with no questions asked. The best I can do is to be honest with her. "There might be people from the U.S. looking for us. Police. Maybe the Feds. I don't want to bring any trouble into your community…"

She stops me with a hand on my wrist. Despite the heat of the day, her touch is cool and soft. She looks deep into my eyes as if speaking all the way into my soul. "Peace begets peace," she reminds me.

I clasp my hands into a prayer at my heart and bow my head to her. "Peace returns peace."

When I call to Angel to gather her things together to leave, she protests. Among the goats on the property is a young kid, all legs and friskiness, whom she has named Baby. "I want to stay and play with Baby," she announces.

"I know, honey, but we have a long drive today. We need to get going."

She makes an elaborate scowling face—she mimics the drawing of a Gorgon on one of my old feminist posters—and turns her back on me, running after the young goat. Her feet kick up a fine layer of dust on her new sandals; her brown curls spill over her shoulders. She's wearing one of her new T-shirts, teal green with bright pink turtles on the front. I feel Amara watching me, to see what I will do.

At times like these, Yoli's inclination is to yell, or to run after Angel and corral her to the car. My own mother would have gotten behind the wheel and pretended to drive off without me. Instead, I lean against the back doorway of Amara's house and I begin to sing "Yellow Submarine." It's one of Angel's favorite Beatles songs. I sing neither very loudly nor very softly, nor particularly on key, but midway through the first chorus Angel has stopped running after the kid and has turned around to look at me.

Before I've finished the second verse, Angel has started singing too, and comes over to stand beside me. She knows all the words, and sings more loudly when I mess up, as if to cover my mistake. I let her sing the little "oom-pah" instrumental part before the final chorus, then lead her down the hallway to the guest room where we spent the night. She double-checks to make sure DogBear is in her knapsack, then reaches for my hand to walk outside. I lead her out the front door to avoid a reunion with Baby.

She's still humming the song under her breath as I swing open the passenger door of the Caprice.

"That's not our car," my daughter informs me, alarmed.

"Honey, it's going to be our car for a little while." I attempt to convey enthusiasm about this.

"Maggie, what did you do?" she scolds, sounding so much like Yoli that I'm tempted to look around for her. "Where's Silver Cloud?"

It's as if she intuits all of it, the car gone for good, traded away in some illicit deal, and she opens her mouth and wails. A mother becomes an expert on her child's cries—which sound means she's overtired, which signals a tantrum, which indicates there may be bleeding. This is not a cry I believe I've ever heard from her before, the bleat of a dinosaur, the mourning of some primal creature on the edge of extinction, upon seeing its world passing away. And the look in my daughter's eyes tells me it's my fault, my fault, and she will never forgive me.

Angel turns around and looks at the house from which we've come, as if seriously considering whether it might be better for her to stay there. Then her shoulders sag in a defeated way, and she makes an elaborate show of disgust as she climbs into the car, scarcely willing to grace the seat with her butt, though I've laid a blanket across the upholstery. She sniffs loudly, letting me know that the smell of oil that permeates the car does not escape her either. She coughs pointedly, to demonstrate that it irritates her throat. The old seat belt barely has any elasticity as I pull it across her chest. She avoids my eyes.

There is nothing for me to do but turn the key in the ignition and aim the Caprice down the road in the direction Amara has mapped out for me. Just before we turn to go to the highway, I see Amara walk out into the road to watch our departure. Is she memorizing the license plate of this car to report it later? *Spirit, I have to trust someone here.* Amara presses her hands together in a little bow, and with this blessing, sends us on our way.

Chapter 3

"Mrs. Havisham, I need your cooperation," I say to Angel as I maneuver the unfamiliar vehicle down the unfamiliar streets of Ensenada back to the highway headed south. Her arms are crossed over her chest, her back already slumped in boredom. "We've got a long way to drive, and it's going to take us all of today and most of tomorrow."

"Where are we *going?*" Her voice is a whine, and lets me know that her support is not available at this moment.

I check my own snappish response, remembering that neither of us has had much sleep, and that her ordeal began weeks ago. *Spirit, let me speak to her from my heart.*

I pull the car to the side of the road, park in a shady spot under a tree. I unfold the map I've purchased, and show her where we are. "See, this is how far we came last night. And by the end of today we'll probably be here." I point to a spot at the very bottom of the map. The Baja peninsula is so long—1,700 kilometers, over 1,000 miles—it takes both sides of the map to show the whole thing. "Tomorrow," I flip the map over, "we need to go all the way to here."

Her eyes follow my index finger. "Todos Santos," she reads, sounding it out. She was reading before she ever got to school. "What's that?"

"In Spanish, the name means 'All Saints.' It's a little town where lots of artists live. And there's also a community of Light Beings."

Angel knows about the Light Beings; she's been to services with me a couple of times in Los Angeles, much against her mother's wishes.

"You're trying to get her involved in that cult?" Yoli accused, the first time Angel went with me. "Besides, she'll be bored to death!"

"No, Mommy," my girl had protested. "I liked all the candles and the music."

In fact, many parents bring their children to those gatherings, even babies, and they usually behave surprisingly well. I asked a Light Being once about this and he told me, "Everyone is meditating, so the energy is very calm. Children perceive this immediately in their central nervous systems and they relax too."

Only once did I bring Yoli to a Light Beings gathering. It was early on in our relationship, and I took her to one of the Sunday evening meditations. I've always liked these, close to a hundred people, mostly civilians like myself in street clothes, coming together to connect to Spirit. The evenings begin with someone giving a talk about living in Spirit, connecting to the divine in each of us, the way doing so can help to resolve the things that trouble us; then we meditate together in silence, and finally close with singing and chanting. Most of the year, it's still daylight when we enter the ashram and, as the two-hour service progresses, we can watch the sunset through leaded windows and then finish in darkness, the room lit only by candles.

Yoli's first problem was having to take her shoes off before entering the room; her second was being asked to sit on the floor. Even though I'd begged her to wear loose pants, she'd gotten herself all dressed up—as if she were going to church, I suppose—and her tight skirt made a cross-legged posture nearly impossible. All during the service, she squirmed back and forth, shifting her legs one way and another, sometimes kicking me softly in the thigh as she tried yet another position. At the end, the only thing she said was, "The day you start wearing one of them turbans, I am *definitely* out of here."

It would be easy to blame Yoli for my not getting more involved in the Light Beings community; she thought it was some crackpot cult and would routinely admonish me, "If they offer you Kool-Aid, don't drink it!" In the early years, she also didn't like me to take time away from being with her, especially on a Sunday evening. But, tempting as it might be, I know that saying it's her fault is just another self-delusion. Even after Yoli moved out, I still remained on the fringes of the Light Beings, going to Sunday night services and usually once or twice more during the week, but almost never staying after for the communal supper and fellowship. I think I'm just not a joiner, in general. I preferred to buy the books, buy the CDs with the songs and chants, but mostly practice on my own at home. I grew accustomed to seeing people at services, and we'd smile or nod at one another, but I never tried to make friends there.

I think, too, that I never quite knew how to find my place in that community. Although they are welcoming of everyone, and I occasionally would see a few other gay men or lesbians at services, the actual structure of Light Beings society is unquestioningly heterosexual, the union of man and woman being the central focus of social relations in all the texts. I was willing to screen that out from the talks, to distill the essence of what was meaningful to me and discard the rest, but I had little enthusiasm for testing it out in actual interactions.

"Why are we going there?" Angel asks, more complaint than question. "And what did you do with Silver Cloud?" Angel named my car and Yoli's car when she was about three. Yoli's orange vintage Karmann Ghia is called Tiger.

I don't say anything, just put my hand on the back of her

head; at this moment, my daughter is less in need of answers than a chance to discharge her feelings of upset. "And where's Mommy?" she continues, "When is Mommy coming back?"

I take a deep breath. "Mommy's in Chicago, honey, she's singing. You know that."

"Let's call her!"

"Honey, we can't."

"Why not? I wanna talk to Mommy!" This last is a full-decibel shriek as tears erupt in a sudden shower over her face; she hops up and down in her seat, only partially restrained by her flaccid seat belt.

I take her hand and let her cry, nervously glancing down at my watch, conscious of all the miles we need to cover today. I'm aware of how frayed my patience feels today—I'm never very good when I haven't had enough sleep—and try to breathe myself into a state of calm. I try to think of what to say to my girl. She probably could call Yoli; supposedly a prepaid cell phone can't be traced, but what would prevent Angel from just telling her where we are? And how could I ask her to lie to her own mother?

I wait for the storm to subside, and hand her a Kleenex. I run my hand lightly down the knobs of her spine, pausing with my palm flat against the area at the back of her heart. I send her soothing energy.

When she is calm again, I turn, pulling my Ray-Bans from my nose so I can look her right in the eyes. "Angel, I told you yesterday that I could get in trouble for taking you away. Right now the police are looking for you, but they don't know where we are. If you call Mommy, she's going to ask you. And I don't want you to lie, ever, but if you tell the truth, then we'll have to go back and you might have to stay with Lurlene again." *And probably I won't get to see you anymore*, I think but don't say to her.

"I won't!" Another squall threatens in her eyes. "I'll run away!"

"What do you think we're doing?"

This hasn't occurred to her; the notion of the two of us running away makes her giggle in a dangerous way. Then she grows plaintive.

"When *can* I talk to Mommy?" She's got hold of DogBear now, her hand clutched tight around his neck. She's whispering in his rather worn left ear, *"It's okay, DogBear, I'm here. I'm not leaving you. I promise. Not ever."*

"I'm not sure. Maybe once I figure out what to do." The enormity of this fact—that I have no concrete plan, no clear sense of what comes next other than to get to Guru Tam—feels suddenly like an impossible weight. *This is where faith comes in*, I remind myself. *Spirit hasn't brought you this far just to leave you by the side of the road.*

"You don't know?" As shocked as she is alarmed, Angel presses her hands over DogBear's ears, so he doesn't have to hear this latest betrayal.

"I know some things, honey. I know where we're going; I know how to get there. I just don't know yet when we're going to come back." *When or if*, I think. "And I know that I love you more than I love birthday cake."

"I love you more than I love…meatloaf." Angel is a vegetarian, much to Yoli's displeasure. My daughter hates meatloaf. This is how she plays the game when she's not happy with me: she loves me more than dog doo, more than throw-up, more than going to the dentist, or more than meatloaf.

"Well, I'm certainly relieved to hear that," I say mildly. I refold the map, take the opportunity to re-apply some lip balm, then rummage in Angel's backpack for her Walkman. I find the CD of Yoli singing, produced by last year's boyfriend. I hope this will be comforting to my inconsolable girl; I fit the headphones around her ears, and press "Play."

Her face lights up when she hears the first notes of "Boogie On, Reggae Woman," the opening cut. "It's Mommy!" she exclaims, then closes her eyes to listen, shutting me out. I pull away from the curb and head for the highway.

On the outskirts of Ensenada, the highway is lined with makeshift *tiendas*; they sell olives or baskets, unfinished wood furniture and household items. Arrayed on wooden shelves, jars of honey glisten gold in the sunlight.

"Look, sweetie," I try to engage Angel's attention, but she's determined to hate every part of her experience in Mexico today, especially any part that has to do with me. She directs her eyes away from where I'm pointing, and turns up the volume on the Walkman. I can hear Yoli's voice scratching through the headphones—it's her soul-tinged cover of Britney Spears' "Oops, I Did It Again," which I strenuously argued against her including—the boom of bass behind her.

Heading south from Ensenada, it's a pretty desolate drive until you reach Baja Sur, which we won't do until early evening. The road veers inland from the ocean and past poor farms and shambling towns where scrawny chickens sometimes wander into the road. The smell of animal manure and other less identifiable odors is ever-present. But of course, that's just how my United Statesian sensibilities perceive it, accustomed to a certain level of presentation. Could I swear that the people here are any less content than the denizens of Los Angeles?

Yoli grew up welfare poor on the east side of Detroit, the oldest of two other sisters and three brothers, mostly all with different dads. One of her brothers is dead, another's in jail for armed robbery; both of her sisters were on welfare until Clinton's reforms trained them for minimum wage jobs. But her brother, Raymond, the next oldest in the family after Yoli, worked his way through medical school and is almost done with his residency. He and Yoli are the only ones who've been to college. She just went for a couple of years before she dropped out to seriously pursue her music. But she always says, "Mom hadn't given up yet when she had me and Raymond; she still had some dreams and she passed 'em onto us. The other kids didn't have that." I know what Yoli wants more than anything is to make a ton of money with her music, and use it to try to help her family.

I grew up secret poor in the San Fernando Valley. I was about nine when Dad lost his job, but nobody was supposed to know. My mother used to drive all the way into Hollywood to shop for groceries, so that none of her friends would see her paying with food stamps. I always had to pretend that I'd forgotten my lunch money, or the money for the school outing. The kids in my class thought I was the biggest space cadet on the planet, but even that I turned to my advantage, claiming it was because I spent every night smoking weed. And some nights that was true; the older kids down the street from me thought it was a riot to get a nine-year-old stoned. The end of the hippie era worked well for me too; everyone thought my thrift store clothes were really far out, that I was too cool to care.

The whole idea of family has always seemed like a bad joke to me, anyway. A bunch of people who don't really like each other but are thrown together by an accident of birth. Guru Tam has always said, *You choose your family; you choose parents who will help your soul grow in the ways it needs to this lifetime,* but I remain skeptical. My dad died when I was in my early twenties, and I haven't had much contact with my mother since I moved out of the house. I don't think she minds; my mother is sort of ashamed of me. I guess she hoped I'd make a bundle and buy her a mansion.

My grades weren't nearly good enough for any kind of scholarship to college. I took a few classes here and there at community college, but there was never anything I wanted to do so badly that I thought I should get a degree in it. I liked jobs I didn't have to get dressed up for, working as a cook at a daycare center, cab driver, dispatcher for a courier service, clerk at a health food store. One day in about 1991, a redheaded woman dressed all in purple went through my line—I remember she bought only white foods, rice, cauliflower, vanilla ice cream—and when I went to give her her change she grabbed my hand and said, "You have a gift! You need to be using these hands. Do you know you're a healer?"

There were about seven other people in line behind her, so I couldn't go into it then, but she actually came back later that day with a brochure about massage school. Guru Tam says that sometimes Spirit will send someone for the sole purpose of affecting your destiny, and I guess that redheaded woman is an example of that for me. Since the day I started doing bodywork, I've had more clients than I knew what to do with. I figure that once I get us situated in Todos Santos, I can make the hour-plus drive to Cabo a few times a week and do massages for the gringo tourists. I wish I'd thought to bring my portable table, but I'll figure that out later.

Though I'm happy to have a skill that allows me to work for myself, in truth bodywork is getting old for me. When I was first starting in the business, a teacher referred a couple of her clients from the entertainment industry to me. She was cutting down her practice; she'd just gotten married and didn't want to work as much. "Easiest dollars you'll ever make," she'd told me at the time, "and the more you charge them, the better they'll think you are." I was initially scandalized by asking one hundred and fifty, or two hundred dollars an hour for my work, but I soon realized they expected it, that they did equate price with value.

But I've grown tired of clients who never want to go deeper than the surface level, who don't perceive the subtleties of their own energy. Healer, indeed! I'm nothing but a muscle masher. It's time for a change, but to what? This was what preoccupied my worrying mind before Yoli took Angel to stay with Lurlene.

About twenty miles out of Ensenada, I see the first checkpoint. Even though Amara had reminded me about them, even though I've been through them before, I can't help being startled at the sight of soldiers in green uniforms with loaded rifles stopping cars on the road.

This, Angel can't ignore. "Maggie, look!" she gasps, "Who are they?"

"They work for the Mexican army," I tell her, trying to disguise the fear in my voice.

The Mexican government has set up several army checkpoints on the road that traverses the Baja. Normally they are looking for drugs or guns. But what if somehow they've been alerted to look for Angel? I tell myself that I'm being ridiculous; no one even knows yet that we're in Mexico, do they?

Approaching the roadblock, I'm startled to see how young the soldiers are; there are about eight of them standing on the road. Some of them look as if they've barely entered their teens, but there is no youth in their hardened expressions. The soldiers' lives are difficult; a little way back from the road, I can see the makeshift tents where they sleep at night. In the day they stand by the road in the hot sun, with nothing to shade them.

Two cars ahead, there's a VW van. Six white teenagers—they look like teenagers anyway, the boys bare-chested and skinny in shorts, the girls in bikini tops—disembark and stand at the side of the road while three guards tear the van from top to bottom. Each time they pull out another box or suitcase, they open it up, seeming to want more to disrupt its order than to find something in particular. The passengers look too scared to object. A fourth guard plies them with questions in rapid-fire Spanish, which apparently none of them speaks. The driver, sandy-haired with a scraggly goatee, tries his best to explain himself in English.

"What are they gonna do to them?" Angel wants to know. My pity for the teens is mitigated by the selfish hope that the amount of attention paid to their vehicle might result in less focus on mine. Perhaps they only check every third vehicle or something. I watch the guards confiscate a watermelon, which the young surfers seem only too glad to relinquish.

It takes a few minutes for them to re-pack their van, during which time the *Federales* move on to the small white pickup in front of me. This car has Mexican plates, and one guard leans into the front window to chat it up with the driver, then waves him on with a grin. The white pickup maneuvers around the van, throwing up dust as he accelerates.

Then the guard motions me forward. He has a scraggly mustache, and eyes that show no spark of recognition of a fellow human being.

In a whisper, Angel asks, "Are we in trouble?"

"No, honey," I tell her, although I wish my own hammering heart would listen to my reassurances. "It's gonna be okay. *Buenos dias*," I greet him.

He peers into the car, staring fixedly at Angel.

"*Mi hija*," I tell him. My daughter.

He studies her longer, unconvinced of any family resemblance. His is not a world of turkey basters and insemination clinics and third world adoptions. His eyes go next to my fingers on the steering wheel. No ring. I should do something about that before the next time we're stopped.

"*Divorciados.*" I smile ruefully, hoping to elicit pity. I feel Angel's eyes on me; does she think I am lying to him? The guard looks me up and down, as if his appraising eye can see why a man would want to leave me.

"*¿Adonde van?*" he wants to know.

"*Vamos a Todos Santos.*" I explain. Here my Spanish fails me. "To see friends, uh...*amigos.*"

"*¿De donde?*" he questions further.

"*De Los Angeles.*" Then I wonder if I should have told him another place. What if he's been instructed to watch for a woman and a girl from Los Angeles?

"Your passports?" He holds out his hand. I stare at him for a moment, hoping the syllables will assemble themselves into something that makes sense. Then it occurs to me: he's asking for our papers. What if he's been told to watch for people with our names?

Still, I hand over our documents, hoping that maintaining eye contact will make me seem more trustworthy.

"Passport," he says more insistently, looking at Angel, who hides her head behind DogBear.

"*No hay,*" I tell him, "*solamente un* birth certificate. But the man at Immigration said it was okay." I realize that babbling in English is worse than futile; he doesn't understand a word.

He stares at me some more, and I expect him to order me and Angel to get out of the car. Instead, with no word of explanation, he turns on his heels and disappears into a small wooden shed by the side of the road. The other guards remain clustered around the car. They look at me and make some remarks and for once, I'm glad I don't understand them. There are no other vehicles behind us.

"Can we go?" Angel whispers.

"Not yet."

"Why? Is he mad at us?" She is gripping my hand in the way she only does anymore when she's afraid.

"I don't know." I try to keep the tremor out of my voice. A fine sheen of sweat has sprouted along my hairline. Maybe the

FBI has sent our pictures to the Mexican police. Maybe in this shed is a desk, atop which is a fax of my picture with the word WANTED emblazoned underneath. But then I look out at the desolate landscape, the smoke rising from the campsite cook fire. It doesn't look like there's even electricity at this outpost, let alone a phone line.

"Are they gonna shoot us?" Tears are welling in her eyes as my daughter stares at the automatic rifles.

"No, of course not." I make myself sound firm, confident. The whole idea of this trip was to keep Angel safe, not to put her at greater risk or terrorize her further. *Spirit, protect her. Do whatever you want to me, but keep this little girl from harm.*

In a minute later the soldier returns, zipping up his fly. Did he really just need to take a piss? He strides back to the car window and hands us back our papers. "*Señora,*" he says, then to Angel, "*señorita,*" and gestures for us to pass.

Before I do, I reach into the food bag for an unopened package of chocolate chip cookies. "*Por ustedes.*" I offer them. He snatches them eagerly and rips the plastic; the other guards crowd around to make sure they get their share.

It is only once I start the car and drive off in a cloud of dust that I notice that the hands gripping the steering wheel are shaking, that my teeth are chattering, even though I am still sweating.

"Maggiemama, are you okay?" Angel wants to know.

I start to answer in the affirmative, but tears come unbidden, so hard that I have to pull to the narrow shoulder of the road because I can't see. It's like a sudden storm come upon the landscape; my shoulders are racked with sobs and I press my forehead against the steering wheel. Perhaps it's years of accumulated grief: the loss of Yoli; the way she's turned into someone I can't even recognize anymore; the threatened loss of Angel; the idea that anyone would dare to beat my child, any child; the long drive; my desperate strategy that could put everything at risk; the skinny, hungry sixteen-year-olds with guns.

Angel unbuckles her seat belt and wraps her slender arms around me. "Don't cry, Maggiemama, don't cry." She rummages on the floor beneath her, then presses DogBear into my neck. I smell the musty, sour smell of the well-loved stuffed animal, and that somehow brings me around.

I lift my head from the steering wheel, wrap Angel in a hug and kiss her cheek. "Thank you, Mrs. Havisham. Thank you, DogBear. I don't know what I'd do without you."

About an hour past the checkpoint, Angel announces, "I hafta pee." The road has gotten mountainous, and it takes me a while to find a place to pull over, during which time my daughter keeps repeating "I hafta pee, I hafta pee." When I finally reach a turnout that seems safe, my daughter takes pride in her newfound talent for roadside urination. With ceremony, she deposits the wad of toilet paper in the inside trash bag.

Once on the road again, she asks, "What if I hafta poop?" She giggles in a way that lets me know her interest is more academic than urgent.

"Better if you can give me a little warning about that," I tell her, "so I can find an indoor place."

"But what if I really can't wait?" There is a scream of delight in her voice, the delight of torturing her mother.

"Then you poop by the side of the road like a bear."

She forms her hands into claws, starts scrabbling at the dash and growling, "I'm a bear, I'm a bear." Since the incident with the army, she seems to have forgotten to be mad at me.

"I'm a bear and I'm going to eat you up!" She has risen up on her knees; one hand then another softly gouges at my neck.

"Careful," I warn, "I'm driving here." The difficulty of the road, coupled with driving an unfamiliar car, puts an edge in my tone. She scoots herself back into her own seat. "Are you a hungry bear?" I ask, not wanting her to get mad again.

"Starving," she growls, still in bear persona.

"And what does a hungry bear eat?" I quiz her.

She stops to think. "People?"

"I don't know. Maybe this bear is a vegetarian," I suggest.

"Oh, yeah, this hungry bear is a vegetable-tarian." She holds DogBear by his two front paws and dances with him.

"Does this hungry bear eat animal cookies?" I wonder.

"Yes, we do!!!!"

One hand on the wheel, I rummage behind me for the food bag in the backseat. My fingers find the small box by its shape, the health food store version of the snack I remember from my own childhood, and she sets to work, feeding herself and DogBear.

"Not too many," I caution her.

"I hafta eat DogBear's too, because he doesn't have a mouth!" She collapses into giggles, crumbs flying from between her lips. I rifle through the cooler, find her a box of juice.

"And I hafta drink DogBear's juice too," she's near hysterical with laughing, "because he doesn't have any lips!"

"Okay, breathe," I remind her. "Calm down there in the front seat." I feel guilty suddenly, for making her stay cooped up this whole long car ride. She has no outlet for her energy, her worry about what we're doing.

I'm torn by competing needs to move as fast as we can and wanting to stop at different places so that Angel can get out and stretch her legs, to see the places we are flying past. The Caprice is not nearly as responsive as my Accord, and I'm afraid to drive as fast as I normally would. The trucks and buses have no such inhibitions, however. They whip by me on this two-lane road, passing close enough that I could reach out my window and touch them. I worry about whether we'll make it to Guerrero Negro, the spot where I'm hoping we can stay tonight.

"Why'd you give away our cookies?" My daughter's mood shifts suddenly, and she's accusing me.

"I don't think those boys in the army get paid very much," I tell her. "Those cookies were probably a treat for them."

"Why don't they just get another job?" she wonders, with a snotty cast to her voice.

It's times like these, when Angel is so unconscious of her privilege, that I feel the urge to shake her. It's one of the few aspects of my daughter's personality that I really don't like. It's not her fault, I remind myself. Yoli and I have protected her from want.

"It isn't that simple," I try to explain. "This is probably one of the best jobs they can get."

"Are you gonna give away everything?" she asks darkly. I know this is a reference to my "giving away" Silver Cloud, but maybe also indicates some deeper anxiety about whether she can count on me. *Spirit, I pray that she can! Don't let me screw this up, please.*

"Only the things we don't really need," I tell her gently.

"Do we really need DogBear?" she asks, holding up the toy for my inspection.

"You betcha we do!"

Driving inland, the temperature gets hotter, the air dryer. The town of Santo Tomás is like an oasis, with olive groves and vineyards nurtured by the river that flows through. Before long, we are back in chaparral country, once again in mountainous terrain.

It takes all my concentration to navigate the two-lane highway. Some cars zip along, passing with impunity, but there is no shortage of vehicles that barely crest forty mph on the inclines. It's my tendency to speed, but the Caprice won't cooperate, and I have to be careful about recalculating my margin for passing.

"Look, Maggiemama." Angel points to a small structure, just two feet high, like a doll's house by the side of the road. A cross pokes up from its angled roof, and flowers are arrayed around the outside. "What is that?"

"It's a shrine, honey." Seeing from the corner of my eye her uncomprehending expression, I explain, "Somebody had an accident on this road, and they died. Their families build these so everyone will remember them." I remember Dagmar telling me that sometimes these shrines will include part of the car and a beer can, but I edit this from my explanation to Angel.

"Look, there's another one!" The alarm in my daughter's voice increases. In truth, there are many on this highway. I tighten my grip on the steering wheel as an eighteen-wheeler traveling north passes and the Chevy sways.

In that uncanny way children have of sensing adult anxiety, my girl asks, "Are *we* gonna have an accident?"

"No, sweetheart, we're not. Mama's an excellent driver." I force my lips into a smile. I feel the skin crack, and reach once more for my lip balm.

It's my intention to get us to San Quintín, about another hour south, before we stop. According to the map, we can take the access road down to the bay. It will be a nice break for both of us, I figure, to stretch and eat some lunch, to stick our toes in the ocean.

The Caprice doesn't get the same kind of mileage as my Accord, but I still figure we can make it to the Catavina before I need to get gas again. I can only hope the station will be open because the next gas after that is too far away. If I were driving this with Yoli, she'd make me stop at every gas station we saw; she's always afraid of getting stranded "out in the middle of nowhere." And it is true, there's no Triple A out here to bail you out if your car breaks down, although I've heard that there's something called the Green Angels, operated by the *Secretaría de Tursimo*, trucks that patrol the road every so often to offer roadside assistance to the stranded. But in the time we've been on this road I haven't seen anything that looked like that.

That is not going to happen, Spirit, I tell myself firmly. *Get us safely to our destination without mishap, please.*

"What *is* this place?" Angel wants to know. "Why don't they plant grass so it's green?" Again that tone of disgust that reminds me of Yoli.

"There are parts that are really pretty," I assure her. "And this afternoon, when we get to the Catavina, it looks like a garden of boulders, like dinosaurs could be walking around there."

"We're not gonna see any dinosaurs," she says, suspicious, refusing to be tricked into seeing something positive.

"No, they're extinct, remember? But you can imagine them in this place. You'll see."

"When do we get there?" She's bored again, petulant.

Patiently, I explain, "I told you, we drive all day today and all day tomorrow..."

"I'm hot!" She's furious.

This ignites my own temper. *You're going to get a lot hotter as we go south,* I long to answer back. *You think I'm not hot too? Don't you know I'm doing this for you?* I'm so grateful that my meditation has at least taught me silence, to not speak back in anger.

"Drink some water, honey," I tell her instead, handing her a bottle. "That'll help to keep you cool." As she hands it back I decide to take my own advice, and draw a long swig.

The town of San Quintín is one long strip of tacky shops, restaurants, food vendors, auto parts places. By the standard of what we've passed through since leaving Ensenada, it seems a major metropolis, but it's really two towns that seem to stretch into one. We drive through the second, Lázaro Cárdenas, before we find the road that promises access to the bay.

But the dirt road is much worse than I could have imagined, and the Caprice shudders so badly I fear it's going to come apart.

"Maggie, what's 'a matter?" Dozing for the last twenty minutes or so, Angel has been shaken awake.

"It's a rough road," I tell her, as if that wasn't already obvious. Up ahead is another sign—in English, for the tourists, I suppose—telling me to turn left for the bay. When I do, the tires almost immediately sink into soft sand. The engine makes a horrible whine. I progress only a few feet before it's clear that this car will never traverse this road. The wheels spin but we aren't moving forward.

Shit! *Spirit, please! Don't let us get stuck out here!* No Green Angel is ever going to find us on this forgotten stretch of road.

"Maggie!" There is panic in my daughter's voice. "What is it?"

It's all I can do not to scream at her, my daughter's anxiety igniting my own like a match in gasoline. I bite down hard on my tongue to keep myself quiet.

Spirit, this was stupid, I admit it, but please get us out of here. I just wanted Angel to see something pretty.

"Maggie!!!" she's shrieking now, that high-pitched sound that puts my teeth on edge. It reminds me of Yoli, how auto emergencies always made her come completely undone.

"Honey," I say tersely, "I need a minute to concentrate here."

From a million years ago, I have a dim memory of something my father said. It was during one of L.A.'s winter rains when the San Fernando Valley is turned into a giant mud puddle. It must have been when he was teaching me to drive, because he was in the passenger seat, and I hear his voice say calmly, "Okay, you're just going to rock it out of here, a little bit forward, not too much, and now in reverse, a little bit back."

And as on that forgotten day so many years ago, I follow his instructions, and little by little, I gain traction. All I want to do is back up a few feet, get back on the road from which I turned, pitted and potholed but at least passable. *Spirit, help me, let us get out of here!* In a few more minutes, I for one am grateful to be bouncing our way back up the road toward the highway.

Angel, however, doesn't see it that way. "This is the most terrible trip anyone ever went on!" she rails through her tears. "You don't even know how to get there, and I want Mommy!" She is kicking her heels against the seat and flailing her fists against the dash. It's a full-blown fit.

Ordinarily I would stop to comfort her, let her cry out her feelings until she was calm, but what I am noticing now is that the temperature gauge in the dash has moved way into the red and I can see steam coming up from under the hood.

Fucking piece of shit car! *Goddamn it, Spirit, I asked you to protect us! Is this your idea of a joke, to lure us all this way and then have us break down?* The part of my mind that is trained in meditation, that can hold neutrality, marvels at the way I will abandon faith the minute something doesn't go my way.

I know enough about cars to know that if I keep driving, I could blow the whole thing up. And while part of me is mad enough to do just that, I know I am still responsible for this little girl. *Acceptance is the only path to peace*, Guru Tam always says. I pull to the side of the road; there is no shade as far as I can see, but there is a little breeze from the ocean.

"What are you doing?" my daughter seethes.

Very calmly, I tell her, "The engine is too hot. We have to stop for a while, and let it cool down."

"Why?" she demands, more accusing than curious. It's a catchall inquiry: *Why* is the engine hot? *Why* do we have to stop? *Why* did you buy this piece of junk in the first place?

I consider telling her the next bit of news, that we're going to need to go back to town to find a mechanic, but even I can't face that yet.

"As long as we have to wait, let's have lunch," I suggest, trying to make myself sound normal, a nearly impossible task. I pull out some of the sandwiches I made—was it only yesterday? The long trip in the hot car has done nothing to improve their freshness.

Angel sighs deeply with each mouthful, washed down with mouthfuls of soymilk. "I knew you shouldn't give away our cookies," she grumbles ominously.

After finishing the dry peanut butter on stale bread with a now overripe banana, and against my daughter's protests, I step outside the car. I want to call Charlie. I want to find out what the developments are, what the television is saying about how the police are pursuing the case. How close they might be behind us. I want ask his opinion of whether it makes sense to be paranoid about the checkpoints. But of course, my cell phone doesn't work out here; I can't get a signal to save my life. Those of us who live in the United States are so spoiled with our technology, our assumption that we are entitled to access anyone from anywhere. Besides, I shouldn't draw Charlie any more deeply into this than I already have. Even if he does find the danger thrilling, he's got too many other people who need him.

After a while, I turn the engine back on. The indicator has gone down a bit, but not all the way to cool. Still, there's no more steam pouring out, so I decide to open the hood. Still channeling my dad, I manage to find the radiator cap. Just in time I remember to grab yesterday's T-shirt before scalding myself. A plume of steam rises up from the radiator, but I manage to step back.

Angel has gotten out of the car. "What are you *doing?*" she asks in that same voice of complaint.

"Stand back, honey, it's very hot," I warn her, and leaning away I pour the contents of one of our water bottles into the radiator. More steam, and this liter bottle doesn't fill it. I don't want to use all our water, in case we are stranded again—I imagine the headline "Kidnapper and daughter found dead of heat stroke in Baja desert." I wonder if this is enough water to get us back to town.

I have to surrender my timetable; I can't even predict how long this detour will take. *Spirit, just let us get to a mechanic, and then I'll go along with whatever you have in mind.* I know it's ridiculous to be bargaining like this; still, that's where my mind goes.

When I ask my daughter to get back in the car, she looks at me for a moment as if she will defy me. She has no more faith in this program, and I believe if she saw *any* other option, she would take it. But no other car has passed since we've been sitting here, and what else is she going to do?

With great reluctance she gets back in the passenger seat, deliberately turning her back to me. Her coppery hair is wild from neglect and from sleeping at odd angles against the window; it looks like an ill-trimmed bush.

She doesn't say a word to me as I inch us back to the highway, and then turn back north.

Once we reach a repair shop, Angel pretends to sleep while the balding mechanic from Lázaro Cárdenas removes the radiator and puts in a new one. He has a little English, but not enough for me to really understand all he says to me as he points with dismay to various things inside the hood. He tugs at hoses, shaking his head.

Finally I tell him, *"Vamos a Todos Santos."* I show him the distance on the map. "Do what you need to do to make sure we get there."

Who knows what he thinks I said? But he does replace some hoses and who knows what else. He adds oil and transmission fluid. An hour and fifteen hundred pesos later, he tells us we are ready to go. I wonder if the police will come at some point and question the mechanic about us.

"*Necessitas* gasoline?" he asks.

I explain that I plan to get it in Catavina.

"No," he objects, "*no hay. Sólo a veces.* Only sometimes. Get it *aquí* or in El Rosario."

I agree to let him fill it up. Was this what Spirit had in mind, I wonder, bringing us here to spare us running out of gas in the Catavina? Was I being taken care of even when I thought I wasn't?

Angel continues her pout as we get back on the road. Despite the near-breakdown, I'm feeling a little more confident about the Caprice now that it's gotten the once-over from someone other than the Ordoña brothers. I'm willing to drive a little faster, all the while keeping one eye on the temperature gauge, which stays mercifully out of the range of boiling over, and the other on the rearview mirror looking for the police.

North of El Rosario, we are stopped at another checkpoint. Angel and I both seem to hold our breath, but the bored young soldiers barely make a pretense of looking at our papers; then they wave us through. After El Rosario, the road heads southeast, into the interior of the peninsula. It's nearly five o'clock, but the air is warming the further we head inland. We probably have four hours to go before we reach Guerrero Negro. I had promised myself I wouldn't drive this road after dark.

Angel still isn't talking to me. I don't think I've ever known her to be this angry with me and it shakes me in my core. Perhaps she is thinking that I never before put her through such a grueling ordeal.

As we drive deeper into the desert, I try to point out things I think might engage her attention. "Look, Mrs. Havisham, see those cacti?" I point to the tall, spindly *cirios,* crowned with foliage like green splayed fingers. "They're called 'boojums.' Isn't that a funny name?"

On any other day she would repeat the name, perhaps several times, giving it multiple inflections like an actress trying out a line. On any other day we might burst into a spontaneous song about "boojums," until we were laughing too hard to go on.

But on this day, she listlessly cranes her neck, then sighs deeply and lapses back into her funk. Even the Catavina does not seem to make an impression. It's always been one of my favorite parts of the drive through Baja, the stark beauty of its massive boulders, so artfully strewn. I always think of it as a garden of boulders, as if they had somehow sprouted out of the dirt.

"Can you believe that people would graffiti here?" I ask, trying to elicit her indignation, if nothing else.

"Everybody sucks," she says dully. I wonder if she picked this up at school or at Lurlene's house. Angel sighs again. *Especially you*, I'm sure she is thinking.

But at least she's talking to me. I try to take advantage of the opening. "Honey, I know the drive is long. There isn't anything I can do about that. What do you think would make it more interesting for you?"

Yoli has often told me that I don't understand what it's like to be a kid, that it's wrong to expect Angel to be like a little adult all the time. To me, I would think she'd be fascinated with the newness, a place different than anywhere she's been, but maybe that's a different level of maturity than an almost-eight-year-old can possess.

"If Mommy was here," she answers in the quietest little voice, as if she's afraid to let me hear her. It punctures my heart, and for the first time I start to really feel like a kidnapper. Perhaps this thing I'm doing, supposedly for her benefit, is not what she wants at all.

I imagine getting to La Paz, sometime tomorrow afternoon, calling Yoli, and putting Angel on a plane back to L.A. on the condition that Yoli fly in to meet her. No more Lurlene. No more me either, not in Angel's life. The thought of it is almost more than I can bear. But that's still not reason enough to keep my child against her will.

Maybe, just maybe, Yoli would fly to meet me. Maybe when she sees the bruises on Angel's legs, she'd be willing to talk about this, come up with some better solutions than unilateral decision-making and Daman's sister. To call her is a risk, but maybe, just maybe, it could pay off so my daughter can be happy again.

"Sweet pea, it may be a little more time before this can

happen, but I promise you you'll get to be with Mommy again."

"How long?" She refuses to be placated.

"I don't know that, but you have my promise. Have I ever broken a promise to you?"

She grudgingly admits I never have. Now there is nothing to do but keep going, whether the destination is La Paz or Todos Santos. It would be almost as far to turn back.

Still, it's a long stretch of driving for a seven-year-old to endure. Her Walkman batteries are dead. I wonder how long we'll have to drive before we find a town with a store that will have them. We play Twenty Questions for a while, my daughter scrupulously keeping track of the number of queries posed. She is insulted by how easy it is for her to guess "DogBear"; she stumps me with clues about a geode on my desk at home, even after granting me five more clues. Home seems impossibly far away, another lifetime. That geode seems as irretrievable as expelled breath.

Still, I've disappointed her. "You used to be good at this," she complains, turning her body away from me, away from the game, away from my whole crazy plan.

She dozes as the sun sinks below the horizon, as the desert sky begins to purple and darken, sleep the only refuge from boredom, frustration, fear. For myself, I use driving as a meditation, letting myself be emptied out by the vast open landscapes.

It's only my faith that keeps me moving down the road after dark, following the wan headlights of the Caprice. Brighter headlights of faster moving vehicles loom menacingly up behind me, and our car is rattled with the speed at which they pass. *Spirit, don't let us crash on the road and in the dark. There's no one here who'd build a shrine to us.* I'm grateful that Angel is sleeping; I don't think I'd be able to hide my fear from her.

Just before Guerrero Negro, we encounter our third checkpoint, on the border between Northern and Southern Baja. There's a big building, maybe an army base, with an enormous Mexican flag.

A soldier wearing eyeglasses waves for us to stop. He asks

for our documents and I pass them over. With a gesture of his rifle, he indicates that we should exit the vehicle.

"*Mi hija esta dormiendo*," I protest, indicating the sleeping girl.

He's unconcerned with this, just repeats the same gesture.

I get out and walk around to Angel's side of the car. Opening the door, I say, "Don't be scared, Mrs. Havisham. These men just want to look in our car." I wrap my arms around her and pull her up from the seat, trying to disturb her as little as possible. Lifting her from this position wrenches my back, but I'll deal with that later.

The April night is cold, and I clutch my daughter close to me. With her head pressed against my neck, I can hear her whimpering in half-sleep. Three men go through the bags in the front and backseat and the trunk. They find bananas and take them. Fine, it's all fine. Just let us go.

I'm too tired and too numb to muster the fear that they will identify us. My body and brain feel as if they're in a cocoon as the young soldiers dig through our meager belongings. Once we're back in the car, they motion us to roll up the windows and drive forward a few feet, and spray a stream of liquid insecticide under the Chevy. For this they charge us ten pesos. Then they motion us on our way.

"How many times do we hafta do that?" Angel is now awake.

"No more tonight," I tell her.

It's only a short time before the road splits and I take the turnoff for Guerrero Negro. There's a decent motel here with a slightly better than decent restaurant, right off the highway. My head is buzzing from the engine whine, the tires rolling over the road; my throat aches from the stench of oil that still permeates the car; my eyes are blurry from focusing too hard through the dark.

As we enter our modest room, Angel's face lights up.

"They've got TV!" she exclaims, and races to turn it on.

I've always taken pride that my daughter was not hooked on TV, and I wonder if I am witnessing the effects of her three weeks with Lurlene. But perhaps it's just the longing for something predictable after so much strangeness and uncertainty.

But rather than the cartoons or sitcoms or whatever she might have expected, what greets her when she turns on the TV is a Mexican talk show, entirely in Spanish. She turns her crestfallen eyes toward me, as if once more I have betrayed her.

I don't try to bullshit her. "Today has just been a total bummer, huh, Mrs. Havisham?"

She nods, but seems slightly relieved to have her reality confirmed.

"Let's go get some dinner, then go to bed and see if tomorrow isn't a little better, okay?"

The host tries to discourage us; it is late and they want to close. I had forgotten about the change from Pacific to Mountain Time that happens crossing from northern to southern Baja.

"But *la niña*," I point shamelessly to Angel, "she hasn't had any dinner." He might say no to me, but I'm betting he won't say no to my daughter. It is only after we are seated that I think perhaps I'm being stupid to call attention to her. Now he'll remember her for certain when the police ask about us.

I am thankful that the menu has cheese enchiladas; we both order them, and find them passable. I am almost too exhausted to chew.

"You drive tomorrow," I tease her, "I'm tired of having to do everything around here."

"If we still had Silver Cloud, I would!" she complains.

"What name should we give to our new car?" I ask, dipping a corn chip into not-bad salsa.

"Poo-poo Box," she grimaces.

"Poo-poo Box, it is!" I smile at her, and she can't help but giggle.

After dinner we stroll through the gift shop, which has a poor sampling of "Mexican" items, carelessly displayed. But as I'd hoped, there is a small tray of cheap silver rings, and I buy the simplest one I can find, place it on the ring finger of my right hand. I believe there will be more frequent checkpoints, now that we are entering Baja Sur.

"Can I get something?" Angel asks.

I like that she is polite, not greedy the way some kids are. I would rather buy her something better than the cheap merchandise arrayed here, but I think she needs to feel like she's gotten something today. "What do you want?"

She looks around; suddenly the shop is full of possibilities. Energized by her mission, she re-examines each item she has previously rushed past—T-shirts and shot glasses and ashtrays and embroidered blouses—searching for treasure. I make up my mind that I will say yes to whatever she chooses, be it the woven hammock or the coffee mug with the marlin on it, so I'm relieved when she comes back to me clutching a single shell, plucked from a basket of shells on a low table. It's speckled brown, curled as a small fist, with a faint pink tinge at its opening.

Back in the room, she has a brief meltdown because there is no bathtub. In my memory of the Baja, I'm not sure I ever encountered a bathtub, even the one time I stayed in a fancy hotel. Every muscle in my body is screaming with tiredness, yet somehow I find the patience to convince her that a shower might be fun.

"Like running through the sprinkler," I tell her, "only it's warm." I wait in the bathroom while she showers, calling out phrases of encouragement. I let her use the sole towel provided, and get her settled with DogBear in one of the room's twin beds.

The pillow is a flat hard mound, the sheets are scratchy, not soft, and as my hands tuck the thin, cheap blanket over her, I feel how foreign and overwhelming this must all be to my girl.

Once she drifts off, I tiptoe back outside, locking the door behind me. I stand in the motel parking lot clutching my cell phone, debating with myself whether to use it. I decide that if I can get a signal, I will. Amazingly, the call I dial goes through, and I hear the ring of a telephone, sounding small and far away.

When Yoli answers, I say, simply, "It's me."

"Goddamn it, Maggie, what have you done with her?" I hear the exhalation of cigarette smoke.

"Yoli, she's safe now. That was the whole point." The wind cuts through my thin jacket, stings my face.

"Where *are* you?"

And I want to tell her. It seems crazy to me that suddenly we are on opposite sides, we who once told each other everything. I choke on the words, "I can't tell you."

"Let me talk to Angela." Her voice is imperious, clipped.

"She's asleep now. Look, she misses you a lot…"

"You're goddamn right she misses me," she interrupts. "I'm her mother."

"I'm her mother too." I will myself to say this without rancor.

"No judge is going to see it that way," she replies with rancor enough for both of us.

It's worse than I'd hoped. I remember Charlie's encouragement from this morning, his belief that after what's happened to Angel, I have a good basis for a custody case. But I don't want to threaten a legal battle long distance with the possibility that the FBI is listening in.

Instead I say, "Yoli, it doesn't have to be that way. I'm not trying to keep her away from you. But you have to promise me you won't leave her with Daman's sister again…"

"I have to promise *you?* I have to promise *you?*" She is shrieking into the mouthpiece, and I have to hold the cell phone away from my ear.

"Yoli, someone in that house hurt her, hurt her bad. You didn't see the bruises, but I did."

But I don't know whether she hears this or not, because all of a sudden it isn't Yoli on the phone anymore, but Daman, and he's yelling, "We're gonna find you, you fucking dyke, if we have to tear this country apart. We're gonna trace this call and find you, you psycho-bitch, and if I don't kill you myself, we're gonna put you in jail so you never get out…"

I push the button to end the call. The whine of the wind seems to carry the echo of his yelling, pushing against me under this Mexican sky. I try to assimilate what has just happened, but there's an odd numbness that makes it hard for me to think. I can't tell if I'm more distressed by Yoli's estrangement from me or her tunnel vision regarding Angel's well being. Or her total surrender to Daman's will.

I suppose some part of me thought I could work this out with Yoli, send Angel back to her with an assurance of her safety, and then deal with the wreckage I've made of my life. But I have no willingness to negotiate with Daman. Nor, apparently, he with me. If he's running the show, no way will I send Angel back.

Because I called Yoli's cell phone, I have no way of knowing whether they're still in Chicago or back in L.A. That's something I wanted to find out. It's equally hard for me to imagine Yoli quitting the touring company as it is to imagine her not doing so.

From Daman's comment, it may be that everyone thinks I am still in the U.S., and that would be a very good thing. But if the FBI was able to trace the call, I've lost that advantage. There are things I want to know, but after this exchange I definitely can't risk calling Charlie. Not tonight, for sure.

I am suddenly desperately tired, and feel more alone than I can ever remember feeling, even when I was a kid. *Spirit, take my hand*, I whisper softly. *Please guide me; I don't know what to do.*

The wind has blown away some cloud cover, and the sky above is cluttered with stars. More stars than we ever see in L.A. They glimmer above me, out of reach, cold and distant comfort.

Chapter 4

I am already sleeping fitfully when I am awakened by Angel's crying. It's a sharp, spasmodic sound that seems to punch its way out of her chest. Nearly eight years of motherhood have taught me to wake at a moment's notice, and I am out of the covers and at Angel's bedside before my body even registers the chill of the unheated room, the tile floor icy under my feet. It's still early enough in spring for the mornings to be cold.

"Sweetheart, what's going on?"

She's crying in her sleep, a trail of drool pooling in DogBear's ear. I slide my body beside hers, and take her in my arms.

"It's okay, my sweet girl. It's okay." I wonder: *is that a lie?*

Her eyes slowly open and take me in; they are still awash in tears.

"Did you have a dream, baby?" I smell the soft wool of her hair.

"It was Mommy. I couldn't find her," my daughter sobs again. "She was singing, but I couldn't see her."

Now the reality of the day comes crashing in on me: where we are, the reason for this mission. My mouth floods with bile as I recall the phone call with Yoli last night, her willful lack of concern about our daughter's welfare.

The thought enters my head: *You're better off without her, little girl,* so full of venom it takes my breath away.

Spirit, fill me up this morning with your essence, your kindness. May I never speak an unkind word to my daughter about her mother.

I look at Angel. "Mrs. Havisham," I tell her, "what say we blow this pop stand and get on the road in time to watch the sunrise?"

She gives me a little smile that seems to have been assembled on my behalf. "Yeah," she agrees, "let's blow this pop stand."

It's my turn to stand under the trickle of the shower, shivering, feeling a headache begin to drill through my temple and behind the left eye. As I try to warm myself under the water, my body's overwhelming thought is *Please, don't make me drive another mile.* But my mind argues, *I've got to get Angel out of here. I've got to get us both to Guru Tam.* This thought propels me out of the shower and into clothes. I hastily toss our belongings into our bags. Angel has already gathered DogBear and her shell and is sitting on one corner of her bed. Her shoulders slump with such dejection that it breaks my heart.

Spirit, please give her a better day than yesterday.

With a quick glance to make sure we haven't left anything behind, we're out the door and into the Caprice, which I can't help but regard now as the Poo-poo Box. I wrap a blanket around Angel, take a peek at the map just to make sure of my game plan, slide some lip balm onto my lips, then start the car. It shudders and chokes, threatens to stall, but then at the last minute decides to cooperate. We are on the road. It's about five thirty. The sun will be up by the time we reach San Ignacio.

Angel dozes against the passenger door. I can't see very well in the grainy light of predawn, but luckily there is no other traffic. We are driving east across the peninsula, through a road carved out of desert, and with each mile the color of the sky lightens, mauve to pink to blue.

It reminds me of the sky the morning I first met Yoli. People used to laugh when we'd tell them we'd met in an all-night coffee shop in the moments just before dawn. Neither of us should have been there, at that place or that time. In fact, sometimes I think we got involved, despite the overwhelming evidence that weighed against the reason of it, because it seemed that Spirit had gone to such elaborate lengths to bring us together.

In those days, I was volunteering in a program Charlie was running to provide free massage and bodywork to people with AIDS. To me it was a great relief from the parade of actors and directors who paid so handsomely to lie on my table yet never really yielded to my touch.

One of the clients I saw regularly in Charlie's program was a former priest whose name was Angus. His once auburn hair had fallen out from the regimen of drugs he was taking, and he'd grown thinner than any man ever should. When, near the end, even the lightest massage would leave bruises on his ravaged skin, I switched to energetic work with him, holding my hands just inches from his body, helping to dissolve blockages and regulate the flow of *qi* through his body.

"Can you heal me with that woo-woo?" he'd once asked with a wry grin.

"I don't know," I replied. "How would you know if you were healed?"

"I wouldn't be angry at God anymore," is what he answered.

On this particular night in June of 1992, his caregiver had called about midnight; Angus was having a bad time, and was asking for me. Would I come?

Though I always say no when my industry clients call me at odd hours or on a moment's notice, a sixth sense provoked me to say yes. By the time I got there, Angus had already slipped below the surface of consciousness, and his breathing was labored and shallow. Still, I talked to him as though it were a regular session. I used my hands to help calm his body when it started to panic, to fight the transition his soul was trying to make. He'd once told me his favorite hymn was "Amazing Grace" and, though I'm no singer, I began to sing it and kept on until my throat was raw. Angus left his body around four a.m.

When I was certain that no more breaths would follow his final exhalation, I stared into his face, no longer wracked with pain and fear, and whispered, "Now, Angus, now you are healed."

His caregiver and I wept a bit; then he began making the appropriate calls and there was nothing more for me to do. Still, sleep was impossible, and I couldn't face going back to my apartment to be awake alone. That's how I ended up in a West Hollywood coffee shop at five o'clock in the morning.

I've always been a bit more fuzzy about the events that brought Yoli to the Tick Tock that night. She'd finished a gig, closed the club; she'd partied at little with someone—a promoter? Her manager? The bassist? It had ended in an argument. It's possible she'd been dumped out of the guy's car. Yoli had a lot of these stories and over the years they tended to run together in my mind.

I had noticed her only briefly when I sat down on the leatherette booth, one of the few other patrons in the post-bar, pre-breakfast hours. An attractive Black woman still dolled up in last night's finery—something glittery, maybe gold lamé. Still working off last night's high. My hands and heart were still full of Angus and his journey from this life, and I probably would have just drunk the burnt coffee and gone home, had the woman not started to sing "Amazing Grace."

Los Angeles is a place where almost no behavior is considered that out of the ordinary. A hymn sung in a diner, sure, why not? A voice began to pervade the coffee shop. Not just any voice, but the voice of Spirit herself, I was convinced at the time, sent to offer me some solace at the end of this sad and miraculous night.

And that is the only reason I can come up with for what I did next, because unlike many denizens of L.A., I was never one for trying to draw attention to myself. But in this brightly lit diner, mere hours since I'd shepherded Angus's passage from this world, my throat already raspy and torn, I opened my mouth and I began to sing along with her.

Most any other time, Yoli would have had a fit that anyone would dare to horn in on her act. But the events of her night had broken some armor she ordinarily wore, and she just smiled at me as we finished the verse. Then she came over to my booth.

"Are you my angel?" I asked her.

It wasn't meant to be some cheesy pick-up line. By this time the sun was just starting to rise and in my sleepless and broken open state, I'd begun to feel ecstatic. I bought her a hot butterscotch sundae—it's what she wanted—and then I drove her back to my apartment and we just slept, huddled together like children in wartime. Somewhat later it would become clear that Yoli was probably not my angel, but then she gave birth to one, and I could never doubt that Spirit had intended our lives to be connected. It's a belief I've had a hard time shaking.

"Angel girl," I reach to gently shake my daughter's shoulder, "don't you want to see the sunrise?"

She squints through the windshield and sleepily murmurs her appreciation at the light show unleashing itself before her in the eastern sky.

"Are you hungry yet?" I ask, but she mumbles no and drifts back to sleep.

I had planned to stop in San Ignacio for breakfast, but we're making better time than I expected; it's only six thirty and Angel shows no signs of wanting to wake up. I know she'd like this little town, an oasis built on a river surrounded by date palms, with a centuries-old church, but instead I keep driving into the sun.

Had we gone into town I would have gone into the church to pray, untroubled by its being a Catholic church. In our teachings, Spirit listens to everyone everywhere at all times. So I pray anyway, to the sky in front of me, to the sun ascending higher in the sky. *Spirit, thank you for keeping us safe thus far. Thank you for this new day and the opportunity to serve you. Let our journey be easy today, and may our destination welcome us. Peace begets peace.*

In another thirty minutes, the Sea of Cortez comes into view, and I have to awaken my girl again.

"Angel, honey, look!"

We're still in the mountains, but as we come around the curves the sea looms ahead. Where the Pacific is largely gray and a little forbidding, the Sea of Cortez is a calm and glimmering turquoise jewel.

"Maggiemama, where *are* we?" My daughter is awed by the vista. She continues to "ooo" and "ahh" each time we round another bend, as if seeing it for the first time again and again. It has the same effect on me, a beauty that seems to heal my heart.

Another twenty minutes and we reach the town of Santa Rosalía, built right on the sea. Much of the town was originally built by a French mining company, which drew copper out of the surrounding mountains. For Central Baja, this is a large town, with a wharf and industry and green public parks. But I drive through the town and a little farther south before I stop for breakfast at the old Hotel Moro, which I remember from a long-ago trip with Dagmar, with a restaurant right on the sea.

Angel is captivated by the aviary built just outside the restaurant; it houses three to four dozen parakeets whose songs make a powerful racket. She watches them, rapt, for several minutes but eventually I coax her into the dining room to breakfast. This early, it's still a little chilly to sit outside, but we eat our *huevos rancheros* and tortillas at a table by the window, savoring the panoramic view and watching the fishing boats bobbing far out on the water.

My girl sighs, looking more at ease than at any time since we started the trip. "Maggiemama, this is so pretty!"

It's as if the beauty is a kind of vitamin tonic for her, and I watch my daughter unwilt.

"I told you, Mrs. Havisham. Some of the Baja is stunningly beautiful." I spoon more salsa onto my eggs.

"Will it be like this where we're going? Todos Santos?" She shows off for me how well she remembers the name of our destination.

"Parts of it, absolutely," I assure her, "although we'll be back

be together, you and Maggie and me. Anyway, DogBear is here too, and we're okay. I love you, Mommy. Don't be sad."

She hangs up and hands the phone to me, but a second later asks, "Can we call her back?"

"Did you forget something you wanted to tell her?"

"No, I just...I thought maybe I could listen to her voice again." She says this apologetically, as if she thinks she's asking too much but can't help herself.

I press redial and hand the phone back to her. Once more she listens through the message, but says nothing after the beep. She hangs up again, returns the phone to me, then walks a little way off by herself. Her hunched shoulders tell me there might be tears. I marvel at the elaborate care she took, saying what was most important to her without giving us away. More than any little girl should have to manage. I turn the phone off and wonder whether I've made anything better or whether I've made everything worse.

Before we leave town, I stop at a *tienda* for batteries. I buy lots of them, and Angel is content to listen to her mother sing for long stretches at a time. The morning passes in a dream as we follow the Sea of Cortez south. It occurs to me we could just remain here, in Mulegé or Bahia Concepción or Loreto, basking in sunlight and the tranquility of this body of water. Gradually the sun would burn away our histories, and we would become two other people. It's a tempting vision, but I am still pulled to seek the counsel of Guru Tam.

North of Loreto we are stopped at another checkpoint, but it seems in the southern Baja the soldiers are much less aggressive about these searches. About half an hour south of Loreto, the road turns west again, and we must leave the Sea of Cortez behind to drive the interior of the peninsula. We don't stop for lunch but instead rummage in our cooler and shopping bags for whatever hasn't gone bad.

I do need to stop for gas in Ciudad Constitución. Angel needs to use the restroom, and I accompany her into the station.

It's an older building, and not one of the cleaner ones we've been in. My daughter is vocal in her disgust.

"Maggiemama, there's no toilet paper!" she protests.

I produce a roll from my backpack. It's amazing we haven't encountered this before. "It's BYO," I tell her.

"What's that?" she pouts. She both wants her privacy and doesn't want to be left alone in this dirty little room. I turn from her to a scarred mirror and reapply lip balm to my cracked lips.

"Bring Your Own!" I tell her. "And remember, don't flush the paper down the toilet. Put it in the trash can."

"Ewwww!"

Truth be told, these restrooms are a lot cleaner than they used to be when I traveled the Baja in the '80s.

As we pull out of the station, Angel turns to me. "Tell me a story, okay?"

"A made-up story or a true story?"

"A true story. Something from when you were almost eight."

This was the time before my dad lost his job, when we were, I guess, a prosperous, middle-class family in the San Fernando Valley living the California dream. It was the 1960s, and we had no idea what was ahead of us.

"Okay," I agreed. "I'll tell you the story about my dog Edgar. He was some kind of terrier mix—a little black, a little brown, a little white. And he used to swim with us in our pool."

"In the pool?" Angel giggles in amazement.

"All the neighborhood kids used to come over. We'd be in there with our inflatable rafts, our flippers, our diving masks— all that paraphernalia, balls, the works, and Edgar would run along the side, run along the side, trying to keep up with us as we swam back and forth. Eventually he'd get to the point where he couldn't stand it, and he'd dive in, and paddle those little legs as fast as he could."

"Did it gross people out to have a dog in the pool?" This was exactly the kind of question Yoli would have asked.

"No. Everybody loved Edgar. Sometimes the kids from down the street would come to our fence and call out, 'Can we come swimming with Edgar today?'"

"What happened to Edgar?" my daughter wants to know.

Now I'm sorry I brought it up. It may be there exists no animal story with a happy ending, and that was certainly true of this one. When my dad lost his job, we got so we couldn't afford to take care of Edgar anymore. I asked all the kids on the block and everyone at school, but no one wanted to adopt a six-year-old mutt, aquatic skills notwithstanding. He went to the pound, almost certainly to a dire fate.

"A couple years after that, we had to give him away." This was my end-of-the-story voice, the one that discouraged any further questions. Although Angel seemed disappointed, I gave no further details. Not lying doesn't always mean disclosing every ghastly fact.

There is one more checkpoint, north of La Paz, as the road turns east to the sea again. This stop, too, is routine and without incident. I wonder if the cheap ring on my finger does the trick, or whether it's my continual prayers. Angel and I high-five each other as we drive away. Just outside La Paz we run into road construction. There are signs posted but I can't read them; I'm not the only one. I'm about to follow a blue Toyota onto the side of the road when I see it get stuck in sand, wheels spinning helplessly.

"Go that way," Angel points, and I follow a truck down the mounded middle of the road; it's watering the dirt to keep the dust down. A man in a hard hat curses us in Spanish and gestures wildly, but we make it past the construction without getting stuck.

"Good navigating," I congratulate my daughter.

She giggles and says, "That man was really mad."

We bypass the metropolis of La Paz, heading into the last hour of our journey. We are traveling west once more across the narrowing peninsula toward the Pacific. We drive past burning mounds of trash, huge fires sending up dark plumes of smoke that can be seen for miles.

"What *is* that?" Angel asks.

It's been decades since you could burn anything outdoors in Los Angeles. I explain that the environmental laws of this country are not as stringent as in ours.

"That's just stupid!" she opines.

We drive through a town that has six sets of speed bumps in the twelve blocks of its total expanse. We bounce our way over sections where the arroyo washed out the road in last season's rain. We pass yet one more roadside shrine, this one with candles in glass jars and baby clothes.

"Does that mean a baby died in the accident?" Angel asks somberly.

"I don't know, honey. It might." I am struck that this is a culture, unlike that of the United States, which does not seek to shield itself from death or similarly harsh realities. Maybe it's because Mexico is a poorer country; maybe only the wealthy can afford the luxury of denial.

Down a hill, we see a farmhouse with a windmill, unexpected in this desert. Then I realize that the desert is nearly all planted, tomato farms encroaching on once-open space, usurping scarce water for the people who live here.

It is late afternoon when we see the sign announcing *"Bienvenidos a Todos Santos."*

"That means 'Welcome,'" Angel declares.

Once a thriving farm community in the 19th century, the town had lapsed into a modest decay, its historic buildings crumbling, until the 1970s, when relatively prosperous gringos, seeking unspoiled vistas and cheap real estate, claimed it as an artists colony.

Now it is two towns, the Mexicans going on with their lives pretty much as before or, at best, finding new employment opportunities with the gringos, and the gringos opening art galleries and inns and restaurants and meditation centers. There's a mostly amiable but distant co-existence, rather than true camaraderie, between the two communities. Some of the gringos make the effort to learn Spanish and involve themselves in projects to improve the life of the town, but others bitch about the backwardness of Mexico and wall themselves off with amenities trucked in over the border.

As we approach, we can see houses dotting the hillsides. We pass a few small *tiendas*, a taco stand, and *La Dulceria*. On the west side of the road we pass palm groves and *la huerta*, which as

I explain to Angel means garden, but is actually farmland, where mangos and chilies are thriving. On our left is the Tropico de Cancer Sports Bar, an open-air establishment shaded by a *palapa* or palm-leaf roof. A sign proclaims that it has TV.

As we enter town, the highway becomes Calle Benito Juarez, one of just a few paved roads, eventually landing us in a block of the commercial strip. The street is festive, the façades of its buildings whitewashed or painted in desert pastels, with shops and restaurants catering to tourists. I slow the Poo-poo Box, find a place to park, and turn off the car.

"Are we here?" Angel wants to know. Since her call to Yoli this morning, she has seemed both more subdued, but also more solid, more at home inside herself. Now she is slightly curious to see this town to which we have driven all this way, and in which we will sojourn for an undetermined amount of time. Not to mention relieved at coming to the end of the longest car trip of her life. She scampers out of the passenger seat and is halfway up the block before I call to her, "Angel, stay with me please!"

She stops but does not retrace her steps. I look up and down the street, trying to figure out where to go. Determination and adrenaline have brought me to this spot, but I don't know what to do next. I haven't been in this town since long before Angel was born, and I barely recognize the street before me. *Spirit, show me what to do now.* When I used to travel, I never had any problem just showing up in a town and finding my way to whatever accommodations might be available.

That would always drive Yoli nuts. *What if there aren't any rooms available?* she'd protest. *What if the only place with a vacancy is a fleabag?* That never made much difference to me—I liked the spirit of adventure, not knowing what you were going to get. But now that Angel is with me, I feel more responsible to ensure her a good environment, someplace where she will feel comfortable and safe.

Perhaps the nicest building on the street belongs to a realtor; the façade boasts tile work and bent verdigris copper gates. Its glass picture window displays color photocopied photos of properties for sale in the area. Across the street is the

Centro Cultural. This building takes up the whole block. We step into a sunny open courtyard, around which are arrayed rooms housing museum collections and a library. I half expect this to snag Angel's attention, but neither of us has the required concentration after spending all day in the car.

Staring back across the street, I note a bank next to the realtor's, a pay phone on the corner. It's a Friday, and many tourists seem to be on the streets, carrying bags of cheap treasure, or driving through on their way to Los Cabos.

Up in the next block, several people sit in a shaded area outside a café. I notice a sign in English, "Tourist Info / Eco Adventures." This brightly whitewashed building also houses the town's bookstore, which stirs some vague recognition in me. I call once more to my daughter, who has wandered ahead without me.

"Take my hand," I instruct her before we cross the street.

A low metal gate across the entryway, no more than knee high, turns out to be a barrier for a litter of puppies that scamper across the floor beneath the cash register, black and brown and of indeterminate breed. Once I've helped Angel over the barricade, she squeals, "Oh!" and drops to her knees, her two hands around the chubby belly of a black pup.

"Bookstore and animal shelter?" I grin at the silver-haired woman behind the register. I'd overheard heard her speaking English to her previous customer, with a slight trace of British accent.

She gets a rueful look on her sun-seamed face. "Taking care of the abandoned dogs of the southern Baja is more than a full-time job." Then she switches to a more purposeful demeanor. "Have you just arrived in town?"

I nod. "We drove from Guerrero Negro this morning."

"And do you have a place to stay here?"

I shake my head. "The decision to come to Todos Santos was a little spontaneous." I feel grateful that Angel is not listening to me.

The bookseller's clear blue eyes blink, as if to take this in. If she thinks it's odd that a woman traveling with a seven-year-old should come to the southern Baja on a whim, she keeps it to herself.

"I haven't been here in several years," I explain, "But I wanted to show it to my daughter. Could you suggest a place that would be nice for her?"

"I'm Penny," the silver-haired woman introduces herself and extends a hand with long, delicate fingers.

I grasp it. "Maggie," I tell her, "and this is Angel." Too late I wonder if it was necessary to give her our real names. My daughter is too preoccupied with her newfound friends to do more than wave distractedly in our direction. "She's rather an animal lover."

Penny grins. "If you were staying a while I'd try to get you to take one of these pups home with you."

This captures Angel's attention. "Oh, Maggiemama, can we?" She grasps her current favorite, a female with a tawny coat, and holds her up. The puppy squirms in my daughter's grip.

I shoot Penny a "see-what-you-started" look that is not entirely forgiving, but she is unruffled. I realize she must do this all the time. Her job is to save animals and find them homes, and if she has to put a parent or boyfriend on the hot seat, so be it.

"Angel, let's talk about it once we get settled, okay?" There is an edge to this response my daughter recognizes; she decides a delay is better than an outright "No."

Turning back to Penny, I ask, "Where would you recommend?"

"How long will you be staying?" She seems to hold no grudge that I've undermined her adoption strategy.

I shrug, again feeling a little foolish. "I'm not completely certain about that," I say. "It's kind of…open-ended."

She doesn't miss a beat. "A lot of places rent by the day or the week or the month, and it gets cheaper the longer you stay. People value long-term tenants because of the steady income. But you'd probably have to know that going into it."

"Do you know about a community called Light Beings?" I ask.

At this, Penny's pleasant face slams shut. "I know who

they are, yes, and I know where their property is." Her tone is strained. "It's none of my business, but I can't imagine that would be a good place for your daughter."

I find her response curious and slightly alarming. I make a mental note to come back and ask her more about it at another time.

"I was just wondering." I try to erase this misstep. "I'd read something about their community here. So, where is a good place for us to stay?"

"What's your budget?" Her tone regains its cordiality.

"Cheap and cheerful." It's my mother's voice coming out of my mouth, my mother after we'd lost our toehold on luxury. I cringe at the ingratiating tone, the laughed-off apology at being poor.

"You might like the Oasis," she offers. "The owner's a woman named Tina Downs, moved here about three years ago from someplace in California. Her *casitas* are very nice, one bedrooms with a little kitchenette. It's about a twenty-minute walk from here, but just a couple of minutes in the car. Tina popped in earlier today, said she had a vacancy."

On the back of a map of the town, she pencils directions about where to go. It's clear that in addition to functioning as the animal shelter and resident bookseller, she is also accustomed to providing tourist information.

"Would you like me to call and tell her you're coming?"

I nod gratefully. Penny picks up the phone behind the counter and dials from memory.

"Tina," I hear her say, "I've got a woman in the store who needs a place." There's a pause while she listens. "Just two, a woman and a little girl."

Penny turns away to curtail my eavesdropping, but still I hear her say, "Now, don't be that way, Tina. It's a very nice little girl. She's on the floor of the bookstore playing with the puppies as we speak, being ever so polite."

There is a very long pause. I want to signal Penny to forget it, we'll try someplace else, but the bookseller's back is impenetrable. At last she says, "Right, then, I'll send them around directly. Bye-bye."

"We really don't want to put anybody out," I tell her.

Penny presses the map into my hands and won't hear my protestations. "Tina's bark is worse than her bite. You'll like the Oasis."

I nod, if a bit hesitantly. Trust Spirit, I remind myself. After all, it's gotten you this far. "Come on, Angel," I call to her, "Maybe we can come back another day and you can play with the puppies then."

Reluctantly, my daughter picks herself off the floor, but not before giving the tawny dog's ear a final nuzzle. "That's Edgar!" she announces, as we step back onto the sidewalk. "Edgar Sue, 'cuz she's a girl."

After overhearing Penny's end of her conversation with Tina Downs, I am already predisposed to be on the defensive, and as we drive up the rutted dirt road to the Oasis, I again wonder what I've gotten us into. While the center of town has been spruced up for the tourists, this neighborhood belongs to the other Todos Santos—tiny houses with yards full of debris, a few rusted-out cars and packs of underfed dogs.

"Maggiemama, look! That dog is too skinny!"

Indeed, the white dog's skin is stretched thin over its bones.

"Angel," I say ruefully, "the dogs of Mexico will break your heart." I can't find a positive spin to put on this one.

"We can't let that happen to Edgar Sue," she protests.

I can hear a whine starting that lets me know she's building up to a full campaign. "Look, I hardly know how we're going to manage ourselves," I snap. "I can't really think about taking on a puppy right this minute!" I hate the sound of my tone, and the way it registers in her eyes.

"You said we could talk about it," she protests.

Spirit, give me a little more patience. She's not even eight years old and her world is totally turned upside down.

"I know, honey," I manage, "and we will. Just not anymore today, okay? Your mama's way too tired."

As we pull up to the tall wooden gate, where a hand-painted

sign announces "Welcome to the Oasis," a very large and healthy looking dog tries to jump into my driver's side window, its loud bark harsh against my ear. With paws on the window ledge, the dog stands taller than the car.

"Loba, calm down." I hear a drawling voice from behind the gate. "I've told you a hundred times, don't eat the guests! It's bad for business."

The gate swings wide, revealing a woman in a long turquoise dress with a mass of flame-red curls piled on top of her head. Several strands of different colored beads swing from her neck. On her feet are fuchsia flip-flops; her toes are painted orange. On her fingers are six or seven jeweled rings, of such size and magnitude that I wonder she can lift her hand.

She doesn't trouble to restrain the dog, just calls to me, "You must be who Penny called about."

"Yes, I'm Maggie." I want to get out of the car, but Loba is still blocking my way, still perched on her hind legs, massive paws perched on the window ledge. Angel is keeping a respectful distance. The dog regards me with a kind of friendly aggression until the redhead pushes her away to peer across to the passenger side.

"This is Angel," I tell her.

"Angel, huh? Well, she better be a little angel, 'cuz I don't usually allow any kids here."

I bristle. "Listen, we don't want to put you out…" I start to shift the Poo-poo Box into reverse.

"Aww, don't get all sensitive on me, Maggie. The maternal gene just passed me by." She sticks her face halfway through my window, much as Loba had done a moment before. "I'm Tina," she tells my daughter.

Angel stares doubtfully, eyes big, lips in a pout. Still, she is polite, "Yes, ma'am."

"Oh, don't call me ma'am," Tina warns. "Nothin' makes a woman feel old like being called ma'am. You'll find that out in about forty years!" she cackles. "Just call me Tina. You, too," she tells me. "Come on in, now, I'll show you the room."

With a grand sweep of her long skirt, she turns her back, expecting us to follow. I look at Angel, she looks back.

"Whaddaya think, Mrs. Havisham?" I don't want her to feel like she has no choice. Maybe I'm hoping she will get me out of this situation, which already seems rife with dissonance.

"She's weird," Angel affirms, "but I think she's okay. She barks, but her tail was wagging."

My smart girl. Sometimes she just knocks me out. I bend to give her a quick kiss on the nose; she pretends to wipe off slobber.

Tina Downs reappears at the gate. "Did I run you off that easy?" she bellows, and we exit the car and, this time, follow her through the gate.

We enter a wide, lushly planted patio, draped with palm trees. The stucco walls enclosing the property are painted in vivid oranges and golds. Each of the *casitas* is painted an equally vibrant hue—from green to turquoise to lavender.

In the middle of the patio is a large fountain, its burbling a kind of music. On a perch in the corner sits a bright macaw. Angel rushes toward him. "Maggie, look, a parrot."

"You watch your fingers, little missy," Tina cautions. "Old Mac could bite one right off."

My daughter hangs back, but continues to regard the bird as if not believing he would really do her harm.

"How long have you had this place?" I ask, not really caring about the answer but feeling some pressure to appease this force of nature with whom we will be residing, at least for the night.

"I guess I been here about three years," she looks around as if she's just considered this for the first time.

"Where did you come from?"

"I think I pretty much lived everywhere else, before I ended up here." Her eyes have a mischievous spark, but I'm not up for hearing the story of her life. Without further prompting from me, she doesn't pursue it. I'm grateful for that.

She leads us into the farthest *casita*; the outside is painted cobalt blue. Inside, the walls are brick red with orange accents, the room furnished with a pleasant mishmash of second-hands. A beaded curtain separates the sitting room/kitchenette from the bedroom, one wall hung salon style with thrift store paintings of children. I hear Angel's intake of breath as she sees them, then draws closer to study them. A small bathroom with shower, painted lime green, completes the accommodations.

Tina points to the shower. "No tub," she proclaims. "People from the States are always put out about no tub." She shakes her head. "You could count on one hand the number of bathtubs in this town. It may be the thing I miss most about the States."

"And how much is it?" I want this part to be over. I want to lie on the bed and close my eyes and rid my senses of road motion and fear and these assaultive colors.

"That depends." She smiles, catlike, "How long do you want to stay?"

"I'm not sure." I tell her awkwardly. "Our plans are kind of...indefinite. I'm not sure when my partner is going to join us here." I wonder if Angel is listening.

Tina knits together her eyebrows, already drawn into sharp auburn points with plucking and pencil. "Angel, honey, would you go out and see what Loba is doing? It's all right," she turns to me as if anticipating my objection, "that dog'll be gentle with her."

Angel looks at me uncertainly, but I nod and say, "It's okay, sweetheart, I'll be right here." She bangs through the screen door and I hear her voice calling, "Loba! Loba!"

Tina eases herself onto one corner of the orange bedspread, and indicates that I should do the same. I shrug and remain standing, leaning against the doorframe to the bathroom. Tina looks me right in the eye.

"A lot of us from the States come down here to get away from something. Probably every third person you meet here has some kinda secret. Now, me, I don't ask a lotta questions. I have a few secrets of my own." She raises one eyebrow and snorts delicately.

"So I'm not gonna ask you why you're driving a car from a Mexican chop shop and how come you don't have a better story about what you're doin' here with that little girl."

I should be alarmed at her words, or rather, at my own seeming transparency. But whether it's the straight-shooting style of Tina Downs or sheer exhaustion, I don't seem to be able to muster the adrenaline. *Spirit*, I offer wearily, *you're in charge here*. Outwardly, I say nothing, just keep meeting her startling eyes, green as new olives.

"Two things you should know, though," our innkeeper continues. "Todos Santos is a small town, especially the *gringo* community. People *love* to talk, because there isn't that much else to do. As somebody new in town, they're gonna be talkin' about *you*. I'd get out in front of the story, if I were you. Don't leave it to them to dig up. Or make up."

"I appreciate that," I tell her. I can't help but wonder how much she already knows. "You said there were two things; what's the other?"

"Don't lie to me." There is no hostility in her tone; she doesn't raise her voice, yet the words crack against my ear like whiplash. "That doesn't mean you have to confide in me, but just don't go outta your way to mislead me." She picks her body off the bed. "Now in the morning, after you've had a good night's rest, you can figure out if you wanna pay the daily rate or get the weekly discount."

Angel bangs in then, with Loba right on her heels. There is unfettered glee on her face, a look I haven't seen since before the night Yoli took her to Lurlene's. "Maggie, it's so pretty here."

"How'd you get all wet?" I ask her.

"Loba was showing me how to drink out of the fountain!" she announces proudly.

"Honey, you shouldn't drink that water..."

"It's all right," Tina interrupts. "Since my damn dog drinks out of it all the time, I put a filter on it. Same with your kitchen and bathroom sink. But you still might find the bottled water *tastes* better—I haven't figured out what to do about that yet.

"Oh, I almost forgot to show you the best thing!" Tina Downs leads us back into the front room, and draws back the orange curtains. "There's the Pacific." She points, and true enough, we have a little sliver of an ocean view.

"You'll be able to hear it at night," she promises, "once my goddamn neighbors turn off their music and things quiet down."

She turns to go. "Let me know if you need anything; I'm

over in the purple house," she gestures. "Oh, do you need me to recommend a place for dinner?"

Angel perks up. "Yeah, Maggie, what are we gonna eat? I'm starving!" She rubs her belly with the flat of her hand and widens her eyes pathetically, as if it's been weeks, not hours since her last repast.

I'm grateful to see my daughter so animated, but I feel now as if my blood has been drained, as if I haven't a drop with which to continue on. My knees don't seem to want to hold me upright anymore. If I have to go out again, I might just fall down and die.

Tina Downs must have read this on my face, because she says next, "My *amigos* dropped by today with a huge Dorado. What if I throw that on the barbeque and we can eat on the picnic table outside? Caught this morning—you won't get any fresher. Will she eat fish?" She gestures with her head toward Angel.

"I'm a vegetarian," Angel responds.

Tina frowns, or maybe she's only pretending. "A vegetarian, huh? That's a big idea for a little squirt like yourself. Well, I think I probably have some cheese in the refrigerator. I could make you a quesadilla."

"I don't want you to go to any trouble…" I protest, but even to me it doesn't sound convincing.

"Sometimes we just have to be trouble for one another," she declares. "Look at you, you're half dead with that drive. Just say, 'Yes, thanks,' and I'll make some supper and maybe some day you'll go to some trouble for me."

"Thank you," I murmur.

"Angel, you come with me and let your momma have a moment's peace. We'll see if she even stays awake long enough to have dinner!"

Angel giggles. "Tina, do you have TV?"

Tina rolls those olive green eyes. "Yes, darlin' I do." To me she says, "Most gringos that are permanent here have some kind of satellite setup, so they can get TV from the States. I hardly ever watch it—one of the things I came here to get away from."

I am startled out of my lethargy. Again I fumble for words, wanting to sound credible. "There…ah…there might be some things on TV that I don't want Angel to watch." I'm too fried to care if I'm giving myself away or just sounding like an over-controlling lunatic.

Tina doesn't register any surprise. "How about a video? I think maybe I can find something around that isn't X-rated!" She cackles at her own joke, then, with my daughter and the massive dog in tow, departs my *casita*.

Now that I am here there are a million things to think about, to do. I need to make some kind of longer term plan. I should let Charlie know we are safe. I should find the Light Beings community and see if they will let us stay with them. I need to find out when I can talk with Guru Tam. But even running a toothbrush through my sour mouth is more than I can manage right now. So I fall back on the bright orange bedspread, let my aching head find the soft down of the pillow, and sink into blessed oblivion.

Chapter 5

I had forgotten about the roosters. Dagmar used to like to stay out until the surfer bar closed, and she'd always let loose a torrent of curses when the roosters crowed before dawn. If the roosters didn't awaken me, my hung-over girlfriend certainly would.

This morning the light is still a dense gray when their cries begin, plaintive and relentless, severing me from sleep. Not the "cockle-doodle-do" of the American barnyard—at least as depicted in the cartoons of my childhood—but an eerie warble, as if each carries the spirit of *La Llarona*, the ghost woman who cries for her dead children. How could they know when to begin, not even a crack of daylight on the horizon? And if I remember right, they continue for hours, until what could be more properly called sunrise.

It takes a moment to fully recall where I am and then to realize that I have not stirred from this spot since before dusk the previous day. My shorts chafe the skin of my groin, my T-shirt stinks of me. Bra straps cut into my shoulders. Someone had taken the trouble to throw a blanket across my body and, I notice with chagrin, to remove my shoes. Angel? Or, more likely, I cringe to think of it, the formidable Ms. Downs. My head throbbing, I sit up and groan.

What kind of mother am I, to dump my child on a complete stranger and lapse into unconsciousness for hours? Anything might have happened to her.

Before I have the chance to wonder where Angel might be, I hear my daughter stir; her feet skitter across the tile floor in the next room and in a moment she joins me under the blanket. "What's that noise?" she complains. "Is it ghosts?"

"Roosters," I tell her. "Lots of the families keep chickens for the eggs."

"But they're so loud! It's too early to get up, isn't it?" She sighs deeply and burrows her body into the curve of mine. She used to do this a lot when she was younger; not so much since she started school.

I drape an arm around her, let the soft frizz of her hair tickle my nose. She smells of soap; surely Tina Downs didn't give her a shower? "You know how the Light Beings get up really early to chant?"

"Uhm hum," she says, but I can tell she is already drifting back to sleep.

"That's what the roosters are doing too. They're saying hello to the day."

I'm wide awake now, shot through with adrenaline after ten or so hours of being dead to the world, but I make my body stay still, as if to create a protective shield for Angel's slumbering. My mind, however, will not match the calm; thoughts jostle and bombard one another for my attention.

Even in my sleep, I've been obsessing about the TV. How widespread is the television coverage of Angel's kidnapping? How many people here with satellites get the local news from L.A.? Undoubtedly the news will be broadcasting pictures of both of us; how long will it take some boob tube addicted *gringo* to recognize us? I feel a sudden compulsion to watch the news coverage, to understand how my actions are being interpreted to the rest of the world. But how can I ask Tina to let me watch her TV without Angel watching it too? Or, without arousing Tina's suspicion?

I'm not gonna ask you why you're drivin' a car from a Mexican chop shop, or how come you don't have a better story about what you're doin' here with that little girl. Tina's words from yesterday afternoon replay on a loop in my brain. What is it about the car that gives it away? What am I not seeing? She probably already knows. She could be ready to call the *Federales* as soon as the sun is up; there might even be some kind of reward.

But then I remember she said *I hardly ever watch TV—one of the things I came here to get away from.* Maybe she doesn't know. Maybe it's just really obvious that I'm doing something I'm not supposed to be doing. Guru Tam has always said, *Reality isn't determined by what you say. Reality is reality, whether your words acknowledge it or not. There's no such thing as lying, because truth is evident to all who open their eyes to see it.*

Spirit, I begin to pray, *you've brought us to this town, gotten my little girl and me here safely. What is it you have in mind for us now? Whatever it is, let me have the courage to meet it, and the blessing to be grateful for it. Let my trust in your plan never waver, for you are the maker of miracles.*

I begin to use my deep breathing to calm my mind, slow my heart rate. Silently, I chant:

Peace begets peace
As day begets night
Peace begets peace
As darkness yields to light.
Let me dwell inside the circle of peace.

I can't tell how long I chant these words before I too drift back into sleep, my own breath falling into sync with my daughter's soft exhalations.

It's Loba's bark that next awakens me, and sun is pushing in through the bedroom window. Angel is nowhere to be found. How could I sleep through her getting up? Then I hear a sharp knock on the door, followed by Tina Downs' cheerful, "Hey, is anybody alive in here?"

I sit up and Tina comes in with two mugs of steaming coffee, one of which she holds out in my direction. She's wearing loose flowing pants and a top of lime green, a jangle of bracelets on each arm. Angel follows behind, wearing a bright yellow T-shirt a million sizes too big for her; its hem falls past her knees. A large fish adorns the front, along with the words, "I caught it in Cabo." Angel is munching a piece of toast smeared with peanut butter.

"Ohh," I groan apologetically when I see this. "Providing dinner for Angel was more than enough. I'm so sorry you had to serve breakfast too. Much too much for someone without the maternal gene."

To Angel, I say, "You should have woken me up."

Tina grins. "I told her not to. That's okay, I'll put it all on your tab." She winks. "Who wants to go to the beach?"

"I do, I do!" Angel begins jumping in time to this repeated affirmation.

"What time is it?" I wonder, pulling the watch from my wrist to squint at it. Its band has left a perfect braid of red marks on the skin.

"Seven forty-five. If we hustle, ours can be the first footprints on the sand this morning."

"I shouldn't. I have things to do today."

"Maggie!" Angel's whine is outraged.

"Relax," Tina says, "you're in Baja. There's nothin' to do today that can't be done *mañana*."

"I wanna go with Loba!" Angel looks ready to throw a full-blown fit.

Still, I demur. "We can't put you out. You've already done so much…"

"I have to go anyway. This big dog needs to run every damn day of her life and at least at the beach I know she's not going to get hit by a truck."

Angel has jumped on the bed and is pulling insistently on my arm, as if it were a pump. "Come on!!!"

"Little missy, get those dirty feet off of my clean comforter,"

Tina Downs cheerfully reprimands her. Then she turns to me and says, "Train's leavin'. All aboard!"

"Can you wait five minutes while I shower and change?"

"Whaddaya think?" Tina confers with Angel. "Shall we wait for her?"

"Yes, please," my daughter says with aching sincerity, not yet accustomed to Tina Downs' sense of humor.

"Okay." Tina feigns reluctance. At least I think it's feigned. "Let's go hunt up a ball you can throw for Big Missy at the ocean."

The two of them bustle out, leaving me to feel like the one who's out of it. How did they get so chummy overnight, and what might my daughter have confided in her? And, if Tina dressed Angel, she has surely seen her bruises. What could she possibly think? Or did Angel tell her what Lurlene had sworn her to tell no one, what she hadn't told me?

These thoughts make my hands clumsy as I pull new underwear and another bra, a fresh T-shirt and my last clean pair of shorts out of the suitcase. I drop the bottle of scented oil I use for deodorant, but luckily it doesn't shatter on the tile floor. I fumble for my toothbrush and toothpaste.

Then hot water is streaming over my naked skin: the too-big boobs, the round belly, the long legs. It feels like a baptism, water giving me new life, temporarily cleansing me of fear and discouragement along with dust and grime. I towel myself dry, swipe some lip balm across my mouth, and peer into the mirror above the sink; my dark blue eyes stare back. It is only beginning to register that I have irretrievably and completely changed my life in the past seventy-two hours. And of course, my daughter's life as well.

Angel needs a boost up as we all three climb into the front seat of Tina's old Chevy truck—by this time it doesn't surprise me that it's painted lavender—while Loba paces in the truck bed. The Apache's shocks have seen better days, and bouncing along the uneven dirt roads of the neighborhood makes my boobs hurt. It flashes through my mind that I'm due for a period in another day or two, and briefly wonder how I will negotiate a purchase of tampons at the local *tienda*.

"Ms. Downs?" my daughter ventures. Seated between us, she cranes her neck to see out the windshield.

"I told you before, call me Tina!"

"Tina?" she tries again. "What's your truck's name?"

I think I may have to explain this concept to Tina Downs, but she doesn't hesitate before a broad smile cracks her face and she answers, "Maybelline," so pleased with herself. Then she breaks into song, "Maybelline, why can't you be true, oh, Maybelline…"

She breaks off with feigned apology, "That's probably more than you need first thing in the morning."

My daughter, though, is captivated with this new name and continues to warble, "Maybelline, oh, Maybelline."

We're on the highway headed south of town, the road once more humming beneath the wheels. Tina waves to, and Loba barks at, every vehicle that passes by; the innkeeper seems to know everyone in town, *gringo* or Mexican.

She turns right at an unmarked passage, and then we're bumping down a severely rutted road through desert landscape. "We had a helluva hurricane season last year," Tina comments, "and now the wildflowers are to die for!" And it's true: against the gray-green of the plant life are blossoms of pink and yellow and white, hidden and unexpected treasures. Loba greets every leaf rustle, every flush of birds, every lizard dash with enthusiastic barking. Tina slows as a jackrabbit scurries in front of the truck, pointing him out for Angel's benefit.

"Ooh," my daughter exclaims, "can we stop to pet him?"

"You'd have to catch him first," Tina replies dryly. Pointing to a dark swoop of wings on the horizon, she adds, "But it looks like Mr. Hawk may beat you to it."

"No!" Angel protests. "He'll get away."

Tina shrugs and doesn't press it, for which I am grateful. I am thrilled to see my daughter transfixed by the landscape, alive to the possibilities of this place to which I've brought her.

Despite the nagging fears still roiling beneath the surface of my thoughts, it is a glorious morning, the sky a blue never achieved in Los Angeles, the sun brilliant but not yet hot. I allow the beauty to soothe my ragged nerves, relax my spine. *This too is part of your gift, Spirit.*

Tina drives right to the end of the road, just at the edge of where the stretch of sand begins. Beyond it, the Pacific, but not the cold gray body of water from the north, crowded with surfers and partiers, families and garbage, but a deep blue green ocean gentled by this palm-ringed cove. Completely empty but for us.

"This is extraordinary!" I gasp. On none of my previous trips to Baja had I seen this. Surfers would of course not be drawn to this calm lagoon.

"Palm Beach," Tina offers with a proprietary sweep of her bejeweled hand. She kicks off her purple thong sandals, leaves them beside the truck. Angel and I follow suit.

"Are we going swimming?" Angel wants to know.

"Too cold this time of morning," Tina advises. "We're going to walk."

"It's safe to park here?" I worry.

"As long as the tide doesn't come in and float her out to sea." Tina laughs. I see how I must appear next to her ease—uptight and nervous, wracked by the energy of the big city.

Tina opens the back panel and Loba leaps down, immediately beginning to dart after seagulls that wait until she is nearly upon them to sail into the air out of reach. Angel takes off to run after the dog, barely acknowledging my admonishing call, "Stay away from the water!"

"Do people ever drown out here?" I ask Tina. I hate sounding like such a worrywart; I'm accustomed to Yoli filling that role.

"Not at this beach. Some of the other beaches have riptides and people drown all the time." We begin walking north along the sand, my own footprints square and solid, hers long and pointy.

"I can't believe we're the only ones here."

"Give it another few minutes. A lot of people in town walk this beach; they all have their rituals around it. Sometimes there are fishermen at the south end of the cove, but I'm often the first one here in the morning."

"Early riser?" I inquire, not because I really care but more to have something to say.

"Truth is, me and sleep are not on the best of terms."

There must be a story here, but I'm not that eager to hear it. I don't want to start exchanging confidences with this woman. I have to remind myself that I can't afford to trust anyone here, at least not until I get to the Light Beings' ashram.

"By the way," I ask her, doing my best to sound offhand, "what do you know about the Light Beings community?"

She raises her already arched eyebrows, stares at me appraisingly. Then she nods, "I guess that makes sense," she says, as if confirming something to herself about me. "They're not very popular here in Todos Santos, not with the gringos and not with the Mexicans either."

"Why not?"

Tina wrinkles her brow, as if trying to summon an explanation. "It's hard to know how it all started. People are narrow-minded, don't like anyone who's too different. Which is kind of a crack-up, because people from the States who pick up and move down here aren't exactly your run-of-the-mill, if you get my drift. But those robes and headpieces make the Light Beings stand out. Plus they got a really prime piece of land, south of here, goes all the way from the mountains to the ocean, land that both gringo and Mexican developers were after. The rumor is they paid off somebody in the government big time, so there's resentment about that. Twenty years ago, property used to be cheap here, plentiful. Now it's at a premium."

"So the problem is about money?" Down at the other end of the beach, I see my girl dancing on the sand. Her borrowed bright yellow shirt is a beacon that helps me keep a eye on her.

"Well, the Light Beings haven't been all that smart about their relationship to this community. In my humble opinion, anyway. They keep to themselves, they don't invite their neighbors over, they don't support the local businesses in town. They don't participate in the local charities—none of the things that would have greased their entry into the society of Todos Santos, such as it is."

"That seems strange to me." I'm thinking about the ashram

in Los Angeles, how the community is invited in, how active the Light Beings are in feeding homeless people, bringing meditation programs into prisons.

"I don't know. I'm a live-and-let-live kind of person, but not everyone follows my shining example." Tina's grin is self-deprecating. "There's a lot of gossip."

"Like what?"

"Oh, ugly stuff, like everyone has group sex together, or the head of it, whatchamacallit?"

"Guru Tam."

"Yeah, like the Guru's hypnotized everyone into giving away all their money, that kind of thing. The kind of crap that people project onto those they've decided not to accept." She sounds angry.

"So is it a totally *gringo* community?" Early as it is, the sun is starting to sear the back of my neck.

"By law, *gringos* can only operate a business here if they hire Mexican workers, so there are Mexicans on the land. But according to Juanita, who cleans for me at the Oasis, they've all been told not to talk about what goes on there if they want to keep their jobs."

Loba runs up then, charging straight into Tina and nearly knocking her over. Rearing up on her hind legs, the dog places her sandy paws on Tina's lime green shirt.

"Get off me, you bitch," she yells affectionately. She fishes a graying tennis ball out of her pocket and throws it up the beach, a surprisingly decent throw for a woman wearing that much jewelry. As if reading my mind, Tina brags, "I used to be an outfielder on a team in Texas."

Once Loba retrieves the ball, Angel wants to throw it, but Loba doesn't want to release it from her jaws. Tina pries it away from the dog, then coaches my daughter in her pitch. Angel squeals with glee as the ball sails a few yards and Loba leaps to catch it. In this manner we make our way along the shore and back ("A half mile each way," Tina informs me.) On the return trip, there are a few more walkers on the beach: an elderly woman putters along the sand with a cane and three ancient wooly dogs; a middle-aged man in a Panama walks a black Lab.

Tina waves to the woman, and the dogs all rush to sniff and greet one another. The black dog starts scuffling with Loba for the ball. Loba bares her teeth and snarls until Tina grabs her collar in one hand and the ball in the other.

"Hey, Jim," she greets the man.

"Your dog is a bully," he complains in a desultory fashion. His blue eyes stand out in his deeply tanned face.

"What can I say—it runs in the family!" She waves and moves on. To me she mutters, "What about *his* damned dog?" I follow her, but something makes me turn around. I find the man still staring at us with a peculiar expression on his face. My fingertips grow cold at the thought that he may have recognized Angel and me.

Once we are back in the truck, I ask Tina, "So can you give me directions to the Light Beings' community?" Angel is sprawled across the backseat, singing her version of "Maybelline."

"Sure," she says. "I was out there once. Juanita's oldest son was working for them, and there was some kind of dispute where he didn't get paid what he was owed. Juanita thought I'd do better than Carlos at negotiating with them."

"And did you?" This is something I really want to know.

"Well, just say this. Carlos got his money, but lost his job. And I would not be welcome there a second time."

"Really? That acrimonious?"

"First off, nobody gets onto the land without going past these guards. If you ask me, that's part of the problem right there. So I had to be pretty aggressive just to get in the damn place. Then there's this one woman who seems to be in charge of everything, what was her name? Suma or Sita, something like that. And she's all in this pale blue gown and everything but let me tell you—what a battle-ax! She reminded me of some of the nuns back in Catholic school, supposed to be all holy and everything but meaner than snakes!"

On the drive back, Angel peppers us with questions: "What's Loba's favorite food?" "Why is there sand by the ocean?" "Can we go back to see Edgar Sue today?" "Where can we find puppets?" I am relieved that Tina is willing to field most of these, as I try to sort out all the information I've gathered since we arrived in town, the frightening news about the town's access to U.S. television, the bewildering reports about the Light Beings' community.

I feel stupid for even imagining I could pull this off. Yoli always said she could read whatever I was thinking on my face, that I couldn't hide my feelings to save my life. What made me think I could pull off a kidnapping across international borders?

Kidnapping. Such a harsh term for trying to save my girl from being brutalized.

Spirit, I am so grateful for your guidance and your light. If I am meant to persist in this, please give me a sign to shore up my courage. Please show me what to do next.

Although I've barely paid attention, I notice we are not going back to the Oasis. Instead, Tina is driving us into town.

"It sure has changed a lot since I was here last."

"How long ago was that?" Tina wants to know. She honks her horn and waves at a man with a neat beard and a straw hat who is walking along the street.

"Probably twenty years." I can't seem to calculate precisely. "There were hardly any gringos here at that time, just surfers."

"Well, that's all changed now!" She makes a right onto Calle Militar. "I'm going to show you the best breakfast place in Todos Santos," she promises.

I want to protest, but she hasn't phrased this as a request. My feeling is that Angel and I should get out of this town and make our way to the Light Beings as soon as we can. Their isolation from the people of Todos Santos is starting to seem like an advantage, and if Tina will keep her mouth shut, nobody needs to know we have gone there. Except the woman in the bookstore might remember. Damn, I've been too careless.

Tina pulls up in front of Karla's *Loncheria*, an open-air café with a *palapa* roof, red plastic tables and chairs arrayed on a covered patio, a counter at one end, behind which the kitchen is visible. Loba stays in the back of the truck, her water bowl filled from a plastic bottle kept for that purpose. The rest of us pile out, and Tina greets a woman behind the counter in a snug pink tank top, *"Buenos días."*

To me she says, "Are you ready to taste the best *huevos rancheros* of your life?" and I nod. "And what about you, little missy?" she asks Angel. "Another quesadilla?"

"Do they have cereal?" my girl asks.

"Cheerios? Frosted Flakes? Something like that?" Tina consults me.

I have always tried to feel Angel healthy food—whole grain bread, granola from the health food store, honey instead of sugar. I do have some granola in the car, along with soymilk, but we're here now and Angel wants to eat. I nod wearily. I'm sure Lurlene wasn't shopping at Whole Foods for Angel's breakfast.

Tina handles the ordering in what sounds to me like fluent Spanish; we take a seat at the far end of the patio. The red plastic tablecloth is emblazoned with the Coca-Cola logo. I choose a chair that will shield me from visibility to the other patrons. Tina talks to everyone: two Mexican men in work clothes huddled over coffee, an elderly gringo couple whose new and carefully tailored clothes announce them as tourists.

The woman in pink brings our food, two mismatched platters of eggs covered in steaming red sauce that bleeds into a pile of refried beans, a covered plastic tortilla holder, and a dish of thick, fire-roasted salsa. In a moment she returns with Angel's cereal, with which my daughter begins to play more than eat.

"Whaddaya think?" Tina wants to know how I like her recommendation.

The truth is, I'm too anxious to really savor the taste of my food. "Mmmm," I answer, hoping to project enthusiasm.

A bus pulls up and people spill out of it, crowd around the counter to buy coffee, cigarettes, gum, candy and chips. Tina explains that this is a designated rest stop on the bus that travels north.

"And could you buy a ticket and get on here?" I wonder.

"I guess so." Tina is distracted by a tall woman who enters the patio just then, her dark hair in a long braid that falls past her waist. "Carmen!" Tina rises from her seat to greet the woman, whose very slender frame is encased in black Capri pants and a sleeveless black shirt. She seems all points and angles. "How's the work for your show coming?"

They chat a bit on the patio, and I hope to escape the ritual of introduction, but Tina drags her over. "Maggie and Angel are staying at the Oasis," she explains. "Carmen is an amazing artist. A lot of people in this town *think* they're artists, but Carmen is the real thing."

Carmen regards me intently, her dark eyes brooding in her narrow face. Her accent is European. "Welcome to Todos Santos," she offers with a faint smile. "You look very familiar to me; we have perhaps met before?"

"N–no," I stammer. To cover my discomfort, I add, "I just have one of those faces—I look like everybody." I am convinced she's seen me on the news; any minute she'll put two and two together. Reflexively I reach to apply a new coat of lip balm.

"Not at all," she disagrees. "Your look is very distinctive. Perhaps I might paint you sometime?"

"Down, girl." Tina swats at the arm of her friend.

I grow more flustered, but now it feels different than fear. Could this woman be flirting with me? I can feel my face reddening to the roots of my hair.

"Uh, we're not going to be in town that long," I demur.

"That's a pity." Carmen hasn't taken her eyes off me this whole time.

"I'd like to be painted," my daughter pipes up. She stops playing with her cereal, her face beaming up at the artist.

Still gazing at me, Carmen widens her smile. "And who are you?" the dark-eyed artist asks my daughter.

"I'm..." Angel begins with enthusiasm. Then her face clouds as I see her recalling our predicament. Then she doesn't know what to say.

"She's my daughter," I answer for her.

"Really?" I feel Carmen's eyes appraising us now, trying to discern the family resemblance. Then to Angel she says, "You are a very pretty little girl. Perhaps you can convince your mother to bring you over to my studio."

"Could we, Maggie, could we, could we?" In her excited pleading, her elbow knocks over her bowl, sending a cascade of milk and soggy flakes onto her chair, the patio floor and the borrowed bright yellow T-shirt.

"Oh!" Carmen takes a small leap backward to avoid the flying cereal. She's not someone accustomed to being around children, that much is clear.

I am relieved to turn my attention from her to petitioning the pink-clad waitress for a wet cloth to wipe off my chastened daughter, the table and chair, and the floor.

"I didn't mean to..." Angel apologizes. Tears threaten in the corners of her eyes. She's profoundly embarrassed; she prides herself on her grown-up behavior in public places.

"It's okay," I tell her. "We all spill things sometimes." To Tina I say, "I'll wash out that T-shirt..." but she has already begun walking Carmen out to the road and is hugging her goodbye.

Before returning to our table, she stops at the counter and pays for breakfast.

I hand her a fistful of pesos. "I was planning to pay for this," I tell her, but she waves them away.

"You certainly made an impression on Carmen." She grins as if she's in on a secret.

I say nothing. I can feel my expression hardening. "Listen, I should get Angel home and out of her wet clothes." I grab for my girl's hand and begin moving toward the truck.

Amused, Tina regards the day. The sun is brilliant in the sky. "I don't think she's in danger of catching a cold."

"Well, we have things to do, I told you that, and we've already taken up too much of your time, I think."

She picks up her coffee cup and drains the lukewarm remains. "Hey, I live in Todos Santos. I've got nothin' but time."

On the short drive back to the Oasis, Angel interrogates Tina about Old Mac. I only half-concentrate on the conversation. He's a blue and gold macaw, ten years old, but Tina's only had him for two years. A friend of hers had to give him away; something in her tone of voice makes me wonder if the friend died.

Tina promises that when we get back to the Oasis, she'll take Mac out of the cage and he and Angel can get acquainted.

"He won't bite off my finger, will he?" Angel hasn't forgotten her warning from the day before.

"Not if I'm there," Tina reassures her. "He's really sweet, but he's not too crazy about new people. That doesn't make him the ideal pet for an inn, does it?"

As we pull in through the gate, Tina turns to me and asks, "So, have you decided how long you're staying?"

"Let me pay you for last night and tonight," I tell her. "If we want to stay longer, do you have space for us?"

"Sure, season's coming to an end down here. Most of the snowbirds are back up north after the middle of April." She grins. "I'm in a position to be flexible."

"Can we visit Mac now?" Angel has jumped down from the cab and is hopping up and down with excitement.

"Hold your horses, missy. Your mom and I just need to do a little bit of business. Why don't you help me by feeding Loba her breakfast?" Tina instructs Angel on how to accomplish this. "See that green plastic cup? Just dip it in the food and fill it up, then put it into her dish." For the moment, this task redirects my daughter's attention.

"You don't have to keep her occupied," I say apologetically. "You didn't even want a child here in the first place."

"Most kids are fucking little brats. Your daughter is scarily well behaved. She's like a little adult. I don't know if it's good for her, but it makes it a lot easier to be around. She's an only child, right?"

I nod as Tina leads me into the office of her large house. The room has many windows, but the overhanging palms shield it from the sun. From another room, I hear the sound of a television.

Tina sighs as she opens a ledger book and picks up a pen. "Mr. Corrigan lives here year-round, in the *casita* on the other side of the house. He's about a thousand years old, but he still manages to get himself out to the beach once a day." With the pen, she gestures toward the noise. "His TV's on the fritz, and it makes him completely anxious to be out of touch with what's going on in the States, so I let him come in to watch mine. But the poor bastard's deaf as a post, so he cranks it up. Then he wanders off for a snack and just leaves it blasting."

She starts to rise. "Let me go turn that off."

"I'll do it," I offer hastily.

I follow the sound into a central foyer, through a bright gold kitchen and up three steps to a raised living room with a full view of the Pacific. The walls are painted chartreuse, and one of them is hung chock-a-block with thrift store paintings of flowers. The television is set into a wooden entertainment center in one corner of the room.

It's tuned to a midday news broadcast, and with a queasy feeling, I recognize the daytime anchors from the local ABC affiliate in Los Angeles. Suddenly I see my picture flash on the screen. It's a picture from almost a decade ago; Yoli must have given it to them. My hair was still long, and I wear the perpetual sneer of dissatisfaction that was typical before I started meditating with the Light Beings. It was taken the first Thanksgiving after she moved into my house. Then there's a picture of Angel, her school picture from this past year. I'd taken her to have her hair done in cornrows, and Yoli was pissed that she looked "like such a pickaninny" for her school picture.

In the upper right corner of the screen is text spelling out a description of my silver Accord and its license plate number. My knees threaten to give out; I sink into the worn purple velvet plush of the antique sofa. I long to look away from the screen, but as with a freeway accident, I can't help but stare.

Now there's a clip of Yoli who, despite her grief, has taken the time to get herself into full makeup. The newscaster describes her as an actress and singer, and mentions that she's in the road company of *Aida*. Yoli stares into the camera and says, "Please, just bring my baby back to me. Don't let this personal vendetta against me ruin my daughter's life, Maggie."

It's hearing my name, spoken aloud and blaring through this room that releases me from my spell. The anchorwoman, whose lipstick is too pink, is saying, "If you have any information about this missing child, call this number..." I click the remote and the screen goes dark and blessedly silent.

Tina comes to the bottom of the stairs. "I thought I lost you." She chuckles at the sight of me with the remote in my hand. "Goddamn TV eats your brain, doesn't it?"

Then she looks at me more closely. "Are you okay?"

I nod. Now I am the one who has been in the accident, at whom onlookers gawk. I'm in shock, deeply recessed into myself. I move off the couch and down the stairs as if underwater; my limbs feel both heavy and weightless at the same time.

Back in the office, Tina says, "Let's see, then, two nights at the per night rate, that's thirteen hundred pesos."

I peel them from my wallet. I don't bother to count them, just hand her a stack. All I can think of is how fast can I get us out of here without arousing further suspicion. Tina counts the bills, returns a smaller pile to me. She scribbles something in the ledger, then says, "Can I just see your driver's license, hon?"

"What do you need that for?" My esophagus seizes up, threatens to return my breakfast. "Sorry," I say, and pull the ID from my wallet. I attempt to laugh it off. "I'm just on edge today, PMS, I guess." My voice sounds hollow, like it comes from the bottom of an empty well.

She glances at the license quickly, doesn't study it in the way I'd expect her to. She folds my pesos into her pocket, returns my license, and closes her ledger. "Okay, that's it! Now I better go see that Angel doesn't feed my dog the whole bag of dog food!"

I nod, barely registering her remarks. I need to call Charlie. I hear Tina and my daughter on the patio with the macaw as I slip into our *casita*. I hunt in my wallet and find the scrap of paper with the number of the cell he'd given me.

He answers on the second ring. "Maggie, is that you?"

"Are you sure it's safe for me to call?" In the front room of the *casita*, I perch on the futon where Angel spent some of the night. There is a bookshelf to my right, its shelves stuffed with a hodgepodge of trashy paperback mysteries.

"Are you okay? It's been two days and five some hours since you last called me, and all I can do is imagine you in some police shootout by the side of the interstate."

"I thought I was okay, but Charlie, I just saw the news."

"Yeah, they're playing it up. It's a slow news cycle; the president hasn't invaded anybody today."

"Fuck, Charlie, this isn't a joke. Are you sure this number is safe?"

"Don't you be snippy with me, Miss Thing. I'm on *your* side. This number has been safe in the past, dumpling, that's all I can tell you. And you got a prepaid cell? Want to give me the number?"

I fish for the scrap of paper where I've written the country code, district code, and then the number. With no explanation, I rattle off the sixteen digits.

"Wait a minute—isn't that too many... Maggie, where the fuck are you?" It takes him a few seconds to put the pieces together, then he whistles long and low.

"Is that good or bad?" Staring down at my arm, I see a burn developing from this morning's walk in the sun. I touch my palm to my cheek; it too feels hot.

"Well, if I can go by the TV reports, I'm pretty sure the cops aren't looking for you south of the border yet, so that's a good thing. But I'm pretty sure the U.S. has an extradition treaty, should they figure it out. And if Yoli decides to prosecute, this isn't going to help."

"Oh, Yoli will definitely prosecute. At least, if Daman is still in the picture. I talked to her the night before last."

"You what?" For the first time, he sounds genuinely upset with me.

"Listen, Angel was getting really sad about missing her mother and I started to feel like maybe I was doing something terrible and that I should just send her back to Yoli."

"*Hello?* Yoli is the one who left her with Cruella DeVil in the first place!"

"I know, but I have to believe she thought Lurlene would take good care of her. Anyway, I called, but she's not even paying attention to what happened to Angel. She's just acting like I did this to get back at her for taking Angel away from me. God, Charlie, I saw her on TV."

"I know. The grieving mother betrayed by the dastardly lesbian—it's the role of a lifetime. So how are you getting the news down there?"

"Satellites, Charlie, satellites. Apparently, most of the

gringos who stay down here can't live without reruns of *Friends* and the nightly news. It is indeed a global village."

"I can't do anything to contradict Yoli's version until I get those photos. Did you send them to me?"

"Yes, but from Ensenada. It could take a while to get to you. So have the cops talked to you?"

"Not yet. You know how Yoli never liked me? I'm hoping she's totally forgotten that I exist. Your mother, on the other hand, has been on TV. I sincerely hope you missed that one."

My mother. I'm flabbergasted that she would agree to be interviewed. I would expect her to be more worried about what the neighbors will think. On the other hand, maybe the attention was too irresistible.

"She was wearing her fur!" Charlie can't refrain from telling me. "In April!"

"And her best jewelry, I'm sure." It occurs to me how thoroughly I have managed to put my mother out of my mind; I'm startled by the sudden reminder of what she's like. With a sick feeling, I ask, "What did she say?"

"Nothing you haven't heard before, sweet cheeks. 'Maggie's always been difficult, never considers how her actions might affect other people...'"

"It's all about *her*, right?"

"Pretty much. And Maggie, I talked to a lawyer."

"Do you think that was a good idea?"

"Trust me, sugar pie, you're gonna need a lawyer. And this lesbian is totally trustworthy. I've worked on a bunch of cases with her—medical marijuana busts, families who try to deny survivorship rights to the partner of their son who's died of AIDS. She's on our side."

"Family—what a fucked-up institution! So what did she say?"

"Depends on what you want to do. If you stay out and don't get caught, you don't need her, although she might be able to recommend someone who could help you get phony documents, etc. She was careful not to suggest this, of course, but alluded to it as one of the possible scenarios."

"What else?"

"Option two, you decide to come back, and she can help you surrender, handle your case, and try to get you at least partial custody. Although, she says, the longer you're gone, the harder this becomes.

"Option three, you get caught, and she represents you. Of course, when I talked to her, I didn't know where you were."

"I'm not going to get caught," I say. Where this determination comes from I don't know, but I feel it like a rod of steel running the length of my spine.

"I hope you're right." Charlie sighs. "I don't think Mexican jail is much fun."

I can hear Angel's voice moving closer to our *casita*. "Listen, Charlie, I should go."

"Do you need any money or anything?"

"No. I'm good."

"Okay, then call me again soon, okay? You don't want me getting any more worry lines over you."

"Thanks, Charlie. I'm sorry to drag you into this."

"Are you kidding?" he says lightly. "Without smuggling medical marijuana and alternative AIDS treatments and running interference for international kidnappers, I'd be just another pretty face!"

Angel skips into the room as I'm tucking the phone into my backpack. "Maggie, Old Mac sat on my shoulder! He ate pineapple right out of my hand! He spread his wings, but Tina says she clips them so he doesn't fly away."

"Great, honey," I say distractedly. "I want you to change out of those clothes right away. We need to take a little ride."

"NO!" she shrieks. "No more driving! I want to stay here! I want to go see Edgar Sue!"

"Honey, I can't leave you here." I can hear how my patience is frayed, "I need you to cooperate with me. We need to go now!"

"NO! NO! NO! NO! NO!"

Never get into a power struggle with a child. I know this, and whenever I forget, it is always disastrous. I reach for her and begin to pull the borrowed T-shirt over her head. I'm not rough with her, but I am handling her against her will. She sets up such a howl that Tina comes and knocks on the door.

"Everybody okay in here?" She peeks her head in, perhaps to make sure no child abuse is going on. I just want my daughter to shut up and for Tina to get out of here.

My daughter sobs in the middle of the room, naked but for her underpants. The bruises are completely visible.

Tina Downs looks me right in the eye. "I saw those earlier. You didn't do that, did you?" She gestures toward the backs of Angel's thighs.

"Of course not." I stare right back at her.

"But you're trying to keep her away from the person who did?"

Angel is still crying. I can feel my shoulders start to collapse. How I long to confide in the big, gruff, flamboyant Tina Downs at this moment, to dump the weight of this responsibility onto her shoulders. But I don't dare.

Instead, I harden my face into a mask. "I thought you never asked questions."

She shrugs. "Suit yourself. Just seems like maybe you could use a hand." She goes back out the screen door.

"Thank you. We'll be fine," I insist, despite the evidence to the contrary. I go to my daughter, sit on the floor, and wrap my arms around her. She cries a little harder, pounds on my shoulders a bit, but I just hold her closer, until she relaxes into my lap.

"I'm sorry," I tell her.

And of course, I'm sorry for everything. I'm sorry for Yoli and me breaking up, sorry for letting her stay with Lurlene, sorry for dragging her on this trip, sorry for losing my temper. I am sure I will have much more to be sorry about before this is over. "Will you please come with me for a little bit? We don't have to drive a very long way."

"Where is it?" she wants to know.

"It's where the Light Beings live."

"Will they sing like they sometimes do?" My daughter is very like her mother; she always loves to sing.

"Depends on when we get there, I expect."

I watch my daughter's face assume its own mask, one of duty, resigned to once more being the good child, doing what she doesn't want to do to please the adults in her life. She looks weary. I think about her effervescence just minutes ago, skipping in to tell me about the macaw. She needs the chance to just be a little kid. Maybe I've robbed her of that, with all my expectations. With this crazy scheme.

Parenting is all about second-guessing oneself, being haunted by what you've done, what you didn't do. There will be plenty of time for remorse. First, though, I need to get her someplace safe. Despite Tina's ominous warnings, I pray to Spirit that the Light Beings' community will prove to be that place.

Chapter 6

I'd felt torn about asking Tina Downs for directions to the Light Beings community—the fewer people who know where I am, the better, I figure, and I've already blown it by bringing it up to the bookstore woman, who I'm sure can be counted on to remember it when the FBI comes to question her—but now I'm glad I did, because there is no marker, no sign, no indication whatsoever that this dirt road off the main highway leads to anywhere at all. Without Tina's instructions—"After the Art & Beer sign, go exactly half a mile and turn left onto a road that looks like it's goin' nowhere"—I would be still driving south.

My urgency to see Guru Tam is now greater than ever. If the gringos of Todos Santos are watching the news from L.A., it is only a matter of time before someone calls that number on the screen and says, "That woman and the kid you're looking for? I've seen them!"

Angel has gone into full sulking mode beside me, not talking, not looking at me, but full of copious sighs and squirming in the passenger seat. She's kicking the dashboard, testing me; I never would have allowed this in my Accord, but with the Poo-poo Box, what difference will it make? I'm stretched too thin to even try to fix things with her right now; I cannot trust myself to emit kindness and comfort.

Guru Tam has always said, "The opposite of fear is love. If you fill yourself with love it will drive the fear from your mind." But what happens when the fear takes over? What happens to love then?

I have another bout of fury at Yoli, for her selfishness. If it weren't for her pathetic need for fame, she wouldn't have to suck up to people like Daman, and if it weren't for Daman and his macho need to control Yoli's life, Angel would have never gotten hurt. And if Angel hadn't gotten hurt, and if Yoli weren't so blinded by what she thinks Daman can do for her career, we could all be home now and Lurlene would be behind bars.

These thoughts spin so feverishly in my brain that I forget to breathe. I don't know how long we've been traveling on this road because I haven't been present. Of course, Angel feels this energy, just as I so clearly read hers, even when she hasn't said a word. *Spirit, deliver me from this poison of negative thought.*

The road is too dusty to keep our windows down, despite the heat of midday. Without air conditioning the heat is blistering. I remind myself to bless this Poo-poo Box; if we were still in my Accord we would be one step closer to being identified. This part of the desert looks barren, even this early in the year. I wouldn't like to have to travel it on foot.

After a mile or so the road takes a turn, and in the distance I see what looks like an oasis. Suddenly the road is superbly maintained, with a small barrier of orange and yellow cannas planted along either side, not a shred of trash evident. Beyond the cannas are carefully cultivated fields, although I'm not close enough to identify what produce is being grown. Farther down the road I can see structures, including a gleaming white building with a golden spire on its roof. The energy of the air itself seems to shift as we approach the complex. Not that it's any cooler, but it does feel a bit lighter. Out of the corner of my eye, I see Angel sit up a little straighter. She too seems aware that we've entered a different kind of space.

As we near those buildings, three bearded men in pale blue robes step into the road and motion us to stop. Their heads are draped in turbans of the same color. All wear silver hearts on chains around their necks. Making sure my own necklace is visible, I roll down my window to I greet them. "Peace begets peace."

They study us with suspicion. Finally one of them, whose beard and eyebrows are gray, says, "Peace returns peace. What is your business here?"

I finger my own silver heart. "I practice at the ashram in Los Angeles. I stayed with Amara in the Light Beings community in Ensenada. I was hoping to find temporary sa– sojourn here for my daughter and myself." I almost said "sanctuary." "I'm here to ask the counsel of Guru Tam," I add.

"That's impossible!" pronounces a man in wire-rimmed sunglasses. "Guru Tam no longer receives visitors." He is short and rotund, barrel-shaped, his facial hair still dark. There are sweat stains under the arms of his robe.

"Our Teacher is ill," explains the tallest of the three, lanky, with a thin blond beard. His tone is more conciliatory than the other two.

"We've come such a long way," I plead, "and we really need help. Guru Tam has said, 'Never turn your back on an opportunity to serve.'" Perhaps they will think I've gone too far, quoting their teacher to them. They are the ones in robes, after all, not me. I'm only someone who read the books, and went to meditation once a week. *Spirit, don't let them turn us away*.

"We don't allow visitors," insists the black-haired man in the wire rims. The backs of his hands are also covered with thick hair. He has stepped in front of the car, his arms crossed at his chest, as if to make himself a barricade to keep me from driving forward.

"You have to turn around." He is making pushing motions with his hands, as if he could force the car backward with his will. "If not, we will be forced to call the authorities."

"Are we gonna get caught?" Angel whimpers beside me.

"Hush!" I mutter, under my breath. I don't want them to sense our desperation. Given what Tina told me about the way the Mexicans regard the Light Beings, I wonder whether the police would respond to such a call, but I don't want to risk it.

"Stay here," I tell my daughter.

I turn off the car and open the door to stand in the middle of the road.

"What are you doing?" The hairy man is incensed. "I told you to go!"

I take a moment to call upon Spirit, to allow a flood of light to enter through the top of my head and fill my body. "Please," I say, and my voice is very calm. "We mean no harm. My daughter and I need the Guru's help. Can't you at least ask if we might see Guru Tam for a short interview."

The blond man goes to the angry man, places a hand on his forearm, whispers something in his ear. The shorter man argues, but I sense it is just for form's sake. Perhaps the blond man has some greater status? The gray-bearded man stands impassive, watching, as he has since we arrived.

"Maggie," Angel leans over the driver's seat to ask, "why won't they let us in?"

"They're going to let us in," I say quietly, and a little grimly.

"But, they said…"

"Shh! Just wait!"

She recoils from the bite in my tone.

The blond man comes back to me. "You will need to talk to Sumati. She's the Chief Assistant to Guru Tam."

"And where will I find her?" I smile in appreciation of his assistance.

"Drive up the road until you reach the main building. There's a fountain in front. Go on into the office. We'll call ahead and let Sumati know to expect you."

"Thank you. Peace begets peace."

"Peace returns peace." He smiles, then begins dialing something that looks like a large walkie-talkie as I climb back into the front seat of the Poo-poo Box.

The dark-haired man is scowling, perhaps because he lost the argument. He barely moves out of my way as I drive slowly past him. My small relief in clearing this hurdle is dampened by my dismay at our reception. In Los Angeles, the Light Beings community is open, friendly; anyone at all is welcome to come to its events. Even in Ensenada, they took us in with no warning whatsoever. What's going on here, I wonder, that has led everyone to be so closed and mistrustful?

"How did you know, Maggie?" Angel tugs at my arm.

"How did I know what?" I drive past a number of smallish stucco structures that might be houses, each surrounded by a pocket garden. Each dwelling is painted a bright white, although they have different accent colors, coral or turquoise or sage.

"That they'd let us in." My daughter's mood seems to have shifted, aligned with me once more against a perceived opposition. "How did you know?"

"It was the right thing to happen, that's all."

"Does the right thing always happen?" she wants to know.

I take in a long breath. These are the kinds of questions kids spring on you when you're least prepared. "When you have faith," I tell her, "you know that everything is the right thing, even when it seems like it's not."

A small frown puckers her caramel forehead as she takes this in. I drive up in front of the building with a large fountain cascading into a circular tile pool. The water burbles, even in the dry desert air. I check my judgment about the environmental consciousness of this object and bring the Poo-poo Box to a stop in front of the building.

I move around to the passenger door to get Angel. "Do you have faith?" she demands. Her eyes seem green as beach glass at the moment, light shining through them.

I gather her in my arms for just a second, inhaling the milky scent of her spilled breakfast. "Yes," I tell her, although really I'm speaking to myself. "Yes, precious girl, I do."

I reach for her hand and she lets me take it, and we walk beneath a tiled archway and enter the coolness of the thick-walled building. Immediately I can smell the rich scent of cloves. Polished wood floors echo with our footsteps. Potted palms line the pale blue walls. A large anteroom boasts a domed skylight in the center of the room that beams over a circular pool, perhaps five feet in diameter. Angel kneels at the edge of the water, lets her fingers trail through it. Colorful pillows are stacked in two corners. One open door reveals a large room beyond this with a low, silk-draped platform at one end, probably used for meditation or workshops. Above the platform is a large photograph of a much younger Guru Tam. I feel an immediate recognition, even though I have only ever seen the Guru in photographs. Even in pictures the teacher emits a radiance that at once fills and soothes me. Two other closed doors off the anteroom lead to unknown destinations.

It is through one of these doors that a woman now treads heavily. I recognize in her gait a woman self-conscious about her size; like me, she is tall and broad. Her pale blue gown stretches across her shoulders and over the girth of her belly; it does not flow gracefully like water. Her head-covering drapes over a square, plain face. The pale flush of her skin suggests to me that she must suffer here in the desert climate.

"Peace begets peace," I greet her, and am surprised to hear Angel echo my words.

"Peace begets peace," my daughter says solemnly.

A tiny smile escapes the thin grip of the woman's lips. "Peace returns peace," she answers, acknowledging both of us. "I am Sumati."

"I'm Maggie, and this is Angel." I hold out a hand to shake, but Sumati does not grasp it. It drops limply back to my side.

"I've come to ask your help," I blurt. "Two things, really…"

"Let's not talk here," she commands, and leads us through the door from which she came.

On the other side of it is an office, a scattering of desks and file cabinets, computers and fax machines. We move to another door that leads to an outside courtyard, a tiled patio shaded by a woven *palapa*, a roof of palm fronds. The gardens are florid with color. She indicates a group of low wooden benches and we sit. With no evident signal to prompt her, a younger woman appears with a tray and three glasses.

"Iced lemon ginger tea?" she offers, seemingly shy with strangers. She hands a glass to each of us and bows slightly toward Sumati before she disappears.

"Jagadeep told me you were persistent down by the gate," Sumati gives me a penetrating stare. "Persistence may be a virtue or may indicate an unwillingness to obey. Which is it for you?"

Angel regards me curiously, unaccustomed to seeing me called out by someone other than Yoli.

"I suppose it is both," I tell Sumati.

She nods in grudging appreciation of my honesty. "And what is it you have come here so urgently to seek?"

I meet her gaze squarely. I have everything to lose and in accepting this, I am oddly fearless. "Angel is the daughter of myself and my former partner, who is the biological mother. When my ex had to go away on business, she put Angel in the care of her new boyfriend's sister. This was painful for me but I worked to accept it as a teaching."

Sumati's face remains expressionless; I have no idea what she thinks about what she's hearing. Maybe this community of Light Beings is more vigorously opposed to homosexuality than their counterparts elsewhere. But that's out of my control.

Across the garden, Angel spots a tortoiseshell cat. "Maggie, look!" she exclaims.

"Is it okay if she plays with the cat?" I ask Sumati, who simply nods in response.

"Okay, honey, go ahead, but go slow, okay? If you rush up to her, she might run away." Angel crouches a bit, makes her way slowly across the garden, calling, "Kitty, kitty" in a soft tone. The cat watches, then slowly begins to creep in my daughter's direction.

Observing this, Sumati remarks, "That cat doesn't usually like children."

I'm relieved to resume my story out of Angel's earshot.

"Three days ago, I learned that this woman was beating Angel. My daughter has severe bruising on the backs of her legs. My fear was that the police would either do nothing and leave Angel with this woman or they'd put her into the foster care system. My only concern was that she be safe. So I took her out of school, and brought her to Mexico. I informed her mother that she is with me and is safe, but she's convinced I did this out of vengeance. Now the police are after me. I don't think they yet know that we're in Mexico, but it's only a matter of time."

"And exactly how do you imagine the Light Beings can help you?" Sumati's tone does not sound very sympathetic.

"I thought this might be a place where we could stay... undiscovered for a bit. And I was hoping Guru Tam might counsel me, help me to better understand what is the right action to take."

Sumati's lips grow even thinner. "And do you concern yourself at all with the possible danger and upheaval you might bring to this community?"

"Of course I mean to do no harm."

The woman's laugh is bitter. "Isn't the gravest harm always done without intention? You are asleep, Maggie. You have committed a crime, you have caused great heartache to a number of people, you have put your daughter in danger, you have risked your life and your future. Your delusions lull you into believing you have done all this for good, that you are a hero, like a Hollywood movie, but that is just ego, Maggie, the biggest delusion of all."

I can feel my face reddening to the tips of my ears. What I most want to do is to say, "Fuck you, you bitter old prune," and storm out of there. But how can I? Where would we go?

Sumati smiles. "Oh, this isn't what you came for, is it? You wanted comfort and justification, not consciousness. The Light Beings are not about comfort, Maggie; we are about the development of the soul. It's hard work and it often isn't 'nice.'"

Across the garden, the tortoiseshell cat has rolled onto its back and is allowing my daughter to rub her nose in its white belly. Perhaps I should have let Angel handle the conversation with Sumati as well.

"I want to learn," I say simply.

"You want to be relieved of the consequences of your actions," Sumati snaps back.

I inhale slowly. Keeping my voice very neutral I say, "So are you saying we can't stay here?"

"Were it up to me, I would definitely say that. It is my job to protect this community. The Mexican politicians are just looking for something like this to drive us off this land!" As she stands, her eyes take in the sweep of property surrounding us.

"But it is not up to me. I must take this question to our Teacher, even though Guru Tam is very unwell and should not be having to engage with such an issue at this time." She says this reprovingly, as though mine will be the request that puts the Beloved Teacher in the grave.

I feel utterly flattened, crushed into the ground, but now the tiniest bit of hope begins to stir again. I can only hope that the Guru will view my situation with more compassion.

"You must wait here," Sumati says. "I cannot tell you how long it will be, because I will not wake the Guru if the Guru is sleeping."

"Thank you," I say, and watch her waddle back into the building, her movement made more ungainly by her rage.

Angel comes up to me, then, the cat scooped into her arms. "Maggie, she likes me!"

"Of course she does, my sweet girl. Who couldn't like you?"

"Tell me what this says," she fingers the silver disk hanging from the cat's collar.

I strain to read the etched letters; at forty-five, my eyesight isn't all that it once was. "I think it says Jyoti."

"What's that?" my daughter wants to know.

"It must be her name, but I don't know what it means."

"How come everybody has such funny names?" She pouts a little.

"Those are spiritual names," I explain. "They're Indian names, I think. Probably most of the people had regular

American names when they were born, but when they came into the Light Beings' community, they were given new names." I take a moment to savor the prospect that Sumati once moved through the world with the name Brunhilda.

Angel drains her ice tea, with Jyoti sprawled in her lap. Then she announces, "Maggie, I hafta pee."

"I didn't see a bathroom when we came through."

"Should I do it here?" My daughter is now an old hand at outdoor urination.

"No, I think that's not a good idea." I look around, then remember the door through which the shy woman came with our tea. I get up to knock on that door, and the shy woman pokes her head out. She has very pale skin and pale eyebrows; her eyes are light gray.

"I'm sorry to bother you..." I begin but she interrupts me.

"Peace begets peace," she insists on the formal greeting.

"Peace returns peace," I respond. "My daughter needs to use a restroom, and I was wondering if you could show us where to go."

"My name is Amrita," she says.

"I'm Maggie, and my daughter's name is Angel." I can see her on the bench, getting squirmy, and I know she's not going to hold it much longer. "Please?"

"Yes," Amrita says, "come with me."

"C'mon, Angel, she'll take us to the bathroom."

My daughter reluctantly eases Jyoti to the ground, then scurries to join us. "I hafta go real bad," she confides to us.

Amrita leads us through an industrial-style kitchen, all chrome, polished to a perfect shine. Besides Amrita, the other three workers—cooks and dishwashers—are Mexican men, dressed identically in navy blue T-shirts and pants. I surmise that they wear a uniform to complement the robes of the Light Beings. There is a great frenzy of lunch preparation going on and a strong scent of garlic, but I don't stop to ask any questions.

Amrita leads us out of the kitchen to a hallway, and shows Angel the door.

"Do you want me to go in with you?" I ask.

My daughter answers impatiently. "No, I can do it!" The blue door closes in my face.

Amrita waits with me. I take the opportunity to spread a new coat of lip balm on my chapped lips.

"Have you lived here a long time?" I ask her.

"I moved from the Light Beings' ashram in Oregon. That was eight years ago."

She looks so young to me. I guess that thought must register on my face, because she explains, "My parents are Light Beings; I was born into the community."

"How many people live here?" I wonder.

She's about to answer when Angel pokes her head around the door. "Can I flush the paper?" she asks, holding up a wad of tissue in her hand.

"No. Please put it in the basket right next to the toilet." Amrita smiles as I roll my eyes in apology. "It was one of the hardest things I had to get used to in Baja as well." The toilet flushes and Angel reappears.

Amrita flashes a shy grin. "I need to get back to organizing lunch. You're both welcome to stay and eat if you'd like." She begins hurrying us back down the hall.

"What's for lunch?" Angel pipes up.

I stop and bug my eyes out at her to let her know that her question is rude.

Amrita isn't the least bit fazed. "Lasagna and salad and garlic bread. Daya's been baking this morning."

Angel turns to me to stage whisper, "Maggie, does lasagna have meat in it?"

"Not here, it doesn't," Amrita answers her. "All of our food is vegetarian."

This announcement makes my daughter's face stretch into a grin. "I'm a vegetarian," she announces.

We are back at the kitchen; the men in navy blue are chatting in Spanish in a little huddle near a long chrome prep table. When they see Amrita, they immediately disperse and resume their tasks. To me she looks too young and too sweet to inspire that kind of obedience; she looks like the nervous substitute teacher that the class knows it can roll over as soon as she walks in the door.

"Is it okay if we stay for lunch here?" Angel wants to know. "I love lasagna!" She asserts this despite the fact she's never actually eaten this dish, at least, not to my knowledge.

"That depends on what Sumati has to say to us after she talks to Guru Tam."

Overhearing this, Amrita says, "I shouldn't speak for her, but she isn't likely to be back with any news before then. In fact, I better set aside a plate for her; she'll be cranky if she misses lunch."

I'd hate to see her cranky, I think, recalling her formidable demeanor this morning.

"Doesn't Guru Tam live here on the property?" I ask.

"Nearby," she answers vaguely, before turning to spread handfuls of fresh nasturtium blossoms on the tops of four enormous bowls of salad. When she's done, she bends down and says to Angel, "I know, why don't you come help me while I sound the call for lunch."

I trail them back outdoors into the courtyard. The cat has disappeared. Two other Mexican men, also dressed in navy blue, are just finishing setting up a series of long wooden tables and benches. The men from the kitchen are in the process of carrying out steaming pans of lasagna, platters of bread and the bowls of salad. A round table boasts large metal coolers of what I presume to be more cold ginger tea. Another holds stacks of plates and bowls and cups and a tray full of cutlery.

Amrita leads Angel over to a large brass gong, the metal hammered into a perfect curve. It's about the size of one of the round tabletops, hung upright from a sturdy metal frame. Guided by Amrita, my daughter picks up a yarn-wrapped wooden mallet; the young woman slowly guides her arm back, and then forward again, striking the gong with a resounding blow. Its tone is deep, resonating throughout the courtyard.

"Can we do it again?" Angel asks.

"Three times," Amrita promises, and they strike the gong again and then once more.

From doorways and diverse paths, people make their way

into the courtyard. Most are clad in pale blue; a couple of men wear jeans. There must be forty or fifty of them. A group of children comes in a herd, perhaps from lessons; fifteen or sixteen of them, looking to range from age three to about twelve. Almost everyone has white skin, except for a dark-skinned couple and two of the children. Those children spot Angel right away and go over to her. One is a boy, about Angel's age, the other an older girl.

I check my impulse to go over and monitor their interaction. I tell myself we're safe here; my daughter needs time with peers, time away from me. That's part of what will be valuable about being here, *if* we're allowed to stay.

Before anyone picks up a plate, the whole group gathers around the food in a loose circle. At an unseen signal, everyone sings:

Thank you, Spirit, for the blessings of the earth and sky.
Thank you for your gifts, may I use them to serve You.

This is chanted three times; even the Mexican workers stop to participate. Then everyone bows. Only then do people form lines on either side of the food tables, and begin to serve themselves. Not certain where I should be, I walk over to Amrita, who shoos me toward the group. "Go ahead, get in line. Get a plate of food," she urges, then bustles back to the kitchen. I realize she's busy with the responsibility of feeding lunch to sixty or seventy people, but by the looks of it, the system is seamless.

I notice that the children go first, with the older ones helping to serve the youngest. I watch my daughter carefully load her plate, hear her boast again, "I'm a vegetarian, too!" She goes off with the other children to a table set aside for them, but first she checks to make sure she knows where I am.

"Is she with you?" a voice behind me asks, and I see it belongs to the African-American woman. The light blue of her head covering sets off the cocoa of her skin. Standing behind, the man I presume to be her husband is tall and wears wire-rimmed glasses with a blue tint to the lenses.

"She's my daughter," I say with a smile. I am more than accustomed to people's slightly perplexed looks, and I long ago stopped feeling the need to explain. "Her name is Angel, and mine is Maggie." I put out my hand to shake.

Instead of taking my hand, she brings hers together in front of her heart and bows slightly. As she does this, I see many lengths of cobalt and gold beads wrapped around her wrists, a stylish addition to the Light Beings' traditional robes. "Peace begets peace." She smiles. "My name is Bhanupriya, and this is my husband, Haroon."

"Peace returns peace," I respond, and don't know what to say beyond that. A square of lasagna is ladled onto my plate, followed by a large serving of salad and a hunk of garlic bread. Even after the *huevos rancheros* this morning, I find I am hungry.

"I figured you were together because you are both in western clothing," Bhanupriya continues.

Her husband chimes in, "It is rare for us to have visitors to the community." He pours two glasses of ginger tea, hands one to his wife. Then he asks if I would like one as well.

I decline the tea, but say, "I'd heard that the community discourages nonmembers from entering."

"Oh, no," Bhanupriya protests. "Where did you hear such a thing?"

I'm reminded of the three guards at the gate placing their bodies in front of my car to prevent us from coming in and of Sumati's forbidding reception.

"We're here to spread the teachings of our beloved Guru," Haroon insists. "Of course we want to invite our fellow humans into the community."

This disconnection between my perception and theirs is curious to me. I follow them over to a table not far from where the children are clustered and slide onto a bench across from them. I take a forkful of lasagna; the sauce is rich and spicy, a perfect contrast to the softness of the noodles and melted cheese.

"So," I continue, "what is your experience when you go into town?"

"Oh," Bhanupriya's laugh is musical. "We don't go into town."

"What do you mean?"

"Most of us do not leave this land. Only Sumati and Pramesh are authorized to go outside the community." There is not a trace of distress about this in her tone.

"And Jayadita, too," her husband amends. "He handles the sale of our crops and other products," he explains to me.

"Are you saying," I am trying to control the distress in my own tone, "that you're not allowed to leave?"

Haroon looks at me curiously. "Allowed? It is not like that. Sumati has said that our Teacher wishes us to stay and provides us with everything we need. Why would we not be happy to do as our Teacher wishes?"

"I don't know. Don't you ever have a desire to do something different?" I wonder.

"In the United States," Bhanupriya adds, swallowing a bite of her garlic bread, "there is such struggle, all because everyone feels he must follow his individual desires. Everything is a conflict of wills—between husband and wife, between parent and child. 'What *I* want is not what *you* want' and such suffering comes from this."

"We have no such conflict here," Haroon agrees. "We are not here to serve ourselves, our own desires, but to serve Spirit, and we are blessed to have our dear Teacher to guide us."

"But what if something were to happen? What if you learned your mother was ill and didn't have much time? Wouldn't you want to be able to leave and go to her?"

"We consider this community to be our family," Haroon answers.

"But if there were some compelling reason," Bhanupriya assures me, "we would talk to Sumati and she would talk to Guru Tam, and it would be worked out. It's not as if we are prisoners," she says and smiles.

I nod, unconvinced but not wishing to be the sower of discord, especially as an uninvited guest. I cannot silence the alarm bells going off in my head, because "prisoner" was pretty much the exact word I was thinking. I try another tack.

"How long has it been since Guru Tam was here?"

Bhanupriya offers me a curious smile, the kind you give when someone has said something you don't comprehend.

"Our Beloved Teacher is always with us here," she tells me.

Does she mean this symbolically? Is it a mass hallucination? Or did Amrita lie to me about the Guru not living on the property? Not wanting to commit another faux pas, I nod politely and bend my face toward my plate of food to concentrate on finishing my lunch. I feel like Alice in Wonderland, as if I've landed in a world where nothing is as I expect it to be.

In Los Angeles, the Light Beings open their doors to nonmembers every day of the week. I've seen them all over town in their blue robes—at the Farmer's Market, at concerts, even at shopping malls and at the movies. What is going on here that gives rise to the need for this community to be sequestered? And what does it mean for Angel and myself? Would it make it safer for us to be here, or would it mean we are much less likely to be allowed to stay? And if allowed to stay, would we also be permitted to leave?

I don't foresee myself ever being able to accept someone telling where I can and cannot go. How can these people agree so readily? Are they brainwashed, or just way more spiritually evolved than I am?

My daughter is having no such misgivings. She's over with some of the children, including Bhanupriya's son, teaching them the Electric Slide. I didn't even know she knew the Electric Slide; it must be something she picked up from the television, or maybe her mother taught her. Her face lights up as she twirls. Sometimes I can see Yoli in her so strongly, it makes me ache.

Haroon glances over at the children. He gets up from his bench and goes over and says something to his son. He does it quietly, without making a scene or making the kids feel bad about what they've been doing. His boy nods and says something to the other children, who stop dancing with Angel and return to the table to clear their dishes.

Lunch is ending. Everyone rises to scrape their dishes into one of three large plastic garbage cans, then rinses them in large pans of hot soapy water. The navy-clad workers begin folding up the tables. The Light Beings are drifting back to their activities, whatever those may be. The oldest children are rounding up the younger ones.

Angel comes racing up to me. "Maggie, can I go with Prem and the others?"

I look at the group, starting to move out of the courtyard. Bhanupriya's son hangs back, expectant, gazing at us.

"May I," I correct her. "I'm not sure it's allowed, honey. Who said it would be okay?"

"Dhwani did. He's the tall one." She points out a gangly boy who seems to be a leader of the children's group.

I rise and walk quickly across the courtyard to the group; Angel has to run to keep up with my quick stride. Approaching the older boy I greet him, "Peace begets peace."

"Peace returns peace," he says, looking down at the toes sticking out of his sandals. He's at that shy stage where interacting with a strange adult is nearly unbearable. He's not old enough to have facial hair, but his pale eyebrows signal that he might be towheaded underneath his turban.

"My daughter and I are visiting today. Angel told me you said it would be okay if she joins the children for the afternoon?"

The boy looks as if he's been caught off-guard. He cuts his eyes sideways at Angel with a glance that is unreadable to me. He still won't look me in the eye.

"I'm sorry, did she misunderstand?" Now I am eager to save face, either for the boy or for my daughter.

The younger boy, Prem, comes up. "Come on, Dhwani, you said it was okay."

It's occurring to me that perhaps Dhwani does not have the authority to make this decision. I say to my daughter, "Angel, I'm not sure when Sumati will be back. Maybe you should just wait here with me."

"Maggie, no!" She stamps one foot and folds her arms across her chest.

The others stand wide-eyed; is it possible they've not seen a child say no to her mother? If the parents are as obedient as Bhanupriya and Haroon, what must the children be like? I have a fleeting image of my daughter corrupting the whole bunch, sowing the tendency to act out and a penchant for dance crazes among this placid and orderly community. It's a notion I find delicious.

Dhwani sees the need to exert some control over the situation. "She may join us," he says solemnly, "but she must do as we say." He looks directly at her, as if waiting for assurance that she is capable of this.

"What will you be doing?" I ask. "Do you have lessons?"

"Morning is for lessons," he explains, looking back at his feet. "In the afternoon, we work."

"What kind of work?" I want to know. Child labor?

"We keep bees on the land, and we sell honey. But they're too young to work with the bees. We also melt the beeswax and make candles, and that's what the young ones do—prepare the molds, clean them after, decorate and wrap the candles."

"They're not working with hot wax?" I press him further.

"Maggie!" In a high whine Angel protests what she considers my overprotectiveness.

"No," he says.

"May I see where she's going to be?" I ask. I don't know how I feel about putting kids to work as part of their education. It's better than watching TV, I suppose, but I don't want my daughter to end up in some sweatshop either.

Dhwani is nonplussed. It occurs to me that since visitors are not allowed, they have no policy for what visitors may and may not do. It is left on the shoulders of this thirteen-year-old to try to intuit what would and would not be permissible.

"I just want to know where I can find her later," I add, trying to assure him of the harmlessness of my request.

"Okay." He abruptly turns and begins to lead the group out of the courtyard. Angel clasps Prem's hand and begins skipping. I am left to trail behind.

We walk a little ways to an area behind the courtyard. In the distance, mountains loom over the desert. The children head toward one of several outbuildings, also shaded by a *palapa*. A long row of windows faces the mountains, allowing light and air to enter the space. At one end of the room is a stove with four burners, each covered by a large metal vat. The scent of wax thickens and sweetens the air.

A red-faced girl, herself perhaps twelve or thirteen, looks up from the stove as we enter. "You're late," she confronts Dhwani.

"Peace begets peace, Chhaya," he teases. She huffs and turns back to the vat she is watching.

Prem leads Angel to a stool beside his at a long table, its surface covered with new butcher paper. Eight others join them. Dhwani brings a box full of aluminum molds and hands them around the table, along with steel wool and other implements to scrape away any wax residue left inside. He turns on a CD player perched atop a cabinet, and I recognize the music that spills out as something I've heard before at the Light Beings' center in L.A.

It doesn't seem to me like a particularly fun way to spend the afternoon, but it doesn't seem like Angel will be harmed by it either.

"Sweetheart, if I'm not back here by the time you're finished, get Dhwani to bring you back to the courtyard to find me, okay?" My daughter nods, impatient for me to be gone. I reiterate, "Don't go anywhere else without telling me, promise?"

"O-*kay*," she says with complete annoyance. Around her peers, she is eager to display her independence.

I repeat the same instructions to Dhwani, who mutters to the floor, "Of course, ma'am, I'll make sure of it."

My daughter has completely forgotten about me as she bends to her task, gripping a star-shaped mold, so I depart, heading back to the courtyard. When I get there, the chairs and benches have been returned to the same configuration as when we first arrived.

I sit for a moment, but feel restive, not wanting to be alone with my thoughts. I imagine Yoli searching for me in her mind, tugging on me, wanting me to reveal our location to her. *It's your own fault, Yoli*, I telegraph her in response. *You're the one who left me. You're the one whose career is more important than your child...* I feel awash in a stream of resentment, corrosive as acid in my system; for a moment it seems like I won't be able to hold down my lasagna.

The only thing to do is try to meditate, to restore my connection to Spirit before my mind spirals completely out of control. I would have expected to feel closer to Spirit around the Light Beings, but at this moment I am steeped in the illusion that I am alone in the world, without support, with no resources from which to draw. It is this illusion, Guru Tam has always said, that causes human suffering.

I lower my large body to the ground, cross my legs, straighten my spine, close my eyes and begin to direct my focus to the third eye, the spot between my eyebrows. After a moment, it begins to tingle. Consciously I slow my breath, drawing the inhalations all the way into my belly, making sure to exhale completely until I am emptied out. I try to quiet the thoughts that charge through my brain—the police searching for us, my mother on the news, how many people in Todos Santos might have recognized us, whether Tina Downs can be trusted, the Light Beings at the gate determined to keep us out, the formidable countenance of Sumati telling me what a bad person I am, the image of Yoli's accusing eyes. I try to breathe these thoughts away, find my way to a place underneath them, a place where the matters of the world don't touch me. I feel a breeze ruffle my hair, hear birds conduct their daily business.

I concentrate on the mantra, "Peace begets peace," repeating the sounds again and again as the focus for my mind. Thoughts intrude and try to pull me away from this deeper place; the mantra reminds me to bring myself back. I sit this way until my legs begin to prickle. In the time I've been meditating I've been able to extend the amount of time I can sit before my legs go to sleep, but I never understand those who can seem to sit for hours without trouble.

Just as I'm unfolding myself and struggling to stand, I hear a rustle behind me. I turn to see Sumati striding across the courtyard. I quickly brush the dirt off my behind, wishing I could make a more decorous presentation. Her mouth is dour. The expression in her eyes in unreadable.

Guide me, Spirit. I gratefully surrender to your will, I pray silently as I turn to meet my fate.

Chapter 7

"Amrita tells me you had lunch."

Sumati sounds as if she'd like to snatch the crumbs right out of my mouth, so I just nod. "And your daughter?" she continues, "where has she gone?"

I gesture toward the direction of the building where I left her. "She wanted to help make candles with the other children." I fear it looks as though we've just inserted ourselves into the community in her absence. I try to keep my voice from sounding defensive. Or impatient, although anxiety constricts my chest. If she's going to turn us away I wish she'd just hurry up and do it. I remind myself to breathe.

"I missed lunch," Sumati says, her expression unchanging.

"I heard Amrita say she would make up a plate for you," I assure her. I remember the younger woman's assertion that

Sumati would be cranky if she didn't have lunch. "Maybe you'd rather eat before we talk."

Sumati's thin smile could just as easily be a grimace. It's foolish to try to mollify her and we both know it. The decision, whatever it may be, is already made. Ignoring my offer, she begins to speak.

"I've been with my Teacher since Guru Tam first arrived in the United States. That was nearly thirty-five years ago. I was just a child myself, all caught up in the commotions of the world, the wars that were tearing my country apart."

Sumati has settled her body into one of the lawn chairs and, feeling rude and awkward standing over her, I do the same. I cannot imagine why she has chosen this moment to confide the story of her life to me, but I attempt to quiet my own fretfulness and bring my attention to her words.

"Guru Tam could have remained in India and lived a quiet life of practicing and consolidating the powers of a Master. But the Teacher saw great anguish in the Americas and came to alleviate it, to teach us tools to develop our minds and our souls. It has been exhausting; it has literally drained the Teacher's life blood, to take on the suffering of so many for so long."

She again looks at me reprovingly, as if by my very existence I have siphoned this precious elixir drop by drop. "Days upon days our Teacher cannot rise from bed. Each breath is an effort; each might be the last."

She sighs deeply and shakes her head. "I have devoted the last twenty years to protecting my Teacher, but my Teacher will not be protected." Sumati draws her spine even straighter, like a judge pronouncing a verdict. "Make no mistake: I would have turned you away. The trouble you bring and your lack of discipline is not, in my view, what the community needs now.

"But part of my lesson is to bow to the greater wisdom of my Teacher. Guru Tam will see you within three days. Maybe sooner. It might be any time of day or night, whenever our Teacher is up to it. Until then, you and your daughter may stay in our community. I have been instructed to welcome you as one of our own."

"Thank you," I whisper, even though it is clearly not by

her grace that this decision has been made. Still, I want to throw my arms around her in relief and gratitude, but I restrain myself. "Where will we stay?" I'm imagining a little guest cottage, like one of Tina Downs' *casitas*, and hoping it has its own bathroom.

"Your daughter will be housed in the children's quarters," Sumati decrees.

"Oh no..." I begin, but Sumati stops me.

"'No' is not in the vocabulary of this community. If you are our guest here, you will do things our way. In this community, children do not live with their parents. While they maintain a special relationship with their mothers and fathers, they are encouraged to see themselves as belonging to the whole community."

After prevailing over this woman's objections to our sojourn there, I know I shouldn't complain, but I can't help myself. "Surely you can see, after all that has happened, Angel shouldn't be separated from me. She's in a foreign country, she's in an unfamiliar community..."

Sumati stops me with a flash of her eyes. "Surely, Maggie, you do not expect the Light Beings to change our way of life to accommodate the extremely questionable decisions you have made." We stare at each other for a long moment in the hot afternoon breeze that is sweeping dust throughout the courtyard.

"There are consequences to everything, Maggie, especially to getting what one has asked for."

My eyes begin to sting, and my closing them is a gesture of defeat. There appears to be no one to whom this decision can be appealed.

Sumati stands then, preparing to conclude the conversation. "You will stay with me in my room," she continues, seeming certain that the matter of Angel is settled. "I have an extra cot. You will work with Harshada in the laundry."

My mind cannot begin to grasp the implications of rooming with this woman who so strenuously disapproves of me, so it moves instead on the work assignment. Could she have chosen an activity more hateful to me, to which I am worse suited?

Let me work on the garden, on the farm, in the aviary, in the kitchen, just not the laundry. Sumati prepares to walk away.

"Excuse me," I rise too now, to interject.

Sumati turns to look at me with undisguised annoyance.

"I don't mean to keep contradicting your plan, but I wanted to let you know that I am a licensed bodyworker and masseuse, and I might better serve the community with this skill." I show her my hands, as if she might visualize the power in them.

"You came to us this morning quite uninvited and asked for a very substantial favor, a favor that will cause us disruption, inconvenience, and possible jeopardy. Do you think you are in a position to negotiate? Do you imagine that being a masseuse is somehow better than doing the laundry, more valuable, more necessary?"

"No." It's all I can do to keep from calling her ma'am; I feel that young and disempowered before her stern countenance. "I just thought I should offer something I'm good at."

"We shouldn't always do the things we're good at," Sumati advises me. "We can so easily get caught in our egos." She turns again, barking over her shoulder, "Go and get your things from the car and come back inside to the area where you first met me."

"My things aren't here," I tell her reluctantly. "I left Angel's and my bags in town at the bed-and-breakfast where we stayed. I'll need to go back for them."

The woman wheels around and charges toward me. For a moment I'm reminded of the Gorgons, the three sisters in Greek mythology whose faces would turn a man to stone. She grabs both of my arms in the tight grip of her hands. For a moment I think she's going to shake me. "Look here, Maggie. I know you are accustomed to a life of commotion and chaos, but in this community we adhere to the discipline of spiritual practice. Love, service, *obedience*." Tiny flecks of spittle fly from her mouth and sprinkle my cheek; she is that close to me. Her breath smells of cloves.

"We're not a way station or a motel you can just traipse in and out of. Once you enter this community you will stay here until your audience with the Guru. That is the same for everyone who lives in this community, but it is even more imperative for you. If you and your daughter are discovered by the police, it's not only disastrous for the two of you, but it will bring this community down. Do you have the capacity to understand this?"

She lets go of my arms. The skin feels bruised where her thumbs have dug in.

"Look, I appreciate all you are doing to help us," I assure her. "I will drive right to the bed-and-breakfast, collect our things, and come right back. Then I will come back and do whatever you ask of me until my time with Guru Tam." I make my voice contrite, submissive; I may have to spend three whole days with this woman who seems to be antagonized by my every word.

"You try to bend the world to your will," Sumati chastises me. "You make every excuse for why it is necessary; you justify to yourself that you are not in fact doing this, but it is in every thought that flickers through your head. How to manipulate, how to get your way. You tell yourself it is all right because you are on the side of good, but you haven't surrendered yourself to the goodness of Spirit. You are lost, Maggie." She looks at me sorrowfully. "I don't know if the Teacher has the strength for one more miracle or not, but nothing short of it will be of help to you." With these words, she departs the courtyard, entering a door in the building facing north.

I want to go get Angel and drive us both the hell away from here, but Sumati's words have pulled the ground from underneath my feet. Is she right? Am I an ego-driven manipulator, blind and deluded? *Spirit, am I so far from you? Have I used you all this time to justify my bad behavior?*

Though I am shaking with anger, I try to concentrate on the tasks in front of me: getting back to Todos Santos and reclaiming our belongings without being apprehended, then getting myself once more past the dragons at the gate. Explaining to Angel why we won't be sleeping in the same place. And enduring Sumati's tirades for the next three days. I wonder if Guru Tam is even aware of the abuse being perpetrated in the Teacher's name.

Crossing the courtyard, I notice the angle of the sun tilting westward. I need to hurry; I don't want to be on that road after dark. Tina Downs was telling me earlier that cows frequently wander onto the highway after sundown, an unhappy surprise for the motorist with bad reflexes or bad brakes, and for the unlucky bovine as well.

My brain begins to concoct a story to tell Ms. Downs—"We decided to go on to Cabo; it will be easier for me to get work as a masseuse there"—but as I catch myself I hear Sumati's scolding. Here I am trying to "bend the world to my will." Exiting the courtyard, I stride toward the building where I left my daughter. As I approach, I am struck by the quiet that emanates from its windows. When I step inside, the room is empty, the long table bare of tools and molds. The burners in the corner are cold.

For a moment I wonder if I've gone to the wrong building, but except for the absence of children, everything is the same as when I was here before; the same scent of beeswax pervades the air. "Angel?" I call, as if she might still be there despite the room's emptiness. "Angel?" I call again. With each repetition of her name, an irrational dread overtakes me; my daughter has disappeared and it is all I can do not to start screaming for her so that all the desert will hear.

With controlled panic, I begin to methodically search the other outbuildings, four of them, barely registering what I see there once I've determined that Angel is not inside. I walk quickly back inside the courtyard and begin to try every one of the doors. I interrupt first a yoga class and next some kind of meeting where four Light Beings are poring over ledgers. A few doors open into unoccupied rooms; some doors are locked.

With each thwarted attempt to find Angel, I have an increased sensation of falling through an endless sweep of space. It's not exhilarating but terrifying, and my chest is so tight I can barely breathe.

When at last I stumble into Sumati's office, tears are streaming down my cheeks. "Where *is* she?" I demand. "She's not in the candle room. What's happened to my daughter?"

"I wonder if you can empathize with what your former partner must be feeling?" Sumati asks.

How dare she? It takes effort not to slam my fist down onto the desk. "The difference being that Yoli knows Angel is with me!"

"The difference being," Sumati contradicts, "that *this* crisis is only in your mind. The children go to the ocean at this time every day." Sumati looks up at me from her desk without emotion. "They need to spend time outside but it's too hot for them midday."

"Dhwani promised he would bring her back to me when they were done with the candles." I know she sees me as overwrought, chaotic. The Light Beings believe that one shouldn't be driven by emotions, or "commotions," as Guru Tam calls them.

"Dhwani has no authority to promise anything, and you have no authority to ask for that promise," she replies evenly.

Being in Sumati's presence is forcing me to compose myself. She's not the kind of person you want to be upset around. I snuffle the snot from my nose and square my shoulders. "She needs to go with me into town."

"She can't do that." It is a flat statement, completely calm but unassailable.

"You can't expect me to leave her?" My voice lifts an octave.

Sumati remains unruffled. "I expect you to stay here as well. I thought I had made that clear."

A streak of red is throbbing through my vision, and I fear if I start screaming I will never stop. Yet I'm choking on the tears I don't want to let her see.

Observing my deepening distress, Sumati counsels, "Find your breath."

I want to tell her to fuck herself, but I recognize her advice as sound. I close my eyes and notice how shallow my inhalations have become. The effort to send air deeper into my belly forces me to relax the muscles in my shoulders, face and chest. I gain a bit of detachment from the terrified, furious part of me.

"Drink a little water," she instructs further. A bottled water cooler stands in the corner behind me.

This direction, too, I follow, mostly because I don't know how to rescue myself from the feelings roiling within. The cool water seems to help dispel them, or at least, diminish their intensity.

Finally, I face her again, restored to some degree of self-possession. "Please, Sumati, I need to go to town to get our stuff. It's everything we have. Please don't make me leave Angel here."

"Maggie." Her tone is not unkind. "You came to the Light Beings to ask for our help. How can you receive the help we offer if you don't trust us?"

This strikes me as a reasonable question, and makes me aware that I don't feel anything like trust—not of Sumati, not of the Light Beings, perhaps not of anyone since I left L.A. Even with Charlie, in whom I've confided, I've still held back.

Yoli used to complain that I didn't trust her. Of course, it turned out I had excellent reasons. But what Guru Tam teaches is that trust is all about the truster, one's own ability to be open-hearted, to be guileless. "When we fail to trust it is because we have failed to be trustworthy," the Guru has said.

Even Angel I haven't fully trusted, afraid she will unwittingly betray us to some stranger. That's why lying is always such a bad option; it corrupts one's connections to everything.

"And of course," Sumati adds, "I'm trusting you. I'm trusting that you're not just planning to dump your child and make a clean get away."

My face must betray my incredulity.

"I know, that's not in your character, but I'm trying to make a point. We are now bound together in a mutual opportunity that requires trust on both our parts. Do you understand this?"

I nod.

"Your daughter will be fine with us," Sumati assures me. "You'll only be gone an hour or so, yes? You'll see her at dinner."

How can I agree to this? How can I fail to agree? I feel like I'm stepping off a precipice, hurling myself into a void. "Will you tell her where I've gone?" I beseech her, "And that I'll be right back?"

"She may not be as anxious as you are," she counters. "Children at that age are resilient. Despite the ordeal she's been through recently, she has always been a loved child, and that gives her a foundation for independence." Seeing the distress return to my face, she adds, "But yes, I'll tell her when the children return."

"Thank you," I say.

As I turn to leave, I wonder what I'm thanking her for; she's done nothing but give me grief since I first laid eyes on her. But something in me feels stronger from her confrontation, more inside myself than I've felt in a while. I guess that's something to be grateful for.

"Dinner's at six," Sumati tells me on my way out. I look at my watch; it's after four. I'll be lucky to get to Todos Santos and back again before dark.

I want to be sure I have a full tank of fuel, since I can't know what lies ahead of me, but there's no gas station between the Light Beings' land and Todos Santos. I remember seeing a station on the main drag in town, just a few blocks from Tina's. Reluctant as I am to transact any more business here, I pull in and stop at a pump. The attendant is stocky and has a burn that's robbed one side of his face of pigment. I try to avoid staring at the mottled pink oval as, in my awkward Spanish, I ask him to fill it up. The smell of gasoline spills in through the window; no fume-recovery nozzles in this country. I stare at my hands in my lap, eager to keep my face down.

I am weighing my desire to make another call to Charlie, to let him know the plan. It feels like every call I make on that cell phone is another spin of the chamber in this Russian Roulette; I still don't know for certain that my calls won't be traced. And maybe it's better if he doesn't know where I am. Still, if I can't get calls on the Light Beings land, and if I'm forbidden to leave that land, I might be out of touch for three days, and I don't want to worry him any more than I already have.

So lost am I in this contemplation that I don't see anyone approach the car.

"Maggie! What a pleasure to see you again!"

Startled, I turn to see Carmen's sculpted features peering in through my passenger window. My shock must register on my face, because she says, "Sorry to sneak up on you. I was trying to wave but you were so deep in thought."

"Sorry." I match her apology, my cheeks reddening as they had this morning. "I just wasn't expecting to run into anybody I know." The gas pump seems to be running unbearably slow; the mechanical numbers seeming to take years to drop, one over the other, as the liters seep into my tank.

Her arm, resting on the sill of the passenger window, is tanned to a deep walnut color, a rich background for a copper wire bracelet that winds its way up and up and up from wrist to elbow. The thin wire is strung with colorful beads and other trinkets of copper that add a musical jangle to her movements. This afternoon her braid is wound into a dark halo at the crown of her head.

"It's good to have friends," she insists with a wide smile. "Don't you find it hard to be in a place where you know no one?"

"Well, I have Angel. She keeps me company."

This rebukes her, and the smile dims, not on her lips but in her eyes. "Of course," she says, "your daughter. Where is she?" she queries.

The impulse to lie leaps to my lips, but I say instead, "She's playing with some other children," and pray the Carmen won't ask for the details.

"Would you like to come over?" Her eyes have regained their light. "I could show you my work, we could watch the sunset." The lilt of her voice promises more.

Something stirs to life in my chest, something so long absent that I'd forgotten it until just now. Saliva floods my mouth and my tongue tastes sweetness. So deeply buried has this feeling been, I scarcely recognize what it is, but my survival instincts know I cannot surrender to this woman's invitation; there is no place in my life for this feeling now. I must give it a quick, painless death.

The pump at last switches off. The attendant removes the nozzle and comes to my window to collect. After handing him pesos, I turn back to Carmen. "I'm sorry," I say in a clipped tone, "I have to get back to her now."

With a look of bemused regret, she says, "Ah, yes. Well, good to see you, Maggie."

She backs away from my window and climbs into a lime green Volkswagen Bug, aged but in pristine condition. Its engine makes a little roar as she floors it out of the station.

I feel guilty, letdown, on edge, relieved. It's been years since a woman made me blush. I didn't mean to hurt her feelings, but I certainly can't afford another complication at this time. I can't even afford to spend the time to analyze my response to her.

I make my way up the rutted streets to the Oasis, aware of the deepening shadows as afternoon begins to give way to evening. I park a half a block away. It's my plan to slip in, take our stuff, and leave a note for our hostess. But I've forgotten about Loba, who sends up an alarm to summon the dead the minute I open the gate.

Tina Downs is not far behind, dressed in bright purple overalls with a shocking pink tank top underneath. "Thank heavens it's you!"

She subdues the dog with a quick, "Loba, quiet!" The animal circles me, sniffing, tail wagging high in the air. "Where's Angel?" There's alarm in her tone.

I don't have a moment to answer because she's grabbing me by the arm and propelling me into the cobalt blue *casita*. "Is Angel all right?" she demands.

"She's fine," I say, as if I'm completely convinced of this fact, as if her asking is a ridiculous imposition.

"It's my habit to stay out of people's business," Tina declares as she paces before the futon. "People come, people go. With any luck they take their troubles with them." She seems to be trying to formulate what it is she wants to say. Then she looks me square in the face. "Maggie, I watched the L.A. news this afternoon."

There's an odd relief when the very thing you've been afraid of actually happens. You can stop being afraid of it and just try to deal with it. My heartbeat doesn't quicken at her announcement; instead, I just feel tired as I plop onto the futon and say, "Don't worry, we're leaving."

"I'm not worried about *myself*, Maggie. I'm half-sick with

worry about you and your little girl. What the hell made you come to Baja?" She sinks into one of the kitchen chairs.

I lean my head back against the upright cushion, stare at the ceiling through closed eyelids. "I don't know. When I found out Angel was being hurt, I made all these huge decisions in about an hour and a half. It was instinctive, not rational. I knew I had to take her away. I wanted to go somewhere we couldn't be easily found. I thought: Mexico. And then I had a flash of this town. I hadn't been here in fifteen years, but it just came to me. There weren't that many gringos in residence when I used to come here, and they certainly didn't have satellite TV. In those days, it was remote." I lift my head to smile ruefully.

"Then I remembered that the Light Beings had their main center down here. I'd always meant to come visit, and then it occurred to me that I could see Guru Tam who would help me know what to do. In the moment I guess it seemed like Divine Guidance."

"You really believe all that stuff? Gurus and Divine Guidance?" She cocks her head in curiosity, reminding me a little of Old Mac.

I just shrug. Right now I don't know what I believe. I don't feel like the person I was when I got up this morning, nor do I any longer have confidence in my ability to do what I've set out to do. The Light Beings' community is not what I expected, and I don't know what that's going to mean to me. But clearly it's not safe to spend any more time in this town.

"I wish I could believe in something." Tina's face puckers in genuine regret. "I've tried all kinds of stuff over the years, some of it much weirder than the Light Beings," she teases, "but in the end it seems like the only thing I can ever count on is common sense."

"Maybe I should try that," I say wryly. "Common sense sure wouldn't have landed me here."

"Yeah, but if you hadn't landed here, we never would'a met," she says with a smile. "So maybe there is something to this Divine Guidance after all."

She takes a breath; her gaze wanders toward some unseen horizon. She seems to be weighing something in her mind.

Evidently she decides to take the plunge and her eyes snap back to my face.

"Maggie, I'm gonna tell you somethin' that I haven't told anybody else here," she begins.

I want to tell her to stop. I don't know how to bear the burden of this confidence on top of everything else I am carrying. But after the trouble I've brought to her door, how can I refuse?

"Right before I came here I was livin' up in Big Sur. You ever been there?"

I have. Yoli and I spent New Year's Eve there once, before Angel was born. A rare New Year's Eve when Yoli didn't have a gig, it must have been early on in our relationship.

"I'd been livin' for a little while with this guy named Antwonne. He was a biker, a big guy, built like a bear. Not Hell's Angels, but he ran with a tough crowd. He could be a mean sonofabitch when he was tweekin', but I think I kinda got off on bein' tough enough to take what he dished out, y'know? It was like a test to not let him get to me."

I say nothing, just watch the shadows gather in the room.

"He had a kid who lived with him, a little boy named Jake. I guess his mama had her fill of Antwonne, and just took off one day. As you might imagine, Antwonne was never gonna win Father of the Year, but he stuck around and tried to do right by that boy. Made sure there was food, got him to school. I know he made an effort to stay off crystal. That was a lotta structure for a man like Antwonne."

She breaks off suddenly, as if reconsidering whether she wants to go on. Then she does.

"I guess Jake must been five or six when I was livin' with them. We've already established that I wasn't put here to be nobody's mama, but kids have a way of being persistent with their needs. If Antwonne didn't come home some nights, Jake still needed his dinner.

"Don't get me wrong, he was a sweet kid. Kinda sad, and who could blame him? He missed his mama." Tina looks up, her eyes round, imploring me to understand. "But I didn't have that to give him."

"Not everyone does," I say. I'm thinking of Yoli. I'm afraid of where this story is going to end.

"Then this guy came to town, some buddy of Antwonne's from the old days, and suddenly my boyfriend was tweekin' every day, getting strung out and mean. He started to let things slide with Jake, and I was picking up more and more of the slack, and really starting to get a resentment on about it.

"He came in one night, really wired, and started to break the place up. He dislocated my shoulder and started in after Jake." Her eyes are once again staring at a point in the distance. Her voice has grown thick with the effort to control tears.

"I knew where Antwonne kept his gun, and I knew he kept it loaded." By way of explanation she adds, "When you live with a guy like Antwonne, you always check for weapons."

Her voice flattens, grows terse. "I shot him. In the thigh. Didn't kill him, but I definitely slowed him down. He kept lookin' at me, all surprised, and sayin' 'The bitch shot me.' And Jake was hysterical."

Tina presses her eyelids shut. "I looked around that trashed-out shit hole of a house. I looked at Antwonne bleeding and Jake screaming, and I thought 'This is somebody else's mess, and I do not want to waste my life trying to clean up somebody else's mess.'

"I told Antwonne I was gonna drive out to the pay phone to call the paramedics. And I *did* do that. I shoved the gun into my purse, and walked out with nothing but the clothes on my back. After the pay phone, I got back in the car and started driving south. Except for gas, I didn't stop until I was over the border, and then I didn't stop until I was nearly at the end of the peninsula. I had some money stashed away from my divorce settlement, and that's how I bought the Oasis."

She looks fully into my face then, looking for the condemnation she's already given herself. "I just left that boy."

"Maybe you shot some sense into his father," I offer. "Maybe it turned him around." Although I grieve for this unseen Jake, I have no wish to add to Tina's suffering.

She exhales, and some tension seems to leave with her

breath. Her shoulders soften, her faces relaxes. "Anyway," she says, "thanks for listening."

It's a comfortable moment, perhaps the first between us. The room is dimming as the light fades, and I almost feel like we should be sharing a beer, talking past nightfall like new friends. Nightfall. I am jolted by this realization.

"I'm sorry, I've got to go." I jump up and begin to gather up our belongings, Angel's and mine, and shove them into our bags. I empty the contents of the refrigerator into a shopping bag, make a run into the bathroom to grab my comb and toothbrush.

"Wait a minute." Tina stands to protest. "You need to make a plan."

"I have to get back," I insist, flying through the rooms, taking one last check on everything. I pull DogBear from underneath the futon, double-check the hidden inner pocket in my duffel bag to make sure my wad of cash is still there.

"Do you need anything?" Her voice is plaintive as she leans against the counter by the toaster oven. Bright colors dimmed in twilight, her large able body appears smaller, helpless. "Can I carry something?"

"No, thanks," I dismiss her. I begin loading my arms with several bags. "I don't know if the police have yet figured out we're in Mexico or not. I just hope you don't have any problems from our having been here."

"I *lost* the card for the satellite dish." She casts meaningful eyes at me. "So there's no way anyone can prove I knew anything. Mr. Corrigan will have to figure out something else to do with his time."

I want to hug her for her unflappable nature, her common sense, but my arms are completely laden. I push through the screen door, head for the gate. Loba follows me anxiously.

Then I change my mind, and walk back. It's as impulsive and as certain as the decision to pick up Angel from school and drive her over the border. "Tina!" I call.

From his shadowed corner of the garden, Old Mac responds, "Tina!" in a granular imitation.

She comes out, wiping at one corner of her eye. "You forget something?"

"Listen, I don't know if you really want to be any more involved in this than you already are…" I begin nervously. "After all," I tease gently, "it's somebody else's mess."

"Just tell me," she says, a smile of relief breaking over her face.

"I have this cell phone," I confide, "prepaid, I don't think it can be traced. Can I give you the number?"

She disappears back into the *casita*, emerges with a three-year-old issue of *Baja Life* and a stub of pencil fished from her overalls pocket. She scrawls the numbers on the back cover.

"If something comes up here that you think I should know about…" I trail off. "I'm not even sure I can get phone reception where I'm going."

"I know how to get there if I need to," she reminds me dryly.

"Well, if for some reason you can't get hold of me, I want to give you another number too. It's my friend in the States. He's got a lawyer lined up if we need it and…he's willing to help."

Tina copies Charlie's number beneath mine. Then she hands me a card from the Oasis. "Here's how to get hold of me."

"Thanks," I say, and wish the word could swell to contain everything I mean by it.

She grins. "Are they gonna make you wear one of those blue nun's habits?"

"I'm sure there will be rules to follow." I grimace. "They've said I can stay three days or until Guru Tam is well enough to meet with me, whichever comes first."

"And after that?" she wants to know.

"I hope by that time I'll know the answer to that question. Look, I really have to go. I wanted to get back there before six."

Tina Downs consults the sky. "You better drive like hell." She hustles me through the gates. Just before I reach my car she calls, "And watch out for cows on the road!"

The residue of Tina's story clings to me like a clear plastic raincoat, invisible but enshrouding me all the same. It's probably not the smartest idea in the world to drive this road at dusk while talking on a cell phone, but I need to call Charlie before I'm too far from town. I don't want him to freak out if Tina should decide to get in touch with him.

"Child abduction hotline," he answers, which signals me that nothing too scary has happened on his end since we last spoke.

"Is that supposed to be funny, Charlie?"

"Listen, aside from watching your dear old mum on TV, there haven't been a lot of chuckles in this episode so far. Just trying to lighten things up, darlin'."

"I know, I love you for it." I'm stuck behind a slow moving panel truck, its bed piled high with tomatoes. I have to jam the phone between my ear and shoulder while I carefully pass. "Any news?" I'm hoping the answer will be no.

"Actually, yes." His voice grows more serious. "A detective came to see me this afternoon."

"God, Charlie, that's awful!" My panic at this information is offset only by my regret for dragging him into this.

"Well, yes, because he wasn't my type at all. Paunchy—hasn't he ever heard of The Zone? I wanted to take him shopping, spruce him up a bit."

"Forget that! What did he say?"

"It seemed routine. They seem to be working their way through everybody they can find who knows you. They asked when I'd last seen you, and if I'd heard from you."

"What did you *say?*" It's only as the car swerves dangerously on a curve that I realize how hard I've been pressing the pedal in my agitation. I take a breath and make a conscious effort to slow down.

"I told them the things they could easily check anyway: that you'd e-mailed me on Wednesday and told me Angel had been hurt. And that you'd called me Thursday morning. I had to tell them that, because you called my home phone."

"But Charlie, I was already over the border by then. They're gonna see that." My hands on the steering wheel are sweating.

"I'm sorry, sugar. My whole take on this is that your actions are defensible, and that there's nothing to hide. By the way, the photos came today."

"How'd you get them so fast?" I remember Amara telling me mail to the U.S. could take up to two or three weeks.

"Your friend in Ensenada had them personally delivered," Charlie answers. "I guess someone was driving north anyway. A very handsome man, I might add, even with the turban!"

I send up a quick prayer of thanks for Amara, going out of her way to help a virtual stranger.

"By the way," Charlie continues, "if someone had done that to *my* kid, I would have done a whole lot worse than just take the child away. I showed them to the detective, and it made an impression. It'll help to have someone in law enforcement who believes your story."

"But what about this number?"

"I believe it's safe, darlin'. That's why I gave it to you. But you're probably not going to be able to run forever. I'm trying to pave the way for your return."

I don't know how to process any of this. I don't know whether I want to return. Maybe I could be like Tina, and just stay here under the radar. A car comes speeding up behind me way too fast; it's only luck there is no oncoming traffic so he can quickly swerve into the other lane.

"Fuck, Charlie, fuck. How did I go from boring, predictable Maggie to being a fugitive?"

"I've never thought you were boring, sweetheart, just overly responsible and with a weakness for wild and wildly irresponsible women."

I think about Dagmar and Yoli. No doubt Carmen too fits that profile. But I don't have time for this kind of reverie. I'm going to lose the signal any minute.

"Listen, Charlie, two things: I gave your number to somebody down here…" The fading light makes it nearly impossible to distinguish the highway from the desert on either side and the road is unlit. "Her name is Tina and she's trustworthy."

"Sweetie-pie, I don't mean to criticize, but are you *sure* you're the best judge of that? Think about Yoli…"

"Charlie, I don't have time for this. Any second now we might get cut off. She'll only call you if it's an emergency. The other thing, I'm going to be inaccessible for the next three days."

"If you didn't have your child with you I'd say that sounds promising," he quips.

This time I ignore him. "Do you remember the Light Beings?"

"Do you mean those droning people with no fashion sense who made me sit like a pretzel for three hours? Please! How could I forget?"

Normally, I love Charlie's patter but between his news, the driving, my lateness in getting back to Angel, the growing darkness, and my concern that the phone signal will die out, it's all I can do not to scream at him.

"They have a community down here. That's where Angel and I are going to be staying for a few days. My cell doesn't work there. If you find out anything, I need you to call Tina. Do you have a pencil?"

He does. Now I somehow have to figure out how to read the lavender typeface on the printed card Tina gave me. I reach for the map light overhead; it's no surprise that it doesn't work. I'm squinting through the dimness when a semi passes way too close. The Poo-poo Box sways dangerously. I drop the phone to grab the steering wheel with both hands. "Shit!"

"Maggie? Maggie!" I hear his disembodied voice coming from the floor. Up ahead it looks like there's a little shoulder; I ease myself onto it and retrieve the phone.

"You still there, Charlie?" I scrabble around until I find a match. As it flares, I read off the number on Tina's card.

Something of my situation—the quickening dark, the bad road, my growing sense of being completely out of control—must have communicated itself to Charlie; he is notably subdued as he asks, "Are you and Angel going to be okay staying there?"

"I hope so, Charlie. Right now it feels like my last option."

"It isn't, though. There are people who can help you if you come back."

Grateful as I am for his hopefulness, I find I can't share it.

"But how would I get back? They've got to be watching the border by now."

"Gumdrop, how many people sneak across that border every day?"

Maybe he's right, but I can't contemplate it now. Whatever the momentum that has driven me to this point, I've run out of it. What I've set in motion must now play out.

"Charlie…" I begin, but a vacuum of sound comes back to me; I've lost the signal. I try redialing; the call fails. I try again; nothing. I won't be able to reconnect unless I turn around.

In the darkness I peer at my watch. Six thirty. I'll never make it back in time for dinner. What is Angel going to think? Will she worry I've abandoned her? Or is she, as Sumati suggests, more resilient than I give her credit for?

I can't count on Sumati's theories. I need to get back to my girl. If the police come and find us, we need to be together. The last wedge of golden light is being squeezed into the Pacific; the sky is now dark tourmaline overhead.

I study my rearview carefully, looking for the right moment to pull back onto the highway. The road is heavily trafficked, day-trippers headed back to Cabo for the night, workers headed back to who-knows-what little hovel. Eventually there is a spot and I slowly ease myself back onto the asphalt still heading south.

Everything looks different now than when I passed this way in daylight. Have I passed the Art & Beer sign and just not noticed it? If I miss that landmark, how will I ever find that tiny road in the dark?

Panic makes me slow down. This caution serves me, because the road bends and suddenly my lights reflect something dark, a boulder-like shape directly in front of me. I press the brake, managing to come to a full stop before a big bony cow hunkered in the middle of my lane.

The animal turns her head, regards me with great, indifferent eyes, before she lazily rises and picks her way back to the road's shoulder.

My heart is pounding at the near miss. Had I been on the phone, had I been speeding, I would have hit that creature and maybe killed us both. Then where would Angel be?

Spirit, thank you for all the ways you are looking out for me. Thank you for Charlie, for Tina, for Sumati, for Amrita. Thank you for all the things I can't even comprehend that you are putting in my path for my benefit. Please, Spirit, help me to do what's best for Angel. And help me to keep faith with you.

I am shaking as I press the accelerator and continue down the road.

Chapter 8

I miss the turnoff for the road to the Light Beings' community, but before I've gone too far past it, a nagging alarm begins to prod my nervous system, and I decide to trust it. Then the challenge is to find a way to turn around on this two-lane highway. Ever since my close call with the cow, I feel a renewed sense of faith. *Spirit, show me how to get back to my girl.* Within just a few miles there is a wide shoulder and a break in the traffic. Although the turning radius on the Poo-poo Box is nowhere near that of my Accord, I manage to get myself pointed back northward. Another gift from Spirit: there's less traffic headed this way, so I slow to a crawl and look carefully to my right. Dark as it is, this time I'm able to find the rutted road that leads once more to the Light Beings' gate.

I have been doing no small bit of praying that the guardians will not give me a hard time about re-entry. I've practiced my entreaties and I've rehearsed my arguments. But as I pull toward the complex, what I find instead is a locked gate attended by no one at all. I get out of the car into the balmy night, leaving my headlights on and the engine running—something I would never do in Los Angeles, for fear of carjacking. The temperature has cooled a bit with the sun's departure, and even the breeze is mild. I call "Hello," a few times; only the wind answers back. I wait a while, concocting an explanation to myself: at night there's only one guard, and he must have needed a bathroom break. I shout a little louder.

The gate is far enough away from the main buildings that I can't count on anyone hearing my car engine, and I hope to avoid antagonizing everyone by honking the horn. I can only imagine Sumati's response to my making that kind of ruckus to get their attention. "If you'd done what I told you to do in the first place, you wouldn't have this problem," I hear her scold me.

The wall is too tall to climb over, and I can see strands of barbed wire on the top. The group certainly takes their security seriously. I wonder if it's warranted.

I recall that earlier one of the gatekeepers used a walkie-talkie to contact the main office. I pull out my cell phone again to see if I can get a signal, only to remember that I don't have a number to contact the office, even if my phone did work.

I walk closer to the gate illuminated in my headlamps. It's a beautiful piece of workmanship, some kind of elaborately carved wood, inlaid with tiles the same blue-green as the Sea of Cortez. The iron latch is locked into place.

The breeze, which just moments ago felt pleasant, is starting to make me feel chilled. I have a fleeting impulse to just drive the Poo-poo Box through the gate. I am about to reconsider my reluctance to use the horn when I notice a small black buzzer installed in one side of the frame. I press it once, then a second time to make sure I pushed it hard enough the first time, then a third time because I'm feeling desperate. There's no intercom, so I can't tell if pushing the button creates any result, or if it's just there to give the hapless and unwanted visitor something to do. And if someone were to respond, would that person drive down or walk down from the center? And how many minutes would it take?

It takes enough minutes to allow me to work myself into a froth about Angel. *She won't know where I am, she won't understand why I left her there.* I have already begun the argument with Sumati in my head about why she has to let me see Angel, even if I'm late, even if the children have gone to bed, when I hear footsteps approaching from the other side of the wall. The owner of the footsteps is whistling the tune of a chant that sounds vaguely familiar to me. He's a great whistler, full, vigorous notes and on key. This gives me encouragement, and I call out, "Peace begets peace. It's Maggie. Sorry I'm late."

The gate swings outward, and the blond man from earlier today, the friendliest of the three gatekeepers, pokes his turbaned head through the opening. "Peace returns peace," he greets me. "We were concerned you might have gotten lost."

"I nearly hit a cow on the highway," I tell him, "And I missed the turnoff." These things have nothing to do with my lateness, and I think back to Sumati's earlier indictments of me, how I try to manipulate to get my way.

My rescuer seems untroubled by any of this. "Well, you've nearly missed dinner as well, but I don't think Amrita has closed the kitchen yet. Come on in," he tells me. "Do you mind giving me a ride back up to the center?"

I steer through the open gate, remembering to thank Spirit for helping me to surmount this latest obstacle. As the tall man relocks the gate, I begin throwing my pile of belongings from the passenger seat into the back. Noticing this, he says, "If it's a problem, I can walk."

"No, no, get in." I insist, even though I'm embarrassed about the torn dashboard and the filthy floor mats, the smell of exhaust that pervades everything. I fear to infect him with my chaos.

He settles in beside me. "I'm Jagadeep," he informs me with a slight bow of his head.

"Does that name have a meaning?" I wonder, thinking about Angel's question earlier.

"In Sanskrit," he grins self-consciously, "it means 'The Light of the World.' Our Teacher believes a name is designed to point to one's destiny."

I wonder to myself about the destiny of *Maggie*. "What about Sumati?" I ask, "What does that mean?" I pass the little cluster of stucco houses, now lit from within.

"Good minded, or strong minded," Jagadeep replies. "Or even tough-minded."

I stifle my urge to say, "You got *that* right!" After all, I remind myself, I am a guest here. I circle the fountain, about to stop as I did earlier today, but with a wave of his hand Jagadeep directs me to drive around behind the main building, where a scattering of other cars and some trucks is parked.

"This community wouldn't have lasted without her," he adds. "That fierceness you find so off-putting—" He says this as though I had spoken, or as if he'd read my thoughts, "—has helped us maintain the fortitude and the discipline to stay here and stay together. She is a Saturn teacher, and we've needed that kind of structure."

"Saturn teacher—what is that?" I hope it's not a stupid question.

"The energy of the planet Saturn is about structure and discipline, strictness, learning through hard tests," he explains.

"But what about Guru Tam?" I wonder if this is going too far. I park beside a VW van, turn off my engine.

Jagadeep is quiet for a while, fingering his long, blond beard. I think he is trying to find a way to deflect my question, but eventually he answers, "Our Teacher is the visionary, the light. Without Guru Tam, we would not have this philosophy, these tools. But for a community to function requires more than vision. And Guru has been ill for a long time."

I wonder how much of the weird vibe of this community is the result of Sumati's leadership. That could explain why it feels so different here than in Los Angeles or even Ensenada.

"May I help you bring your things in?" he asks.

"Should I do that first? I really want to see Angel."

"I'll just carry them in and leave them in the office," he says. "That's where you'll find your daughter as well."

This creates a prick of alarm, so I hastily load his arms with a couple of bags, then grab the rest myself. I make sure I have my cell phone and the bag that contains my money and the scraps of paper with Charlie's and Tina's phone numbers.

"This food?" he says delicately, peering into one of the shopping bags. "I'm going to have to take that to the kitchen. All food is shared here. No one has a private stash in their rooms."

It makes me long for the opportunity to rifle through a few rooms to see how closely this policy is obeyed, but this is not a battle I'm going to fight. I shrug and nod.

We enter the main building through a different door than the ones I've used before. There's the scent of cinnamon and ginger in the hallways. I'm grateful when Jagadeep leads me to the office—I still don't have my bearings.

Entering, I see Angel sitting on a chair, a downcast expression on her face. This changes the minute she sees me. "Maggiemama!"

"Mrs. Havisham!" I bend down and fold her into my arms.

"I thought you left me," she moans into my neck. "That's what *she* said."

I glare at Sumati who is sitting behind the desk, her mouth twisted into what seems its customary sour expression.

"You told her *what?*"

"Your daughter has a great deal to learn about cooperation and discipline," Sumati says. "Not that I find that completely surprising."

I turn my attention away from her to console my daughter. "Mrs. Havisham, I went back to Tina's to get our things. I came to look for you, but you'd gone to the beach. Do you remember that I asked you to come back and find me once you were done with the candles?"

Angel nods, sorrowfully.

"So I couldn't find you and I needed to go before dark. Sumati *promised* me she would tell you where I'd gone and that I'd be back." I overemphasize this last for Sumati's benefit.

The stern woman chimes in. "That is what I told her. And *you* said you'd be back at six p.m. for dinner. Once that time came and went, I thought perhaps you'd made other plans."

I am shaking with anger, but I don't want to scare Angel any further. So I speak to her instead of Sumati, my voice soft but filled with passion. "Angel, most precious to me of all beings: I promise you, I will not leave you. Not ever." I remember Tina's story as I gaze deep into my daughter's eyes. "Do you believe me?"

I would have always said this to her, the way any mother reassures her child, but I recognize in my words a new depth and commitment. Whatever the ultimate resolution to our situation, it is going to have to spring from this.

She looks at me and nods, a grin breaking out over her face. "That's what *I* told her!"

"Did you get any supper, honey?"

She scowls. "No, I had to sit in here."

"And *I* had to sit here with her," Sumati adds.

I note that it's the second meal she's missed today due to Angel's and my presence here.

"Your daughter insisted we shouldn't serve dinner until you got here. She became quite distraught about it. In fact she threw her plate against the wall. It's a bad example for the other children, except to point out to them what happens to children who are not fortunate enough to be raised inside this community. So I asked her to come sit in here until she calmed down."

"Don't the children of Light Beings ever get upset? Don't they ever misbehave or act out?" I'm remembering the older girl from this afternoon, Chhaya, with her bad temper.

"Just as we use breath and meditation to control the commotion inside us," Sumati explains, "we teach our children these techniques from an early age. We work with infants to help build their nervous systems, to develop the nonreactive parts of the brain. They are raised with Divine love, not just personal love, so they are not desperate or insecure. And of course, we teach them to serve the good of the community, not simply to seek to have their personal wishes gratified."

It all sounds good in theory—strong, calm, secure children who place their faith in Spirit. But what about independence?

Creativity? Rebellion? Individuality? It's likely she would argue that these are not qualities that produce a peaceful and serene world.

I turn back to Angel. "You were sweet to want to wait for me, and I'm really sorry I was late and made you worry. But for the time we're here, I need you to do what Sumati tells you to do."

She makes a face.

"I mean it, honey. We're guests here and we need our company manners, okay?"

My daughter neither agrees nor disagrees. "Did you go see Edgar Sue?" she wants to know.

"No, I didn't. That would have made me even later." Angel looks crestfallen, so I add, "But I saw Tina, and Loba. And I saw Carmen."

"Is she going to paint my picture?"

"Someday, maybe. I hope so," I tell her. I go to one of the bags and retrieve DogBear. "Look who I brought you!"

Angel's arms encircle the stuffed toy in a great embrace.

Sumati looks like she is about to object; no doubt they have some rule against toys or who knows what. My eyes plead with her to let this one go, and to my amazement and relief, she does. I ask her, "Is it too late for us to get something to eat?"

"Amrita sends the kitchen staff home at seven thirty," she says. A quick glance at my watch confirms for me that it's just past that time. "But, if you're willing to clean up after yourself and leave the kitchen as you found it, I suppose we can heat up the leftovers."

I wonder if this sudden willingness to bend the rules is related to her own state of hunger more than compassion for ours, but I decide it doesn't matter and to just be grateful for it.

"Now I suppose I'm going to be awake all night after eating so late," Sumati complains, though with no real rancor, as we prepare to hunker down for the night.

It's true: I do feel a little stuffed from the gingery mung beans and rice that was our dinner. Happily, Angel ate it without complaint. She put up a pretty big fuss about going to sleep in the children's quarters, but I promised her it would be for no more than three nights. First I showed her Sumati's room where I would be staying, then had her note the landmarks as I walked her down the hall to the children's wing. A woman I hadn't met yet was there with her guitar, singing songs with the other girls. Angel was immediately entranced, and went to sit near the hem of her blue gown. By the time I waved goodnight, my girl was singing her heart out, barely focused on me at all.

We are upstairs from the rooms I was in earlier today. One side of the C-shaped building houses the unmarried women and the girls; the other side houses the single men and the boys. The stucco houses I saw from the road are for couples, and there is apparently another cluster of such houses farther from this central complex. What would happen, I wonder, if a single woman wanted her own little house?

Sumati's room is small but pleasant, and very tidy, painted not light blue but a deep gold, which has a very soothing affect once inside it. Tonight the hue is deepened by the glow of a small lamp. Her single bed is in one corner; a small desk sits beneath the sole window, which looks out on the courtyard. An armoire perches against another wall. She explains to me that Light Beings don't accumulate many personal possessions, since most items are shared by the community. My cot is wedged into another corner, opposite Sumati, and even with my vagabond status, I've got way more personal possessions crowding her room. I do my best to stow everything under the cot, but the bags and bundles still seem to spill forward as if willfully encroaching on her careful order.

We've each taken turns visiting the communal bathroom at the end of the hall. Sumati thoughtfully provides me a towel and soap, and I duck into a shower to wash away my day. But I haven't thought to bring any other clothes with me, so I have to climb back into the grimy clothes I first put on this morning, a lifetime ago. After brushing my teeth, I pad back to Sumati's room.

I wonder if it will seem too immodest to sleep only in a T-shirt. I wait to take my cues from my roommate. I watch her lift off the pale fabric of her headdress and fold it neatly into the drawer beneath the armoire. Then she unwinds a coil of hair—once rich chestnut, now streaked with gray—that falls almost to her knees.

"Your hair is so long," I can't help but exclaim.

"Light Beings don't cut our hair. Hair conducts energy," she explains. In her room, no longer in her role as Chief Assistant, her tone is softer, her manner more relaxed. It's as if she's lifted off the armor of her persona, and revealed the soft skin underneath. She retrieves a brush from the desk drawer, and begins working it through her hair, long sensuous strokes, and as she does, her face takes on new dimensions, eyes closed, lips gently curved. I almost feel as if I am witnessing something intimate, private, and wonder if I should turn my eyes away.

Then she astounds me by pulling her gown over her head, stripping off the undergarments beneath, and walking naked across the room to place these in the armoire. Her body is ample, as I knew from seeing her dressed; large breasts rest on a round belly, and flesh pads her hips, her butt and thighs. Her skin is unexpectedly creamy and delicate. Unselfconscious in the flesh Spirit gave her, she recrosses the room, slips between the sheets, and turns out the lamp. I assume from this that it's safe to slither out of my shorts, but I do this when already hidden by the bedclothes.

"You must be tired," she says, but her tone clearly wants me to refute this.

"Well, it's been a challenging day," I concede, "but it's still pretty early. Isn't it about nine o'clock? You're welcome to keep the light on if you want."

"I was just having a memory of sleepovers when I was a girl. I had only brothers, so it was a treat to have another girl in the house, to lie awake and tell secrets."

This revelation belongs to the woman who'd dreamily brushed her hair a few moments before, not to the stern overseer who'd wanted to kick Angel and me out of the complex. I struggle to reconcile these two versions of Sumati.

"I never did that," I tell her. "I felt more comfortable being friends with boys when I was growing up. I didn't like dolls and I didn't like dress up. Boys liked to have adventures." I hold back the detail that inviting anyone over after we got poor was strictly forbidden by my mother; she didn't want anyone to witness our diminished lifestyle.

"But what about with your former partner? Yoli, did you say her name was?" She appears to have no inhibitions about asking anything.

"Short for Yolanda," I say, hoping to discourage this line of inquiry.

"Weren't there nights you'd lie in bed with the lights off and talk?"

I have a fleeting impulse to say, "No, we were always too busy fucking our brains out," but that would be both untrue and hostile. And there seems to be no reason to be antagonistic to this version of Sumati. She may ask inappropriate questions, but her curiosity seems without guile.

"I thought the Light Beings weren't too keen on same-sex relationships," I say, still hoping to deflect her.

"Where did you get that idea?" She sounds surprised. "Of course we believe that one's first and most important relationship is with Spirit. But we support everyone to have a healthy relationship with whomever they choose."

"Why then, in all the books and all the literature, are couples only depicted as man and woman?" She can't deny this.

"Tradition, I suppose," she says, as if it's never before occurred to her. I find that's true of most straight people; they seem to exist in a bubble, as if no other possibilities exist. "But are you going to answer my question about Yoli?"

Does she think she's entitled to pry into my personal business just because I am sleeping on a cot in her room? I bristle at the intrusion, but I don't have the energy for another conflict tonight. I give in. "Sure we did. We'd talk about our days. She's a singer, so she often had some pretty wild stories. Sometimes we'd tell stories of when we were kids, although those weren't very happy stories for either of us. And we'd talk about Angel." I turn over onto my stomach; the cot's thin mattress is hurting my back. "Before Angel was born, sometimes Yoli would sing to me when I couldn't fall asleep." I haven't thought about this in a long time.

"How is it you're no longer with each other?"

My sigh is audible in the dark room. "She knew I loved her. And I knew she loved me too, in her way. But Yoli is a very practical person, and a relationship with another woman simply couldn't provide her the security and opportunity she's looking for." For years now I have practiced this statement until now I can recite it matter-of-factly, keeping the bitterness out of my tone. There is a longer and more complicated explanation, but I've somehow never been able to quite figure it out.

Sumati says, "You didn't fight for your family." For a moment I can't believe I've heard her right.

"I don't believe in family," I tell her, and this time I don't bother to disguise the anger in my voice.

"You didn't believe in *yourself*," she continues, "enough to fight for your love, for your family. You didn't feel entitled enough as a lesbian to stake your claim."

Now she's really crossed the line. Bad enough that she pokes around uninvited in my private life, but now she's going to presume to criticize me for it? And what does she know about lesbians and entitlement?

"I thought the Light Beings don't believe in fighting," I retort. "Doesn't Guru Tam say the path to serenity lies in acceptance?"

"Yes, but acceptance doesn't mean you just roll over and take whatever anyone does." She sits up in the bed to further emphasize her point. "Acceptance means you acknowledge what is happening, you don't try to deny it, or hide from it, or pretend something else is happening. But you still advocate for what you believe."

I want this conversation to be over. Too much is staring me in the face right now without sifting through ancient history. I stage an elaborate yawn. "It wouldn't have mattered what I did," I mutter, "her mind was made up." I deliberately turn on my side, with my back to Sumati.

"You lost faith," she persists. "Maybe you didn't believe that a same-sex relationship deserved to prevail." She waits several moments for my response, but when my only rejoinder is silence, she too rolls over and settles her hips into the mattress. After a little while I hear a gentle snore arise from the other side of the room.

I, however, am left wide-awake, vexed and pondering in the dark.

I think I am dreaming of the sound of a gong, but then Sumati is shaking my shoulder and I realize the sound is resonating through the hall outside the door. The room is still fully dark, but Sumati is already dressed in her blue gown, headdress in place.

"What time is it?" I rasp, straining to hold onto the tail of a swiftly fading dream.

"Time to salute the morning," she announces crisply, and I can see that she has already resumed her role as Chief Assistant. "Do you have a proper covering for your head?"

Clearly my participation is not viewed as optional, as it was in Ensenada. "No," I confess. "I might have a baseball cap somewhere, but that's the extent of it."

The Sumati from last night might have been dimly amused, but not the one who looms over me now. She "tsks" in annoyance, then says, "You can borrow one of mine. I can't have you running around in shorts and a T-shirt anyway."

Before I can protest, she has pulled from the armoire another blue gown and headdress. "Hurry up, now, we begin in five minutes." She whisks out of the room.

What will they do to me, I wonder, if I come downstairs in my own clothes? Or even better, if I just stay in bed? Will she send a posse of Light Beings upstairs to force me into her blue gown? Will she kick us out?

Then I reflect that I am doing just what she has accused me of, trying to manipulate the situation to get my way, refusing to surrender my will. Will it kill me to play dress-up for a few days? It's not like anybody will see me except a bunch of other folks in identical drag. *Spirit, help me to change my attitude!* I pray. *Help me to be grateful for this place of shelter and respite.*

I grumble to my feet, find clean underwear, and load my boobs into a bra. Then I regard the hated gown, drop it over my head, and thrash my way into it. Since I was a kid, I've hated dresses. It's probably over forty years since I last wore one. I look down. Its pressed lines immediately start to wrinkle. It's a little tight in the chest, but roomier in the waist and hips than Sumati's appeared on her. There's no mirror in the room and I'm grateful for this small reprieve.

The headdress, on the other hand, eludes me. It's supposed to tie and then tuck somehow and then be tied again, but my fingers can't manage it. The best I can do is knot it under the nape of my neck like a *babushka*, dig for my flip-flops and clop on down the stairs. *Spirit, by your grace, maybe Guru Tam can see me today, and then we can get the hell out of here!*

Gratitude, I remind myself, as I shuffle in the direction of the music. If I think these rules are impossible to follow, imagine how well I'll do in Mexican jail.

I find everyone in the large room off the foyer, seated on blankets or cushions. The low platform glitters with lit candles and a trio of musicians is seated to one side. One is the woman who sang to the girls last night; her guitar is once more strapped across her chest. Haroon sits before a *tabla*, a large drum. A third man I don't recall seeing before holds a harmonium.

I haven't thought to bring anything to cushion my seat on the hardwood floor, so I find a wall against which to prop my back. I think I was about eight when I absolutely refused to wear a dress any longer, so I have no idea how to descend gracefully in this getup. I'm relatively certain I'm not supposed to show this much skin.

Just then the children enter in a gaggle, carrying blankets, looking sleepy. I easily spot Angel; she too is wearing a pale blue gown. She's looking for me too, and I stand up so she can find me. She makes a face and laughs at my attire; I grab both sides of the gown and curtsy. She starts over to sit next to me, but Chhaya gently guides her with the other children to the opposite side of the room. I can see her about to rebel, but I gently shake my head and remind her to do as she's told.

Then a man with a gray beard climbs up onto the teacher's platform; I recognize him as one of the guards at the gate yesterday. He was the most neutral of the three, neither firmly opposed to my entry nor particularly helpful about resolving the situation. It is he who will lead us in prayer this morning.

Bhanupriya comes over and sits next to me. "Peace begets peace," she greets me.

"Peace returns peace," is all I have time to say before the musicians begin to play again. It's a song clearly familiar to those assembled, but I've not heard it before, so I sit quietly while the others sing. I scoot myself a little to the left so I can watch Angel, who joins in as if this were an audition for "Star Search."

Then the gray-bearded man begins to recite a prayer in Sanskrit. Quickly I whisper, "What's that man's name?" hoping she won't be annoyed by my interruption.

"Pramesh," she says kindly before she returns to praying. I remember this name; Bhanupriya had told me yesterday that Sumati and Pramesh were the only Light Beings "authorized" to leave the community. And Jagadeep.

I want to ask her what his name means, indeed, what her own name means, but this is not a time for conversation. I lean back against my wall, grateful for the support of the rough stucco, and close my eyes. I only hope I will appear deep in meditation, and not falling asleep.

Before I am caught snoring, we move to our physical practice, which requires me to once more hoist myself from the floor in the awkward costume. The exercises are much more rigorous than the simple routine at the ashram in Ensenada, and I am confounded by trying to tug the gown back down over my legs while keeping my butt high in the air as I try to execute a downward facing dog pose. The other women seem to handle it so gracefully, as if they were born to float and drift, while I am destined to clomp and struggle and sweat.

After our heartbeats are elevated, we sit once more for the hour of chanted prayer to follow. I no longer feel like I will doze off, and I try to invest myself in the spirit of the practice, even without understanding the words. I enjoy watching the musicians, especially Haroon, his dark hands flashing over the paler skin of the *tablas*. I wonder if he once played other music, and pass some time imagining him in a jazz club.

Periodically I steal a glance at my daughter, but she is as deep in concentration as a Method actor on opening night, sitting up tall, eyes alert, doing her best to follow the string of unfamiliar syllables, an expression of devoutness on her face. If Yoli could see her now, she would want to skin me alive. Although I've never wanted to deliberately use Angel to get back at Yoli, I can't seem to help but relish the thought of her upset.

As always, my legs go numb after an extended time of sitting, and I take turns stretching first one leg, then the other, doing my best not to kick my neighbors who are clustered around me. If they find my fidgeting annoying, there's no evidence of it; no one else breaks their concentration. Finally, a gong announces that we are done.

"What happens now?" I ask Bhanupriya.

"We have an hour now before breakfast. Perhaps you want to go for a walk and watch the sun rise?"

What I want to do is to spend some time with Angel. I thank Bhanupriya, and hurry over to the other side of the room, where the children are gathering up their blankets and belongings. I am about to talk my daughter into breaking the rules with me, when Sumati intercepts me.

"Come with me," she whispers sharply in my ear. "Guru Tam may be able to see you now."

I'm startled; I didn't expect the opportunity to come so soon. *Thank you, Spirit,* I offer up, but at the same time I wonder if I am prepared. I should have meditated more carefully this morning, instead of letting my mind wander all over the place.

"Let me just tell Angel..." I say, but Sumati is not in a mood to negotiate.

"We have to go right now!" she hisses.

I gesture to Angel that I will see her later, and that I love her. She waves goodbye without evident distress. Her complexion looks darker against the pale blue; she breaks my heart in her little gown.

Sumati hustles me out the back entrance and over toward the parking lot. It's still cool from the night; the sun has only just risen. She swings open the door of a battered Jeep. I climb in, awkward in my dress. Sumati glares at me with mocking amusement. "Look at you," she points to a streak of dirt at the hem of my gown, "you've already got that stained!"

I decide not to let her get the best of me this morning. "Do you have any idea how many years it's been since I wore a dress?" I respond.

"My, my. Spirit is giving you no end of things to challenge you!" She observes this without scorn; I'm reminded more of the teasing camaraderie of the locker room.

Her driving is more adventurous than I would have given her credit for, and as we bounce along a dirt road leading up to the mountains, I am reminded that I am due to start my period any second. Tampax was one thing I neglected to get in town. I cross my arms over my chest to surreptitiously keep my boobs from rebounding.

I wonder what kind of menstrual product Light Beings use. I pray that it isn't one of those natural sponges that you're supposed to wash out and reinsert. But maybe we will be out of here before I have to face that.

As we ascend I get a view of the Pacific, stunning in the early morning light. Tina had told me yesterday that the desert floor is green from last fall's hurricanes. I don't blame Guru Tam for wanting to live up here, but I wonder what members of the community feel about the disparity. I don't want to risk setting Sumati off by asking.

Instead I inquire, "Has Guru Tam lived up here since the community first moved to Baja?"

"Yes," she says. "Our beloved Teacher was already unwell before we moved here. Living in close proximity to the others puts a constant demand on Guru's energy, which we are trying to preserve."

"I guess I don't understand that," I venture. "Do you mean that people are always asking for Guru Tam's time and attention?"

"That, but also on a more subtle level. Like an air filter," she explains. "The air comes in with all its toxins and pollutants, and the filter captures those and returns the air clean. Our Teacher has been filtering the energy of the planet for too long."

"But isn't...? I mean, as a bodyworker, I filter energy for my clients too. But one of the first things they teach you is how not to take on a client's energy." I don't want to make it sound as if I'm being critical of Guru Tam, but this puzzles me.

Her response edges toward defensiveness. "But you're only concerning yourself with certain levels of energy—physical, maybe emotional. You're not attempting to clear someone's karma."

"I wouldn't even begin to know how to do that," I concede, and this admission softens her.

The road has narrowed to a single lane and Sumati is taking it a lot faster than I would. I remind myself not to look down. I try to frame in my mind what I will say to the Teacher, and how I will plead my case. I suppose I know deep down that I am going to have to go back, and admit what I've done, and turn over the outcome to Spirit. Have I come all this way to just hear what I've been reluctant to accept?

Finally, Sumati makes a sharp left up a steep driveway and comes to a halt under a large and leafy avocado tree. "Wait here," she instructs.

As Sumati departs the Jeep I turn to follow her movements. Behind me is a large whitewashed house, Mediterranean style with a redtile roof, multi-storied, built even higher up the slope. A wide patio sweeps around the front side, providing what I would imagine is a spectacular ocean view. Aloes and other cacti are planted amidst desert wildflowers in the terraced landscaping that spills from the front door down to the flat expanse on which we are parked. The air smells sweet and dry, grassy.

As the sun climbs a little higher, it begins to warm the day, and I register the fact that the Light Beings must be having breakfast now. Hunger stirs my belly; the arid wind sucks moisture from my tongue. I hope that Angel isn't worried about me.

Just then a figure begins to descend the steep flight of stone steps. She is not wearing pale blue, but a sari of deep saffron that offsets rich olive skin. Her head is draped loosely in another saffron fabric, but beneath it, black hair frames her face. As she approaches, I note a dot of crimson between her eyebrows, at her third eye point. She approaches me, bearing a tray.

"Peace begets peace," she greets me.

"Peace returns peace."

"I am Kundanika." she smiles.

"Maggie." It feels like a lackluster response. "What does your name mean?" I inquire.

"Golden." Her smile grows wider.

I wonder whether that's why she's allowed to wear this blazing color, so appealing to the eye. Equally appealing are the grapefruit and strawberries arranged on her tray, along with a baked roll that smells of cinnamon, and a cup of lemon ginger tea. She offers this to me, explaining, "I'm sorry that your wait may be extended."

"Is the Guru feeling poorly again?" I ask.

Kundanika smiles but does not engage the question. "I'll be back for the tray in a little while, and to see whether you need anything else." She turns and glides back up the stone steps and disappears into the house.

Curious as I am about what's going on inside, my appetite is compelling, and I'm grateful for tart fresh fruit and the still-warm bread. It was kind of my hosts to consider that I was missing breakfast, and I hope Sumati is feasting in a similar fashion.

From some window drifts the sound of a flute, a haunting Eastern melody. Once I've eaten, the warming sun and extended wait make me drowsy. I know I should be thinking about how to present my case to Guru Tam, and the questions I want to ask. I don't know whether, once I am let in, I will have one minute or five minutes or thirty to receive what I am seeking from the Great Teacher.

But waking so early has turned my mind to a thick soup, and the more I try to think, the more my eyelids sag, until my limbs are spread across the worn leather upholstery of the Jeep's front seat. I am having a dream about Carmen, who is somehow dancing with Old Mac on the patio at the Oasis;

Angel is riding on Loba's back, and everything is so pleasant until Daman appears, dressed in a suit of red like the devil. A gun has appeared in my hand and I am pointing it in his direction, when something grabs my arm...

It's Sumati, shaking me awake. Her face is red with agitation; she's got the kind of pale skin that can't hide her emotions. Her grip on my arm is not gentle.

"Maggie, wake up," she booms into my ear.

"I'm awake," I protest, retrieving my abused limb. "Sorry, it was warm and I got sleepy."

"I have news," she pronounces importantly, but it doesn't look as if she's happy about it. "My Teacher has decided that you will stay here."

I'm not as awake as I'm pretending to be. "Stay here? You mean with the Light Beings? Forever?" I was afraid of this. I attempt to steel myself for the next battle. Guru or no, this is definitely not something that anyone gets to decide for me.

Her eyes widen with surprise. "Forever? I hardly think so! No, I mean you are to stay here at the Guru's house for the next few days."

"But, I thought Guru Tam was really ill? Won't two houseguests just be in the way?" I'm addled by the thought of another move, more change, not just for myself but also for Angel, and I don't really know if this is a good thing or not. It might give me more freedom than being under Sumati's watchful eye.

"Two?" Sumati looks puzzled.

"Angel and me."

"No," she hastens to disabuse me. "Just you. Angel will remain with the other children at the center."

I jump out of the front seat. If I have to walk all the way back down the mountain I'm willing to. "No, Sumati, absolutely not! Every time another decision comes down it serves to put more distance between my daughter and me. First we can't stay in the same room. Then you tell her maybe I'm not coming back. Now I'm supposed to just leave her there where I can't even check in on her and see if she's okay? Where she can't come to me if she needs to? I *promised* her, you heard me! No!"

I expect her to explode, but she gazes at me calmly. "Get hold of yourself, Maggie. You can't keep flying off the handle every time something happens that's different than what you planned." She is firm, but not mean. "You cannot come here seeking the Teacher's help and then refuse to follow what's asked of you. Nobody's looking to hurt you or to hurt your daughter. I told you yesterday, you have to trust us."

I feel like a fish on a hook, flopping against air. Do I fail to trust because I have good reason for suspicion, or do I fail to trust because of a lack in myself, and will that lack end up endangering my daughter?

"There's something else," Sumati tells me. "The FBI now knows you're in Baja."

"How do you know that?" I'm astonished by this bolt-from-the-blue news.

She points upward, and I suddenly notice the satellite dish mounted on one side of the house.

"Guru Tam watches TV?" Nothing is sacred. The Dalai Lama's into off-track betting. Pope John Paul's addicted to Internet porn. Guru Tam watches *Fear Factor*. Cynicism is easier to focus on than the panic that's branching through my nerve endings at the implications of this news.

Sumati shrugs. "According to the news report I saw, they don't yet know exactly where you are. They're searching for your car."

"That's not my car anymore," I interject.

"Still, people have seen the two of you. They're offering a reward, Maggie. People are greedy, or desperate. You can't count on everyone staying quiet. And the *Federales*, though maybe not as high-tech as the FBI, have their ways of finding things out."

A reward? Where would Yoli get the money for that? Or maybe it's Daman's. "How much?" I ask.

"Fifty thousand dollars," Sumati tells me.

People commit reckless acts for a whole lot less money than that. I wonder if Tina knows about the reward. Or Carmen? Fifty thousand dollars would mean a lot to either of them. Suddenly I wonder if I've been rash to place my trust in anyone.

"We should get out of here." I'm thinking out loud. "We can take a ferry to the mainland, and get a boat someplace—maybe Cuba. Surely *they* have no extradition treaty with the U.S. *And* no satellite TV."

Sumati places her hands on my shoulders; this time her touch is soothing. "That's the same kind of reaction that got you here in the first place. Maggie, you can't drag that child all over the planet. You can't keep running for the rest of your life." She places the palm of one hand on my back, just at the level of my heart. I feel the energy pouring into me, a rush of bright light. It radiates through me, relaxing my shoulders, helping my breath to deepen. Tears begin to stream from my eyes.

"Maggie," she says softly, "you came to us for help in figuring out what to do. In all my years with the Teacher, I've never seen anyone fail who follows the Guru's guidance." Her hand is still pressed against my mid-spine, her light still blessing me. "Let Guru help you now. Just because you cannot understand the plan, doesn't mean it's not a good plan. Do as you're being asked, Maggie. Come inside. Have faith."

Chapter 9

Having only barely acclimated to the austerity of the Light Beings' complex, I am struck by the lavishness of Guru Tam's house. The bright white rooms are festooned with heavy carved furniture from India, while thick Persian rugs cushion the tile floors. Walls are adorned with framed paintings of deities and gurus; vases of fresh flowers fill every room. Colorful fabric filters the light that streams through leaded panes, many of which capture an ocean view from atop this mountain. Wind chimes sway on the house's many terraces, creating a constant music.

On the downstairs level, I've wandered the large living room, the even larger dining room, a comfortable sitting room, an immense industrial kitchen and, in addition to the wide front porch, a vast patio around the back of the house, with a pool and landscaped gardens. Upstairs, I've only seen the guest room where I will be staying, the bed with its downy white comforter, the private bathroom and deep tub.

I wonder how many of the Light Beings have been up to this house and whether they're aware that their labor down below is buying their Teacher a higher standard of living than they enjoy. Or perhaps it would not trouble them. Perhaps they are happy to sacrifice for their Guru. Maybe it's only me with my craven worldview who is disturbed. I suppose I can afford to be craven with a price on my head. Still, I'm not so troubled by the disparity that I can't appreciate the beautiful surroundings. If only Angel were here with me.

The only way I could accept Guru Tam's invitation was to insist I talk it over with my daughter first. For once, Sumati didn't argue with me, but drove me back down the mountain so I could consult Angel and retrieve some of my possessions. She even agreed to let me pull Angel out of lessons in order to talk to her.

Angel was happy to see me. "Maggie, you didn't come to breakfast! I looked for you, then Yamini told me it was time to go to school." Her tone was more scolding than anxious, which I took as a good sign.

"Mrs. Havisham, I went to see Guru Tam this morning. I'm hoping to find out what to do to get us out of this pickle."

She giggled at the word pickle, no doubt at its funny sound but maybe too at its gross understatement of our situation.

I explained to her that the Guru wanted me to stay at another house.

"No!" she protested. "I don't wanna do any more moving around!"

I explained to her that she would stay here, and I would stay in another house, just a little bit away.

"How far?" my daughter wanted to know.

"Come with me." I took her little soft hand in mine, noticed the flash of her darker skin against my paleness, and walked her outside into the courtyard. "See that mountain?" I pointed and her eyes followed. "Do you see the road? It goes around and around the mountain. The house is up there."

"That's a long way," she said, and her lower lip trembled. "I can't even see it!" Her eyes grew stormy, as she accused, "You told me you wouldn't leave me!"

"Sweetheart, I'm not leaving you. And I won't do it if you don't want me to, I swear." I meant it, no matter what the consequences to our stay with the Light Beings. "I just think maybe the Guru can help us."

"Why can't I come?" Angel wanted to know.

I thought of a few ways to respond—"Guru Tam is sick and we want to protect you," or "You'll have a lot more fun staying here with the other kids"—the kinds of small lies adults routinely tell. Instead I told her the truth. "I don't know why."

She considered this. "How long?"

"I think just for a couple more days." It occurred to me this was a question I hadn't asked. But that had been the original agreement.

"What if something happens? How can I find you?"

This was a question she asked when we first took her to school. That time we told her to go to her teacher, and her teacher would find us. And over the years I've made a few mad dashes to school when her teacher called to tell me Angel was sick and needed to come home.

Now I needed to be very careful in answering this question. I definitely didn't want to promise something that I couldn't deliver. So I walked her back inside and into Sumati's office.

When she saw Angel, impatience flashed through Sumati's eyes, but she quickly rearranged her face into a neutral expression.

"My daughter has a question to ask you," I announced then, encouraging Angel, "go ahead, honey."

"Peace begets peace," my girl says reminding me that I've forgotten the polite greeting.

"Peace returns peace," Sumati replies. "What is your question?"

My daughter's expression is concentrated, her lips pursed together. "If Maggie goes to stay up on the mountain, what do I do if I need her?"

Sumati knelt down to speak to Angel at eye level, and I was grateful to her for doing that. "First of all, if you need something you can go to anybody here for help."

From the look on my daughter's face it was clear that this did nothing to allay her concerns.

"Second, if you really decide it's something only Maggie can help you with, come to me and I'll go up and get her."

"Sumati, please don't promise that if you don't mean it," I couldn't help but interject.

"Do you actually think I would do that?" Her eyes penetrated mine until I had to look away. "Angel, I give you my word."

"Anytime?" my daughter pressed.

"Day or night," Sumati promised.

"I guess okay then," she said with hesitation.

What else could she say—it was so clear what Sumati and I wanted her to do. Had we left her any room to refuse?

"Are you sure?" I asked her, but she just nodded stoically. She didn't want to revisit the issue.

As I walked her back to class, I said to her, "I love you more than sunny days."

"I love you more than Edgar Sue," she replied. Her meaning was clear: she was doing this for me, the least I could do was get her the puppy.

Then I was treated to another thrill ride around hairpin curves in Sumati's Jeep. When she deposited me back atop the mountain, I asked, "What am I to do here?"

"Kundanika will give you instructions," she explained. "And of course, Guru Tam may make requests of you." Sumati frowned and shook her head. "Harshada is really going to miss your help in the laundry." Her expression was deadpan, but I could tell she was ribbing me.

"And you know how sorry I am to miss that opportunity," I teased back.

"Your daughter will be fine," she assured me. "She's seven, yes, almost eight? Children that age need to test themselves in other environments, to face things without their parents' mediation. This time will be good for her."

And then I watched her Jeep head back down the hill in a cloud of dust.

I'd wanted to drive my own car up here. I hated the idea of being stranded, but Sumati insisted I'd be safer this way.

I can't see how it's safer to be without transportation when people are after you; I suppose this is another thing I just have to trust.

I'm starting to see now that ever since I was a kid, I've done everything I could to be self-sufficient. Trust isn't a big issue when you don't need anything. But being in a position where you're forced to rely on others—terrifying. No doubt this is part of my lesson.

But the answer isn't to trust indiscriminately either. That woman from the bookstore in town would definitely sell me out, even if there weren't a reward involved. What was I thinking when I mentioned the Light Beings to her? I might as well have drawn a map and captioned it, *This is where to find me.* And Carmen—what kind of idiot am I to think a woman like that would be interested in me? She must have heard about the reward and figured she'd find a way to get under my skin. Artists always need money, don't they? Even Tina—she seems like a really great person, but what do I really know about her? I know she shot her boyfriend and left a child in danger. I can't believe I gave her Charlie's number. Charlie, the one person whose loyalty I don't doubt.

At one time I wouldn't have doubted Yoli's, despite her infidelities. But the lessons here have been harsh and brutal. Now when I think about her, instead of feeling tenderness, my mouth floods with saliva, sharp and sour.

Now I almost wish I *were* at work in the laundry. I need activity to distract my mind before I drive myself crazy. Kundanika just told me to "Relax for a little while." What a joke that is.

As if my thoughts had evoked her, a flash of saffron appears in my open door. "Peace begets peace," the young woman greets me.

"Peace returns peace." I lumber to my feet.

"Guru Tam has asked to see you. I'm to take you there now."

Panic erupts in my belly. How long have I been moving toward this moment—days or a lifetime? Suddenly I'm terrified; what makes me think I'm ready to meet the Teacher?

Kundanika grins. "Don't be nervous." Her brown eyes steady me.

I pad after her down a long hallway; it is the custom to go barefoot in this house. I admire her grace as her hips sway gently in front of me, as if she is moving to a music only she can hear. We step through French doors to the outside, cross a stone terrace, and enter another set of doors into a large and low-lit chamber. Here the walls are painted in deep colors, brick red and burgundy; the windows are hung with velvet. The first room has a hardwood floor, upon which a few embroidered meditation cushions are placed. These are set before an altar that takes up an entire wall. More than two dozen candles are flickering amidst fresh flowers and statuary, crystals, bundles of herbs and small paintings of deities unknown to me. In one corner a brass gong is suspended from the ceiling, round and large as a kitchen table.

The next room is even darker, its only light coming from two candles on either side of the bed. Although incense burns— I think it's cedar—the smell of sickness hangs in the room, the odor of the body's decay.

In a wide bed with a carved headboard, an olive brown face rises from a sea of white—white pillows and bed linens, white head cloth, white garments. The Guru is nearly unrecognizable from the many photos I've seen, the body wizened, skin wrinkled, features drawn. She appears so tiny to command so much power. But the obsidian eyes still glow with a light that seems to ignite my spine, and her voice, when she speaks, rings clear.

"Maggie," Guru speaks with a trace of an accent, "I need a glass of water."

"Of course, ah…" I falter, not knowing how to address her.

"Call her 'Guru-Ji,'" Kundanika murmurs in a low voice. "It means 'Beloved Teacher.'" The young woman also shows me the cabinet in one corner on which a silver tray is set with a crystal pitcher of water and four glasses. A ceramic plate bears thin slices of lemon in perfect rounds.

"Would you care for lemon, Guru-Ji?" I ask, and Kundanika nods at me approvingly.

"Thank you," Guru Tam responds.

I pour the water, careful not to overfill the glass, and bring it to the bed. I don't know whether she will need help to sit up, help to hold the glass; I don't want to assume her incapable, nor do I want to force her to instruct me.

"Yes, help me to sit up," she answers my unasked question, "and we'll both hold onto the glass."

I perch on the side of the bed, and slip my left hand behind her back. Her garments are damp with sweat, her bones sharp beneath flesh that seems to have thinned to parchment. I can feel the breath as it enters and leaves her body; in some ways the breath feels more substantial than the flesh that contains it. Her body seems to weigh nothing, perhaps no more than Angel, as I carefully tilt it forward. Her fingers wrap around my grasp on the drinking glass with unexpected strength, and together we bring it to her lips. In the candlelight I can see how dry they are, cracked at the corners. I should offer her some lip balm.

She drinks the entire glass, then I feel her weight rest back against my hand. I gently lower her to the mound of pillows that elevate her head.

"Lip balm is a good idea. I never remember to use it," she admits.

Kundanika nods her encouragement to me. It's as if we're all engaged in a conversation that's being carried only in my head.

I reach for the tube in my pocket, but the blue gown has no pockets, yet another reason to hate it.

I excuse myself and hurry back across the patio, down the hall to my room, where I fish it from the pocket of my shorts. I spread a thick coat on my own lips, then decide to offer her a fresh tube, which is tucked into the pocket of my backpack.

I retrace my steps to Guru Tam's room, once more feeling ungainly in Sumati's blue gown; as the day has grown warmer, I feel like I'm sweating in a tent. Kundanika has disappeared, and the Guru's eyes are closed. I hesitate in the doorway, wondering if she has fallen asleep. This time I notice the television set across the room, it's eye momentarily dark.

"Come in," she says, without opening her lids. "By the way, you don't need to wear that uniform while you're here. I don't mind if you wear your own clothes."

I approach the bed. "Would you like to apply this yourself, or shall I put it on for you?"

"I want to smell it first," she says, and I open the little plastic tube and waft it under her nose.

"It's supposed to be cherry," I say.

"Almond oil," she counters. "Almond and coconut."

I squint at the tiny print that lists the ingredients and indeed, almond and coconut oil are both there. I use the pad of my middle finger to scoop a bit of the unguent and spread it gently over the cracked surface of her lips.

"When I was just a girl in India, my *ayah* would rub coconut oil into my hair until it shone," she reminisces.

I imagine her about Angel's age. I have read that Guru was only eight years old when her gift was discovered. The story told is that a dove was found dead on the balcony outside her window. The servants wanted to dispose of it but the little girl cried so hard they relented and brought it to her. As she held its lifeless body in her hands and wept, her tears dropped onto its gray breast and soon its wings began to stir. Soon the bird was flying around the room, cooing its gratitude. It is considered Guru Tam's first miracle. I used to tell Angel this story when she was small. For a while, whenever we were out in the yard she would look for a dead bird to revive.

"You have been a good mother to this daughter," Guru says now. "Even though her soul did not take root in your body, she still came here to be with you."

There is so much I want to say, but the simplicity of her words renders it unnecessary. Tears spring to my eyes.

She pats my hand. "I'm tired now. We will have time to talk later. You need a task to occupy you, yes? So your mind does not spin like a crazy monkey? Go see about the garden; there is much to be done there."

Like that, she is asleep. Not knowing the proper protocol, I bow my head before I take my leave. I scarcely know how to describe the power of her words to touch me, as if she can read what is written on my heart.

I stop in my room to change my clothes, surveying with dismay the streaks and stains I have visited upon Sumati's pristine gown, so crisp just this morning when I first put it on. It feels heavenly to free my head from the shroud that's surrounded it; I put my fingers to my scalp and scratch deliciously. I pull on one of my last clean T-shirts, and rummage to find my least soiled pair of shorts. I decide to take advantage of the private bathroom and run some water in the tub with a squirt of shampoo, and toss my soiled clothing beneath the suds. I leave everything to soak and wind my way back downstairs.

I'm on my way to the garden when Kundanika finds me; she hands me a plate of rice and steamed vegetables and succulent cubes of sautéed tofu. "You'll need lunch before you tackle the garden," she says with a smile. It is both comforting and deeply unnerving that everything seems to be known around here without having been spoken. Why would they even need TV?

I walk the plate outside to the back patio. I lower my body to the edge of the pool and immerse my feet in the water. The sun on my scalp and skin feels delicious, though I know I should take care not to get more burned. My arms and face are still pink from yesterday morning—is it possible that just thirty hours ago I was walking on the beach with Tina?

Chewing perfectly steamed broccoli and green beans, I try to reestablish chronology. It was Wednesday when I left Los Angeles. Two days driving. I got to Todos Santos on Friday afternoon. So today is Sunday. It seems a meaningless designation, sitting in this timeless garden. Except perhaps I am less likely to be apprehended on a Sunday. This comes, no doubt, from some romantic fantasy about the Baja police; I imagine them going to church, having dinner with their families, having a beer while watching *futbol* on TV.

As I gather the last grains of rice, I can't help but muse about the contradictions of life—here I am, a criminal wanted by the FBI and now the *Federales*, sitting in the sun in an utterly bucolic setting. Will I remember this scene when I am behind bars in a filthy Mexican jail? Or is Spirit trying to show me that everything will be all right?

Leaving my plate by the side of the pool, I survey the garden. My original intention was to get an overview, make a checklist and work through it, but my eyes fall first on a stand of roses in need in pruning. Some bushes produce bright red blooms; other yield yellow flowers, or white. Spent blossoms have been allowed to go to rosehips. I wonder if Kundanika collects them for tea?

In one corner of the garden I find a small wooden shed. Inside are clippers and plastic bags, along with an array of other tools, all neatly organized. Everything in the house is so well maintained, I find it odd that the garden would be in need of care. Still, I turn my efforts to the task.

Though I'm not much of a gardener, I do know something about roses. When I was growing up, my mother prized her rose garden. When my dad lost his job and we had to let the gardener go, the roses were the one part of the yard that faithfully got my mother's attention. She had several bushes, all in varying shades of pink, from pale blush to near magenta. She would always clip fragrant bouquets and display them in glass vases around the house. My mother knew all the fancy names and their pedigrees, which have long ago escaped my memory. But I do recall that she taught me how to prune them, looking for stems with five leaves, cutting a quarter inch above them.

I can almost smell the perspiration mixing with my mother's face powder as she'd oversee my task, "Be careful! Make a clean cut all the way through. Don't tear it." I used to resent the interest she would lavish on the roses, and later considered it a pathetic affectation of her long-lost economic status, but now I feel glad that my mother had something in her life to make her happy.

Although I don't know how the growing season in Baja compares with that of Los Angeles, it seems to me that these should be the first blooms after a period of dormancy. That would counsel a light touch with the pruning. But the presence of rosehips suggests that no heavy pruning was done in the winter, and I don't honestly know what will serve these plants best. I decide to strike a middle course; the days are too hot now to prune all the way back to bare canes.

I cut away the rosehips first and gather them to present to Kundanika. Next I clip the blooms, careful not to disturb the new buds, and carry them to the kitchen along with my bag of rosehips. Kundanika is pouring batter into a baking pan as I appear in the doorway, displaying the blossoms along with the dirt on my hands. She smiles and opens a tall cabinet, from which she produces three vases. She takes the roses from me.

"Careful of the thorns," I warn her. I have already punctured my hands in several places, and have a long scrape on my thigh.

"I'll put these in water," she offers. "You can take them up to the Guru later."

I leave the bag of rosehips at the doorway and return to my task. Now I can cut back the stems. I rummage in the shed until I find a bag of rose food, which I scatter on the ground beneath the plants. The soil is dry, and cultivating the food into the ground is arduous. I am bathed in sweat, slowly burning under the sun, covered in dirt; I feel happier than I have in a long time. The work is soothing to me after days of driving and waiting and worrying.

As I sprinkle water from the hose onto the ground, careful not to wet the leaves in this afternoon heat, I think of Yoli. I'm remembering one particular night shortly after she found out she was pregnant. She was defensive in those early weeks, sure I was going to change my mind and kick her out, guilty maybe; at any rate, she practically snarled at everything I said to her. We weren't being intimate; I was too hurt for that, but I was trying to feed her better nutrition and get her to take vitamins, buying books on natural pregnancy and childbirth, and going with her to her doctor's appointments. I grew resentful—she was the one who'd had the affair, but nothing I seemed to do was enough.

I was preparing myself for a confrontation. "Either lose the attitude or maybe you should go," I would tell her. But before I got around to it, I went to a meditation at the Light Beings session. Quoting Guru Tam, the leader said, "It is usually better to be kind than to be right." I felt the truth of this statement resonate throughout my molecules; it seemed to speak to me directly, to rearrange the patterns in my brain.

That night, when Yoli came home from her gig, I had a bath waiting for her. The bathroom was lit with candles. I massaged her shoulders and her legs, her hands and feet while she soaked in the fragrant tub. Immersed in water up to her neck, she began to cry, and I leaned over and slowly kissed the tears away.

"How can you forgive…?" she started to ask, but I kissed her lips quiet.

When the water grew tepid, I dried her off, running the towel over every inch of her body, kissing her breasts that were starting to swell, her brown belly with its now unmistakable curve.

Then I led her to our bed. I had spread rose petals over the sheets, and gently guided her down onto them. I lay beside her, and opened myself to her, taking her into the cave of my body. Later I would remember the music of the beads that adorned her braids as she swayed above me.

When Yoli left me, four years later, I put away memories like this one. I've worked hard since that time to cultivate neither nostalgia nor bitterness. "People go," I've told myself, "everyone must follow her own path. Release and bless her." It has been easier to relinquish the good memories than the bad, which I gnaw on like an old bone. But standing on this terrace littered with the debris of roses, I feel an ache of missing her so palpable that my body sinks to earth with it. A few tears add to the water streaming from the hose. I grasp a fistful of mud and let it wash through my fingers. I long to cover my face with it, cake my hair, streak it over the planes of my flesh.

I feel an energy swirling in my head, in and around it, through and outside my limbs. There almost seems to be a color to it, although no color I can describe, and a sound, but not a sound I've ever heard before, like the long tone of the universe, as I kneel in the dirt of Guru Tam's garden.

Time passes, minutes or hours. The sun is lower in the sky the next time I notice, and the breeze has picked up. My knees are stiff and my shorts are soaked through. Water pools in the rose beds. I hobble to my feet, turn off the hose, and quickly clean up. I feel different, lighter, more empty. I remember Sumati talking about how the Guru acts as a filter, clearing the karma out of people, and wonder if she is working even now, even as she sleeps.

Following directions from Kundanika, I take an outside staircase back up to my room, and thus avoid tracking mud through the entire house. Once there I wring out the clothes I'd left soaking and hang them on the balcony to dry. I run a hot bath to soak myself clean and to ease the muscles that have already started to ache.

My hands and arms are covered with scrapes and thorn splinters that sting as I slide my body into the steaming water. I think of my daughter, and wish she too could take advantage of this bathtub. Angel has always loved her bath; being immersed seems to bring forth her imagination and she becomes a mermaid, alive in this element. I hope her day has been okay; I hope she hasn't pissed off Sumati.

I keep soaking, nearly dozing off, until the water cools. After patting my body dry with a thick towel and sliding into underwear and a T-shirt, I collapse on the white comforter into an exhausted and dreamless sleep.

Most of the light is gone when Kundanika taps lightly at my door. "Peace begets peace," she greets me. She bears a tray of spicy cheese enchiladas, their sauce seeping into mounds of rice and black beans. There is crisp salad and cornbread with kernels of real corn.

"Peace returns peace," I answer, quickly sliding my legs into shorts. "But you don't have to serve me," I protest. "I could come down for dinner."

"It's just the two of us," Kundanika explains. "Whenever I cook, I tend to nibble, so I'm not having a meal now."

"And Guru Tam?"

"My Teacher hasn't eaten solid food for a long time. Clear broth, sometimes. Maybe a little fruit once in a while."

"Is that in the best interest of her health?" It seems that someone so weakened would need the nutrients.

"Guru often says that she's just visiting her body, like staying overnight in a motel. She doesn't consider it her home." The young woman does not seem to have particular concern about this.

"So you made this food just for me?" I hate to put her to the trouble.

"Guru likes to have cooking going on in the kitchen, even when she herself doesn't eat. She says the kitchen is the heart of the house, and we can't let it stop beating." Kundanika smiles. "Often Sumati will take the meals I've prepared to families in the community who are in need." Then she adds, "Besides, Guru says you're going to need your strength for what's ahead."

"Does that mean Guru Tam knows what's ahead?" My mouth is salivating from the smell of the plate in front of me, but the conversation is too intriguing to stop to eat.

"Go ahead and eat," Kundanika encourages me. She slides into an elegant squat against the stucco wall. Then, answering my question, "Guru says that everything is already known."

I can't help but slide a forkful of the enchilada into my mouth, so flavorful it nearly brings tears to my eyes. "This is sooo amazing," I compliment her. I pray that Angel is eating something this good tonight too. I feel guilty enjoying this without her. "But is Guru Tam saying the future is already known?"

"My Teacher says there is only one Energy and we are all part of it. There is no disconnection from that Source. Everything it contains we contain, forever and throughout all time. Most people live as if they are separate from that Source, and this is why they forget what they know, what they have always known." She radiates conviction.

I wonder to myself how I lost that connection, that knowledge. It seems it must have happened a long time ago.

"The world encourages us to live in our egos," Kundanika replies to the question I have not voiced. "It's all about making people like us, or trying to prove ourselves, or trying to survive and best the person next to us. The practice Guru Tam brought to us, the meditation and yoga and diet and the whole way of life—it reconnects us. That's why so many of us are happy to stay within the community, to limit our involvement in the so-called real world."

To myself, I think that it might be relatively easy to maintain that connection if one is spared the ordinary challenges of life. But wouldn't the true test of one's spiritual practice lie in the ability to maintain one's connection even while being in the world?

"We each have different paths," the young woman answers as if I'd spoken. "For some it is their karma to do just that, to try to balance themselves between ego and spirit. Perhaps that is your karma," she adds, kindly.

She pauses, her face concentrating as if listening to something from a distance. I can't hear it.

Then she says, "Sumati's on her way."

"You can hear her Jeep driving up?" I ask. Then, anxiously, "Is my daughter all right?"

"Your daughter is just fine. She had pizza for dinner," Kundanika assures me. "I guess you could call it hearing, or maybe listening, though it doesn't really have anything to do with the ears."

"That 'knowing' thing?" I tease her.

"Yes," she smiles, "that 'knowing' thing." She rises to her feet. "I need to go fix another plate." Her forehead puckers again. "Or maybe three."

Without explaining, she leaves me to finish my dinner and dare to hope that Angel might be one of the people Sumati is bringing with her.

I devour every bite of the delicious meal and, with no one to set an example for, I use the remnant of my cornbread to mop up the last of the sauce. Now I begin to feel nervous. What is Sumati coming to tell me? Who is she bringing with her? Is she planning to take me back to the Light Beings complex before I've had a chance to really speak with Guru Tam? Or maybe something has happened to Angel, and Kundanika wanted to wait for Sumati to tell me.

I wonder if I can *know* in the way that Kundanika does. I

make myself put down my fork, swallow the remnants of the last mouthful, and try to make myself quiet. I concentrate very hard. I furrow my forehead and wait. At first there is just density, as if the conduit were impenetrably clogged. Then it is like the car radio when you're way out in the boondocks— too many signals trying to come through on one channel, scraps of country tunes and radio preaching and oldies rock, so that nothing can be truly listened to. It bothers me that all the meditating I've done, albeit inconsistently, hasn't left me emptier and more receptive.

The evening is cooler on top of the mountain, and I need to find a pair of long pants and a shirt with sleeves. The cotton knit shirt I pull out is a soft lavender, and every time I wear it, Angel asks me if she can have it. Last time she said, "It's the color of my dreams." I resolve to give it to her.

It is another ten minutes before I can hear, with my pedestrian ears, the whine of the Jeep engine coming up the steep driveway, tires crunching on the dirt as the vehicle pulls to a stop. My fingertips are ice cold. I remind myself to take a few deep breaths before I leave my room and descend the stairs.

I expect to find people in the living room, but it's empty. So are the dining room, sitting room and kitchen, although the sink and countertops bear witness to Kundanika's most recent ministrations.

Walking outside, I see she has set the table on the patio. Sumati is in the chair facing me, but seated on either side of her are Tina Downs and Carmen. I gape at them. Light from a dozen candles shows me that Tina is wearing bright turquoise silk. Carmen is in red, her shoulders bare, black hair loose and streaming down her back. All three are talking over their plates, as if dining *al fresco* at an elegant restaurant.

I have the strangest sensation of wanting to retreat, as if I might just slip back up the stairs, the guests would finish their dinner and depart, and this moment would never have to happen. Seeing different aspects of my world, each one new to me, converge is unnerving, like those French comedies in which the wife meets the mistress, and the unfaithful husband stands disempowered and revealed.

My mind flashes on the reward; can any of the three of them be trusted, especially now that they're in league?

Slipping up behind me, Kundanika murmurs quietly, "Don't be nervous. They're all here to help you."

I am awkward in my body as I plod onto the patio, shy when all three look up from their plates at me.

"Peace begets peace," I greet Sumati. Oddly, she is the easiest of the trio for me to focus on. "Is Angel all right?"

"Peace returns peace. Your daughter spent the afternoon teaching the younger children to sing the Sponge Bob song. She's fine, although she loves the spotlight a little too much."

I smile at the image of my girl.

I watch Sumati's eyes register that I am no longer wearing her Light Beings gown and headdress; I hear her sigh inwardly. Have I too suddenly developed this strange ability to read people's thoughts?

"I'm surprised to see you here," I say to the other two.

"That's the understatement of the year, isn't it?" Tina retorts. Her lack of pretense puts me at ease.

"Your friends are persistent, or perhaps relentless is the better word, in their determination to help you," Sumati observes.

From her tone, I take it that Tina and Carmen somehow talked their way past the guards.

Then Sumati suggests, "You better sit down." She is devouring her enchiladas with every bit as much gusto as I did earlier.

I take the fourth seat at the wrought iron table, waiting to be briefed.

Sumati gestures to Tina to speak, but Tina says, "Carmen, why don't you begin?"

Carmen gives me a penetrating look, as if she could unlock the door to my soul. "This afternoon I was in the Hotel California. The owners have been wanting me to do some paintings for some of the rooms and I've been putting them off, but finally I thought, okay, I'll meet with them."

It is clear that Sumati has already heard this story and would prefer Carmen to cut to the chase, but she holds her tongue. Is it her body language that tells me this, or do I *hear* what she is thinking?

"I'm waiting in the lobby when these two people come in…"

As she says these words I see a picture of them, standing in the sour apple green lobby of the hotel. Daman and Yoli. I know this without having to be told.

"A white man and a black woman. They're arguing," Carmen continues, "and making no effort to keep from being overheard. She's saying, 'Let's just go to the police,' but he's saying, 'No, let's not bring the cops into it unless we have to. Let's ask around. Someone must have seen them.'"

How did they find me? If it was from tracking the cell phone calls, wouldn't the police already be involved? Did Charlie somehow let something slip? No, he wouldn't; he's too gifted at subterfuge. It must be that when the FBI said "Baja," Yoli remembered that I used to talk about coming down here. But why did they come by themselves? Why not just let the authorities handle it?

Carmen is still speaking. "Then I hear her ask the clerk, 'Have you seen a tall white woman with short gray hair, and a little African-American girl in town in the last few days?' The clerk hadn't, but I realized they must be talking about you.

"I didn't know anything about what had happened," Carmen assures me. "I don't have TV, it bores me. But their energy was very hard, very harsh. I felt you were in danger, so I didn't say anything to them. I walked right over to Tina's, and she told me to get in the truck. We came straight here."

"Well, first I called Charlie," Tina interjects. "He told me to tell you he was calling your lawyer and they would be on the next plane down here. Do you know about the reward?"

I nod, feeling my panic rise again. It's all happening too fast. I'd thought I would have my time with Guru Tam, and then I would know what to do next. I would be in control of the next step—whether to go back, whether to take Angel someplace else. This afternoon and evening at the Guru's house, it was easy to believe that time was one continuous flow, past and future an illusion. But Kundanika was right; the world barrels in and catches you up and pushes you off that place of balance.

"The timing is always perfect, Maggie. Don't doubt that," Sumati counsels. Her voice is gentle. "Here's what we'll do: Tina and Carmen will go back to town. Tomorrow morning they will find your daughter's other mother and her partner and invite them to the Light Beings' center in the afternoon. You will meet and talk with them there."

"I can't!" I object. "They'll take Angel away and I'll never see her again."

"Not to mention toss your butt in jail," Tina concurs.

"They don't seem to be much in a talking mode," Carmen agrees.

Sumati holds up her hands to call for silence. One commotion-filled person is enough; three is just too taxing. She takes a deep breath. "Maggie, when you came to us for help, what did you imagine we would do?"

"I hoped we'd get a safe place to stay for a couple of days, and that Guru Tam would be able to help me to see something I couldn't see on my own." My voice breaks. My plan sounds so flimsy, as if I believed the Wizard of Oz would fix some missing part of me.

"Don't be embarrassed that you put your faith in something, Maggie." Sumati again speaks to my unvoiced thoughts. "Now, find your breath. It's impossible to panic when you're breathing deep."

She waits for me to do this before she continues. "In order for you to be shown something new, you have to allow for the possibility that options exist that you cannot imagine. Where there is no faith, there are no miracles."

Carmen is looking at Sumati with deep interest. I can tell the Light Being's words are having an impact on her. Tina is rolling her eyes at me, not meaning disrespect, but asking silently if this is really the course of action I want to follow.

"We can have you on a ferry to the mainland first thing in the morning," she offers.

I remember Sumati's words from the other night. *You didn't believe in yourself enough to fight for your love, for your family.* I hear her say *You can't keep running.* I know this, at least, is true.

"Would Angel have to be at this meeting?" I ask Sumati. I don't want her to have to see how far apart her family has been blown.

"Not at first," Sumati answers. "Although later on, of course, your daughter will want to see her mother."

All three look at me to see what I am going to decide. I feel myself standing on the edge of a precipice, trying to summon the courage to jump. My toes curl against the ledge, my body paralyzed.

And yet, the choice is simple: I can live in fear or I can choose to live in faith.

Chapter 10

Of course I can't sleep. Nerves thrum, hours seep by, fits of abject terror only momentarily alleviated by bouts of prayer as darkness wanes to soupy gray. Worries layer my mind like advertisements on a wood construction fence, each papering over the one beneath: the prospect of facing Yoli now that she thinks I kidnapped her child, the chance she and Daman will show up with *Federales* ready to cart me off to jail, the potential that I might never see Angel again.

Of course this last is the worst threat. Even though Sumati says I must be prepared to accept *any* outcome as the benevolent will of Spirit, my heart feels like shattering each time I try to contemplate it. Last night I seriously considered taking Tina up on her offer to smuggle us to the mainland, where we could try once more to disappear, but if Yoli and Daman have found us in just five days, I figure I'm not much good at life on the lam.

The breeze through the windows is chilly and damp. Under moonlight, my watch informs me it's three a.m. Nine more hours before the appointed meeting time. Will the meeting even happen? Maybe Carmen won't be able to find Yoli and Daman in town. Maybe they won't go to the bookstore and ask that proprietress, who will surely remember us and recall my asking about the Light Beings.

It would be worse, I realize, if Daman and Yoli show up at the Light Beings' on their own. Certainly worse for the Light Beings. Once more I wonder if Sumati can be trusted. Has she suggested this showdown just to protect her own community? To rid herself of the problem of Angel and me? And what about Tina? Or Carmen? Maybe for them this is all about the reward.

Spirit, release me from this tumult. Show me what I am to do.

There is a knock at my door. It's Kundanika.

"Don't they let you sleep?" I ask her. I fear it's my pacing that's awakened her. Or my agitated mind.

"I sleep when I'm not needed." She smiles. Her dark hair is loose, and she wears a floor-length shift over her slender body, but in the dim light I can't distinguish its color. It's pale enough to give off a faint glow. "Guru Tam is asking for you."

My heart lifts with this summons. I'd been praying that I would be allowed to see the Guru before I had to face Yoli and Daman. Perhaps she will tell me what to do to break through Yoli's veils of denial and self-righteousness.

Then Kundanika continues, "Guru's been having a bad night in terms of pain. We are hoping your skill as a bodyworker might bring some relief."

A wave of disappointment makes my shoulders sag. She's not going to help me.

I inwardly chide myself: I should feel honored to be asked to serve in this way, but all I can think about are my own troubles. At least I'm not confined to my bed, riddled with pain, facing disablement and death.

As Kundanika leads me back across the upper patio to the

Guru's quarters, I try to put myself in the frame of mind to work. I need to empty myself of all my concerns in order to be a pure channel for any healing. I can't allow my frantic energy, my real and imagined trepidations, to further burden this already sick woman. *Spirit, use me as your instrument. Calm me, empty me. Cleanse me of fear and desire, so I might serve you.*

Entering the Teacher's bedroom I can smell the rotting sweetness emanating from her pores, sickness a palpable presence in the room. In my work with AIDS patients, I encountered this presence of bodily decay many times.

"Guru-Ji," I address her, keeping my voice soft in case she might be sleeping. Her eyes are closed, her mouth a grimace in her shrunken face.

"You're having a bad night too," she acknowledges.

"At least my pain is only in my mind," I say sheepishly.

She opens her fierce black eyes; the fire still rages there. *"All* pain is in the mind," she counters emphatically. With a loose hand she pats the mattress beside her, indicating that I should sit.

Her head is wreathed in perspiration; her sheets are damp. I should change these for her.

"No, I can't get up right now," she dissuades me. "I need to just lie here." Her voice sounds weaker than it did this afternoon; her breath is raspy and effortful.

How ironic it must seem to her, to have had such powers in her life and to now be so helpless.

"You misunderstand," she corrects me. She does not speak these words out loud, yet I hear them as clearly as if she'd shouted them. "No one *has* power. And no one is helpless. Power is always there to be used." Then, a moment later, "More is happening than you can see."

What, I want to ask her. What is happening that I can't see? But the energy around her does not invite these questions.

"I hope someday to understand," I murmur.

I rise then, and enter the small bathroom that adjoins the Guru's room. It is painted a deep periwinkle that reminds me of Tina. I wash my hands in the oval sink; water will clear the residue of my frenetic energy. Then I return to her side, remove my watch, and lay it by the side of the bed. "Guru-Ji, may I touch you?" I murmur.

I sense her agreement and take just a moment to prepare. Rubbing the palms of my hands together, I deepen my breath, and offer a prayer to Spirit. *Use me. Make of me a channel for your love, your light.* Then, bending over the mattress, I slide one hand underneath her spine, my open palm cradling her heart center from behind. The other hand slips under her sacrum. Her body feels so light in my hands, as if made of cloth or paper. I have decided to begin with some energy balancing; I fear her ravaged body is too brittle to withstand any pressure from my hands. I feel the quiet energy of her pulses and bring my breath.

As I do this, her breathing begins to ease, air flowing more smoothly in and out of her.

"Ahhh," she moans in soft relief. "You hope someday to understand but already your body knows."

"Thank you, Teacher," I whisper. I seem to enter a sort of dream with her. Images flow like water into my mind then, like fish, slip out again, too quick to catch. Crowded streets, flashes of color—is this India? A river, a temple, candle flame. These merge and commingle with pictures of Angel, and then her bruises, of Yoli, the vacancy of her face the last time she looked at me. I see Edgar Sue, Loba, Old Mac. Carmen's penetrating eyes. My mother's roses.

My left hip begins to sting, sharp and hot. I breathe out the discomfort, visualize and transform the energy until it leaves my body and disperses, neutralized, into the atmosphere. I hear a drum but it's from far away, perhaps another time altogether, an auditory hallucination. My forehead breaks out in a sweat; soon perspiration is dripping from my scalp, pouring down my face, dropping onto the already soaked-through sheets. My sweat smells of sulphur, eggs left too long in the sun. The soles of my feet itch.

Whatever I know now, I know it in my cells, in the electrical sparking of my nervous system. A storm of energy swirls about us, filling the room, Guru Tam and I vibrating together now, pulsating at a higher frequency. I have never felt so deep inside my body, and yet I feel completely detached from it as well, watching the two of us from high above. Teacher is right. Everything *is* understood, but the mind can't capture or analyze it.

Time passes, but I can't tell how much. In this darkened room, I cannot know if the sun has begun its journey through the sky above us. We are all journeying at this unknown hour.

When at last the vibrating ceases, I am wordless. There is no need for language. I withdraw my hands from under Guru's spine and the sensations begin to fade. My temperature slowly cools. As I have been trained, I move into the purple bathroom and once more wash my hands in cold water, so that I do not carry into my own system any of the energy of disease.

Guru Tam seems now to be truly asleep. Her temperature, too, has cooled, and her face is more relaxed. I feel spent, my legs so heavy I cannot imagine them carrying me across the patio to my room, let alone back down the mountain.

Kundanika appears in the doorway. She carries a large sheepskin, which she spreads on the floor beside the bed. "Sleep here for a bit," she urges, and my body is too exhausted to do anything except obey.

Gratefully, I sink to the floor, cushioned by the soft wool. My bones feel as if they might melt into the floor beneath. Kundanika covers me with a light quilt, redolent of sandalwood. I flash a grateful smile before collapsing into immediate and dreamless sleep.

Five nights I have slept in different beds, five mornings awakened in different places. As my eyes open in the darkened room, I cannot at first recall where I am, cannot even imagine where I might be. Kundanika enters the room as if the mere flick of my eyelashes had summoned her.

"Good morning," she greets me, then reports, "Sumati will be here in an hour." This morning she is dressed in a gold sari, the color of egg yolk.

"An hour? What time is it?" I grope for my watch and squint at its face. Ten thirty. I never sleep in like this. Suddenly I remember to lower my voice, hoping not to disturb the sleeping Guru. "Does that mean Carmen found Yoli and Daman?" I whisper.

"I believe everything is arranged," she answers cheerily, though I find the vagueness of her response maddening.

As I crawl to my feet, I see the bed beside me is empty. "What happened?" I ask Kundanika. *Please, Spirit, don't let me have killed the Guru.*

She is unperturbed. "Guru is having a good morning. She was up when the sun rose."

This seems scarcely possible to me, given her condition just hours earlier.

"When Guru has energy, she likes to take full advantage of it," Kundanika explains. "I believe she was swimming first thing."

"Perhaps she'd be better off to preserve her energy," I suggest, though I cannot imagine there is anyone who would presume to tell her what to do.

"Teacher will do what she is called to do," Kundanika confirms. "May I get you some breakfast?"

I should be too nervous to eat but, at her suggestion, I am suddenly aware of the enormity of my appetite. I do feel a current of excitement radiating from my belly to my fingertips, but nothing like the debilitating panic I had the night before. Now I wonder just who was healing whom in this morning's wee hours?

Kundanika disappears down the stairs, and I pad back to my room to shower. Under the flow of the water, I try to imagine what to wear to this crucial appointment. My choices seem dismal. Yoli always looks as if she's stepped out of a fashion magazine, and neither a sojourn in Baja nor her daughter's abduction are likely to get in the way of that. Daman fancies himself a stud, and dresses the part. In my worn T-shirts and shorts, I tend to appear more like an overgrown child.

At least I thought to wash my clothes yesterday. I don't have to be a dirty child. As I survey my wardrobe options, I find myself thinking that I should wear whatever might serve me best in jail. I choose my jeans, the only pair of long pants I brought with me to Baja, and button a long-sleeve shirt over my T. It cries out for an iron; I've never been one to pull off the rumpled look. I tell myself this protective covering is in case it's cold at night, but also, I don't want my flesh to be uncovered. Not in jail, and not in front of Daman and Yoli.

Downstairs, Kundanika has set a place outside on the patio. She invites me to sit before a plate of cornmeal pancakes ringed with fresh, ripe strawberries. A small pitcher of warm maple syrup waits beside the plate. I am conscious of savoring every bite, deeply tasting the flavors, exploring each texture with my tongue. I allow myself to take in the sky, the green scent of the garden. I'm struck with the awareness that when I leave this house today, I might never return. Although I never did have my conversation with Guru Tam, I feel that so much has happened to me in the short time I've been here.

Something catches my attention then, and I realize I can sense Sumati on her way. It isn't a sound or anything tangible I can describe, just a knowing. As I carry my empty plate into the kitchen, Kundanika and I exchange a look that verifies what I've intuited. We have no need to talk about it.

I walk through the house once more, noticing the exact shade of a drapery, studying the imagery in the art that is displayed. My sojourn in this house is a gift, I understand, and I want to receive it entirely. My breath stays calm.

By the time Sumati's Jeep pulls into the parking area in front of the house, I am already sitting out on the front terrace, letting the sun warm me through.

"Peace begets peace," I greet her.

"Peace returns peace." She seems unruffled about the events about to take place.

"How is Angel?" It's the first thing I want to know.

"She's spirited," Sumati says with a wry grimace. "Last night she told everyone the story of Mulan." *Mulan* is an animated Disney movie about a girl who disguises herself as a boy to become a soldier and save her people, but I wonder if Sumati would know that.

"That's one of her favorite movies." I can't help but smile, but I do add, "I hope she isn't a terrible problem for you."

"She's got a very pure heart," Sumati assures me. "It's just that she's been raised in such a different framework than our children. 'Why would a girl want to dress like a boy?' they wonder. They can't conceive of it."

I nod. I can only imagine.

"Are you ready?" She refocuses on the task at hand.

"Should I bring all my things with me?" I ask. I have already put my money, my passport, Angel's birth certificate, my cell phone and some simple toiletries into a small knapsack.

"I can drive you back here afterward," she answers. I can't tell if this means I will be coming back to stay or not; perhaps she doesn't know.

Before we leave, I go to thank Kundanika. There is not a moment when she hasn't been attuned to taking care of me.

"It is a blessing to serve Spirit," she responds, and presses her palms together at her heart center and bows her head.

I return the gesture. "I wish I could say goodbye to Guru Tam."

"Goodbye?" she repeats, her eyes narrow with curiosity. "There is no goodbye. We are forever united."

This idea delights and perplexes me. It fills me with hope and simultaneously with despair. I want to argue with it. I want to lose that argument. I want to sit and ponder her words, to find a way to take them into my heart, commit to them with the simple clarity the young woman has expressed. I want to learn what these words might mean for Angel and myself. But Sumati is already turning her Jeep around, ready to head down the mountain.

Sumati drives just as aggressively on the trip down as she had when she delivered me here yesterday. I grip the door and try not to look down as the Jeep clips around the curves. Still, I pepper her with questions.

"So Carmen found Yoli and Daman?"

"Evidently they took a room in the Hotel California," Sumati reports.

I wait for her to continue, but she adds nothing. "So what happened?" I nearly shriek. "What did she say? What did they say? Are they bringing the *Federales* with them?"

Sumati sighs. "Americans are so addicted to events. I think it must come from your movies. 'What happened? What happened?'" she mimics me. "As if events could reveal the truth of anything."

"Sumati, *please*. Just tell me what Carmen said."

"Because Carmen knows the owners of the hotel," Sumati dutifully recounts, "she asked them about the American visitors she'd seen yesterday. 'Yes,' they told her, the two were staying at the hotel. 'How awful,' they said, 'about their missing little girl.'"

I interrupt her with a snort. "Yeah, I'm sure Yoli's playing the role of grieving mother to the hilt!"

Sumati gives me a sharp look. "Maggie, if you have no compassion for your former partner, for your child's mother, if you cannot feel what she is feeling, even the Guru will not be able to help you."

"How can she help me anyway?" I say peevishly, "I never even got to really talk to her about it." Just a mile from Guru's house, and I am already lapsing back into my bad attitude. Maybe this is why some people don't mind never leaving the ashram.

Sumati shakes her head, as if confronted with a very slow learner. "Oh, Maggie. More is happening than you can see."

These were Guru Tam's exact words to me this morning. I still don't know what they mean.

"In your dealings with Yoli," Sumati continues, "remember, it is better to be kind than to be right."

I do a double take. I didn't tell her about Yoli's and my history, did I? But Sumati's admonishment makes sense. I suddenly understand that Yoli is acting so truculent because, whether she's aware of it or not, she feels guilty for leaving Angel with Lurlene. I'll have to get past her defensive barriers before I can hope she'll listen to me.

"Please go on," I request. I'm queasy with our shuddering descent, but the conversation braces me.

"Carmen talked her way up to their room," Sumati obliges, "knocked on the door and said she'd overheard them yesterday talking about the child. She said she could help them. Yoli was suspicious, thought she was just trying to cash in on the reward. Daman wanted her to bring them to Angel immediately, but Carmen insisted it had to be done a certain way."

"I bet that went over well," I interject.

"Daman apparently shouted that they were not going to bargain with criminals and cults," Sumati concurs. "But Carmen says Yoli shushed him—she just wants to get her daughter back. He seems to be more focused on vengeance. Carmen explained that to them that we are a religious community and would tolerate no violence or disruption during their visit.

"So," she concludes, "Carmen and Tina are picking them up and will bring them to our center at twelve thirty."

"Does Angel know they're coming?" I ask her. We're down the mountain now, hurtling over the desert road to this fateful moment. It seems like days have passed since I first made this journey, though it was only yesterday morning.

"We haven't told Angel," Sumati replies. "Whether she *knows* or not is another matter."

"Will I have time to see her before this meeting takes place?" My watch reads 12:05. I need to reassure my daughter that I love her no matter what, that I'll continue to fight for her if she's taken away from me.

"I don't think we should pull her out of lessons. Let her have a normal morning."

"What's normal?" I ask, and in that moment, we both have to laugh. I can see the buildings of the Light Beings' complex in the distance. It's hotter here on the desert floor.

"Sumati," I ask suddenly, "did you ever have children?"

"I never gave birth," she replies. "Though since we came to Baja I often feel that I have *many* children."

"Because you feel responsible for everyone?"

"That, and..." She hesitates. "Living in a community like this is not that much different than living in any family. People struggle to get along."

"Even Light Beings?" I tease, but my amazement is only partly put-on.

"Maggie, we're still human beings. We have all the faults, all the negative emotions, all the crazy thinking. We get competitive, jealous, depressed. Our egos make us feel separate from one another, and separate from Spirit. The only difference is that we share a practice that commits us to another path and gives us tools to manage ourselves."

So much for my romanticizing of the spiritual life. Then I blurt, "So, Sumati, were you ever in love?"

Something passes over her face, dimming its light. She does not have to speak a word for me to know all the love she contains has been pledged to Guru Tam. In my own chest I can feel the fullness of love in Sumati's heart, and the ragged longing that's been painstakingly submerged into duty. There is so much I want to ask her about this, but it's private, even sacred, not something on which I feel entitled to intrude.

Suddenly, we are screeching into the parking lot. We bounce to an inelegant stop beside the unfortunate Poo-poo Box. My attention switches abruptly to the task before me.

I wish I understood better what the task is, what Sumati imagines this meeting might accomplish. I wish I knew what to say, or even what to hope for.

Spirit, walk with me now. Help me to embrace whatever you place before me; help me to accept whatever happens as the best possible outcome for me and for Angel.

As we walk into the building, Sumati places her hand on my back, right at the level of my heart. I feel her energy flow into me. I know in my cells that I'm surrounded by light and protection. If only I can remember it.

Sumati leads me into a first floor-room in which I haven't yet been. Before one pale blue wall, a plush, comfortable chair sits before arched windows. Cushions are scattered on the floor in front of the chair. Seeing the cushions, I worry; I know Yoli's going to hate it if they make her sit on the floor. A bouquet of desert flowers has been gathered and fills a vase set on a low table next to the chair. White candles burn in sconces on the other three walls.

I wonder if the men at the gate will have been prepped

for the arrival of visitors. I almost smile imagining Daman's response to the reception I received the first time. But there is nothing really to smile about. If he behaves badly and is turned away, he will only return with the police. Now that he and Yoli know where to find me.

Have I been crazy to agree to this? Have I been lulled into a false sense of trust and safety that will make me lose my daughter for good? I breathe to quell this latest outbreak of doubt and fear. I try to recapture that utter sense of oneness I felt with the teacher in the early hours of the morning.

My watch reads twelve thirty. Amrita comes in with a pitcher of lemon ginger tea and several glasses. These she arrays beside the vase on the small table.

"Peace begets peace," she greets me. Her smile feels encompassing, as if she knows the difficulty I am about to face and wants to convey her support.

"Peace returns peace," I tell her gratefully.

Sumati bustles in again. "There's a bit of a delay," she informs me. "It seems your former partner's boyfriend tried to enter the complex with a concealed weapon, and there's a negotiation going on about it now."

"They frisked him?" I ask astonished. I conjure an image of the peaceful Light Beings in a scuffle with Daman. Would they use force to prevail or just energy?

"Jagadeep is Head of Security. Just because we do not live in the world doesn't mean we are ignorant of the ways of that world." Sumati frowns slightly at the flower arrangement, tugs here and there at a few stems. She moves the cushions around on the floor to form a circle and reorganizes the glasses and vase. Amrita bows her head and leaves the room.

"Are you nervous?" I ask Sumati. I'm surprised to see her fidgety. My own stomach is back to doing flip-flops.

"I feel a stir of anticipation," she admits, "but I trust that the outcome will be for the highest good."

She crosses over to where I stand and takes my hand. "Sit with me, Maggie." We both lower our bodies onto cushions. "Let's meditate on Angel. Let's see her surrounded by the most radiant light."

I close my eyes, turning my gaze inward and up until the point between my eyebrows begins to vibrate. I summon the image of my daughter, envision her surrounded by a golden halo, pulsing and luminous. I can feel my energy supported and magnified by Sumati's; the light around Angel grows more vibrant, as if she is protected by an impenetrable force field, and nothing will be able to harm her.

I'm startled by an uproar outside the door in the hallway; then Sumati and I stand as Jagadeep escorts a truculent Daman into the room. He's arguing, "You better not try to steal my gun, motherfucker."

Jagadeep never loses his cool as he replies evenly, "If you still want your weapon by the time you leave here, we will be happy to return it to you." Despite Daman's menace, the tall blue-robed man appears the stronger, because of his calm and focus.

A few steps behind, Amrita enters, followed by Tina, Yoli and Carmen. Except for the Light Beings, everyone's energy is jangled and frantic; I understand what Guru Tam means by "commotion."

Tina is apologizing, "Sumati, believe me, if I'd known this guy had a gun I never would have brought him here," while at nearly the same moment Daman, wiry and pugnacious, is confronting me, jabbing his index finger toward my face. "All right, you bitch. This trip is *over*. Give us the goddamn kid!"

Truth be told, I am about an inch taller than Daman, and perhaps half again his girth. Although I don't respond to his aggression, neither do I shrink from him. An inhalation draws me up to my full height and he, perhaps without realizing it, takes a couple of steps back. *He's a punk*, I think, *all attitude but no real courage.*

I ignore him and sit back down, in an effort to not get drawn into the hubbub. Instead, I try to really tune in to each person in the room. Tina is directly on my left, uncharacteristically subdued in all white—loose pants and a big gauzy shirt. I wonder if her wardrobe choice was influenced by her visit to the Light Beings. Beside her, Carmen is in a dress of deep tan that is almost indistinguishable from the hue of her skin. Around her neck is an amulet of bronze. Daman sports a calculated spray of blond stubble on his chin. His shiny suit is rumpled; his cologne invades the room.

Yoli is the furthest from me. Her appearance is the most surprising. Her hair is unstyled, a loose and uncontainable frizz that circles her scalp. She wears no makeup. Her eyes are red and puffy. She exhibits the slow unfocused movements of someone in shock, or someone heavily medicated. It is a stark contrast to the Yoli I've known for over a decade, the one who's always scrappy and ready to take on the world to get what she wants.

I take a deep breath and regard the visitors. "Peace begets peace," I greet them.

Carmen bends down to hug me. "Peace returns peace," she answers, the only one to do so. She must have picked this up yesterday. Tina raises one eyebrow, while Yoli barely seems to register my presence.

"Please sit." Sumati gestures toward the remaining cushions. "May I pour you some cold tea?"

Tina and Carmen accept the invitation and slide their bodies to the floor. Yoli looks uncertainly from them to Daman, while he says, "Let's cut the horseshit. We're here to get our kid and that's all we're doing."

I want to say, "How dare you refer to her as *'ours?'*" but I breathe more deeply instead.

To me, Daman barks, "You're lucky we don't have the Mexican police with us."

Carmen contradicts this. "It's not 'lucky' at all. The police are likely to take Angel into custody. The police will also investigate what happened to the child."

"*Nothing* happened to her," Daman insists.

Sumati says again, "Please sit." This time it does not sound like a request.

Awkward in her heeled sandals, Yoli makes her way to the floor, but Daman continues to stand. "I said we're not staying. Get the fuck up, Yolanda. Get the kid and let's go."

Yoli half-rises to her knees, uncertain what to do. I hate to hear anyone speak to her this way, but this is the kind of man she always chooses.

"I don't think you understand," Sumati counters. "We haven't made a determination about the little girl's fate. We're here in the hope of coming to a reasonable agreement that will best serve the child's interest."

"I don't think *you* understand," Daman threatens. "We're not here to negotiate with a bunch of rag heads. I understand the Mexican government is not too fond of having you here. This is *your* one chance not to be dragged into this for harboring a fugitive."

Yoli begins to weep. "Maggie, how could you do this? How could you steal my child and bring her to this cult in the middle of nowhere?"

"It's not a cult—" I begin, but Sumati interrupts me.

"There's nothing you can do to us." Sumati faces Daman calmly. "We are a spiritual community and we are protected by the Loving Spirit. There is a long history of spiritual institutions providing sanctuary to those who are endangered. And the child *is* endangered. I personally witnessed the bruises inflicted on this child while in your sister's care."

"I saw them too," Tina adds hotly.

"How do you know Maggie didn't put them there herself, to try to justify kidnapping?" Daman accuses.

I won't look at him; if I do I will tear him limb from limb. Instead I say to Yoli, "You know I could never do that. Besides, I hadn't even seen her for three weeks before her teacher called me in." My eyes probe her, trying to find a way in, trying to connect to the woman I know so well, who knows me. Is she still in there somewhere?

"That teacher is looking for a new job now. She violated state law, calling you instead of the police," Daman gloats.

"And if she had done that, Yoli," I say, still trying to reach her, "Angel would be locked up in McLaren Hall, and would you really want that?" L.A.'s juvenile justice facility is a notorious hellhole; Yoli herself had spent a couple of weeks there after one of her mother's worst binges.

"Maggie," Sumati reminds me softly, or perhaps she doesn't even speak, "remember your breath. Peace begets peace."

Does peace beget peace when you're dealing with crazy people? I want to ask her. *Evil people who've lost their souls?*

"We cannot produce the child," Sumati continues evenly, "until we've arrived at the truth about how she was injured, and have agreed upon a plan to insure that it will *never* happen again."

Just then there is a knock at the door. It's Dhwani, one of the teenagers who watches the younger children. He looks miserable, and when he sees me his face falls even further.

"Peace begets peace," he mumbles quickly. "Sumati, I...I need to talk to you for a moment."

Sumati rises and walks outside the room with him.

Daman uses this opportunity to continue his assault on me. "You fucking dyke, you're gonna pay for this, I promise you..."

Jagadeep quickly walks toward him, ready to restrain him if need be.

"Knock it off," Tina interrupts him. "You have no say in this."

"What, are you some fat dyke too?"

She jumps up. "Keep up the crap, and you and your girlfriend can walk your asses home through the desert."

Tina's willing to give as good as she gets. I can imagine her now with a gun in her hand, pulling the trigger without blinking.

Carmen is trying to subdue her when Sumati sticks her head back into the room.

"Maggie, will you step outside for a moment?" To the others she says, "We'll be right back."

"This better not be some fucking trick," Daman warns as I leave the room. "I found you once and I'll find you again."

In the hall, Sumati looks at me with a grave expression. "Maggie, Angel is gone."

"What do you mean, gone?" My knees threaten to give way.

"Dhwani says when he went to assemble the children after lunch, Angel wasn't with them. He sent Chhaya up to check her room, and her knapsack was gone. Daman and Yoli haven't been alone since they came on the land, so I know they don't have her. We're getting together teams right now to check all the rooms and all the buildings."

"No," I say sharply.

I need Sumati to stop talking so I can hear something. I close my eyes and breathe. "They won't find her," I insist.

It's eerie how the knowledge dawns on me, but once it does, it is irrefutable. I know it as clearly as if my daughter had told me herself. "I'm the only one who can find her." I know this too.

I'm watching a scene unfold in my head, like a dream, or a movie. "Angel saw Daman. She didn't see Yoli. It scared her. My daughter's gone to look for me," I say. "She's headed toward the mountain now to find me."

"Spirit save us!" Sumati exclaims. It is as close to unnerved as I have ever seen her. "That desert is no place for a child by herself!"

Chapter 11

"I'll go with you; we can take the Jeep," Sumati offers, but I insist on going alone. Angel must be completely freaking out to take off on her own this way. I've been stupid, asking her to put up with way too much, counting on her to handle things that even I've found challenging. Now I've got to find her and let her know she's safe. I'm already running to the parking lot as Sumati jogs behind me.

"But you don't know the desert," she argues as she sprints. For a large woman, she moves quickly. "There's the heat, there are snakes, and who knows who wandering about."

I wonder at her lapse of faith.

"But I know Angel." I call back over my shoulder. When we reach the parking lot, I'm more winded than she.

"Faith doesn't mean that some situations aren't dangerous,"

she answers my unvoiced thought. "We have faith, but we don't let people walk on the property with guns, and we don't think seven-year-olds should roam around the desert by themselves."

"Okay," I say, "but Yoli and Daman are going to tear this place apart if we both disappear right now. I need you to go in there and keep them from calling the cops." How she's going to pull this off I have no idea, but maybe she's still got a few tricks up her pale blue sleeve.

"I don't know," she says. "If I were you I might just as soon plead my case before a judge as try to talk sense into Daman. His energy is very dense. Do you know what his name means in Sanskrit?"

I don't really have time to play What's in a Name. My fingers are trembling as I unlock my car.

Despite my lack of response she answers, "It means 'one who controls.' He doesn't care about Angel, perhaps not even Yoli. He just wants to win."

"Why do you think I ended up here?" I say as I slide behind the wheel of the Poo-poo Box.

Miraculously, Sumati doesn't argue further. As I turn the key in the ignition and the car sputters to start, she pulls two bottles of water out of her Jeep, along with a small parcel about as big as my thumb wrapped in green rubber. "It's a snakebite kit. Do you know how to use it?" she asks as she pushes it and the water bottles into my lap through my open window.

I don't, but I'm already backing out of the spot as I nod my thanks; then I shift into drive and kick up a storm of dust as I head for the road. At first, my anxiety pushes me to speed as fast as I can, as if I had a destination, as if I knew exactly where to find my daughter.

Then I realize she could be anywhere. It's not a matter of getting someplace, but of figuring out where someplace might be. I force myself to breathe then, slow my pace, release my foot's heavy pressure on the accelerator. If I go too fast, I could end up passing right by her. I slow to a creep, and begin scanning as carefully as I can in every direction.

Surely I'll find Angel before I get to the mountain. She can't have been gone that long, and she won't get too far on her own. I try to instruct my mind to think as she might. Would she stay on the road where it's easier to walk, or move into the desert where she's less likely to be seen? Is she still wearing her borrowed Light Beings robe or did she change back into her own clothes? I peer as far into the distance as I can see, but there's no sign of my little girl.

I'm remembering a day three or so years ago. Angel was about four and a half when Yoli and I broke up. When Yoli moved out she took an apartment in one of Hollywood's seedier neighborhoods, and we worked out a custody plan that had Angel spending a few nights a week at each of our places. She wasn't at all happy with this arrangement, and kept asking me when she and Yoli could both come home. How could I explain to her that I'd never wanted either one of them to leave? I don't know exactly what Yoli was telling her, but evidently Angel wasn't satisfied. One afternoon, a couple of weeks after Yoli moved, I got a panicked call from her.

"Where's Angel?" she demanded.

It was a Wednesday, which meant it was Yoli's night to have her. This schedule was new and we both jealously guarded our time with Angel and scrupulously kept to the plan.

"What do you mean?" I barked. "You were supposed to pick her up from daycare today." My tone was, no doubt, accusatory.

"Yes, of course I did." She had that haughty tone she always takes on to defend herself. "But..." I could hear her struggle, fear competing with her reluctance to give any ground to me, to admit she'd lost control of the situation. Finally she crumbled. "Maggie, she's gone. I just went to the store for a minute and when I came back, the apartment was empty. I just hoped that... somehow...you'd come and gotten her."

Then she began to wail as her denial gave way. "Oh, God, she's gone, my baby's out there by herself in this neighborhood. Oh, Jesus, what if she's not by herself..."

"Yoli. *Yoli*, stay calm." I tried to make my voice so focused it would penetrate her rising panic. "I'm on my way over there. Wait for me. We'll find her."

And we did. Angel had decided to register her displeasure

with the choices Yoli and I had made by running away. She'd packed her little overnight bag with DogBear, Yoli's favorite pair of sunglasses, a set of bangle bracelets she'd gotten for her birthday from Yoli's bass player, and a couple of boxes of animal crackers. Resourceful, she'd climbed up on a kitchen chair to undo the lock on the apartment door. Our daughter had made it as far as the bus stop at the end of the street where, remarkably, a Salvadoran gangbanger with tattoos on his knuckles was sitting next to her on the wooden bench. His hands were folded respectfully in his lap, and he was trying with his limited English to find out where our daughter lived. Yoli wanted to rip his face off, but I believed him when he said he was just trying to keep her safe, and gave him twenty bucks.

That day we promised we would always listen to her when she didn't like something and she promised she wouldn't run away again. But of course, we couldn't redress her most basic grievance: that she wanted her two mothers to live together once more. And today, neither of us was there to listen to her. Today she was not even trying to teach us a lesson; she was just trying protect herself.

It's another cloudless day, the sun beating down strongly. I'm much too hot in my jeans, my long-sleeved shirt. I hope Angel is still in her Light Beings gown; at least her head will be covered. She could get heat stroke out here unprotected. Once in a while, I catch a little glimpse of color in my peripheral vision. I stop then to closely scrutinize the variegated greens and browns of cacti and brush off to the side of the road. But the flash of yellow or bright pink or lavender turns out to be a desert blossom, wilting in the afternoon sun. An occasional lizard or jackrabbit darts across the road in front of me, and desultory insects weave through the thick air, but there is no other sign of life. Where in the world has my daughter gone?

I think about Sumati's comment, ...*who knows who wandering about*. Has someone else found my girl first? A chill travels through me, despite the blazing sun.

It takes about fifteen minutes to reach the base of the mountain, where the road begins to wind upward. I wonder if I've driven too fast; did I somehow miss her? I'm torn about what to do next; it seems impossible she would have gotten so far already on foot. Yet if somehow she has begun to climb, this territory will be more dangerous to her.

I decide to park and walk back a little way down the road before beginning the ascent. I'll be able to see things walking that I might have missed as I drove by. And I can call for her. Maybe she would hide from any car at this point, but will come when she hears my voice.

"Angel," I cry out. My voice sounds frayed, ragged in the desert wind. "Angel, it's me, Maggiemama."

Every ten paces or so, I call again. I wonder if I should leave the road, venture into the desert. But I don't know this terrain. I don't want to lose time wandering in a direction opposite the one my daughter might have taken.

Only now do I start to register the significance of Sumati's gift. A snakebite kit means there are snakes. My daughter is not afraid of snakes; she thinks they're cute. Last year she got all excited when her teacher brought in a California King snake for the class to study. She was enthusiastic right up until the day they watched it swallow a live mouse whole. But she still might be more fascinated than scared if she came upon one. Angel hasn't worn her athletic shoes since I bought her sandals in Ensenada. How can I expect her to know to wear close-toed shoes when she goes walking in the desert? She's a little girl who grew up in the city. What does she know about deserts?

Spirit, send your protection to my little girl. I don't care what you do with me—send me to jail, take away my parental rights. Just please don't let her get hurt out here.

It's all taking too much time. The longer she's out here by herself, the more likely that something will happen to her. Still calling her name along the way, I hurry back to my car. The heat on the desert floor is blistering. How long could one survive it without shelter? My mouth, my throat are parched from the dry air. The back of my shirt is drenched.

I drop into the passenger seat and unscrew the cap on one of the water bottles as I begin to steer the Poo-poo Box up the mountain. The transmission whines in protest. *Come on, Spirit, don't let this shitbox die on me now.*

Most of the road is narrow with a steep overhang. If she's on it, there's no real place to hide. If she's fallen over… No, I'm not going to give any power to that thought.

It's almost impossible to go slow without the transmission balking. I'm trying to steer the narrow passage and look for Angel at the same time. Every few seconds I yell her name out the window like a crazy person. My mouth fills with the dust kicked up by my tires. This is not working.

About half a mile up there is a turnout, scarcely bigger than a car width, but I pull into it and stop the Caprice. I'm on the side overlooking where I've come from, and I think maybe I will see her from up above. I scan the road back to the Light Beings' complex, search the desert surrounding this road, but I see nothing moving or stationary that looks like my little girl.

Then all of a sudden I think: What if my intuition was wrong? What if she didn't go toward the mountain at all? What if she tried to walk herself back to the highway? Where would she go? This is almost more than I can stand, the thought of her walking on that busy road, or being hauled into a car by some stranger with who knows what on his mind.

Then it is as if I feel Guru Tam's hands on my shoulders, as if she were standing behind me. I hear her voice—nothing to do with the ears—and it says, *If there is something you wish to find, don't run around after it. Use your energy. Use your power. Use your electromagnetic field. Draw it to you.*

This is part of the vast body of teachings, something I've heard before in meditation sessions. I used to rely on it as my "marketing strategy" for my massage business. I never advertised or went after clients, but somehow they found me. Now, though, I feel the deeper wisdom of the suggestion. I cannot possibly spread my energy across this expanse of land, unknown to me, to arrive precisely at the spot where Angel might be. But my daughter is looking for me; if I consolidate my energy and focus, perhaps I can draw her to where I am.

I perch on the edge of the car's hood. The sun seems to swoop down to blaze over me, perhaps to make a spotlight in which I'll be visible. I close my eyes to focus inside, begin to draw my breath more slowly and deeply into my belly. At the point between my eyebrows, I summon an image of Angel, then a vision of the two of us together. In my mind I call to her, "Angel, don't be scared, honey. I'm right here. Come to me, Mrs. Havisham."

I sit in concentration for a long time. With each breath, I expect Angel to appear, right then, as if by magic. I have to chide myself. Even if Angel is drawn by my summons, it may take her some time to get where I am. But I'm impatient for results, and this causes me to doubt my strategy.

Now I don't know what to do. Panic begins to rise, crowding out my efforts to center myself. I can't go back to Yoli and Daman and say that Angel's gone. I can't abandon my efforts to locate her. A glance at my watch tells me I've already been gone more than an hour. I have no idea how long Sumati will be able to keep them sitting there before they explode.

Then I decide to stop worrying about Daman and Yoli. They will do whatever it is they will do. My concern right now has to be on Angel's immediate well being, on finding her and making sure she's safe. Maybe it would be best if they did call the police, who could probably bring more resources to the task of finding her.

From my vantage overlooking the Light Beings' complex I can see a car travel up the road from the highway to the complex. I'm too far away to be able to tell much more about it. There are no flashing red lights, but who knows how the Mexican police conduct their business?

Maybe someone else has found Angel and is bringing her back. I let the hope of it fill me for a moment, but then I know that's not right. Angel is not going to let herself be found until she's ready. However scared she might be, her resolve is stronger. Of this I feel certain.

Then what is the best thing for me to do? The answer that reverberates in me is "Keeping calling her. Keep sending out signals."

I never really know about that inner voice—when it's real and when it's bogus. How I envy Kundanika her simple certainty, her absolute faith, while my thoughts are an endless spiral of questions, belief always besieged by doubt. *Oh, Spirit, deliver me from the gyrations of my crazy monkey mind.*

I hop down from the hood to stretch my legs. Recalling some of the exercises from the other morning, I let my spine elongate to stretch out the kinks. Circling my head brings relief to the tightness in my neck. I take another long gulp of water, too warm to be refreshing, but still necessary in the arid heat.

It is then that my eyes catch sight of a flutter of pale blue in the dense brush of the steep incline below me. "Angel!" I scream, and hear the echo of my terror in the air. Without a thought, I lower myself over the edge as my feet scrabble for a toehold on the rocks that seem to crumble with the slightest pressure. I am grateful to be in jeans as my knees scrape against the mountainside.

The rock is searing under my hands, and the muscles in my shoulders feel like they're tearing. I don't know how long I'll have the strength to hold my own weight. And if I drop, how far will I fall? Will I die on impact, or will I merely shatter my legs, leaving me to contemplate my fatal impulsiveness as I die of starvation or heatstroke. And who, then, will find Angel?

Spirit, I pray. I can feel my fingers slipping from their hold on the rock. *Catch me!* And I turn my body around before I loosen my grip and let myself fall. Twenty or so feet below, my feet catch a ledge. Operating on pure instinct, I bend my knees and sit, which slows my downward slide. I grasp stinging handfuls of brush, and somehow hold on. I scramble to press my back against the solid face of the mountain as I slow my shuddering breath.

I am only ten feet or so from the pale blue cloth. I gingerly edge my way over to it, fearful of triggering a rockslide that will carry me down and down. When I reach it, I squat down to examine it. It is the fabric of the head cloth worn by Light Beings' women. But is it Angel's? Couldn't it have been lost by accident on one of Sumati's reckless drives up the mountain?

As my fingers stretch to pluck it from the brush, I hear the rattle. It is only then I see the snake, coiled, just inches from the cloth, as if it is the guardian of this fabric. Sumati's snakebite kit, like my water, is on the front seat of the Poo-poo Box. Did this snake kill Angel, I wonder? Is she lying somewhere in the brush, dying of its poison? If that's the case, I will gladly surrender myself too.

I regard the serpent, who looks back at me. "Oh, Snake," I say, as I might once have addressed Spirit. "Did you strike a little girl today? It couldn't have been too long ago. She probably wanted to be your friend and scared you."

It has to be the effects of the intense sun. My brain must be cooking in the heat, because I could swear the snake is answering me. "I did not strike her, though I did see her on the trail."

"There's a trail?" I ask pathetically, thinking of my drop from above. "Where is she now?"

The rattler answers neither of these questions, but he no longer seems interested to attack either. Instead he coils himself to face in another direction and slithers through the brush and out of sight. I begin to have such an odd sensation, as if my limbs are turning to liquid, or as if the energy of my molecules is speeding up and my form is in the process of dissolving. It's not scary or frantic though; it's like accelerating in slow motion, and everything peripheral blurs while I become increasingly still. As the phenomenon persists, my hearing seems to grow more acute; I am aware of the sounds of far-off birds, the soft tread of fire ants in the dust. I hear multiple tones in the wind, a rabbit masticating a leaf.

It is then I hear the music of voices above me on the road, a giddy piccolo and a calm cello. The words are not intelligible to me; they might be in another language altogether, the language of insects or flowers or light. I can hear the crunch of feet upon gravel, two pairs with different gaits, an odd syncopation. It is all I can do not to run toward these sounds, but I don't know how to get myself back to the road. I can't imagine being able to make the climb.

Once the voices seem close enough to be perceived by normal hearing, I call upward, "Hello! Hello! Is someone there?"

From above, I see two heads peek over: the first belonging to Angel and the second to Guru Tam. In the moment, I am so relieved to find my girl that I don't even register marvel at the fact that the Guru is upright, let alone walking down the mountain road.

"Maggiemama!" my daughter squeals, then cocks her head like a cocker spaniel. "What are you doing down there?"

"I saw your headscarf, and I thought…"

"I came looking for you!" My girl is proud of herself.

But the anxiety of the last two hours spills over, and instead of rewarding her initiative, I find myself scolding, "And I came looking for you. Sweetheart, I was so worried! Didn't you promise me you'd never run away again?"

"I didn't run away." Angel's defense is vehement. "I had to find you. Daman's here!"

"I know, honey, your mommy is too."

"Mommy?" Her face lights up, "Where is she? I want to see her now!"

"Maggie, do you need help?" Guru Tam speaks finally. Her voice sounds strong.

"Yes, Guru-Ji," I answer her. "When I saw this scarf, I'm afraid I launched myself down here without thinking about how I was going to get back up."

The Teacher chuckles. "You do that a lot, don't you?" Then she explains, "About twenty yards to your right, there's a trail that will bring you back to the road."

"Okay," I manage weakly, "thanks." She must think I'm a complete doofus.

Keeping a watchful eye out for snakes, I pick my way across the brush and rocky terrain until I find the trail. In the meantime, I hear Angel say to Guru, "My mommy has the most beautiful voice you've ever heard…"

The trail itself is steep; did my girl climb this by herself? Bruised and banged-up as my legs are from their earlier descent, overheated as I am in the afternoon sun, it's an effort for me to make it back to the road. Once there, I kneel at the side of the road to take my girl in my arms, inhaling the damp sweat of her neck, feeling her heart beat loud and strong against mine.

"Maggie, I saw Daman, and I was scared." Angel is spilling over with need to tell her story. "But I couldn't find you, and it was a long walk, and I didn't know where I was. I took my scarf off 'cuz I was hot, but then the wind blew it away. I tried to go get it, but I didn't know how."

I clasp her to me again, once more hug her hard. "Honey, I'm so sorry. You must have been scared."

"But then I found this lady, and she told me not to be afraid," my daughter says. "And then I wasn't."

The halo I envisioned surrounding her earlier—I see it now. She's beaming, radiant with light.

I study Guru Tam then. She bears little resemblance to the wizened woman in the bed from last night. Although her body is thin as air, her eyes are alight, her bearing erect. Her facial muscles are no longer creased with pain, but relaxed. Her white robes billow in the afternoon winds that have begun to blow. A palpable field of energy seems to surround her, extending several feet in every direction.

"Guru-Ji." I bow my head to her. "You're feeling better then?"

"You are an excellent channel for Spirit," she says.

We walk up the road until we reach the spot where I left my car. I offer them water from the second bottle Sumati provided; Guru Tam shakes her head but Angel drinks greedily.

"We saw a big snake!" my daughter says as she finishes her last swallow, eyes round. "It was right in front of us, and it hissed like it was mad, but then she sang to it." She pointed to the Guru. "And it just lied there. Then she taught me Snake language." My daughter begins once more to make the sounds I heard before at a distance.

My daughter's level of comfort with Guru Tam is something to behold, as if they had known each other for a very long time. Angel is ordinarily cautious with new people, slow to let go of her reserve. Her body language now, though—face open, smile easy, torso loose and even seeming to bend in Guru's direction—tells me she is completely relaxed with Teacher.

Although the sun is still bright in the sky, already the afternoon has started to shift toward its ending. My watch tells me it is nearly three thirty. "We should get back."

"I wanna see Mommy!"

Guru looks at my daughter. "Are you ready now?"

Soberly, Angel bobs her head up and down, a gesture with more resolve than enthusiasm. She's clinging to my side.

Guru Tam persists. "And do you remember what we talked about?"

"Spirit is always with me when I tell the truth," my daughter recites.

I gaze down at the top of her head, and wonder to what degree she knows what these words mean, if they have any meaning for her at all. When she was little, she used to mimic whatever song she heard on the radio. It was quite an experience to quiz a four-year-old about her understanding of "Oops, I Did It Again."

Then, as if defending me, she adds, "Maggie always told me to never lie."

Guru reaches out a bony hand and my girl takes it. With exquisite kindness, the older woman says, "Sometimes, dear child, there's a difference between not lying and telling the truth. We can hide and say nothing, and we have not lied, but neither have we been powerful. When we speak the truth we shine our light into the world, and this world is brighter for it."

I have a wave of fear of what Angel may not have been saying. That she doesn't want to be with me? That she's furious that I've disrupted her life by dragging her to Mexico? That she's been hurt in ways the bruising doesn't begin to reveal?

Angel looks at me then, her eyes clear and full of wisdom. "Don't worry, Maggie," she tells me, as if she has read the content of my heart. Her voice is so loving it brings tears to my eyes. "Please don't worry. It's Mommy I have to tell something to."

Angel sits on Guru Tam's lap as I drive them back down the mountain in the Poo-poo Box. At first I worry whether the Guru has the strength to hold her, but she seems untroubled. I wonder when was the last time she rode in a car, or when last she visited the Light Beings' complex.

"It's been over a year since I left my house," she tells me.

I am becoming strangely accustomed to my thoughts being read, even finding a certain comfort in it.

"I made a visit to India in 2002, and when I came back my illness worsened. There were many who wanted me to stay in India, but I felt I could be of better service here."

"In school, Sumiko showed us India on the big globe," Angel informs us.

This time the drive seems to go very quickly, though I do not speed, taking care not to jostle the Guru any more than I can help. My fingers are icy again as I near the Center. Everything is going to change now, though I don't know in what ways.

Since last Wednesday I have had but one focus: to get here and talk to Guru Tam. Looking back, it seems crazy; I should have been thinking more long term, I should have had a plan. Now I am headed back to face my accusers, and it is likely that Yoli and Daman will take Angel from me, and I will be going to jail.

Guru taps me lightly on the arm. "Don't make a home in your fear," she tells me. "It is like building your house on quicksand. Build instead on the mountaintop of faith."

There is nothing to do but surrender, of course. "Surrender," Guru Tam once wrote, "is accepting that things are exactly as they are." Surrender to the unknowingness of what will occur, surrender to the path Spirit intends for me.

I drive into the parking lot, stop once more beside Sumati's Jeep. The crunch of gravel echoes the grating of my nerves. *Spirit, allow me to serve you; you know much better than I the order and balance of this world.*

As we exit the car, Angel comes to take my hand. "I'm scared too," she confides. Her skin is warm in my cold palm. *Thank you, Spirit, for bringing her back safe. Now I will accept whatever you have in store for me.*

"It's okay, Mrs. Havisham," I promise her. "I love you more than this whole world."

We keep hold of each other's hand as we walk into the building.

Chapter 12

No one is in the room I last walked out of more than two hours ago, and the pale blue walls are not revealing any secrets of what might have transpired in my absence. The candles that had burned in the wall sconces have been snuffed out; the refreshments have been cleared away. The pillows have been neatly stacked against one wall.

Angel says, "Mommy was here! I can smell her perfume." Dior's Poison, an aroma of which I've never been fond. I wonder that my girl can distinguish it from Daman's Homme, which still manages to override the faint residue of incense. Then she adds, "I knew she'd come to find us!"

"Let's go find her," I say, still holding tight to her hand. I pray my girl won't have any further disappointment when she sees Yoli. Guru Tam has disappeared; I'm not sure when she stopped following us.

We go down the hall to Sumati's office, now crowded with people. Sumati is at her desk, Carmen and Tina are sprawled in chairs, and Charlie paces nervously before the windows. His hair is bristle-short, bleached blond to offset his salon tan. For the decade I've known him he's been too thin. In a far corner sits another woman I don't recognize, wearing pressed khakis with polished tassel loafers and a pale green polo shirt.

When they see us, everyone jumps up at once, except Sumati and the woman I don't know. The others crowd around Angel and myself, burbling their relief.

"It's about damn time." Tina's gruffness masks her concern. Then she looks at me, "Honey, you look like something the cat dragged *out!* Are you all right?"

"I'm fine," I insist, although I can imagine my appearance tells a different story.

"You were gone so long. I wanted to come look for both of you," Carmen chimes in.

Charlie trumps their expressions of concern. "Dahling, *I've* been worried sick about you for the last week!" he pronounces in his best Tallulah Bankhead, as he wraps his arms around me.

Angel is hugging each one of them like long-lost friends. She shrieks with delight at Charlie's presence; he's always been a favorite of hers. Sometimes he plays dress-up with her, indulging his drag fantasies.

"You better appreciate it, sugar," he teases her. "This desert air is *murder* on my youthful complexion."

In the midst of the clamor, it is Sumati's eyes I seek out, drawn to her calm, steady energy. We share an acknowledging look.

"I trust you found what you were searching for," she says and smiles.

She is not just talking about Angel, but about Guru as well. I shouldn't be surprised that she's aware of Guru Tam's interaction with Angel. I just nod. "And…anything here I should know about?"

Tina and Charlie look like they are dying to tell the story but both incline their heads meaningfully toward Angel and keep silent.

Sumati explains, "Daman is currently with Jagadeep and Pramesh. And Yoli is upstairs in Bhanupriya's room." She pauses before adding, "Everyone needed a bit of a time-out."

I can only imagine.

"I want to see Mommy!" Angel implores, tugging on my hand. "I need to talk to her."

Sumati tells her, "You will definitely see your Mommy in just a little while. In the meantime, the grown-ups need to talk. You missed lunch, didn't you, Angel? Shall I get Amrita to make you something to eat?"

Angel looks at me uncertainly. I tell her, "Angel, we won't decide anything until you've had a chance to say what you need to say. But why not go with Amrita to have a bite?"

To all of us she says, "You won't leave?"

"Not without you," I promise.

As if on cue, Amrita arrives and escorts my daughter down the hall in the direction of the kitchen. I look wistfully after them; it's occurring to me that I missed lunch as well.

"Daman was convinced that you'd given them the slip and that we'd all helped you," Tina bursts out the minute the door is closed. "He went ballistic! That guy is one scary piece of work."

"It's a good thing they took away his gun," Carmen affirms.

"That's why Angel ran away," I explain. "She saw him when he was separated from Yoli, and she just took off."

"Then, when your friend Charlie here showed up with an attorney—" Tina gestures to the woman in the corner, "—hell really broke loose. Daman managed to convince Yoli that you were trying to take away her custody."

"Aided by the photographic evidence that showed the extent of Angel's injury!" Charlie waves a sheaf of color snapshots in my direction. "By the way, Maggie, meet Caroline McGrievy, Esquire."

The trim woman with the ash-blond bob looks like she

doesn't quite know how she got dragged into all this drama, though if she's known Charlie very long you'd think she'd be used to it.

"I hope Charlie explained to you that I cannot represent your case while you remain in Mexico," she says in a crisp though not unkind tone. "But he thought my presence here might be...persuasive. And I am also prepared to talk to you about your options should you return to the United States."

"What did Yoli say when she saw the pictures?" I ask.

"Daman just kept yelling, 'She's trying to steal your daughter,'" says Carmen. "I don't think Yoli had a chance to take it in."

"Daman and Yoli had a shit fit," Tina continues, then quickly glances at Sumati to see how the profanity registers. "They *both* had to be restrained. It took those two big guys to drag Daman out of here."

It's all too much for me. Angel running away. Police and the threat of jail. My ex-lover needing to be restrained. My knees threaten to give way.

"Give her a minute to breathe!" Carmen insists fiercely, stepping between me and the others. "Maggie's already been through so much!" She's assigned herself the role of my protector; she looks ready to take up the sword on my behalf.

All of a sudden I am longing for the peaceful atmosphere of the Guru's home up on the mountain. As much as I appreciate the efforts of every person in this room, their combined energy is hard for me to take. I feel like a circuit being overloaded, my nerve ends beginning to smoke.

To Sumati, I ask, "Do you think I could take a shower before the festivities resume?"

"Go on upstairs to my room and take some time to gather yourself," she suggests. "We're not ready to reconvene anyway. I'll send Amrita up with a tray for you."

I nod gratefully. To Tina and Carmen, I say, "If you want to go back to town, that's okay. I can deal with getting Yoli and Daman back to where they need to go. I'm sure this is already way more than you bargained for."

"Are you kidding?" says Tina. "You couldn't pry me out of here with a crowbar."

"I'm not going anywhere until I know you and Angel are going to be okay," Carmen insists.

She might be in for a long siege, I think, but I just nod with what I hope will seem like gratitude.

Climbing the stairs, I can already feel the stiffening of my muscles from my tumble down the mountainside. I feel exhausted and wrung out, not up for the confrontation to come. *Spirit, help me to find my reserves. Allow my energy to become one with yours, so that I have the strength to face whatever comes.*

Once upstairs in the shower, I am soothed by the warm water running over my sticky flesh. Even though it stings my scrapes and sunburn, I am grateful that it washes away the energy of panic and stress, the dryness of the desert. I let the spray massage my scalp, my shoulders, drown out the snippets of today's conversations that want to replay themselves in my head. I know I shouldn't waste water but I crave its reviving pulse. I brush my teeth under the shower too, then emerge from the stall with my big body wrapped in the towel Sumati left for me. I inspect the impressive jagged, raw scratches on my arms, the back of my legs. By tomorrow I will have my own set of bruises.

It's unfortunate I will have to put on the same filthy clothes I just took off, but at least my skin feels clean. I decide to risk a trip down the hall wrapped in a towel in order to dress in Sumati's room.

Just as I go to pull open the bathroom door, someone pushes it from the other side, nearly knocking me over. It's Yoli.

"'Scuse me," she says, not even looking to see who it is. When she lifts her eyes she gasps slightly. She appears to be as startled as I feel, being face-to-face with her, naked but for a strip of terrycloth wrapped breasts to thighs. Still, I meet her eyes and, when I do, my mouth begins to babble.

"Yoli, I'm sorry this has turned into such a mess." My eyes flood with unexpected tears, so profoundly do I want her to believe me. "You know I would never use Angel to hurt you, don't you?"

"Where is she?" Yoli demands, without addressing my words. "Where's my girl?"

"She's downstairs getting something to eat. You'll see her in a little bit."

"I can't take any more of this bullshit, Maggie, if this is another trick…"

She reaches to grasp my shoulders, as if to shake me, but when her hands come in contact with my skin she inhales sharply and drops her arms back to her sides, as if the touch had burned.

"Yoli, it's never been a trick. I called and left you a message before we even drove out of L.A. because I did not want you to have one minute of worry that something terrible had happened to her. I called you from the road. I even let Angel leave you a message." Why do I so badly need her to approve my actions? "Look, Lurlene hurt her and I couldn't stand by for that, but I did everything I could to make it easy on you. Including *not* going to the police."

She tosses her head, one more gesture so familiar to me. "Yeah, well, excuse me for not being grateful that you 'helped me out' by kidnapping my daughter."

"She's my daughter too!" It sounds even louder echoing off the bathroom tile. "And, Yoli, you weren't there! What would you have done if I'd left her with someone you didn't know and she showed up to school with bruises all over her?"

Yoli sighs, shaking her head. "I don't know, Maggie. But I sure as hell wouldn't have done *this*."

"Oh, Yoli…" My tone is half-beseeching, half-lament.

Her hand swipes at the air, wiping me away. "Maggie, I can't…" Her words barely a whisper, full of exhaustion, defeat. And resentment, as if I'd done this to her.

She turns and departs from the bathroom. There's nothing I can do but I let her go.

Amrita has left a tray for me in Sumati's room with a sandwich of tahini and sprouts and fresh tomatoes from the garden on toasted rye bread. Although I am ravenous, I can manage to eat only a few bites, so nervous am I about the impending showdown. I dress hurriedly, my clothes still damp with my sweat.

I am shaken by my encounter with Yoli. In the last few years I've had to let go of so much of what used to be between us, but even with my bitterness about her choices, I'd always imagined there was some elemental bond, some irreducible connection or, if nothing else, the recognition of our shared commitment to Angel. Now even this seems to have eroded.

Kundanika's words from this morning return to me. *We are forever united.* Can that still be true if only one of us believes it? And what if that one loses faith?

Sumati comes for me then. She makes no announcement, just stands in the doorway to her room, a rooted presence. I simply nod and stand, then follow her down the stairs, heading back to the room where we met this morning. Before we enter, she pauses before a window that faces the courtyard. Drawing back the curtains, she gestures for me to look.

Outside, in the late afternoon, what seems like the entire Light Beings community has gathered on the lawn. I see Bhanupriya and Haroon, along with Angel's friend Prem; I spot the crabby man from the gate the day I first arrived. I notice Dhwani and Chhaya, Amrita, and the woman who played guitar and others whose faces are familiar to me, although I have not learned their names. They are seated in a great circle on the lawn, their palms raised skyward.

I raise my eyebrows in question to Sumati.

"A prayer circle," she tells me, "for your family."

My family. The resonance of this phrase takes me by surprise. My first impulse is to resist it, yet it seems undeniably true. My eyes fill along with my heart. I have no words for my gratitude. I can only press my palms together and bow.

"You've taught me something, Maggie," Sumati adds. "I see that I have held the community too close. It is not enough to benefit ourselves. We need to interact more with the world. There is important work to do. That is what Guru wanted me to understand when she instructed me to invite you in."

"I was surprised when you brought Tina and Carmen up to the house last night." It's an inadequate response to the import of what she's disclosed, but it's the first thing that popped into my head.

"My Teacher instructed me to do whatever was necessary to help you resolve your dilemma," she says simply.

I will ponder all of this later, I promise myself, but now Sumati is leading me back downstairs and into the meeting room. Once more candles flicker against the wall; pillows are arranged in a circle on the floor, gathered before the empty chair. Tina and Carmen are perched on two of the cushions, Charlie and the lawyer, Caroline, on two more. Between the two groups is an empty pillow, and Sumati indicates for me to sit there. Sumati then leaves the room.

I look at my friends. Also part of *my family*. I can't stop my tears from brimming over. "You guys," I say, ineloquently. "No matter what happens, I hope you will always know how much your support means to me."

"Talk about support." Tina points to the window, through which the sound of chanting filters. "Did Sumati tell you what's going on out there?"

"It's amazing," Carmen whispers. "I can feel the power being generated in the atmosphere." Seated next to me, she reaches over to squeeze my hand.

"I feel the power," Charlie quips from my other side, "but I can no longer feel my legs." He shifts uncomfortably from buttock to buttock on his pillow. Catching sight of my face, he camps, "Now, now, don't make Mama's mascara run," to mask his own emotion. To his right, Caroline's smile is a little tight.

Sumati returns then, leading a reluctant Yoli, who sulks into the room, her lower lip in full pout. I've never seen her so devoid of spark, so beaten down. My family. My family is in trouble. *You didn't believe in yourself enough to fight for it, for your love, your family.* Sumati's words replay themselves in my mind. I never before admitted I had one.

Sumati leads her to a pillow directly across from mine. I try to smile apologetically; I know she hates sitting on the floor, but Yoli avoids my eyes.

The door opens again and, Daman enters, flanked by Jagadeep and Pramesh. He hasn't lost his swagger or his sneer. He struts beside Yoli, and refuses to sit. The two Light Beings stand just behind him, waiting.

Then the door opens once more, and the two men press Daman to his knees as Guru Tam enters with Angel beside her. My daughter has shed the Light Beings robe, and wears a pair of the long shorts and an embroidered shirt I bought her in Ensenada. My girl looks nervous, yet her expression seems strangely grown up, her bearing full of purpose as she walks next to the Teacher.

"My baby!" Yoli cries and opens her arms.

My daughter's face opens and she rushes toward Yoli, who takes her in a full embrace. Angel gives herself over to it, but when Daman moves close, she reacts as if suddenly jolted in shock, and backs away. Daman glowers in her direction. Yoli doesn't understand what's just happened.

"What in God's name did you do?" Yoli accuses me from across the circle. "Did you turn her against her own mother?"

"Yolanda," Guru Tam speaks her name. It has the effect of silencing Yoli, as if the Teacher had turned off a switch.

Then Guru proceeds to the top of the circle, with Angel still at her side. She lowers herself carefully into the chair, as if trying not to break something delicate. She seems considerably more tired than when I saw her on the mountain earlier; some of the pain lines in her forehead have deepened. Her breathing seems effortful. I wonder if she has been "filtering" our energy, and I fear what this might do to her fragile state of health.

Still, an unmistakable force field surrounds her. The Teacher's voice is clear and steady, her accent lilting as, pressing her palms together, she begins to pray, "Spirit, You are the source of all. You provide us with this world of matter in which we dwell for a time; You provide us the infinite world in which we dwell for all eternity. You are the container that holds us and You are the contained; You live inside each of us. There is nothing that exists that is not You."

I cast a sideways glance around the circle. Carmen is deep in prayer, her copper skin burnished as if lit from within. Tina has bowed her head and seems to be listening, respectful if not convinced. Even Charlie seems rapt, with curiosity if nothing else. His lawyer friend looks a bit taken aback but doesn't appear ready to bolt. Yoli has clasped her hands together and is resting her forehead against them. The shaking of her shoulders lets me know she's weeping. I try to project my energy across the circle, to be of comfort to her. I don't know if she receives it or not, but I do not feel her rebuff me.

Daman has his head down; I can't read his expression.

Guru continues, "Every day You give us the miracle of deciding who we are going to be in this lifetime, what karma we are going to accrue. At any moment we can remember that we are not separate from You, that we are part of Your essence, the Infinite Consciousness that is unborn and undying. At any moment, we may turn around our fate, make ourselves anew. This is but one of the ways in which you bless us, Oh Loving Spirit."

Sumati has picked up a silver bell; she strikes it with a small wand and a clear note chimes throughout the room, one pure resonant tone.

Guru Tam asks then, "Daman, is there anything you wish to tell us at this time?" Her voice is oddly kind.

His eyes snap to attention. "The same thing I've been saying since we got here. Give me the kid and my gun and let us get the fuck outta here," he growls.

Jagadeep and Pramesh look to the Guru, ready to move to her defense, but she shakes her head to deter their intervention.

"Angel, then it's your turn." She turns to look deep into my daughter's eyes. "Remember what I told you?"

I remember her words to my girl earlier, *"When we speak the truth we shine our light into the world, and this world is brighter for it."* And indeed, I see a clear light emanating all around Angel as she takes two tentative steps into the center of the circle, and turns to face Yoli.

"Mommy..." she begins.

"You better remember what *I* told you," Daman warns, his face darkening.

My girl hesitates, looks back at Guru Tam.

"Don't be afraid." The Teacher smiles at her. "There is never anything to fear from Truth."

"What is it, baby?" Yoli looks more frightened than I've ever seen her.

I can see Angel's lower lip tremble as she turns around, and slowly lifts the hem of her shorts to reveal the bruises on the backs of her thighs. Now six days old, they are still purple as a winter sunset.

"Who did this to you?" Yoli springs forward, takes Angel by her shoulders, and spins her around with a ferocity that I'm afraid will alarm my girl. Indeed, Angel seems unable to speak as Yoli demands, "Tell me! You tell me right now!"

"Give her the chance to speak," Guru Tam instructs Yoli in a gentle but commanding tone.

"This is bullshit!" Daman protests. "Can't you see this is all staged, right down to bringing in a lawyer? This is all an act, a setup."

"They said you'd get in trouble if I told," Angel sobs. "I don't want you to get in trouble, and I don't want Maggiemama to get in trouble."

"Don't you worry about us," I encourage her. "We just want you to be safe."

"*Who* told you that? Who hurt you?" Yoli appears ready to explode.

As if the words are torn from her throat against her will, my daughter cries, "He did," and points her finger at Daman. She can't look at him. She runs to bury her face in Guru's lap.

Yoli wheels around to face him, "Is this true?"

"Of course not," he begins. "Kids are liars. Can't you see she's just saying what they've told her to say—"

But Yoli doesn't wait for the rest his response. "My daughter is not a liar. It *is* true, you fucking son of a bitch!" And then she's on him, screaming and crying and tearing at his face with her acrylic nails. He doesn't try to defend himself.

Several of us head toward her but I get there first, grab her from behind and pull her away from him. Her furious momentum makes me lose my balance; we thump down on the floor. I land on my butt and she lands on my lap, and I just hold onto to her. I hold her fiercely as she wails, trying to contain the immensity of her outrage. "He hurt...he hurt my baby," she keens, inconsolable.

Daman is huddled on the floor in a heap. He's made his body very small. It's a tactic a child might use, when all strategies of denial and lying and blaming someone else have been exhausted, trying to make himself invisible to avoid the consequences of his acts.

Unable to contain herself, Tina taunts him, "Yeah, what a big tough guy! You can take a seven-year-old—does that make you feel like a man?"

Guru Tam looks at her keenly. Without scorn, she says, "Nor is it an act of courage to kick a man when he's at his lowest."

Tina gazes at the floor, which is pretty much the only place any of us feels comfortable to look.

Only the Light Beings appear unshaken by what's just happened. Pramesh and Jagadeep are standing on each side of Daman, seeming now as much to protect him as to guard against a possible outburst from him. Sumati sits, eyes closed, holding a space of neutrality. Guru Tam leans over to whisper to Angel, "You have done very well, my child. You have shown great courage, and this will be rewarded. Now go with Amrita for a little bit, while we get things sorted out."

Amrita appears in the doorway. She glides to the front of the room and holds out her hand to my daughter, who takes it and rises to her feet. As they walk toward the door, my daughter looks back with trepidation. "I'm sorry..." she begins.

"You have nothing to be sorry for, sweetheart," I tell her. I want to go to her now, to kiss her cheeks, but Yoli is still collapsed against me. If I were to leave her now, I fear she might dissolve into the floor on which we sit.

"*I'm* sorry, baby, *I'm* sorry," Yoli repeats again and again as Amrita leads Angel from the room.

Once the door has closed behind them Guru Tam says, "Now, Daman, perhaps you have something you wish to say."

Daman looks as if he too is on the verge of weeping, and it's not a pretty sight, that collision of macho belligerence and boyhood vulnerability, a person at war with himself and someone's going to get hurt.

Yoli springs from my lap. "I do not want to hear a fucking word from him," she announces.

"Sit down, Yolanda," Guru says quietly, but it isn't a request. Yoli thumps down beside me.

"Hey," Daman whines defensively, "I never signed on for the whole kid thing. I didn't even know you had a kid the first few times we went out."

"Then why did you make such a stink about Angel staying with me?" I challenge him. Sumati's quick glance across the circle cautions me not to escalate the situation with my own drama.

But Daman's relieved by the distraction of my question. "It was awkward, y'know, to have my girlfriend so hooked up with some dy—" He stops himself. "With her ex," he amends. "With you."

His discomfort palpable, Daman runs both hands through his artificially lightened hair, then presses his tented fingers into either side of the bridge of his nose, as though drawing on a private source of oxygen.

"I stopped over to Lurlene's one day last week, and my sister's all freaked out and overwhelmed as usual. Everything's a crisis with her. She needs me to watch the kids so she can run out to get something at the store. She's outta Tampax or something. 'I'll just be a minute and I'm watchin' your girlfriend's kid, it's the least you could do.' She guilt trips me. So, all right, I get along okay with her kids, I figure, what's the big deal?" His eyes seem to be focused on nothing in particular as he speaks.

"But Angel..." He now tries to engage Yoli's eyes. "See, Angel's hated me from the moment she first laid eyes on me, and you goin' away for so long didn't exactly help that. Like it's my fault you caught a break with that tour!"

His eyes sweep the room, searching for understanding, but only Guru Tam will meet his gaze with anything like kindness. He looks at the floor. "That day, she really started in on me— 'where's my mommy, what did you do with her?' I was tryin' to explain to her, but she wasn't listenin'. She just worked herself into a fit, and then she was cryin' and screamin', and when I

tried to calm her down she just whaled on me. It was workin'
my nerves, and the other kids were gettin' crazy from it, and
she just kept it up and kept it up. I didn't know what to do. I just
wanted to make her stop. So I hauled her over my knee and I
just started to hit her."

At these words, I feel Yoli's body jerk beside mine, like the
warning tremors of an oncoming volcano. Daman is not close
enough to see it, and he continues.

"I just wanted to spank her so she'd shut up. But she didn't,
she screamed louder. And I hit her harder and harder. I don't
know what happened; I just kept hitting her...until Lurlene
came in and pulled her off me. All she had to do was shut up,
but that little girl never stopped screaming the whole time," he
concludes, as if in wonderment.

Then it's as if he suddenly hears himself, as if he registers for
the first time the meaning of his words, the action they depict.
"Oh, God!" he beseeches. Then to Yoli, "You have to believe
me! I didn't mean to."

The change in his countenance is nothing short of
remarkable. Gone is the aggressive bravado, the menacing
swagger. He seems to have shrunk a few inches; his hunched
shoulders make his body appear narrower. His face has lost its
angry leer, the eyes now disconcertingly naked. "I don't want to
be the kind of man who hits kids," he sobs into his hands.

Listening to the story of what happened to my girl, I feel
like throwing up. Yoli's face has grown dangerous, and I sense
in her a tension that signals she may be getting ready to strike
at him again. I stretch my arms around her once more. It's been
years since I've held her, yet it feels natural, familiar. Not the
caress of the lover but the embrace of one who knows another.
I know her in my being. I feel her muscles surrender just a bit,
abort their planned attack.

Tina looks like she wants to beat the crap out of him. I can
see her clenching and unclenching her fists. Carmen is staring
at Yoli and me, reading some kind of truth about us. Charlie is
keeping his eye on the lawyer, who has retreated to the far wall,
not in distress, but as if to assert that she is strictly an observer
here, nothing more.

It is Sumati who comes up behind Daman and lays her palm on his back, right at heart level. I watch it calm him, almost as if his spirit spills back into his body. She appears steady and neutral, without judgment or emotional attachment to what has taken place. Guru Tam has her eyes pressed shut, deep in concentration, as if her energy alone is keeping the room and everything in it from combusting.

And, by Spirit's grace, somehow we don't self-destruct. As I hold Yoli, my arms full of her struggle and her frailty, I remember to find my breath, inhaling and exhaling deeply, rhythmically against her back. After a while, her breathing begins to fall into cadence with mine as her sobs diminish and her composure slowly returns.

From across the circle, Daman appeals to Yoli, "Baby, I'm sorry. Can you forgive me?" He half-kneels, awkward, appearing lost, as if he's been given a new body and hasn't yet figured out how the parts work.

She stares at him like something crawled up from the sewer. "You rot in hell," she seethes, and her tears renew.

Daman slumps back down, his limbs limp as a rag doll's, his soul laid bare. This man who further estranged me from Yoli, who beat my daughter, who reviled and threatened me, whose actions have caused me to risk everything. I feel Yoli's curse resonate in my own heart.

Sumati rises and walks around the room, gently striking the bell, wordlessly encouraging everyone to return to their places, to regather in the circle.

"Precious Loving Spirit," Guru Tam prays, her voice more ragged than before, "you have given us the Word so we might speak the Truth. Truth is the essence of your love. Where there is no Truth, there can be no healing. We thank you that Truth has now been spoken, that healing can begin."

Not everyone in this room yet appears to share this gratitude for the truth that has been spoken. Outside, the Light Beings' chanting continues to filter through the window.

"Daman," Guru continues, turning to him. "Sometimes Spirit sends us circumstances that necessitate that we dismantle who and what we are, that we take ourselves apart so that we might rebuild on a stronger foundation. It can be terrifying to feel those inner walls shatter, to feel the wind blow through those empty rooms."

Painfully she rises, walks toward him. She brings her hands to each side of his face, cradles him like something precious. "It is a gift, my son. It is a chance to redeem yourself and your life. I cannot know what the material consequences of your actions will be, but I do know that you can heal your karma, and that your speaking the truth in this room is the beginning of doing so.

"You may not believe it now, but you may someday feel grateful to Maggie for bringing you here today."

He avoids looking at me, his expression doubtful.

"Just as Maggie may someday experience gratitude for this journey for which your actions have been the catalyst."

I am certain my lips are similarly twisted in skepticism.

"Daman, I would like to invite you and strongly suggest that you remain here in the Light Beings' community for a period of time. You are going to tell me that your work will not allow it, that you cannot afford it but, should you decline, I can foresee an even bigger disruption in your life."

That Yoli will send him to jail seems certain, if she doesn't kill him with her bare hands.

He looks around, bewildered. Nothing about this afternoon has gone as he'd intended. "I...uh..."

"I'll give you some time to think about it," Guru offers. "And I want you to think very carefully about your options. This is a critical juncture for your soul. In the meantime, we have some other business to attend to."

Jagadeep and Pramesh immediately flank Daman, help him unsteadily to his feet, and proceed to escort him from the room.

Before he exits, Guru Tam offers this. "Contrary to what some religions say, Spirit never judges our actions. It is we who condemn ourselves, and we who condemn others. Spirit has no part in that. You must first look within for your forgiveness," she advises. "No one here can offer you absolution. Only Spirit can ease your burden. Spirit will never abandon us; it is only we who abandon Spirit."

Chapter 13

"How could you do that?" Yoli shrieks at Guru Tam, but only after Daman has left the room. She's on her feet, arms jabbing the air in ardent punctuation. "The man just confessed to abusing my little girl, and you're all like 'Hey, no harm, no foul, come join the community.'"

"What were you wanting us to do?" It's Sumati who poses the question. Her tone suggests curiosity rather than conflict.

"That man has to pay for what he did! He should be locked up."

Guru Tam totters back to her chair, moving as if every step is costing her. "Yolanda, I believe that Daman's staying here with us is the best chance for him to reflect on his actions and develop a practice to keep him from ever repeating that behavior. As temporarily satisfying as revenge might seem, how many individuals actually are uplifted by going to jail?"

"I don't care about if he's uplifted or not! I want him to suffer." Her eyes narrow to mean slits.

The Teacher twists her mouth into a sorrowful grin. "I think you can be assured that he suffers," she says. "But why do you wish this on him? Is it that you do not love him?"

"How'm I s'posed to love a man who would beat a little girl?" Yoli snarls.

Guru sighs. I notice the ochre skin is more ashen now; the rings beneath her eyes are darkening. A glassiness to her corneas suggests the return of fever. I'm starting to feel alarmed for her. She, however, is not thinking about her own well-being, so determined is she to complete her work. "Love is not about what another person does. It is something one gives unconditionally. And once you give it, you can never take it back. Your souls are bound for all time."

"Look, I'm sick of this holier-than-thou bullshit." A sweep of her hand encompasses all that she rejects. "I want my little girl, and I want to go home."

"Yolanda," Guru responds calmly, "we are not finished here."

"*I'm* finished. You damn well better believe I'm finished!" Yoli turns and strides from the room, slamming the door behind her.

Deep silence pervades in her wake. Tina and Carmen, Charlie and the lawyer stare at each other awkwardly, affected but embarrassed by everything they've witnessed. Now that Daman and Yoli have gone, the room seems to contain a vacuum, a dark vortex into which everything remaining might be sucked. Everything except, that is, for Sumati and Guru Tam who appear unaltered.

Finally I recover my voice. "She can't just leave here with Angel!" I protest.

Sumati looks at me evenly. "No, she can't." It's a statement of fact; there isn't a trace of concern in her voice. She hoists her body to standing and begins pouring glassfuls of lemon ginger tea, offering them like a hostess at a summer lawn party.

We, her unlikely guests, down them eagerly, gratefully, feeling parched and depleted from the afternoon's upheavals. The room still holds the late afternoon heat. We stand and stretch, shaking off the residue of negativity, stamping life back into our stiffened limbs.

From outside, I can hear the Light Beings' chant has changed, its tempo slower, melody less stalwart and more plaintive. The window is starting to darken; they must be postponing dinner to perform these blessings for us.

"Did you know he did it?" Tina sidles over to ask me. The others begin to cluster for chatter, although at this moment I crave silence and solitude more than anything. I don't want to be annoyed with them, though; they have all done more to help me than I could have ever asked for.

So I try to engage Tina's question. I try to think about why this never occurred to me. "I never let myself imagine it," I answer. Out of some twisted loyalty to Yoli, I realize. How can the lesbian ex accuse the new boyfriend of being a child abuser?

"It makes more sense that it would be him," Carmen muses, coming over to join us. "It's harder to imagine a woman hurting a child in that way." She has slipped an arm around my lower back, loosely, in a way that might be comradely or comforting, but isn't. I can feel the heat of her skin on mine.

"I don't know," Tina disagrees. "I don't think men hold the patent on cruelty."

Charlie glides over to inform us, "Caroline says the law can't touch him as long as he stays in Mexico. They won't extradite for this kind of crime."

"Anybody want to form a posse?" Tina sounds like she's only half-kidding.

"I don't know," I say, "I think staying here could be a really good thing for him."

"You mean having to wear those lovely blue smocks?" Charlie's grin is wicked. "I suppose that could be considered punishment enough."

"No, I think it might really turn him around," I insist. "He wasn't putting us on in here—he's coming apart. If he goes back home, or even to jail, he'll just close back up again and harden."

Fanning himself like Scarlett O'Hara, Charlie drawls, "As I live and breathe, I never thought I'd hear you stickin' up for one of Miss Yoli's gentlemen callers! Girlfriend, don't turn into a saint on us now, okay?" he pleads.

"You're a whole lot more forgiving than I would be," Tina agrees. "And more, I think, than your ex is likely to be."

"Speaking of which…" Charlie inclines his head toward the door, which Yoli has just burst through.

"Where *is* she?" Yoli bellows. The torpor that had enveloped her earlier in the day has been replaced by frenzy. She is breathing heavily, shallowly, her face and gestures fractured as a Cubist painting.

Moving behind us, with a soft touch on arms and shoulders, Sumati quietly herds the rest of us back to sitting in our circle. We comply like theatergoers not wanting to be late for the next act.

Guru holds out her hand and says, "Yolanda, come here."

Though gentler than a command, there is an irrefutable authority in her words. They cut through Yoli's tumult, seem to shift her emotional state; obediently, she crosses the room to sit by Guru's side. I wonder if she is making a conscious choice or if she is caught in the pull of the Teacher's energy. Guru strokes her hair lightly, as a mother might. Yoli usually hates to have anyone mess with her hair, but I can see her face relaxing, shoulders easing from their armored stance.

"Yolanda," Guru says gently, "I can see by all that has happened that you have been confused about your purpose."

"I don't *think* so," Yoli snarls in that defensive tone she gets whenever she believes she's being criticized.

I have often been on the receiving end of this tone with Yoli. I probably even used it myself with Sumati that first day when I felt she was attacking me.

Guru's expression never falters. She continues, patient, "Yolanda, what's the most important thing to you?"

"Singing," Yoli responds without thinking, and for just a

moment, her eyes spark. For the first time today, I glimpse the sassy, confident, look-out-world-don't-get-in-my-way woman I've known all these years.

"Why?" Guru wants to know. Her voice is warm and encouraging. "What's so important about that?"

Yoli has risen to her knees, staring right at Guru Tam. "When I sing, I feel...full...and whole. I feel that connection you talked about, like God is inside me and I'm His channel to come out into the world."

I've felt that too, sometimes, listening to her sing.

"And Daman? Does he help you sing better? Does he bring more God into you?" Guru asks.

"No," Yoli snaps, sharp as gunshot.

"What about Malique? Or Code Eye?" She pauses to let the questions sink in. "What of Everett? Or Gray?"

I stare dumbfounded. How does Guru know the names of Yoli's recent boyfriends? Yoli is thinking I must have been the one who told her.

Embarrassed, Yoli juts her lower lip. "No-oh," she drawls, impatient. I can tell she doesn't like where this is going.

"Well, then, what do they bring you?" Guru grows more insistent. "Are you in love with them? Do they help you to feel more whole?"

"Look, they helped me...with my career, okay? They helped get me gigs, helped me get some airplay for my CD. Daman got me the audition for this tour." Once so excited about this, she now reports this as if he'd gotten her an appointment with the executioner.

Even to her own ears, it sounds a little grasping, so Yoli grows more defensive. "Look, is it so wrong for me to want to support myself and my child with my music? Am I supposed to be a temp secretary for the rest of my life?" Her voice rises to a whine.

"No one is judging you, Yolanda," Guru Tam assures her. "I just want to help you understand how you find yourself in this situation, so that you don't think it's the result of someone else's decisions or actions, and so you don't ever find yourself here again."

"What are you saying?" Yoli argues. "I didn't beat up my daughter. And I didn't kidnap her either," she snipes at me.

"No," Guru agrees, her voice penetrating as a laser. "But you did leave her to go off to sing, and you left her with Daman because you wanted him to help your career. And when I ask you about what's most important to you, you don't mention your child." Her voice grows gentle again. "You don't think maybe you are confused about some things?"

Now it's Yoli who looks as if the air has been drained out of her.

"I love my daughter," she says hotly to the rest of us.

"And no one in this room imagines otherwise," Guru says. "But to love as a mother is a deeply demanding vocation."

Yoli whirls to face her. "Are you saying that a woman with a gift can't pursue that *and* be a mother too?"

"Why would I say that?" Guru Tam smiles at her. "What I would say is that a woman who has a gift to pursue, as you do, who is also a mother, as you are, cannot parent alone. What do they say in your country? You need 'backup.'

"In our tradition," Guru goes on to explain, "we do not believe in just one or two parents for any child. The child is born to the community; he or she is everyone's responsibility. I know that is not the way in most of the United States, but children are suffering for it."

Guru leans closer to Yoli. Her voice grows softer. "Loving Spirit has provided you with someone who is completely devoted to Angel. If I were to ask Maggie, 'What's the most important thing to you?' what do you think she would say?"

Yoli's eyes glance off me, then lower to the floor. She knows exactly what my answer would be.

"See, here is another area of confusion for you," Guru Tam continues. "Why do you reject the miracle that Spirit has sent you? This is a circumstance that allows your daughter to receive what she needs by way of mothering, and allows you to pursue your gift. Why do you refuse this blessing?"

Yoli says nothing, but I can hear the commotion of thoughts and feelings flying around inside her. Guilt about Angel. Guilt about me. Competition with me for our daughter's affections.

Fear because I know her so well. Ambition. Shame about her ambition. Defensiveness about that shame.

I wish I could just lift it from her, that welter of emotion, draw it out through my hands and leave her empty and clear, so things could be as simple as Guru makes them: Yoli lives to sing, I live to love our little girl. It should be simple, joyous. We are lucky, if we could only realize it.

Charlie and Caroline have scooted themselves back to the wall, the better to support their backs. The circle is not so much broken as lopsided on their end. I imagine the lawyer must be bored to death, plunked down in the midst of someone else's melodrama. But perhaps that is always the fate of lawyers. Tina and Carmen hang on every word, occasionally glancing at me to see how I'm reacting. From the courtyard, the Light Beings' chanting has not flagged.

"Yolanda," Guru Tam continues. Each time she repeats the name it is an incantation, and each time it seems to burrow deeper inside Yoli, excavating another layer. "You have a gift. I don't even need to hear you sing to feel the music that is inside you. If you exalt your gift, if you turn it to a divine purpose, everything you need will come to you. You do not have to strive and struggle and prostitute yourself with men you do not love in order to achieve 'success' or 'fame.' Those are yearnings of ego, not the fulfillment of destiny."

I can't tell what Yoli thinks of any of this, whether enough of her has been hollowed out for this message to penetrate. I can imagine the voices inside her contesting Guru's words. *What am I s'posed to do, sing in some church choir? You don't understand the way it is in the industry. Men have the power and women have to use what we can to get some of it.* As long as I've known her, Yoli has not merely wanted to sing, but has been determined to become a star. Her drive for fame is ferocious; I have never dared question it.

Guru, perhaps sensing resistance, does not press this point, but that doesn't mean she's finished. "Yolanda," she delves further still, "I am going to ask you one more thing. What does love mean to you?"

Yoli crosses her arms over her chest; her eyes grow hard.

I know she wants to say, "None of your damn business." But beneath this defense is utter terror, a panicked flailing as if an invisible net had been dropped over her, the sheer determination to escape. I used to feel this from her at times in our relationship, usually after we had been the most close, but I never understood it clearly as I do now.

Despite her squared shoulders and set jaw, I see her running in a maze, but every path is a dead end, nothing to do but keep running. She is fleeing the question and the meaning behind the question. Minutes go by as Yoli fiddles with her manicure to avoid our eyes. Guru's question still rings with the resonance of a bell.

"Yolanda?"

"I don't know," she finally answers, her tone flattened, desiccated. It is an admission of defeat. It may be the saddest sound I've ever heard.

Guru may think so as well, because she makes a tent of her fingers and presses them to her third eye point, a spot in the forehead above the bridge of the nose. She closes her eyes and appears to pray, silently.

Just then, the door opens from the hallway and Angel steps inside. Someone has taken the time to pick her hair and divide it into several small neat pigtails that form a corona around her head. "Mommy?" she asks tentatively, as she moves forward to the spot where Yoli kneels.

Yoli wraps her arms around Angel, and holds her tight. Fresh tears sprout from the corners of her eyes as she croons, "Oh, my baby, oh my little girl, I've been so worried about you."

From the look on her face, I would venture that Yoli best knows what love means to her when she doesn't try to think about it.

Angel squirms a bit in the tight clutch. "Mommy, you shouldn't worry! Maggiemama took care of me. I met Tina's parrot, and fed him pineapple. And I made candles, and taught everyone how to do the Electric Slide. And, Mom, I found a puppy—Edgar Sue—and, Mom, I want her really, really bad. Maggie said 'maybe.' Mommy, can I get her?"

I marvel at my daughter's uncanny sense of when to press

her advantage, but Yoli seems to have not even registered her words. "Let's go home, now, baby," she says, and rises to do just that.

"Excuse me." It's Caroline, the lawyer, who's barely said a word all afternoon. She is looking at her watch. "I have to get my rental car back to Cabo tonight, and I have to catch a plane to Los Angeles first thing in the morning. Before any of us goes, I'd like to recommend that we take a moment to address the legal issues that have been raised here. There is the question of prosecution regarding both Ms. Seaver and, separately, of Mr. Devereaux. It is also possible that Ms. Washington could be charged with child abandonment and child endangerment. And further, there may be the issue of custody to resolve."

"Custody?" Yoli asks, the snarl returning to her voice.

"Yes," the lawyer continues, unruffled. "Ms. Seaver may have a compelling case for custody, given what happened to the child in the care you selected for her."

"She kidnaps my child and you're talkin' custody?" Yoli turns to glare at me. "You wouldn't dare—"

"Mommy, don't be mad at Maggiemama," Angel begs.

"Yoli, I swear—" I begin, but Guru Tam pushes her body to a standing position. With effort she takes a step, then another, until she stands midway between us. Every gesture is labored, her limbs shaky now, her breath coming in little gasps.

"I am certain these matters can be resolved without involving the courts," she pronounces. Sorrowfully, she asks us, "What have we come to when we place the most fundamental issues of love and family into the hands of strangers?"

It seems such an effort for her to speak, it pains me to listen.

"Beloved Teacher." Sumati rises to go to her. "Please sit down and rest now. We can continue this later."

Guru Tam waves her away with her hand, a gesture almost too weak to stir air. Still she persists. "Maggie, Yolanda. There is so much history, lifetimes of karma between the two of you," she rasps. "And, of course, there is the child. Now is the time to open your hearts. Before it's too late. Talk to one another."

And with this, her knees give way, and she begins to sink. I reach her before she hits the ground. Her breath is shallow; the sulfurous sweat begins to seep from her pores.

"Stay back," I say to everyone who has crowded around her. To my daughter, I call, "Angel, honey, don't be scared."

"Is she sick?" my daughter wants to know.

To Sumati I say, "We have to get her upstairs."

Sumati goes to the window and knocks three times. I hear people in the courtyard running to enter the room.

As I kneel beside her, the Guru's pulse barely whispers under my fingers.

Chapter 14

Guru's chest cavity is a hollow rattle as shallow breath shudders through. She has not appeared to be conscious since she rasped those words to Yoli and to me. Occasionally her eyelids flutter, as do her hands, but these movements seem to be without intention. Although I recommended she be brought to one of the upstairs bedrooms, Sumati ordered Haroon and Rutajit to carry her into the main gathering room, the place we came for morning meditations. There, a makeshift bed has been assembled from piled sheepskins, covered with sheets and a quilt.

All the Light Beings have been called in from the courtyard and now they fill this room, seated in concentric circles around the spot where Guru lies. Their chanting, a persistent heartbeat, resonates under the arched ceiling. Many hold lit tapers; the flames spark in the dim room.

Charlie has left to deliver Carolyn back to Cabo, but has promised to return in the morning. I sense they're both a little frustrated that more was not concretely resolved; neither can appreciate how much has shifted while it appeared that nothing was going on. *More is happening than you can see.* For the first time I think I can understand this.

Before she left, Carolyn said to me, "It's really up to your ex. Unless she decides to be vindictive, I think we can explain the circumstances to the FBI and persuade them not to prosecute." She pressed her card into my hands and made me promise to call her before I tried to reenter the U.S. "Better if you're in control of the process."

When I asked her about money, she told me not to worry, that she and Charlie had a habit of "helping each other out."

I thanked her and I thanked Spirit.

"Charlie," I said as I hugged him goodbye, "what would I do without you?"

He dismissed this. "Just a day in the life of a spiritual warrior, girlfriend. You'd do the same for me.

"By the way," he said, glancing significantly at Carmen, "you didn't tell me about this little find. Have you two…" He pretends to be too delicate to ask the question directly.

"Charlie, my mind isn't even there."

"Sugarplum, you don't need your *mind* for what she's got in mind for you!"

"Please," I begged off, but he didn't quite relent.

"Don't lose your chance at the future while you're holding on to the past," he warned me.

"But time is continuous." I grin at him wearily. "There's no such thing as past or future. It's all happening now, in multiple dimensions."

"Now don't get all woo-woo on me."

"Peace begets peace, Charlie," I bade him goodbye. "And watch out for cows on the road."

Carmen and Tina offered to drive Yoli back to the Hotel California, but she wouldn't hear of leaving without Angel, who, in her newfound autonomy, insisted she was going to stay "and help the Guru." She's sitting with Prem and the other children, while Yoli, Tina and Carmen have taken a spot in the back of the room.

All this seemed to happen in one long suspended minute after Guru's collapse, while Sumati barked at me, "Please, Maggie, help her!"

When I worked with AIDS patients in Los Angeles, I always understood my mission was to bring a greater degree of physical comfort to them in whatever stage of illness they might be. Some were moderately healthy, perhaps just recovering from their first bout of pneumocystis; others were so ravaged and wasted it seemed Spirit alone was keeping breath flowing through them. I never believed it was my job to change the course of their illness or to attempt to arrest their dying process. And yet this seems to be what's expected of me now.

The Light Beings gather around, sending energy to their beloved Teacher and to me, in hopes I might save her. My little girl is among them, watching. I want to say to them, "Please, I am just a bodyworker. A mother. An intermittent meditator. A failed lover. I'm only here because I panicked in a crisis—I let my ego take over and put my child in danger. Don't invest your hopes in me. I have no power over life and death."

But Guru's words from the night before come back to me, so clearly it's as if she were speaking them now: *You misunderstand. No one has power. And no one is helpless. Power is always there to be used.*

So, instead I pray. *Spirit, my training has not prepared me for this overwhelming task. Use me now to achieve your intention, whatever it may be. I cannot know what this is, but I can make myself a clear channel for its expression. Guide me, Spirit. Show me what I am to do.*

Kundanika emerges from the crowd, bearing a bowl of water and a clean white towel so I can wash my hands. I don't know how she's gotten down the mountain in such a short time, but I'm relieved to see her. Her gold colored sari seems to glow against the backdrop of pale blue. I can sense that Guru is aware of her presence too as Kundanika kneels beside her.

"I'm here now, Guru-Ji," the young woman whispers, and the Teacher's breathing seems to deepen a bit.

After washing my hands and rubbing the palms together to stimulate the nerve endings, I am guided to bring my hands first to the soles of her feet, which are very cold to the touch. I visualize sending a beam of red light into each foot, and watch it travel up the legs and through the torso to the heart. I call on the fire element to warm her, to spark energy into her electromagnetic field. In a mechanical sense, one can recharge the body as one might a battery. Guru's feet begin to warm in my hands as I apply gentle pressure to various points connected to the heart, lungs, liver, spleen. With this, I am on more solid ground; foot massage is used in many healing modalities to open blockages in the organs and produce relief from pain.

Still allowing myself to be guided, I move next to her abdomen and place both hands on the hollow beneath her navel. She is so thin this area is concave, and the hipbones feel fragile as twigs. The pulse at her navel point is barely detectable. Working on instinct rather from anything I've been taught, I lower my head and begin to blow against her third chakra, *manipura*, the spot three fingers below her naval. If someone were to ask me, as I expect them to any moment, "What the hell are you doing?" I could not tell them.

I hear a collective stir from some of the Light Beings in the front row, and I lift my head to see that Guru has opened her eyes. She is far too weak to speak, but the focus of her gaze indicates she is conscious and aware of her condition and surroundings.

"Guru-Ji," I whisper to her, "your energy is very depleted. Please don't try to do anything. Please just rest."

She blinks twice, slowly, as if in agreement, then closes her eyes again. As I begin to gently massage her left hand, I feel her spirit is here now with her body. This does not mean I am confident it will remain in this weakened and exhausted shell; it is possible her soul will soon depart for a more hospitable home.

I know the Light Beings believe, as I do, in reincarnation, in an eternal soul that is reborn into various living forms—trees, earthworms, cats, humans. I also know the Light Beings consider humans to be the superior incarnation, but I myself have never been convinced of that. Between a cat and a person—which has the stronger Buddha nature? What karma does a tree accumulate? But even as a human, one reincarnates many times, striving to learn the lessons that can release one from the cycle of material form.

Despite this belief in the soul's everlastingness, the Light Beings in this room are reluctant to see the Guru depart this particular form, to complete this lifetime as their spiritual leader. I am reminded of Sumati's words from this morning: *We're still human beings. The only difference is that we share a practice that commits us to another path.* And what is more human than not wanting to let go?

I wonder what will happen to the community once Guru Tam has left her body. When I first got here it seemed that the Teacher was removed, isolated from the community, far away and out of the loop, but I see now how closely she has held each one of the Light Beings in her energy. Will this enclave be able to maintain itself under Sumati's leadership? Will it choose to? And what, then, will sustain Sumati?

One of the first things you learn in energetic bodywork is that the left hand receives and the right hand transmits. I have been feeding energy to Guru through my work on her left hand, nourishing those places in her that are weak or empty. As I do this, her essence is plumping, growing stronger; her pulses gain depth and resonance. This is not to be confused with curing her, any more than hydration in a hospital can save the life of a terminal patient. But this infusion gives her more to work with, provides her the capacity to fight, should she choose to. Or simply relieves some of the discomfort of surrender.

Moving now to her right hand, I am drawing things out of her. I begin to have pictures flash through me, as they did last night, as if I had wired myself into her memory. They come so fast they are hard to discern, like dreams; I get only occasional glints that seem recognizable: a boat moving through water, a torchlight procession, a perfect wedge of watermelon.

Over time, though, this rush of images coheres into something more like a movie, no longer random but deliberate. It flickers on the scrim of my eyelids, a film about a skinny blond boy stranded in a flat landscape, a charmless suburban slum. His house is empty. There is a mother who puts on lipstick the color of dried blood and leaves the boy alone in those rooms of decrepit furniture and dim, hopeless light. The film loops; always her battered Bonneville retreats down the rutted driveway.

Time weighs heavily as it does in dreams, as if everything were moving in slow motion, underwater. When it seems the emptiness will suffocate him, the boy leaves the rooms, escapes onto desolate sidewalks. He slinks past dilapidated storefronts, padlocked and shuttered. The skinny boy is chased down treeless streets by bigger boys; a part of him is so lonely he longs to be caught. He is caught. They beat him in vacant lots, torture him in abandoned garages. They leave him there. Later, he drags himself home to the empty rooms, now grown dark; he washes his sores best he can, falls asleep at the window, waiting.

This is the boy who grew up to be Daman.

When Guru Tam encountered him, this is what she saw. Not the swagger, the bluster, the brandished gun. Not the scar tissue grown over those wounds. It was the boy she discerned, buried underneath the other layers. He for whom she argued. *Go get him*, she wants to say to Daman, *he's waiting for you to rescue him. Don't consign him forever to those forlorn rooms. Don't let him die in that house.*

These pictures fill me with the heaviest weight; it feels as if my skin might split. Am I cleansing this from her energy field, or is she showing me deliberately? And if so, why? So near to vacating her body, is she teaching still?

"No!" my mind argues, as Guru's purpose announces itself more clearly. "Don't ask this of me too. Not now." *But what is meditation but training for the spirit to override the mind's resistance?*

I feel a shift in Guru Tam's physical condition, perhaps a signal to me. The flood of images stops, the projector goes dark. Her breath eases a bit more, her limbs relax; she seems to drop into a genuine sleep. Having conveyed my mission to me, she can once more rest.

Spirit, why me?

Sumati looks concerned when I rinse and dry my hands, stand up and begin to back away from the Teacher.

"I'm not giving up," I assure her. "Guru has asked me to do something."

This she accepts without question.

"Where can I find Daman?" My voice is quiet yet urgent.

"Upstairs, on the men's side. Room two-fifteen." She gives me a penetrating look as if she understands what I am about to do.

As I leave the room, Angel looks at me to ask where I'm going. I gesture to her that I'll be right back. I notice Kundanika has returned to Guru Tam's side, and is sponging her forehead and neck. The Lights Beings continue their vigil, never flagging in their mantra.

The hallway is much cooler than the room with its crowd and lit candles. A shiver travels the length of my spine, whether from the change in temperature or from my assignment, I don't know. I climb the stairs on the opposite side of the building, the men's side. With each step, my mind records its protest: *He stole Yoli, he stole Angel, he abused Angel, he threatened you.*

When I reach the door of 215, I knock. Jagadeep answers and looks at me with a worried expression, as if he's not sure what I might do.

"Guru sent me," I tell him, and he immediately steps aside to let me enter.

"I'll be right outside if you need me," he says as he closes the door behind him.

The room is the same light blue as most of the rest of the complex. Evidently the men don't go in for decorating their rooms the same way the women do.

Daman sits in a heap at the edge of a cot, his back hunched and head hanging as if he were in a prison cell. He's removed his shirt, and sweat drenches his shoulders. His naked torso looks scrawnier than it does in the fancy clothes he usually wears.

When he sees me, he flinches as if I'd come to strike him. "Nothing you can say can make me feel any worse, so save it," he sneers.

"Shh," I say, as if to a fidgety child, and sit myself down on the woven jute rug in front of him. His discomfort is so painful to witness, I lower my eyes. I wonder if my own uneasiness is as apparent. I could always still leave, and the pull to do so is fierce. *Why are we always given the tasks for which we are least equipped?*

I can't think how to begin, so I pray for guidance. *Spirit, send me the words to help and not harm. Help me to fulfill this mission.* After a few minutes, I get an idea.

"Did Yoli ever tell you anything about how she grew up?" I ask.

"Nah," he replies bitterly. "She was too busy trying to see what she could get me to do for her career." He feels used, and I can understand that. Not everyone is called to devote one's energies toward providing service to great talent. But of course, feeling aggrieved is always a great way to avoid responsibility for one's own actions.

I have to consciously decide I'm not going to get hooked into his melancholy or his rage, I need to stay neutral to be of any use at all. "She grew up in Detroit," I continue. "She was the oldest of six."

"All I ever heard about was one brother, Raymond," he carps. "The doctor, like that's some big fuckin' deal."

He's still not listening, too focused on his own self-pity. It would be so easy to judge him, and split. I have to resummon the image of the boy in the empty house in order to keep going. Daman narrows his eyes at me. He senses something, but doesn't know how to trust his own perceptions.

"I think most of 'em had different dads," I say. "The point is, her mom had a lot of men in and out of the house, all the time Yoli was growing up." I hesitate, wondering how much to reveal. I'm remembering, as I so often have, Yoli's story of going to the library when her mom was entertaining during the day, hiding in the stacks and staying until it was time for the library to close. "Not all of them were nice," I unconsciously parrot Angel's word from earlier.

"What the hell are you saying?" He thinks I'm accusing him of something else.

"All I'm saying," I have to keep my energy calm enough to

soothe his volatility, "is you and Yoli don't really know each other. You don't see where she comes from, and she doesn't know what you've been through either."

His look is suspicious. How could *I* know what he's been through? I can tell he longs to ask, but he doesn't want the answer. Feeling this naked is almost intolerable to him. If a person could die of shame and vulnerability, his vital signs would be critical right now. His instinct is to lash out.

I have to make sure my own intentions are utterly clean, that there is no ego at work in what I am doing now. How can I ever be sure of that? I am doing the last thing in the world I ever expected to do, but even in this, is there not some pride, some self-congratulation? I have to be willing to fail miserably, to look like a fool or worse. I have to give up all illusions of being heroic.

Carefully, I reach to take his hand. I'm not sure he will let me, but he does. The skin is clammy, both cold and fevered at once. The energy moving through him is so bilious that I immediately begin to retch. Just in time I grab for a wastebasket with my free hand and empty the contents of my heaving throat. Only once or twice before have I gotten sick this way from conducting another's energy.

"Jesus, sorry," he says, and jerks his hand away, as if he knows it's him.

"Shh," I pacify him. "We needed to expel that poison."

Working on sick people, not to mention being a mother, has gotten me over any distress about vomit. I calmly excuse myself to the bathroom to sponge out the wastebasket and rinse my own mouth with water. I wash my hands and borrow just a dab of toothpaste from someone who's left a tube on the edge of the basin.

When I come back into the room, Daman has put his shirt back on, as if that could disguise him now. "Listen," he says, like he's been thinking it over while I was gone, "you know as well as me she's never gonna talk to me again."

This very much matters to him, I can see.

Once you surrender to serve Spirit, there's no half measures; you have to go as far as it takes. "Maybe I can help," I offer.

"Not that I have any sway over Yoli…"

We share a fleeting moment of recognition of her formidable stubbornness, and it is both so strange and so natural to feel aligned with him in our knowing of her.

"Why the fuck would you?" he asks harshly. He means, why would I help?

I shrug. "I don't know," I tell him honestly. "It's weird, I admit it. Look, Spirit has a strange sense of humor. I only know it's what I'm supposed to do."

He shakes his head, both discouraged and bewildered, as if he cannot understand one thing that's happened to him since he arrived on this land today.

Suddenly we hear a commotion outside the door. First is Jagadeep's hasty, "No, you can't go in there," followed closely by Yoli's frustrated, "Angel, I told you. Come on, she's not here."

But my daughter instead starts calling, "Maggiemama! Maggiemama!"

"Don't let them in," Daman panics. He's simultaneously trying to find a place to hide and tidy himself up, running his hands through his hair, jamming shirttail into waistband.

I open the door, as I am meant to. Angel says, "Maggie, the sick lady told me to come find you," and I know she doesn't mean they had a conversation.

But Angel gasps when she notices Daman in the room, and backs away from me to hide her face in Yoli's hip.

"What the hell are you doin'?" Yoli demands of me. She pointedly refuses to look at Daman. She raises her palm as if to fend off my answer. "I don't even want to know—Angel, let's go."

"Both of you, please, come in and sit down," I order crisply, "Daman, you sit too. Jagadeep, please close the door." The words seem to be coming from my mouth, but who is it speaking in this tone of command?

And what the hell *am* I doing? Putting my daughter at risk of further trauma? Exactly what do I think I can do with Daman and Yoli—get them back together? And why in fact would I?

We sit for a few moments in awkward and resentful silence. Occasionally one of them flicks their eyes in my direction, waiting for me to do something that will justify their being here against their wills. I ask Spirit for the necessary words, but my mouth remains empty.

Finally I close my eyes and begin to expand each breath, trying to go deeper within myself, down to a solid core beyond this room, beyond those who occupy it with me. I am seeking my own source, a clear golden light, feeling it well up inside. I begin to project it in waves throughout the room, brighter and stronger with every breath, until it fills all four corners. I need it to be solid and powerful enough to hold everyone safe.

Then I rerun the movie of the skinny boy in the empty rooms and, alongside it, the film of the voluptuous girl trying to escape violation among shelves of library books. I don't know how I'm doing this, but I allow it to be done. I let those pictures fill me, project them growing sharper and brighter, so clear and resonant the others can't fail to see or feel them too.

Angel begins to cry. Deep, powerful sobs erupt from her chest. When Yoli attempts to console her, Angel jumps down from the bed, retreats to a corner of the room where she huddles with her arms around her own torso. She sees, and on some level far beyond her years, she understands. She weeps for the boy and the girl, for the two adults who sit before her, whose unhealed wounds have wounded her, have brought her to this moment, this place. Perhaps she weeps for me as well, the boy-girl who has lived by her own strategies of retreat and hiding. Angel, my spirit-girl. Her tears cleanse us.

In silence we listen to her weeping, as we might sit and listen to a rainstorm on a long afternoon. Eventually she calms, quiets, and the air is clearer, as after a thunderstorm. But something is still happening in her; she appears to be listening too. She must be receiving her own guidance from Spirit and wrestling with it, as I had, because slowly she walks over to me, her eyes full of her question: *Do I have to?*

Oh, my girl! The tests we are given, the sacrifices we are asked to make for those we love and for those we haven't yet learned to love. Yes, we are always asked to do the hardest thing, the thing for which we feel least equipped. It is in this way we grow and learn. Even when we are so young.

With only my eyes, I answer her: *For your own sake, Mrs. Havisham, I think so, yes.*

My brave girl squares her shoulders. She turns to Daman, walks a few steps closer, stares at him until he returns her gaze. In a low voice, she says, "I know you're sorry you hurt me."

At first his expression is puzzled, as if he cannot comprehend what she has said to him. Then, as the sound of her words becomes clear, something lifts from him. I watch it rise, dark and heavy, from his shoulders and dissolve in the atmosphere. Some mask leaves his face until the man more closely resembles the boy. He's unable to speak, but he nods, *Yes, oh God, yes I am, I'm sorry,* his eyes never leaving hers, even as they spill over.

Yoli is watching all of it, utterly perplexed. She is lost without the familiar reference points of good and bad, victim and victimizer, blame and righteousness. She is both moved and suspicious, both angry and afraid, both determined to hold up her carefully erected defenses and desperately longing for them to collapse.

Then I find some words. Not my words perhaps, but words that are given to me for just this moment.

"When the worst happens," I hear myself say, "it occurs not to break us, but to build us stronger. It occurs not to separate us, but to bring us together. To give us cause to look into our hearts and heal what needs to be healed. Not one of us would wish for what happened to Angel." *Or to you, Daman. Or you, Yoli,* I think silently. "Still, instead of cultivating mistrust and bitterness, we can use this to bring forward what is best within us, what is loving and strong. We can be grateful for this opportunity to build anew."

The words hang in the air, to resonate or dissipate. This is the kind of thing you either believe or you don't. It is one of two ways we can choose to live, and we are given the choice every day.

I look at Daman. At Angel. At Yoli. My family. I wonder what choice each is prepared to make.

Rushed footsteps outside in the hall disrupt the suspended moment. A quick whispered conference and Jagadeep bursts into the room.

"Maggie, please come quickly," he says. "You're needed downstairs."

Both Angel and Jagadeep accompany me to the first floor. Perhaps, left alone, Yoli and Daman will find some way to each other, now that so much has been stripped away. It's up to them now.

At another time of my life I would have warned someone in Yoli's position, "Once a batterer, always a batterer. Don't be fooled." But that is the belief of another world, and now that I've crossed over into this one, I want to have faith that every soul deserves redemption and forgiveness. Even at seven, my daughter understands this, and I am humbled by it.

"What's gonna happen?" Angel clutches my hand, a child again. There are so many layers to this question, and I have no answers for any of them.

"I don't know, sweetheart." I stroke the soft nap of her hair, as we descend the stairs. "We'll just have to see."

As we reenter the large gathering room, both Tina and Carmen jump up to hug me as if I've been gone a long time, or as if my return had been uncertain. Carmen's eyes are wide with tears.

"What's happened?" I ask.

The Light Beings are still chanting, but their notes are more lamenting. The lights in the room have been dimmed; now the candles flicker in darkness.

Sumati comes to me. Despite her obvious depth of feeling, her tone is calm. "Maggie, we're...losing her. Is there anything more you can do?"

I start to say, no, nothing, but Angel tugs at the hem of my shirt.

"Try, Maggie, okay?" Her eyes are full of faith in endless possibility, after all she has been through today.

"Will you watch her?" I ask Tina, but Angel's not about to stay on the sidelines. She clings to my hand as Sumati leads us through the crowd back to the pallet on which Guru lies.

Even without touching her I can see the Teacher is less vital, her skin color more flat. Her facial features have recessed and her limbs seem to be stiffening.

I kneel beside her. I feel in her no awareness of my proximity. A check of her pulses confirms my fears; they are slow and weakening. The presence I sensed in her earlier is diminishing.

Angel has plopped down at my side. She too looks at the motionless woman before us. This will be my daughter's first encounter with death. Her looking is full of curiosity but respect as well. Perhaps awe is not too grand a word.

"Guru-ji," I whisper, and there is a slight stirring in response.

As I settle into a cross-legged position to take her left hand in mine, I feel her breath deepening, her spirit trying to rouse itself to meet me. And I realize that I probably can feed her enough energy to rally for another hour, another night, perhaps another day. What is ultimately poisoning and draining her life force, though, I cannot cure. I know this, and I'm no longer sure that it's kind or merciful to ask her to remain in this body's house of suffering.

Spirit, surely this decision cannot rest on my shoulders.

So instead, I say to her, soundlessly, "Guru-ji, thank you for all you have done for me and for my family. I know you are aware of everything that has transpired. We can go forward now, without your help.

"You have accomplished miracles beyond what I would have ever asked or expected. I would do anything I could to repay you, Teacher. I would give you every drop of energy I can muster, but I am also willing to let you go, to shepherd your departure. Either way it will be an honor to serve you."

I feel her consciousness suspended, weighing the options. Several minutes seem to pass.

Then, Angel yawns. Unable to keep her eyes open another moment, my daughter curls on her side with her head on my thigh. She faces Guru Tam as she drops into a deep sleep. In a short time, their faces bloom with identical smiles, as if they are sharing the same sweet dream. Still seated, I close my eyes and let myself drift, aware of the hard floor beneath my legs, aware of the drone of chanting that recedes into the background. Times passes and then I am dreaming too.

In this dream, Angel and I are still in Baja. We are in a *casita* at Tina's, maybe we live there, because I have painted the inside walls white, needing respite from the riot of color that rampages everywhere else on the property.

I am on the patio, bending over a massage table in the shade of the *palapa*. I can't see the client, but my hands knead knotted muscles underneath slick skin. From nearby I can hear the chatter of Old Mac. Across the patio, Carmen sprawls on a lounge chair, her breasts naked to the sun and sky. Her body feels familiar to me, a source of pleasure and comfort. A breeze stirs the fine hair on my arms.

Tina, her red hair surrounded by a halo of peacock feathers, starts the truck. She is ready to drive Angel to school at the Light Beings' complex. There are other children in the truck too; the Light Beings have opened their school to other children in the surrounding community, including the children of their Mexican workers.

Daman also lives with the Light Beings, and he is helping them to build a music studio, where children can learn to play instruments, and the musicians in the community can come to jam and record their chants. He's gotten his associates in L.A. to donate equipment and money.

In the dream, I look around for Yoli, but she is not here. "L.A. is where I have to be to do my music," she's insisted, but she comes down every couple of weeks to see Angel. And to visit Daman.

My daughter comes dashing out of the *casita*, breathless and nearly late. She is exuberantly accompanied by Loba and a tan puppy by the name of Edgar Sue.

From inside the dream I feel a shift in the atmosphere outside of it, like something shaking me awake. Angel stirs too, turns on her other side, her curled fingers burrowing into my belly. I hear her sigh in her sleep, a soft sound beneath the chanting that continues still.

The hand I am holding, Guru's hand, is heavy and limp. Its

temperature has cooled; the pulse has ceased its rhythm. I sense from her one final exhalation.

My ovaries, tight and aching these last few days, unclench then and I feel the slow sticky drip between my legs that signals my period has at last come.

The room is swept by sudden wind that seems to rise from its center and spiral to the four walls. The candles sputter out. The chanting stops.

Then we sit together silently in darkness, like the night at the beginning of the world.

About the Author

Terry Wolverton is the author of eight books: three novels, *The Labrys Reunion*, *Bailey's Beads* and the novel in poems, *Embers*; a memoir, *Insurgent Muse: life and art at the Woman's Building*; a collection of short fiction, *Breath and other stories*; and three collections of poetry, *Shadow and Praise*, *Mystery Bruise* and *Black Slip*.

She has also edited fourteen successful compilations, including (with Robert Drake) the Lambda Book Award-winning six-volume series *His: brilliant new fiction by gay men* and *Hers: brilliant new fiction by lesbians*.

Terry has taught creative writing for over twenty-five years; in 1997, she founded Writers at Work, a center for creative writing in Los Angeles, where she offers several weekly workshops in fiction and poetry. She is currently an Associate Faculty Mentor for the MFA Writing Program at Antioch University Los Angeles. She spent thirteen years at the Woman's Building, a public center for women's culture, eventually serving as its executive director. She is also a certified instructor of Kundalini Yoga. Her website is www.terrywolverton.xbuild.com